TAINTED SAINTS

ROSA LEE

DIRTY LITTLE PUBLISHERS LTD

Cover designed by Dirty Little Creations

Cover photograph by Wander Aguiar

Formatting by DAZED Designs

Copyright © 2023 by Rosa Lee

All rights reserved.

No part of this book may be reproduced in any form or by any electronic or mechanical means, including information storage and retrieval systems, without written permission from the author, except for the use of brief quotations in a book review.

*To all those good girls who like to get on their knees for Daddy...
Look at you, you're doing such a good job.*

*Rosa Lee
Xxx*

*"For saints have hands that pilgrims hands do touch,
And palm to palm is holy palmers' kiss"*

— WILLIAM SHAKESPEARE

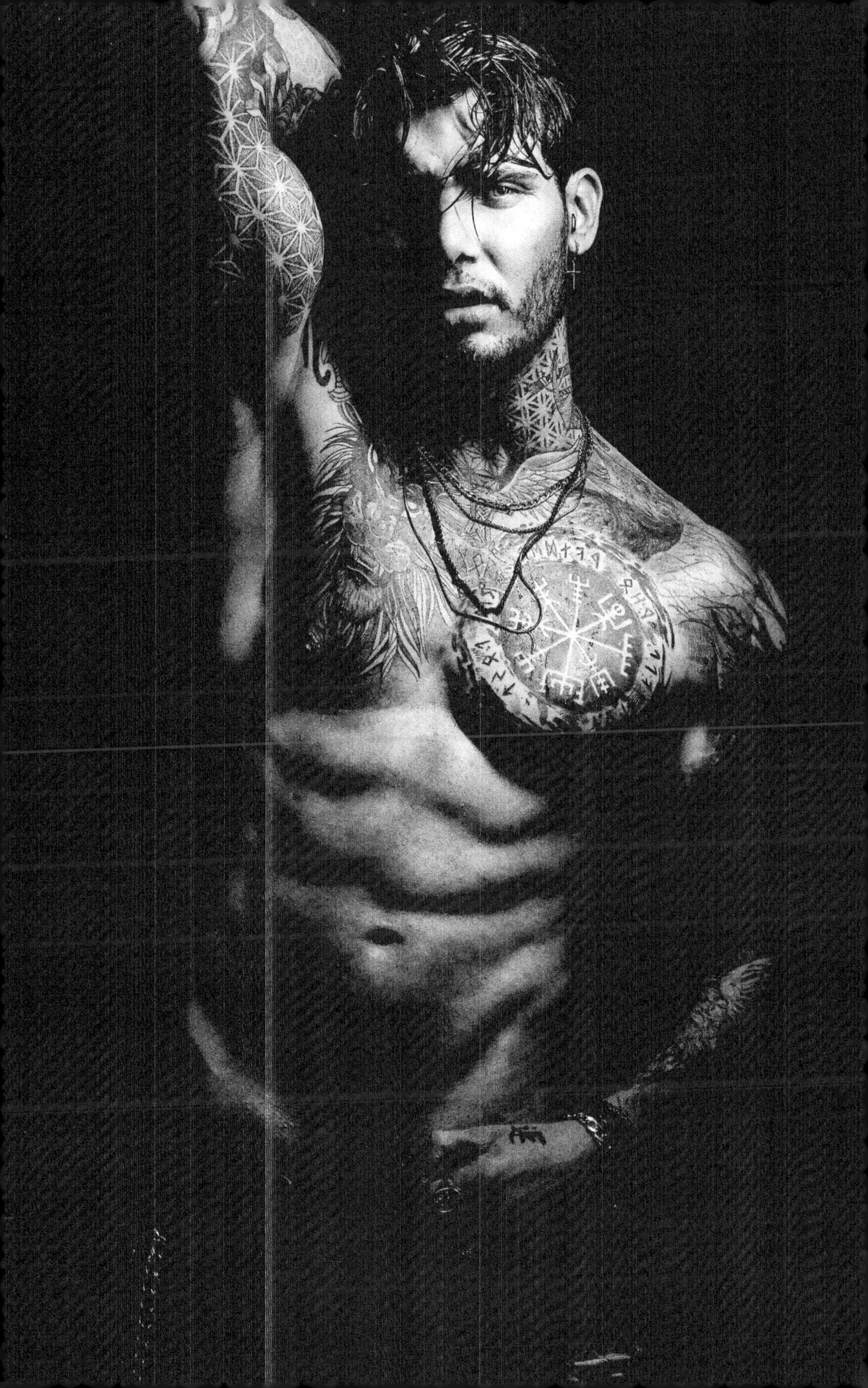

TAINTED SAINTS

What if everything you've ever needed, is everything you can never have?

In the opulent British Ambassador's residence, nestled near Washington DC, an unexpected encounter awaits that will rock everything I thought I knew and change the course of my life. At my new school I meet the enigmatic Tainted Saints—three mesmerising men who become the protectors I never knew I needed.

However, my sordid past unravels as the Ambassador, the man who sired me but will never earn the title of father, reveals his true depravity. With a shocking thirst for blood, he tests the limits of his monstrous nature.

Can I escape his clutches and find true freedom? Or will my life be forever tethered to him instead of the deserving men who have captured my heart?

"Tainted Saints" is a stand alone, compelling retelling, where our fearless heroine need not choose between her impassioned suitors. Discover a world where the boundaries of desire and possibility collide. Brace yourself for a dark romance, but please heed the warnings at the book's outset—this tale is not for the faint of heart.

*****Warning**: 18+ Please be aware that this book may contain graphic scenes that some readers may find upsetting or triggering, so please read the author's note at the beginning. ***

Disclaimer: Please note: Rosa Lee cannot be held responsible for the destruction of underwear of any kind. She recommends you take adequate precautions before reading to avoid any sticky situations.*

TAINTED SAINTS PLAYLIST

I love books with playlists and I listen to my compiled playlist as I'm writing. I've even based some scenes solely around one track, listening to it on repeat to really get into the vibe.

Listen to the full playlist on Spotify HERE

"tired" by das
"Dancer in the Dark" by Chase Atlantic
"dying on the inside" by Nessa Barrett
"Contaminated" by BANKS
"Desert Rose" by Lolo Zouaï
Goddess" by Nation Haven
"Panic Room - Acoustic" by Au/Ra
"Bad Boys" by Azee
"Wicked Game" by Grace Carter
"Anyone Else" by PVRIS
"Smells Like Teen Spirit" by Saint Mesa
"Shameless" by Camila Cabello
"ceilings" by Lizzy McAlpine

"Fahrenheit" by Azee
"Stick Around" by ENVYYOU
"All Mine" by PLAZA
"365" by Mother's Daughter, Beck
"Lavender Haze" by Taylor Swift
"i'm yours" by Isabel LaRosa
"Tidal Wave" by Chase Atlantic
"No Man's Land" by Hands Like Houses
"Counting Stars" by OneRepublic
"more than friends" by Isabel LaRosa
"Pictures" by ECÂF
"Runaway" by AURORA
"Bella Notte" by Peggy Lee
"Gangsta" by Kehlani
"Eat Your Young" by Hozier
"Moonlight" by Chase Atlantic
"We Go Down Together" by Dove Cameron, Kahlid
"Heaven" by FINNEAS
"Don't Blame Me" by Taylor Swift
"when the party's over" by Billie Eilish
"Running Up That Hill" by Loveless
"in the stars" by Sami Rose
"GOOD TO DIE YOUNG" by Elley Duhé
"Hands" by ORKID
"Become the Beast" by Karliene
"Vigilante Shit" by Taylor Swift
"Young and Beautiful" by Scott Bradlee's Postmodern Jukebox

https://open.spotify.com/playlist/6HMqgqQuBmMKSugI5Q5gQs?si=343aaca882474a1f

NOTE TO READERS

Dear Reader,

Firstly, thank you so much for choosing to read Tainted Saints. I hope you enjoy it and that it satisfies all of your dark needs!

This book is full of angst and heartache, plus some very dark parental abuse and neglect is explored so please take care when reading.

For a full list of triggers please visit www.rosaleeauthor.com/trigger-warnings

Also a small word of caution. My books have a lot of BDSM vibes in them, and if they inspire you to dive into that kinky world, please do your research and educate yourself before trying out anything new for the first time. Take care my little smut bunnies!

CHAPTER 1

"TIRED" BY DAS

ASPEN

My palms start to dampen and my breath comes in short gasps, the air thin in my chest. The lights in the pharmacy blaze with sterile brightness, casting harsh shadows on the empty aisles. The sounds of laughter and chatter from the mall—or shopping centre as we call it back home in England—invade my ears, grating and jarring like nails on a chalkboard.

My tongue darts out to moisten my parched lips as I warily scan my surroundings, trying to see if anyone is nearby, but I'm alone aside from the young woman at the till. I extend a shaky hand toward the red nail polish, even though I know I shouldn't. It's not as if I need it. Back at the Ambassador's residence, I have more bottles than I'd ever use, but it feels as though some alien force has commandeered my body, compelling me to act against my better judgement.

Ignoring the crisp dollar bills tucked neatly in my purse, I seize the small glass bottle. It slides smoothly into my jacket pocket, joining five others already concealed there. Then just like that, I find myself on the move, hustling towards the exit with the stolen prizes in my pocket, my heart pounding like a war drum in my chest, the only sound I can hear as I make my escape.

Relief floods my veins, leaving me almost lightheaded as I pick up my pace, the doors within my sight.

"Uh, miss?" a deep voice rumbles behind me, and I freeze, feeling the blood drain from my face as my heart thumps wildly in my chest. Shaking, I slowly turn only to come face to face with a security guard. *Why is there security here? It's just a pharmacy.* "I'm going to need you to empty your pockets, miss."

Swallowing hard past the lump in my throat, I shake my head, my eyes filling with tears as guilt and shame leave a bitter taste in my mouth. I thought I was being so careful, making sure no one saw, and it's almost closing time. The sky was darkening when I entered the mall, desperate for some relief from this itch that I can't get rid of. I wouldn't have kept them, previously I have given them away when the urge to steal becomes too much to resist, but I suppose that doesn't matter anymore.

"I–I c–can explain..." I stutter, suddenly feeling a presence behind me. The crackle of a radio makes me jump just as a large hand wraps around my bicep, squeezing hard, a sharp pain racing up and down my arm as I yelp with shock. Trembles rack my body as his grip tightens, the sinking feeling in the pit of my stomach telling me I've been caught.

"Need some help here, Bill?" another male voice says, his tone nasally and harsh, and I twist my head slightly to catch his blue uniform. Fairview Heights Police. Shit.

"I believe this girl has taken something that doesn't belong to her," the security guard—Bill—states, drawing my attention back to him, his eyes flicking behind me before focusing back on me.

"I–I was going to pay for t–them," I rasp weakly as the officer yanks my hand out of my pocket. There's a clatter as the bottle of red polish I was holding flies from my hand, smashing on the floor and spilling crimson across the white tiles. It looks like blood, and it's only fear that roots me to the spot even as my mind screams at me to run. Tears fill my eyes and I sag in his hold as Bill steps forward and reaches into my pocket, pulling out the other bottles.

"We've heard it all before, lady," the officer states with a sigh, taking my handbag off my shoulder and handing that over to Bill.

"Please, I can pay for them," I beg, tears streaming down my face which feels red-hot and burns with shame. "Check in my purse, I have money." My mouth feels so dry that I have to swallow several times, a pit in my stomach telling me that this time I've fucked up. Badly.

Bill tuts when he opens my bag, and my knees almost buckle when I remember the scarf I took from the shop across the mall and the earrings from the jewellery store. Usually, taking one thing settles the itch, but today, after what happened with the Ambassador this morning, it wasn't enough. I was powerless to stop, promising myself that each item was the last. It didn't work the first couple of times.

"You are under arrest for theft. You have the right to remain silent, anything you say can and will be used against you in a court of law. You have the right to an attorney, if you can not afford one, one will be appointed to you," the officer tells me, the bite of metal around my wrists behind my back making my breaths come in short, sharp pants as they cuff me. He says something into his radio and then there's another police officer beside us, a broad-shouldered woman with short brown hair, taking my bag from Bill. "You'll need to come to the station with me, miss."

He keeps a firm hold on my arm, but there's no fight left in me, I know that the game is up. He tugs me outside of the store, into the mostly quiet mall for which I'm beyond grateful. I don't know how I would cope with a whole load of strangers' eyes on me as I'm dragged away. I've never been caught before, never imagined how awful it would feel to be taken away like this.

Hanging my head, I catch a dark gaze trained on me from the shadows of an already closed store, and my heart pauses for a beat as I lock gazes with the watcher, my steps faltering. For a moment, I drown in his eyes, the colour of them so dark that it's like staring at the night sky. The hair along the back of my neck stands on end, but I'm not quite sure if it's due to fear or something else.

Either way, I'm pulled along by the no-named officer, breaking the intense connection with my mysterious stranger, and for some reason, I don't feel quite as alone as I did moments ago. Hell, as I did this morning when the Ambassador informed me that I would be dating a boy I've never met because, and I quote, *"His family is from good American stock."*

The cool night air hits me as we exit the mall, cooling my overheated cheeks but not easing the turmoil raging inside me. I look up into a starless sky, the sight reminding me of my observer back inside. Who was he? And why do I feel like he was watching me for more than just the drama of seeing someone being arrested?

"DANCER IN THE DARK" BY CHASE ATLANTIC

LANDON

I watch as Officer Jones takes her away, a growl rumbling in my chest at how tightly he's gripping her arm. I don't fucking like it, even though there's no reason for me to feel protective over the rich bitch.

Heat flashes through my body, my teeth grinding when I recall the way I watched, mouth agape as she stole the scarf, then the earrings, and finally the nail polish. What the actual fuck?

When my uncle tasked me with tailing the British Ambassador's daughter, I didn't expect to find her so...captivating. Or to find her stealing like a downtown thief. She's fucking loaded, why would she steal? She probably gets some sort of fucked up, rich botch kick taking things from people who are less fortunate than herself.

My upper lip curls at the thought. No matter how pretty she is, fuck that. She's the most beautiful woman I've ever seen with her softly curling, long, blonde hair and sparkling green eyes, her slender curves only accentuated by the fitted skirt and blazer she wore. Regardless of all of that shit, she's still a thief and there is no reason for someone as rich as she is to be stealing.

Some might say that's hypocritical of me, given my criminal background, but fuck them. I wouldn't lower myself to steal from people who didn't have it to spare, and the shop owners on this side of town aren't exactly rolling in it. Fucking disgusting.

My phone buzzes in my pocket, tearing my gaze away from the spot that she disappeared through, and I reach into my jeans to take it out as Forest's number with a picture of his cock flashes up on the screen. Fucking degenerate's been at my phone again.

"What the fuck is your cock doing on my phone, Forest?" I ask in a low growl, but the fucker just laughs.

"I know you love it, Daddy," he teases back, his Louisiana accent thick when his voice drops that low. Fuck, that boy knows how to get me hard with just a couple of words.

"Was there a reason you called?" I grit out, adjusting myself as I watch the cop car drive off.

"Oh, shit, boy! I almost forgot!" He exclaims, and my lips threaten to tip up at the sound. He's just a ray of fucking sunshine that makes the world a little bit brighter, has been ever since he came to Fairview as a kid, regardless of his shitty parents. "Blaine's been arrested."

Just like that, my almost smile drops. "What? And you didn't think to start with that? Jesus, Forest." I huff out a breath before pinching the bridge of my nose between my thumb and forefinger. "What was it for this time?"

It doesn't surprise me that Blaine has been arrested again. Our boy has so much pent-up rage, always simmering under the surface, which is unsurprising given his damage and the way his shitstain of a dad beat him and his mom. It just bursts from him every so often, usually when someone smaller than himself is being threatened.

"Some pimp was threatening one of his girls and Blaine made him see the error of his ways. It was beautiful, son, blood splatter all over the sidewalk." Forest's tone deepens, and I know he's sporting a hard-on right now, violence gets that fucker off. So does fucking in public, and he always seems to get away with it.

I go to tell him to meet me down at the precinct but pause, a plan forming in my mind as a smirk tilts my lips upwards. "Let's leave him there. Our little Duchess has just been carted off for an overnight stay at our glorious jail so he can keep an eye on her."

Forest whistles. "What for? Why would she be taken there? Surely daddy dearest could stop that kind of shit?"

"Not when she's out alone, stealing," I tell him, and for once, silence greets me. This time, I do smile. It's not often I can surprise Forest.

"What the fuck she stealing for? She's as rich as living in high cotton!" he exclaims, and I chuckle at his Southern turn of phrase. Fuck knows what it means, but it just makes me love him more.

"Probably some kick that she gets from robbing us poor folk," I growl, all humour draining away from me whilst remembering the look of horror on her perfect features when she was discovered. The tears that made her eyes gleam and shine tugged at something within me. Something that recognised another being trapped by a thing that is beyond their control, but they can't help doing it anyway. Shaking my head as if to dislodge any kind of thoughts about how I might relate to Her Highness, I grip the phone tighter in my hand. "I'm heading back now. Let's have some dinner, get some sleep, and pick up Blaine first thing."

"Roger that, Daddy," Forest sasses before hanging up.

Giving a rueful chuckle, I place the phone in my back pocket and stride out into the crisp winter night. It's even colder now that the sun has set, and I stand there, letting the light breeze trace across my face as I gaze out at Fairview Heights, my home and the place that a part of me is desperate to escape from.

Working my jaw back and forth to ease the tension that's gathered there, I sigh, knowing that leaving Fairview is unlikely. I have too much responsibility here, too much to do to ensure my boys and our families are safe from the reach of my uncle and the Cosa Nostra. That's if the poverty doesn't get to us first.

Fuck. When did life get so fucking exhausting?

Scrubbing a hand over my face, I stroll towards my pride and joy, the one thing that my father left me that brings pure bliss. I run my hand along the matte black paint of my Papa's old Chopper, remembering all the time we spent restoring it when I was a kid. A lump forms in my throat, my jaw clenching tight in a bid to stop the flashback, but it's no use.

"Quick, Lan, hide under the bench!" my dad hisses at me, the whites of his eyes showing as he pushes me into the small space. "Don't come out, no matter what."

I nod, my heart thudding painfully in my chest as I do as he says, shuffling to the back behind a box of spare motorcycle parts. I jump, my hand over my mouth to stifle my scream when the door crashes open.

There's a rapid conversation in Italian, too fast for me to follow even though I know the language having been raised to speak it. At first, I think the loud crack in the air is just whoever is here knocking over one of the many piles of parts that litter the garage, but then my father's face comes into view, his eyes open but somehow I know that they can't see me.

My lips tremble as blood begins to pool underneath his head, and even though I remain silent, just as he told me to, my ears are full of *the screams of a little boy who just lost one of the most important people in the world to him.*

BEING CONNECTED TO THE ITALIAN MOB HAS BROUGHT NOTHING but heartache and death to my family, and when their enemies killed my Papa in a bid to send a message to my uncle, I vowed that I would never become a Made Man. That I would sever all ties to the mafia and I would take Mama far away from here.

So much for that plan. It's been a decade and we're still here, trapped by a lack of fucking money with no honest way out. Sure, Papa's restaurant doesn't do too badly, just enough for Mama to get by really, but nothing on the east side of Fairview does that well. The people are just too poor and struggling to make a difference. We've had to resort to less than legal means, accepting the scraps that my uncle gives us, even with Forest's job at the Pound and me helping my mama at the restaurant some weekends.

My hand clenches around the handlebars, the touch bringing me back to the present and the fact that my worn hoodie is now soaked through and clinging to my skin, the sudden winter shower quickly becoming a downpour. Throwing my leg over, I sit down in the moulded seat, not bothering with a helmet as it's an expense I can't afford. Plus, a part of me enjoys the thrill of riding without one, especially in the rain.

Starting the old girl up, she roars to life with a deep rumble that's enough to make any man a little hard, and I tear away from the West Side Mall, the one that's just across the river from DC. I head in the direction of home, the place where more people are crammed into a space half the size of the richer side of town, where the Ambassador and his beautiful daughter live, despite them having a full fucking mansion on Embassy Row in the city.

I gun the throttle, the sound loud over the pouring rain as I sail down the streets, the change almost unnoticeable in the dark, but I know from living here my whole life that the sidewalks here are cracked, the buildings tired and more run down the further I go. People don't have time to look after the outside when they can barely feed themselves.

All the while, I can't get the image out of my head of a blonde-haired Duchess, tears streaming down her face as she begs me with her soulful green eyes to save her.

CHAPTER 2

"DYING ON THE INSIDE" BY NESSA BARRETT

ASPEN

I can't stop shaking, my winter clothes providing no warmth against the shock of being arrested and hauled off to county jail. Fuck, the Ambassador will be so mad, and when he gets mad...

I have to shut down that train of thought, I can't think of what will happen once they call him. The female officer—Officer Anne—told me they would be in touch with my family, her voice soft as if she thought I would break. I wanted to laugh, tell her that she's too late for that. I was broken by my father a long time ago, and moulded into the perfect daughter, fit to be in the public eye.

Not so perfect if she keeps stealing things...

I wrap my trembling arms tighter around myself, trying to practise the deep breathing I read about online when I first suspected that I suffer from social anxiety disorder. It's a form of anxiety that rears its ugly head when I'm forced to participate in the many social engagements that I have to attend being the daughter of the British Ambassador.

I never knew what was worse, knowing what was wrong with me after extensive Google searches as an early teen, or not being able to get the right medical help because heaven forbid we have any mental health issues or craziness in the family. My mother's words when I told her my suspicions. The Buckinghams do not hold truck with that sort of nonsense, no. It's stiff upper lips all the way in our family, and if ever you were to get too out of hand, well, you wouldn't want to end up like Great Aunt Flo, locked away in a private institution, talking to the mice and smearing her porridge all over the velvet curtains. We have more skeletons than we know what to do with in our family's closet, and they will stay hidden come hell or high water, not even our trusted staff are privy to most of them.

The car pulls to a stop and suddenly my chilled body is breaking out in a sweat that only makes me feel colder. The sharp tang of copper tells me that I've worried my lip bloody, and taking a rasping breath, I wait as the car door is pulled open. Officer Anne helps me out, a shiver working its way up my body as the now cold night air hits my face.

"Let's get you inside, shall we?" she asks kindly and I nod, my teeth chattering too much to answer properly.

I blink rapidly at the brightness of the reception, the artificial light almost unbearable after being in the dark car.

"Well, what do we have here? Not our usual clientele," an older man behind the desk states with a chuckle, and I suck my lower lip again, unable to form any words as I try to keep my breathing under control.

"Evenin', John," the male officer, who still hasn't given me his name, greets. "Caught this one stealing at the mall. Thought a night in the cells should dissuade her from doing so again, didn't we, sweetheart?" He turns to look at me, and his gaze leaves a slimy feel

11

along my skin. I cower away slightly from the invasion of his stare, but Officer Anne still has a firm grip on me so I don't get far.

"Do you have a name, darlin'?" the officer behind the desk, John, turns to me, lowering his head so he can catch my eye. He smiles, and there's a warmth in his brown eyes that the other man doesn't have, and it instantly eases something within me.

"A–Aspen. Aspen Buckingham," I tell him softly, his bushy grey eyebrows rising slightly when he hears my name. "M–my f–father, C–Charles Buckingham, is t–the British Ambassador. I–I can't remember our address, we only moved a couple of weeks or so ago." It's like now that I've started talking, I can't stop, and it seems I have all of their attention now, all three officer's eyes slightly wide as they gape at me.

"Right." John blows out a breath, taking my small leather handbag from the male officer and pulling out the items inside, including my diplomatic household passport which is my current form of ID. "Well, I'll be damned. You really are the Ambassador's daughter." I don't have an answer to that non-question, so I remain quiet as he pulls out the other items from my bag, including my phone and the items that I stole. I wince seeing them laid out, John gathering evidence bags to place them into. "Let's get you in the system, and then we'll give your pops, I mean, Mr. Ambassador a call."

My lips lift in a small smile at the term Mr. Ambassador. He'd be so pissed if he heard that, citing that it's not his correct or full title. Dread pools in my stomach, my smile dropping as I wonder just how angry he'll be when he hears that I've gotten myself arrested. What will my punishment be for this infraction?

"Miss?" Officer Anne's voice breaks through my thoughts, and when I look at her and the others, I realise that they're waiting on me for something.

"S–sorry, pardon?"

"Can you give me your age, please?" John asks, fingers gripping a pen and I wonder for a moment why he's not typing it into the computer on his desk.

"Oh, um. I'm eighteen. My date of birth is fourteenth of February, two thousand and six," I answer, guessing that he'd want to record that as well. Though it is all on my passport.

"A Valentine's Day baby, huh?" John comments with a wry chuckle.

"It's not too bad," I tell him, not wanting to go into details about the amount of times I've spent my birthday at a social function, never on a date or even a party to celebrate the day. I prefer it when I am alone, when they go off without me and I can sit and read, rather than being forced to attend one of their parties, like the recent ball held by the Tailors in Colorado. Lark seemed sweet, but Aeron Tailor was pretty scary and there were just so many people there that it took everything in me not to pass out or throw up.

John asks me some more questions, which I answer to the best of my abilities, and then we're done.

"Do you have your dad's number? So we can tell him where you are and how he can arrange to collect you?" Officer Anne questions softly, and I shake my head.

"You'll have better luck with his personal secretary, Robert," I inform her, then give them his number instead. I don't miss the way her eyebrows furrow or her soft blue eyes full of a pity that I don't want or need.

"Thank you, Aspen. I'll take you to the cells now," she says, and my breathing catches, my limbs feeling shaky again. "Have you eaten anything recently?"

I hear the no-name male officer scoff behind me, muttering something about giving preferential treatment to the pretty ones. I choose to ignore him, deciding he's a bastard anyway, and am glad that he doesn't follow us, the place on my arm he grabbed pulsing as the new bruise forms. I shake my head at her.

"Um, not since breakfast. Mother has me on this new diet and today is a fast day, so I shouldn't really eat again until tomorrow morning," I tell her, my brows dipping as her jaw tightens.

"Well, how about I see what I can rustle up for you, would a sandwich work? And maybe a cup of coffee?" My nose wrinkles before I can stop it, and she laughs as she turns to lead me through a door she has to swipe an access card through, and down a corridor. "Not a fan of a good old cup of Joe?"

"Um, well, no, not really. But if you have some tea that would be lovely, thank you," I reply, my cheeks colouring as my limbs start trembling again the deeper we go down the corridor.

"I'm sure I can get you a cup of tea. I won't even microwave it," she jokes, and my eyes go wide as I gasp.

"You microwave tea? And they call the British barbaric," I comment, glancing at her out of the corner of my eye as she huffs a laugh.

"Best not to get into that debate just now, but I have an English aunt who would have my hide if I ever made a cup of tea in the microwave, so I'll make sure you get a proper cup, Your Highness," she teases, and some of the tension loosens from my limbs at the joke, knowing that I sound like a posh twat, my accent giving away my privileged upbringing.

All the tension returns though when we go through the next door and I'm faced with rows of bars, open cells down one side that all seem to be full. My breathing speeds up, my stomach going rock-hard as all eyes turn to us, the majority of them male and with an assessing gleam in their gazes that makes me want to run and hide. Catcalls and jeers start up a moment later, and the lewd comments have me shuddering and grateful for the bars that will keep us separate.

"Settle down, assholes!" she bellows, making me jump, and the shivers are back tenfold as she leads me, stumbling, to a cell towards the back.

Thankfully, one of the sides is the wall, the other being bars that separates it from the cell next door, its occupant sat on the hard-looking bench, leather-clad elbows resting on his knees, his head hanging down.

His tattooed knuckles appear to be split, blood dripping onto the floor between his legs, and I wonder what happened to him tonight. His hair is dark, longer, and slicked back on top, almost like a quiff, and as he raises his head to see what all the commotion is about, I'm caught by a face that takes my breath away completely.

He has a strong jaw covered in light stubble and his skin is the colour of golden sands bathed in sunlight. His plush lips are just begging to be kissed, and thick eyebrows dropped low over chocolate-brown eyes that I could easily lose myself in. There's a deep scar that bisects his left brow, carrying on into his cheek, and a ringed piercing sits on that side of his nose. Ink covers his neck to his jawline, and the hair raises on the back of my neck, all my nerve endings stirring as he holds me captive in his gaze, his dark eyes unreadable.

"Garcia," Officer Anne says as she draws me closer, ignoring the comments of the other prisoners. "I know you'll look after our newest guest." He sniggers at that, and Jesus fucking Christ, are those matching dimples in his cheeks? "You've been here enough times to know how this shit works, so fill her in, would ya?" She takes a key from somewhere, my eyes tearing away from him to watch as she slides it into the lock and then opens the door. Then her fingers are doing something with the metal cuffs on my wrists, which spring free a moment later, the blood feeling like it can move freely to my hands even though I know they weren't that tight. "In you go, Miss Buckingham." My entire body shudders as I walk into the cell, stopping just inside but unable to turn around, and my eyes fill with tears as the door clangs shut, the lock loud even over the noise from the other inmates. "I'll go get that tea, okay?"

"T–thank you," I whisper, unsure if she even heard me, but still not able to face the consequences of my foolish fucking actions. I'm not sure how I'll manage if I see the bars trapping me here. I suppose it's better than the darkened, windowless cell that I know awaits me back at the mansion.

ROSA LEE

My breathing comes faster as her retreating footsteps sound behind me, my hands clenched into quaking fists at my sides, my body flinching when the bang of the other door sounds and I'm left here, in this cell, with the criminals of Fairview trapped with me.

"CONTAMINATED" BY BANKS

BLAINE

I watch her, the most beautiful fucking girl I have ever seen, and wonder what the fuck she's doing in a place like this with people like me? Her entire small frame shakes like a leaf desperately clinging onto the branch of a tree as a gale threatens to tear it off, and something in my chest stirs at the way her eyes refuse to open, at the strength it seems to be taking her to stay standing.

"You gonna give us something to help make the night pass quickly, missy?" someone rasps from across the large room, and my teeth grind as I stand, a growl leaving my chest as I look around at the others in here with us.

Their calls stop as I catch each of their gazes, telling them with a single stare to shut the fuck up. Many know who Blaine Garcia is, and know that my bloodied knuckles are nothing to what the other guy looks like. My reputation proceeds me most places on the east side of Fairview, everyone knowing not to fuck with me or pick on anyone else when I'm around.

I turn my attention back to the beauty in the cell next to mine and, stepping closer to the bars, I allow my gaze to take in her long, tumbling honey-blonde waves falling down around her slender shoulders, a deep-red blazer-style jacket doing nothing to hide the swell of her breasts. It's fitted, highlighting her beautiful figure, and her dark green woolen pencil skirt shows off the curve of her ass but hides everything from hip to just below her knees.

I find, surprisingly, it's the sexiest fucking outfit I've ever seen on a woman before. Something about the way it tells me everything and nothing about her body makes me more desperate to discover its secrets than if she wore something far more revealing.

Even in the quiet, she doesn't stop trembling, just stands there, biting her bottom lip, and my brows lower as I continue to watch her.

"You cold, *mi princesa linda?*"

My own voice surprises me, deep and gravelly with disuse. I don't often use it, resorting to my fists more often than not. She doesn't flinch like I expect her to, instead, slowly turns her head and opens her eyes, frowning at me. It's too fucking cute, but I'm rendered fucking speechless when she locks those stunning green eyes on me. They're swimming with tears, but that only makes them shine like the sea glass my mother used to keep as a memento from the time her father was a sailor. My hand reaches up to my neck, running my thumb over the leather that hangs around it, the glass dangling from it.

"P–pardon?" Her voice wavers, but shit if it isn't the most melodic voice I've ever heard. It reminds me of the old-time singers, another thing I have to thank my mom for because she used to play me old records whenever my shit stain of a Papi was out of the house.

I take a step forward. "Are you cold? You're shivering."

She looks down at herself, as if she didn't notice that her fucking body looks like it's about to shake itself apart. Not waiting for her answer, I shrug off my leather jacket, stepping closer to the bars that separate us, and hold it out for her. She flicks her wide gaze to my hand, licking her lip that looks like she's been biting into it if the fresh scab is any sign, and then shakes her head.

"Oh, um, I'm okay, thank you," she says, wrapping her arms around herself and proving that she is definitely not fine. A growl escapes my lips and her eyes dart back up to mine, but there's not just fear in her gaze. There's a thread of lust that has her pupils wide as she traces up my now bare arms and like a fucking peacock, I want to puff out my chest for her approval. *Fucking hell, you never let chicks affect you like this.*

"Take the damn jacket, *mi princesa linda*, before you injure yourself," I command, my tone brokering no argument. She licks that bottom lip again—*not the time to get a semi, Blaine*—she tentatively steps closer, her fingers brushing mine as she reaches for my jacket.

Sparks race up my arm, and I hear her small gasp as my gaze flicks to her perfect face, her lips open in a way that's far too fucking inviting. *Shit, dude, head out of the fucking gutter.*

"T–thank you, Garcia," she says, the words so soft that it sends a delicate shiver across my skin.

"Blaine," I correct her, not sure why I do as only my boys call me that. Everyone else calls me Garcia. "My name is Blaine."

"Pleased to make your acquaintance, Blaine. I'm Aspen," she tells me, and fuck, even the small smile playing around her lips almost knocks me on my ass. It could also be that sexy as fuck British accent.

I watch as she puts my jacket on, taking a deep inhale, her eyes closing briefly as she snuggles into the huge garment. Shit, it almost drowns her, she's tiny compared to my bulk. Opening her beautiful eyes, her cheeks flush when she sees me staring at her, but I don't look away. I couldn't, even if I wanted to. She's just so fucking enchanting.

Holding out her hand for me to shake, I waste no time in grasping it in mine, marvelling at how much smaller it is than my own. Flicking my eyes back up to hers, I hold her stare as I bring her hand up to my lips, brushing a light kiss across her knuckles. Her mouth opens in surprise and I grin when I notice that she's no longer shaking, in fact, her cheeks are a beautiful rosy colour now.

The door to the cells opens then, and she pulls her hand back, turning to face the walkway as the female officer—Anne—comes back carrying a brown paper bag and a large Styrofoam cup.

"How you settling in, Miss Buckingham?" she asks, and my blood freezes for a second as her full name registers.

Aspen Buckingham, the daughter of the British Ambassador.

The one we've been tasked to watch over by two separate people for two very different reasons. Aeron Taylor, leader of the Tailors gang in Colorado asked us to watch her after their ball at Christmas. We got an invite but couldn't make it due to not being able to leave Forest's aunt and uncle in charge of the Poundfor that long. Plus, I know none of us would have accepted the use of Aeron's private jet, seeing it as too close to charity for comfort.

Landon's uncle also set us the task of getting close to her in order to find out what the fuck her Papi, the British Ambassador, is doing. There have been rumours of a gambling ring having been set up by him and his rich friends, and everyone knows the mafia controls all of the gambling in Fairview.

"I–I'm fine, thank you, Officer Anne," Aspen replies quietly, wrapping her arms around herself again and I find that it tightens something inside my chest to see her looking so vulnerable.

"Good, seems like Garcia is taking care of you, as I knew he would." She winks at me, and I roll my eyes. I like Officer Anne, she's tough but fair, and she may have a soft spot for me seeing as I'm mostly in here defending women from motherfuckers who think it's okay to beat on them. "And, as promised, a sandwich and a cup of tea, not microwaved."

I don't know what the *coño* she's talking about, but it makes Aspen smile, filling the cells with a light that steals the air from my lungs.

"Oh, that's so kind of you. Thank you, Officer Anne," the golden beauty replies, and Anne hands the bag and cup over through the bars. The other prisoners are right to grumble, she's never given us food, but I can't hold it against her, seeing how much the golden-haired *princesa* needs a meal right now.

"No problems, Miss Buckingham. We left a message with your father's secretary. So as soon as we hear back, I'll be sure to let you know." She looks at Aspen with pity in her eyes and my chest tightens as my hands wrap around the bars, a protective growl wanting to escape my throat, and I have no damn idea why.

"Oh, thank you," Aspen mumbles as her hand around the bag clenches, causing it to crinkle. Her bottom lip disappears under her teeth and I want to bark at her to stop abusing it, that only my teeth are allowed to make it bleed.

Coño, no, Blaine. Remember the job, the task we've been set. We're not here to fuck her, we're here to watch. Although, Landon's uncle did say he wanted us to get close.

Officer Anne gives her another sympathetic smile and then turns to walk out, ignoring the grumbles of the other prisoners who are complaining that she never bought us food. I don't hold it against her, the girl looks like a strong wind would blow her down. She's curvy, but she still looks like she needs a good meal or two to see her right.

Suddenly, her green eyes are on me, and I swear to fuck my heart stops beating for a second.

"There's far too much here for me, Blaine. Want to share?" she asks tentatively, a slight blush stealing over the apple of her cheeks and I wonder what else would make them colour up like that. Immediately, the image of her thrashing beneath me while I feast on her dripping pussy fills my sight until I have to blink it away, my dick stirring in my jeans.

"You need it more than me, *mi princesa linda*," I say gently, and her cheeks darken some more.

"What does it mean; *mi princesa linda?*" she questions, and heat steals across my cheeks, which rarely happens. I hadn't realised I'd used the phrase enough for her to take notice.

"My pretty princess in Spanish," I tell her after clearing my throat, watching her reaction. Her lips part slightly, her eyes wide as she just stares at me.

"T–that's beautiful." She replies so quietly that I'm not sure if I heard the words or read them from her lips. Then she takes a deep inhale. "Well, regardless if you think I'm too thin, I still won't manage everything in the bag, so please share it with me. I'd hate for it to go to waste after all the trouble Officer Anne went through."

I sigh, unable to resist those fucking doe eyes she's giving me.

Forest is going to be putty when he eventually meets her, the softie that he is.

"Fine, but I never said you were too thin. You have a stunning body, *mi princesa linda*. You just look like you need some energy, and that maybe you've skipped a meal today." I make a point to glance over her pale face, the way her hands tremble slightly as she sets the cup down on the floor to open the bag, still facing my cell.

"Mother has me on a special diet, so today was, is, a fast day," she tells me, straightening up and opening the bag, the crinkle of the paper loud in the quiet of the cells. Again, I have to suppress a growl. *Why the fuck would she be on a special diet? Especially one that would mean she has fast days?* There's barely anything to her as it is.

She pulls out one half of an overflowing sub that can only have come from Diana's across the street. They have the best sandwiches on the east side, hell, probably all of Fairview, and I'm impressed that Anne went to the trouble. Though maybe like me, she saw that this girl desperately needs some fucking carbs.

Her eyes widen as she takes in the huge portion, but the smell of chicken and bacon with fresh salad has her stomach giving an audible growl. I chuckle, and her eyes fly to my face.

"Seems to me like you are a bit hungry after all," I tease, and then wonder where the fuck this side of me has come from? I don't tease or joke unless it's with Lan and Forest, my chosen brothers.

She giggles and fucking hell, that sound. She needs to make it every damn day. "I guess I am. Here."

Holding out the sub, she steps closer until I can smell her sweet perfume; citrus, hyacinth, and clove, reminding me of a woodland in spring. Letting go of the bars, I reach out and take the sandwich, my fingers brushing hers again and electricity races up and down my arm.

She's frozen, just staring at my hand with a wonder in her eyes that I want to see more of. Blinking rapidly, she shakes her head, then takes her hand away, and I immediately miss the warmth of her touch. *Coño*, this shit is getting real far too quickly but I find myself not giving a fuck, becoming addicted to her all already.

"Thank you," I rumble, watching as she shudders at the sound of my voice, even in her blazer and my leather jacket. I find that I like that I have this effect on her, even if part of it is due to the cold of the cells we're in.

"You're welcome, Blaine," she whispers back, taking out her own half and bringing it up to her lips. I watch, utterly fucking captivated, as she takes a bite, then her eyes close and a small, almost sexual moan leaves her lips.

Fucking hell.

"Good?" I rasp out, and her eyes snap open, her jaw working as she chews, waiting until she's finished before she speaks. A proper lady then.

"Oh my god, Blaine. This is amazing," she gushes, and the words go straight to my dick, which starts to harden in my scruffy jeans. I desperately try to think of old Mrs. Nichols who used to live two doors down from us and would eye us like a snack anytime we passed. "I can't remember the last time I ate bread, and the chicken and bacon? I will definitely need to see where she got this from and come back."

"Diana's, it's across the street and you won't find a better sandwich in Fairview," I tell her, my own half forgotten as I watch her take another bite and her eyes practically roll again. It's going to be a long night if she keeps that up.

I watch her eat every last bite, ignoring my own in favour of observing my golden *princesa*. *Coño*, she's beautiful. Eventually, she sighs, her eyes catching my stare, and another blush colouring her cheeks.

"Better?" I ask, that note of teasing back in my tone. She gives me a wide grin, and once again, the cells fill with a light and warmth that I've not known in a long time.

"So much better," she answers, then she looks down at my hand, her brows dipping. "Are you not hungry? Did you have dinner before you...arrived?" she winces at the last word, and a bark of laughter escapes my throat.

"Nice way to put being locked up in here, *princesa*," I tease, and her cheeks turn a deeper colour, my face softening. "I'm only teasing, and no, I didn't eat before I was arrested."

Anger flares hot and bright inside me when I recall what led to my incarceration. Finding that scum trying to force a woman to her knees. She may be a sex worker, but no one should be made to do something they clearly don't want to.

"W–what happened?" she asks, stepping closer, and I look to see the paper bag on the floor and the cup in her hand. She's taken the lid off, and hot steam floats around her face, making her seem almost otherworldly in her beauty. "Oh, I'm sorry, that was rude. You don't have to answer." She looks down away from me, not meeting my eyes.

Her lip disappears under her teeth again, the skin cracking while a bead of crimson wells up from the broken skin. Without conscious thought, my free hand reaches through the bars and my thumb tugs her lip free, swiping across the blood, that mesmerising gaze snapping back to me. She doesn't say anything, doesn't pull away. Just watches as I bring my thumb up to my mouth and slip it inside, the tangy copper making my jaw ache as if I want more of her. A shiver runs through her, and the idea that she's not disgusted with what I've just done, with the dark desires I might have, makes my dick strain against my pants.

"I caught a pimp trying to force a prostitute to her knees when she was begging him to stop." She's unblinking as she focuses her attention entirely on me, and damn if it isn't like looking into the rays of the sun. Warm yet blinding and almost too much. "So I beat the shit out of him to teach him a lesson about consent."

She goes to suck in her lip again, stops halfway, and then releases it. *Good girl.*

"I think that's very gallant of you," she breathes out, her pupils large and a soft expression on her face that I don't often see directed at me. Correction, that I *never* see directed at me. "To defend someone who is unable to help themselves. You shouldn't be punished for it."

I chuckle darkly. "I'm no white knight, *mi princesa linda*," I tell her, self-deprecation coating my tongue with bitterness. I wasn't able to save the one person who needed it the most, and no matter how many I try to help now, it doesn't change that fact. My uneaten sandwich lies forgotten as I stare at it, my eyes seeing only the lifeless body of my mother before me.

"Maybe not, perhaps a black knight of mediaeval legend then," she suggests, and blinking out of the nightmarish memory, I raise a brow at her, asking without words what she means. "It is believed that there were knights who dressed in black armour that would save cities from unjust rulers and do many good deeds, but the church banned such legends from being spoken of, and any texts that made reference to them were censored. Perhaps you are one of those knights then."

This woman. My body tingles as if I've been seen for the first time in my life. As if my soul has just been laid bare for all to gaze on and a part of me doesn't mind, couldn't give a fuck that she is the one to have stripped me.

CHAPTER 3

"DESERT ROSE" BY LOLO ZOUAÏ

ASPEN

Blaine looks at me with eyes that are bright and a little glossy, like chocolate that is being tempered on marble. I wonder if anyone has ever truly appreciated this giant of a man, and he is huge, towering over me. I have to crane my neck back just to maintain eye contact. His shoulders are so broad, twice the width of me, and he has powerful arms covered in tattoos that disappear under his fitted, black T-shirt which creeps up to the edge of his strong jawline.

As I shift, his scent wafts up from the leather jacket that he lent me, and it takes all of my self-control not to snuggle into it, breathing in the heady scents of ambrox, rum, and tonka bean. It's sweet, woody, and musky, addicting and comforting, and I know that it will forever remind me of Blaine Garcia.

"Why were you bought in?" he asks out of the blue, and I feel all the colour drain from my face. Though, fair is fair, and all of a sudden, I can't wait to get this burden off my chest. For one person to know my dark secret.

I take a deep, shuddering inhale. "I stole some things from the mall." I watch for his reaction, but he doesn't even raise a single brow, just waits for me to continue. "I–I get the urge to take things, and it's like I can't control myself. Like, if I don't steal, I will cease to function. Do you ever feel that way? Like your body is totally beyond your control?" He gives me a slow nod, and something loosens inside me, something that makes me feel that I'm not quite as alone as I was before. "The Ambassador told me this morning that I would be dating a guy I've never met, but who goes to my new school, all because his family comes from good stock." My tone is bitter, and my eyes dart to Blaine when a small growl rumbles in his chest. At least, I think that's what I heard. "Anyway, it sent me into a spiral. I've been so good lately and have managed to avoid any situations where I might be tempted. And things have been easier at home." I've no idea why I'm telling him this, he's a complete stranger, but I can't seem to stop now that I've started. "But today it was like I was possessed. It was the only thing my mind could focus on, nothing else existed. Before I really knew what was happening, I got our driver to take me to the mall...oh god, Bobby!" My hand flies to my mouth. Poor Bobby might still be waiting for me, having no idea what's happened. I made him wait in the car, even though he wanted to come in with me as I'd refused to bring security, but I couldn't have anyone there to witness my shame. Joke's on me I guess.

"And you got caught," Blaine adds, and the sandwich is gone, presumably he ate it while I was talking.

"And I got caught," I confirm softly, hanging my head as tears fill my eyes. Fingers brush down the side of my cheek before a strong thumb and forefinger grips my chin and lifts it up. Then his warm eyes fill my vision, wavering a little as the tears blur my vision.

"You don't need to be ashamed of the things you can't control, *mi princesa linda*," he tells me gently, his voice like a soothing balm over wounds that are festering and won't stop bleeding. "Has it been a problem for you for a while?"

"Yes," I confess, staring into his eyes as if they will save me. "Even when I was a young teenager, I had urges to steal. It started with taking things from my mother and then things from shops in London. I never keep the stuff, usually giving it away to homeless people or charity shops, but I wish I knew how to make the urges stop."

I'm not stupid, I was able to self-diagnose my anxiety and this is no different. Kleptomania. The urge to steal like it's a compulsion. The way I feel a heady rush of pleasure after I've taken something, followed by intense guilt and shame. It's never anything of great value, never pre-planned and I can go for months without taking something. Again, another useless diagnosis, because what's the point in knowing if I can't get the help I need to sort the problem? *"We mustn't have anything less than perfection in the Buckingham household."* My mother's words, again, come to haunt me.

"Have you told anyone about the urges?" he asks gently, his thumb stroking my chin in soothing circles, calming my frantic heartbeat and relaxing my tight muscles. My mind tells me that I shouldn't be okay with him touching me this way, that he's a practical stranger, but the tension leaves my body all the same and I don't stop him.

"I tried, telling them about something else, but having mental health issues is not something that's tolerated in my world," I tell him, hopelessness making my whole body feel too heavy, my shoulders slumping.

"Well, you've told me, *princesa*, and that's a start," he replies, and my eyelids flutter closed, his acceptance like a golden glow that fills my entire being with a lightness that I haven't experienced in many years.

"Yes, it is," I whisper, opening my eyes to see him standing there with the smallest of smiles tugging up his pillowy lips. God, he's so fucking beautiful.

"You should try to get some rest," he tells me, a note of command in his tone that I really shouldn't like as much as I do. As if the world also bowes down to his orders, the lights dim, not going off completely, but enough to make the space feel dark after the brightness of moments before.

"Yes, Sir," I tease, my heart racing when his nostrils flare and his thumb and finger tighten on my chin. He holds me for several long moments, both my hands wrapped around my cup of tea, squeezing it slightly with the need to reach for him.

"Get some sleep, I'll keep watch over you," he eventually says, and a lump forms in my throat at the kindness this stranger is offering me.

"Okay, Blaine," I reply in barely above a whisper, his hand falling away as I take a step back. My breath catches at the loss, and I pause, my body screaming at me to get as close as possible to him.

"I'll be right here, *mi princesa linda*," he assures me, as if he knew the reason behind my hesitation. That should be weird, right? That he knows me so well, can read me so well, after only a couple of hours.

Taking a steadying breath, I nod, placing the cup on the low wall that surrounds the stainless steel toilet pan on the side that abuts Blaine's cell. The front is open, and I shiver at the thought of using it, everyone being able to hear even if they can't see.

Stepping up to the bench, there's a thin, waterproof mattress on top. No blanket or pillow, and tears sting my eyes when I think of how low I've come. Of how angry the Ambassador will be when he learns of this.

Don't think of what will happen, Aspen. Focus on the here and now.

Taking my own advice, I breathe deeply for a breath or two, then turning, I hop onto the uncomfortable bed. Blaine is still where I left him, his massive arms draped through the bars as he watches me, giving me an encouraging nod.

Deciding fuck it, I bring his coat up around my nose and, closing my eyes, take another deep inhale, letting his woodsy scent calm me.

It's enough to allow me to relax and lie down, facing the man in question.

There's what looks like a gleam of satisfaction in his eyes, his features soft as he does as he promised and watches me settle down.

"Goodnight, Blaine."

"Goodnight, *mi tesoro*," he calls back softly, his deep voice like a caress of silk against my skin, even through my clothes. Despite being locked in a jail cell, and regardless of all of the trauma from when my father told me about my new boyfriend, my eyes close and sleep takes me in its embrace.

"MI PRINCESA LINDA..." A DEEP RUMBLE TEASES ME OUT OF MY slumber, and I find my body relaxing into the sound, a small sigh of contentment slipping from between my lips. A gruff chuckle makes me shiver, and my eyelids flutter open to a brightness that makes me wince. "Time to wake up."

Stretching, the creak of leather followed by the woodsy scent of Blaine only makes me want to snuggle back into the depths of sleep, but the hard mattress underneath me, and the sounds of men pissing, remind me that I'm not at the mansion. A mixed blessing, but still.

"What time is it?" I ask, my voice rusty with sleep, and I look over to Blaine, finding him where he was last night, arms resting through the bars. There are violet circles under his eyes, making his honey-coloured skin look a little yellow in the harsh fluorescent light. My brows crinkle. *Did he not sleep at all?*

"Not sure, but I think a little after six," he answers, his soft stare not leaving me as I sit up, brushing my hair out of my face. My teeth feel gross and fuzzy, and my bladder is screaming at me. Biting my lip, I look over at the steel toilet. There's some loo roll at least, and it looks clean enough, but my nose wrinkles at the idea of using it so publicly. I know no one can see me, but it still feels too exposed. "I'll keep watch if you need to go, *mi tesoro*."

I snap my attention back to Blaine, releasing my lip at his pointed look. He gives a small nod of approval, and I flush at the unsaid praise. Some part of me likes doing what he says, even when he doesn't speak the words.

"But everyone will hear me," I murmur quietly, my gaze darting from his as I feel my cheeks heat at the admission.

"You could always sing to distract them," he suggests, and my gaze snaps up to his, my eyes wide.

"Sing?" My heart thuds in my chest at the idea, at the desperate desire to sing in front of someone like Blaine, to sing in front of anyone.

I've always loved to sing, ever since I was a child, and although I was allowed to join the school choir, my parents didn't want any undue attention on the family that might come from anything more. And the idea of actually singing professionally? It was made pretty clear to me that wasn't an option for the daughter of Charles Buckingham.

"No one will mind if it sounds like cats wailing, *mi princesa*," Blaine teases, a slight twitch to his lush lips that stalls my breath in my chest.

I've never been one to resist a challenge. No matter how much my parents tried to make me a meek and mild daughter, there were always small rebellions, ways that I pushed back a little, even if they never knew it. Narrowing my eyes, I stand.

"Will you turn around, please?" I ask him as I make my way over to the low wall that shields one side of the toilet.

He gives me a small nod, taking his arms out of the bars and turning, clearly folding them across his chest with the way his T-shirt stretches across his back. Heat pools low in my stomach at the sheer power he must have in his body, and a flash of just how he could use that power on me has my legs quivering. *Jesus, Aspen, you barely know the guy and you're imagining him fucking you into oblivion already?* Real class act.

Shaking my head at myself, I get to business, hissing when I make contact with the cold metal.

"You okay?" Blaine asks over his shoulder.

"Fine!" I rush out, not wanting him to turn around, even if my bladder is refusing to comply. Taking a deep inhale, I close my eyes, recalling the song by Freya Ridings that I'm currently obsessed with; "Elephant."

I start off quietly, but soon get lost in the song, and it's enough of a distraction to enable me to pee, even knowing that I'm surrounded by strangers. I continue to sing as I open my eyes and lock gazes with a slack-jawed Blaine. My heart thuds in my chest, my cheeks flaming as I hold his stare and I sing the final few notes, a mixture of nerves and pride leaving butterflies swarming in my stomach.

A moment of silence follows and is broken by loud applause and whistles as the other inmates cheer, but all my focus is on Blaine and the look of wonder on his stunning features.

"Not bad for a cat wailing, huh?" I ask, standing and quickly pulling my knickers back up. Thank goodness I didn't put tights on and opted for my usual stockings and suspender belt. It's so much more comfortable in my opinion.

"Shit, *mi tesoro*. That was…" he trails off, and I rinse my hands in the small sink, drying them on my skirt. "That was incredible."

I feel my cheeks burn just as my chest tightens and a smile threatens to split my face in half. "Thank you, Blaine. Do you—"

I'm cut off when the main door opens and in walks two new officers, both men. One is young, maybe a couple of years older than me, and has dark skin, the sepia of the soil back in our gardens at the country house. The other is older with salt and pepper hair and skin weathered and tanned like he's spent a lot of time in the sun.

"Buckingham and Garcia, you are free to go," the older officer states, going to unlock Blaine's cell as the younger officer comes to unlock mine. "Your people are here to collect you."

My heart thuds for an entirely different reason as I step towards the open door. Why does it feel like I'm being led to the gallows instead of my freedom?

"Come, *mi princesa linda*," Blaine whispers gently from outside his cell, holding his hand out, and tears threaten to fall once again at his kindness. Feeling a little braver now that I know he'll be beside me, I slip my hand into his warm one, his large fingers closing around mine and the shock of electricity has those butterflies doing a fucking jig inside me.

The officers don't say anything, the older one just raising an eyebrow, then turning and heading back towards the door, the younger guy at our backs. Blaine keeps a tight grip as we leave the cells and walk back down the corridor. He goes first, like he's placing himself in front of me for protection, never letting go of my hand, the warmth of his palm lending me a confidence that I desperately need if I'm about to face the Ambassador.

All too soon we're back in reception, and I breathe a sigh of relief when I only see Bobby waiting for me, his sandy complexion not dissimilar to Blaine's, although he's older than Blaine, probably in his forties.

"Miss Aspen," he breathes out, rushing over but pulling up short when Blaine steps in front of me, his grip on my hand tightening.

"It's okay, Blaine," I whisper at his back, placing my hand on his T-shirt. His back muscles tense and flex beneath my touch, the heat of his skin underneath the fabric like a furnace. God, the urge to lean into him, to breathe him in fully is almost overwhelming. "That's my driver."

Blaine releases a low growl, his hand still holding mine as he steps to the side. Bobby looks between Blaine and I, rapidly blinking and frowning.

"Your parents have been so worried, Miss Aspen. When we got the call..." His tone is uncertain, and I gulp, unable to contain the trembling that seems to have overtaken my body. My view of Bobby is once again blocked as Blaine steps in front of me, his back to my driver.

Tilting my head, I look up into brown eyes full of concern, his brows dipped low, and the scar across his right eye socket crinkling. His palm comes up, cupping my face, and all the breath leaves my lungs, tears springing into my eyes at the tender gesture. His other hand hasn't left mine, and he squeezes, not saying a damn thing but letting me know that he's worried, that he doesn't want to leave me. I know that I should be freaked out, we've only just met for fuck's sake, but I'm not. Instead, I just sink into his touch, letting the comfort wash over me in a wave.

"I'll be fine, Blaine," I tell him, my cracked tone making a lie of my words, and his brows dip even lower.

"Miss Aspen? Are you alright?" I hear Bobby call from somewhere behind Blaine, but I can't escape Blaine's intense stare or the way he holds me as if I'm something precious that needs to be protected and cherished.

I don't think, just let my body do all the talking like his, and my hand lands on his hard pec as I go up on my tiptoes and press my lips against his. The relief I feel at the contact almost has my knees buckling, and it's like everything in the world finally makes sense. Blaine is frozen, but at the small whimper I make, he uses his grip on my face to pull me closer, kissing me back as if I'm the air that he never knew he needed to breathe.

Kissing Blaine is like walking into a room and knowing that you're finally safe. That none of the monsters in the dark can reach you, and I taste salt as my tears run down my cheeks. It's a bittersweet kiss, and a whine escapes my chest knowing that it can't last and soon I will be without him. Without my new protector. My heart breaks as I try to pull away, but he doesn't let me, sucking my lower lip so hard that the scab I caused last night reopens and copper tinges our kiss.

A deep, male growl thunders from his chest and he laps at my blood, making my knees weak at the thought of how some part of me is inside him now, becoming a part of him. My hand clings to his T-shirt, my other gripping his between us so tightly that it's a wonder my nails haven't left bloody trails in his skin.

It's the hardest thing in the world to let go, and even though my mind knows that this is crazy, that I barely know the man, my body tells me that we've known him for a lifetime and more. That we belong with Blaine Garcia.

"Blaine..." I breathe out against his lips, my eyes closed as if that will help me stay with him longer. "I should go."

A growl vibrates against my lips, making my skin shiver and tingle. "I know, *mi tesoro*, but I don't want you to."

"Me neither," I choke out quietly, aware of the soft conversation behind Blaine. He sighs, pressing his forehead against mine.

"Miss Buckingham?" Bobby enquires, and I briefly squeeze my eyelids tight, taking a deep inhale of Blaine's scent, knowing that once I step away, I'll never feel as safe as I do right now.

"I'm coming, Bobby," I say softly, opening my eyes and taking a step back, feeling like I'm leaving my fucking soul behind.

Blaine refuses to let go of my hand, our arms slightly stretched between us.

"I'll walk you to your car," he tells me, no question, just a simple statement of fact. I don't want to argue, so I just nod and then allow him to pull me along towards the desk where we have to sign something, for our belongings, I think. Well, minus the things I stole, I guess.

I pull up short when I see that Bobby wasn't the only one waiting. There are two other men here, and I have to wonder what the hell they feed the guys in America for them to come out looking like they just walked off the cover of Hot Guys USA.

The one on the left is looking at us with open amusement, the grin on his face infectious and I feel my lips wanting to slide upwards in a smile of my own. His eyes are the colour of a forest at night, his skin a golden, sunkissed tan and he's got honey-blond hair that's longer on top, which is slicked back from his face and cut short on the sides.

"You gonna introduce us to your pretty lil' friend, Big Daddy?" he drawls, his thick, Southern accent turning me into a legit puddle of goo on the tiles. What is it about a Southern drawl? And don't get me started on the way he calls Blaine daddy. The guy speaking is staring at me, his gaze taking me in from head to toe, and rather than find it uncomfortable, I like the heat that makes his green eyes sparkle like dark peridot jewels.

"Aspen Buckingham," I tell him, holding out my hand. He gives me a smoulder that would rival Flynn Rider's, and it fucking works too, all my nerve endings tingling. Taking my hand, practically setting me alight with his touch, he brings my knuckles up to his full lips and places a soft kiss on the back of them.

Blaine makes a deep sound next to me, and that just makes the new guy huff out a laugh.

"Sharin' is carin', Big Daddy," he teases, and my cheeks burn at the implication. "Well, ain't you just pretty as a peach." His gaze burns as he takes me in, filling with a heat that makes my core tingle. He keeps hold of my hand, and it's as though my heartbeat is a war drum for all to hear.

"Forest, leave Blaine's toy alone," someone sneers, and I snatch my hand back. Those words should not make me feel a shiver of pleasure, especially when I catch the dark gaze of the third man. There's something familiar about his eyes, and I can't shake the feeling that I've met him before, even if I'm sure I'd remember a face as fucking beautiful as his.

He has a strong jaw with just a hint of stubble, and his square chin gives him a look of superiority, an air of fuck you that his creased brow and slight lift of his luscious lips confirms. Ink decorates his jawline, and a single hoop with a cross dangles from one ear like some kind of rogue pirate. His hair is a deep, rich brown, longer on the top and styled back as if it doesn't dare look messy for fear of the wrath of its owner.

"Cool it, Landon," Blaine rumbles back, a hint of a snarl in his tone, and it warms something inside me to have someone jump to my defence so quickly. Landon's eyes widen ever so slightly, then with a small shake of his head, he dismisses me.

"Let's get out of here," he says, but it has the ring of an order to it.

"Come, *mi princesa linda*," Blaine encourages, tugging me towards the desk and only letting go of my hand when I need to sign the papers. They hand me my bag back afterwards, and I place the strap on my shoulder.

"Hopefully we won't see you again, Miss. Buckingham," the older officer says, and my face burns, shame stealing my ability to speak so I just nod and look at my feet.

"Don't let them get to you, Little Lady," Forest whispers from close behind me, and I suck in my lips at the way his breath tickles my neck. The urge to lean back hits me so strongly that I sway, but I manage to tamp it down, not wanting to appear any more foolish than I do already. Strong hands grasp my waist, holding me close to his body. "You doin' okay, sugar?"

"Um, y–yes, thank you, Forest," I reply, feeling his hands tighten a fraction even over mine and Blaine's jackets.

"Let's get you to the car, *mi tesoro*," Blaine mumbles, and I nod again like one of those dogs people put in the back of their cars, breathing out a sigh when his hand slides back into mine, our fingers intertwining once more.

Forest lets go but then takes my free hand, shrugging with a smile when I give him a puzzled look. Poor Bobby looks from Blaine to Forest either side of me, blinking as if he can't work out what's happening. *You and me both, sunshine.*

Though, it doesn't take him long to pull himself together, rushing over to the cracked glass door and holding it open for us to pass through. Somehow we manage, even with both guys refusing to let me go, but I don't complain. I know this security blanket can't last, and I'll be heading towards my punishment soon enough. I can stay here in this false safety just a little longer.

The sound of footsteps behind me lets me know that Landon is following us as Bobby leads us down the few steps and across the parking lot to where the Bentley sits. Forest gives a low whistle from beside me as we stand before the vehicle.

"A beautiful ride for a beautiful girl," he states, and my cheeks blaze even as a cool wind bites into me.

Bobby turns and reaches into his jacket pocket, both guys stiffening, letting go of my hands and stepping in as if to block me from him. Unaware as he's looking down, Bobby grabs a thick wad of dollar bills, and I want the world to open up and swallow me whole.

"This is to ensure you didn't see her, she was never here, understood?" he tells them in a voice that's hard and brokers no argument, even as his hand trembles. He's frightened of them, or at least cautious, and it makes me wonder why.

Silence fills the air around us, the tension surrounding us thick. I tug at my hands, but again, they will not release their grips.

"We don't need your dirty money," Blaine spits out, and I flinch at the venom in his tone. His hand squeezes mine briefly, as if in apology, but he doesn't look away from Bobby.

"There's a lot of money here, *amigo*. Enough to help out that dog pound his aunt and uncle own." Bobby nods his head towards Forest, and my bows dip even as my heart aches.

I knew Blaine wasn't from the same background as me, his lack of an actual winter coat and his thin T-shirt were only a couple of signs. Plus, people in my circles didn't get scars like that on their faces, scars that look like they were on the wrong side of a knife.

"We'll do fine without it," Forest growls, and this time I squeeze his hand. Bobby goes to say something else but I can feel the tension around and behind me telling me that I need to intervene before things get heated.

"They won't say anything," I tell Bobby, who looks at me with a slightly softer expression. He's had a soft spot for me since we moved here, looking out for me as though he were family and not just staff. "Will you, Blaine? Forest?" I look at each in turn, begging them with my eyes to let it go.

Blaine huffs before turning his gaze back to me, his free hand reaching out and stroking my cheek. "Of course fucking not, *mi tesoro.*" Bobby's eyes widen at that, and I vow to ask him later if he knows what it means.

"Your criminal antics are safe with us, Lil' Lady," Forest whispers in my ear, his body pressed against mine from behind, our joined hands trapped between us, and god fucking almighty, being between them like this? I don't know if I'm in heaven or hell right now.

"Time to go, boys," Landon states coldly, dousing my lust with embers of anger. *Why is he such a twatwaffle?*

Tears sting my eyes, the realisation that this is goodbye. It's like having a hot poker driven into my chest, but I don't understand why. I only met Blaine last night, Forest a few minutes ago, and yet it feels like they are as crucial to me as the lungs that bring oxygen into my body.

It's just the stress talking, Aspen.

But it doesn't feel like that when Blaine is looking down at me like I mean something to him. Like he will feel my loss as keenly as I know I'll feel his.

"Goodbye, Blaine," I choke out, the lump in my throat making it hard to speak. There's no point in trying to swap numbers. There is no world where I will be able to see him again, no place for anything between us as my future is mapped out in solid black ink and there is no getting away from it.

His jaw flexes, his palm cupping my cheek once more, and for just a moment, I give in to what my body is demanding. Closing my eyes, I nuzzle into it. Then with a deep inhale, I blink back tears and let go of both their hands before I step up to the now open car door.

"I–it was lovely to meet you all," I whisper, then, stepping into the car, I look straight ahead as Bobby shuts the door, knowing that they won't be able to see the tears that track down my cheeks as I wait for Bobby to get in and drive us back to my latest hell.

CHAPTER 4

"GODDESS" BY NATION HAVEN

FOREST

"I did not expect her to be so..." I trail off as the Bentley pulls out of the lot, unable to shake the feeling that I just lost something precious before I even had it.

There isn't a single fucking word that can describe Aspen Buckingham. Sure, I knew she was pretty from the research we did as soon as Aeron Taylor asked us to keep an eye on her, but what are the chances that Lan's uncle would do the same, though for vastly different reasons?

She's a fucking goddess, sent down from heaven above to bless us with her presence. Though, by the way Lan is scowling at the car, you'd think she was sent up from below to tempt mankind into sin. Either way, I'm glad we're the ones who get to watch her.

"You didn't get your jacket back," Lan snaps at Blaine, and I turn slightly to see that he's in just a short-sleeved T-shirt, looking finer than any man has a right to look.

"She caught you good, Big Daddy, huh?" I chuckle while Lan just glares at me, which makes me full-on laugh. "Aw, don't pitch a hissy fit, son. I'm jus' messin' with ya. Look, how 'bout I let you drive Gerti and I'll ride bitch?"

The big guy casts his eyes over to the two bikes; Lan's vintage chopper and Gerti, my pride and joy. She's a beautiful, deep-red Indian. Lan and Blaine helped me restore her from a rusted piece of shit that had been left to rot like yesterday's trash, but we brought her back, Lan, Blaine, and I, and she makes my heart sing every damn time I look at her.

"Let's go," Lan orders like the bossy son of a bitch he is. I roll my eyes at him.

"Yessir," I say, giving him a salute, and his nostrils flare. That man is just too easy to rile up sometimes.

We mount the bikes, and I snuggle into Blaine's hot back, wrapping my arms around him. We don't bother with helmets, why would we when the life expectancy for guys like us isn't the same as it is for normal folk? I'll be doing well to see forty, so why give a fuck about a helmet when I can feel the wind in my hair?

The engine purrs underneath me, and I can't help the holler that leaves my lips as we peel out of the parking lot, heading deeper into the east side and to the place that we call home. It may not be much and we may not have much, but we have each other and our freedom, so as far as I'm concerned, I've got everything I need right here.

"PANIC ROOM" BY AU/RA

ASPEN

The drive back over to the west side is quiet, Bobby not saying anything, and I'm grateful for the silence. It allows me to pretend for just a little while longer that my heart isn't breaking. That I didn't fall in love with a stranger—possibly two strangers—who I can never be with.

I tell myself it was just the stress of the situation, that my connection to Blaine was nothing more than a chemical imbalance in my brain, but my tingling lips make a mockery of my thoughts, and the way my chest aches and the tears that sting my eyes try to make a lie of my denials.

All too soon we're driving down the tree-lined street that leads to the mansion, the perfectly manicured lawns soon hidden behind high walls and metal gates with guards manning gatehouses like sentinels of old. Within mere moments, Bobby is pulling up outside my gate while the security guard opens it as we approach and nausea swirls in my stomach, my palms sweating as we make our way up the long, winding drive. I can't seem to keep still in my seat, all my composure that I know I should have gone, fled from the way my eyes shift around like the Ambassador might pop out at any moment and enact some punishment on me.

The Ambassador has a residence in DC, on Embassy Row, but my mother wanted a place just outside of the city, away from the hustle and bustle of Washington. Fairview Heights, the west side anyway, is the most desirable location within ten miles of the city, so here we are. We have an obscene amount of land; there are rolling, well-maintained gardens as far as the eye can see and a beautiful lake that I've found some semblance of peace sitting next to.

Despite all of this, nothing about what goes on inside the gargantuan house is peaceful. I swallow, trying to clear the lump in my throat, my hands trembling as we stop outside the front of the monstrously huge, red brick mansion. Both my parents are waiting on the elevated front porch, the Ambassador's arms crossed over his chest, his face a blank mask, and his suit pristine as always. My mother is a different story, and although not a hair is out of place—he wouldn't stand for that—she's practically vibrating with anger.

White-hot terror renders me immobile for a few moments, and I don't even notice Bobby opening the car door until he gives a subtle cough. Blinking, I somehow manage to force myself out of the vehicle, my bag clutched in my trembling fingers and my knees threatening to give way beneath me when I lock eyes with the Ambassador, my sire. My tormentor.

I've barely taken a step when my head whips to the side, a sharp, stinging pain radiating from my right cheek.

"You stupid little bitch!" my mother spits at me, and I cautiously turn back to face her, my hand cupping my throbbing cheek, my eyes wide and watery as I stare at her. I've never seen her so incensed, her face contorted with pure rage until she looks monstrous.

"Olivia," the Ambassador snaps in a low tone that has all the hairs along my arms standing on end, and my mother's spine straightens. With a curl to her lip, she turns on her Louboutin heels and stalks back inside, not giving me so much as a backward glance. "That'll be all, Bobby."

I turn slightly to see Bobby a few steps from me, his brows raised and his hand outstretched as if he were planning on intervening. It's probably best he doesn't, the repercussions for him would be swift; he'd lose his job and be blacklisted forever more, or so I overheard the staff saying once when one of our previous drivers tried to stand up for me. It's not the first time my mother has hit me and I doubt it'll be the last, though usually she avoids my face.

Dread pools in my stomach and I have to swallow bile at the realisation of what it means for her to have marked me like this.

"T-thank you, Bobby," I whisper, taking a shaking breath and then dropping my hand. The cold winter breeze soothes my sore cheek as much as it hurts, but it helps to lend me the strength to put one foot in front of the other and face my real punishment.

I keep my gaze lowered, staring down at the cold stone beneath my feet, knowing that if I try to make eye contact the Ambassador will see it as a challenge to his authority and only make my correction worse. I stop on the step below him and we wait, the sound of the gravel crunching behind me as Bobby drives the car into the garage at the back of our property. He keeps me waiting for several long moments, my thoughts threatening to spiral the longer I stand in the chill breeze, my body caving in on itself as I await his decree.

That's his endgame; to make me crack, to show me that I am nothing compared to him. To teach me that I need to fall in line, come to heel, and be nothing short of perfect. Copper fills my mouth as I bite the inside of my cheek in a bid to stop the pleas from falling from my lips. That, too, will only make him angrier; the Buckinghams are not weak. We do not beg for forgiveness and we do not apologise, even when we have done wrong. It took a long time for that lesson to sink in, to understand that I mustn't beg, no matter how bad it got.

"Come."

A single word, spoken with no emotion. It rivals the freezing winter air in its coldness and barrenness.

I watch his shiny black shoes turn and walk back inside with unhurried steps, and I follow, accepting my dismal fate. Our footsteps echo across the large marble foyer, the space full of bland decorations that my mother picked out before we moved in. The colours are muted and devoid of life and energy that makes a house into a home. Or at least, from movies, I think that's what is always missing from the places I've lived. He leads me past the double staircase and down the small side door that leads to the kitchen.

All activity stops when we enter the room, our cook pausing in whatever she is making for lunch, something that I'm sure will be delicious but I won't get to taste a bite of it where I'm going. I catch Bobby's frowning face as I pass the large island in the middle of the room where he and the cook's assistant are sitting, but tear my gaze away before he can see the terror that no doubt shines in my eyes.

My body is wracked with tremors as we go down another corridor, doors off it that lead to various food and wine storage. I briefly look up, which is a fucking mistake, as the door at the end looms before me. No object should have the ability to almost make me pass out, but that door does. The Ambassador brought me down here the day we moved in and showed me my room of correction so I was well aware of what awaited me should I make a single mistake or take a step out of the rigid lines he draws for me.

It's the same wherever we move, and I've lost count of the number of houses we've lived in, none of them feeling remotely like home. A single door now has untold power over me and the ability to render me a sobbing mess, even if it's not one of the doors that leads to my correction. I can barely look at a closed door without my heart crashing around in my ribcage, threatening to burst free like a trapped bird. I flinch hard when the Ambassador turns the key in the lock. I hadn't even realised we'd reached the room of my nightmares, so lost in my terror.

He doesn't say anything, just swings the door open into the pitch-blackness beyond, his hand held out for my purse. I'll have no comfort in that dark room, nothing to help ease the silence. It's all part of his correction, all a way to teach me the error of my ways and mould me into the perfect daughter, something I'm not sure is even possible after all these years. Apparently, the Ambassador went through the same style of punishment at the hands of my grandfather, and he used to tell me how strong it would make me, how resilient I would become. But all it's ever done is given me a deep-rooted fear of the dark, a terror of being anything less than perfect, and a desperate need to escape.

The Ambassador is a master at mind games, in his political career and at home. He has never struck me. Never raised so much as a finger to me. Sometimes I wish he would, for surely that would be over sooner than what he puts me through every time he locks me in the darkness with only my fractured mind for company.

CHAPTER 5

"RIGHT HERE" BY CHASE ATLANTIC

ASPEN

Time loses all meaning when you're in the dark. There are no hours, no seconds ticking down, and no sun to tell you when it's morning, just endless darkness.

When I fumbled around the pitch-black room and discovered seven bottles of water, the panic almost consumed me, but I managed to employ the breathing techniques I'd learnt over the years and stave off a full-blown attack. Breathing in Blaine's woodsy scent from his leather jacket that I was still wearing helped more than I'd like to admit. Reciting what I knew about the situation also helped. There's the water, a bucket in the corner for me to do my business in, and a threadbare mattress with no blankets or pillows.

I'd never been locked in my room of correction, as the Ambassador calls it, for so long before, and I knew that I would be weak like a newborn lamb by the end of it because he never gives me any food while I'm inside. It's a complete and total isolation, and I still struggle to work out exactly what it's supposed to teach me, even after all these years.

I'm lying on the thin mattress when the door is opened, letting in a light that sends agony racing across my head. I can barely lift my hand to cover my eyes, to shield them from the blinding light, but in the next moment, hands are tucking underneath me and lifting me carefully. They're gentle, and I crack my lids to see Bobby, his jaw clenched tight as he adjusts his grip. This is the first time he's come to collect me, the first time he's seen exactly what being the Ambassador's daughter really means, and my cheeks burn, my parched throat tightening at the thought of him seeing me so low.

"Let's get you upstairs, Miss," he murmurs, but he might as well have shouted for the way my ears ring. The Ambassador always makes sure that these rooms are fully soundproofed so no one can hear my cries, my screams for mercy.

I want to thank him, to show my appreciation for his kind touch, but speaking requires more energy than I am capable of right now, so instead, I just rest my head against his chest, letting his steady heartbeat soothe me as he carries me through the silent kitchen.

"Poor lamb," I think I hear someone whisper, but I can't seem to open my eyes again to see if the words were real or in my head. The voices shout the loudest when there is silence, the lines between reality and fiction blurred when you're trapped in the dark, and it doesn't always come back so easily once I'm free from the room of horrors.

Bobby carefully places me on a soft bed, and moments later there's a sharp prick in my arm. I know from past experience that an IV is being hooked up to give me some much-needed nutrition, my stomach unable to handle anything much straight after such a long fast.

"She starts Fairview Academy in two days," I hear the Ambassador state to whoever is in the room. I wish I could open my eyes and see, but it feels as though lead weights are on top of them right now. "Ensure that she's ready."

The sound of a door closing follows shortly afterwards, then silence once more, and I want to beg for some noise, for anything other than the blinding light to let me know that I'm out of my nightmare.

But my body gives up, and the blackness of sleep claims me. I don't fight it, am unable to resist the lure of leaving the hell that is my life for just a little while, the faint smell of a tattooed criminal surrounding me as I give in.

IT'S TOO FUCKING LOUD, I THINK AS I MAKE MY WAY THROUGH the crowded hall of Fairview Academy, conversation pausing when I pass by each group. Smoothing my damp palms down my favourite high-waisted burgundy wool skirt, I take a breath and pull my leather satchel up on my shoulder.

I'm sure the students are similar to every other private school I've been to; full of rich entitled brats that have gotten by on Daddy's money or family name, or a combination of both, never having anything not go their own way.

I suppose, being the British Ambassador's daughter, one could say the same for me. Except, I know what it feels like to be deprived of basic necessities, though not for lack of money but all in the name of correction.

Don't think about that now, Aspen. Just find the office.

Taking a deep inhale and trying to settle the rush of dizziness that I know will be with me for the next few days, I walk in the direction of the administration office. I'm due to collect my timetable—or schedule as they say here—and meet my student guide, who'll show me around the vast campus.

Unfortunately for me, Fairview isn't a boarding school, the students living close by on the exclusive west side of Fairview

Heights and being driven in every morning, just like I was. There is a large car park for the students who have expensive cars of their own, and this morning it was full of Lamborghinis, Bugattis, and a whole load of other supercars that cost a small fortune. I did spot three motorcycles that looked a little out of place, not having the same air of cost-more-than-a-small-island kind of vibe as the rest of the vehicles, but what do I know, maybe they're classics that cost more than all the cars in the lot put together.

A sigh of relief leaves me when I'm finally standing in front of a carved wooden desk. It matches the whole Etonian feel of the school; basically screams old money even though I don't think it's more than fifty years old. There's a woman sitting behind it, a shiny, light pink iMac in front of her. She looks young with neat, light brown hair and glasses perched on the end of her nose as she concentrates on the screen in front of her.

As I approach, she looks up, and her smile seems genuine enough that it puts me at ease.

"Good morning, Miss Buckingham," she cheerfully greets, and I'm taken aback for a moment wondering how the fuck she knew my name. "I've been expecting you. Welcome to Fairview Academy."

Of fucking course she's been expecting me, it's the first day of term after Christmas and I doubt they have any other students joining so late in the year, let alone in their final year—senior year as it's known over here.

"Oh, good morning," I hurriedly reply, giving myself a kick up the arse and closing the distance between the desk and myself. "I hope you had a nice holiday?" When you're trained from birth to be well-mannered and polite, it becomes your default setting. Though I can thank my nanny, Alison, for those lessons as neither of my parents bothered with me unless it was to show me off at some function or another.

"It was lovely, thank you. I got to spend time with my family which is always nice as we live in different parts of the country," she replies, reaching into the side of the desk and pulling out a shiny, new iPad Pro. "And you? Did you have a nice holiday? You were in the US for Christmas day, weren't you?"

"Yes, it was lovely," I reply tightly, my smile as fake as my words.

After the Tailor ball in Colorado on Christmas Eve, we flew back that night on the diplomatic jet, landing in Washington just a little after midnight. I didn't see either of my parents all day, there were no decorations, and they both went out to a party in the evening, leaving me alone after a silent Christmas dinner where not even a cracker was pulled.

As for presents, my mother gave me an hour a day with a personal trainer because, in her words, I looked like I could do with toning up as I wouldn't stay young forever and needed to keep on top of my figure if I wanted to attract a husband. Thanks, Mum.

The Ambassador gave me and my mother matching diamond necklaces, that no doubt are worth a considerable amount of money. I couldn't help feeling that although beautiful, the jewellery was as cold as he is, and I'm pretty confident his PA was sent out to purchase them on his behalf.

To be fair, once they left for the evening, I was able to put on my favourite old records on my reproduction Wockoder portable suitcase player and just relax.

"Miss Buckingham?" The concerned voice filters through my memories, and I blink, coming back to the Academy and the secretary who's looking at me with furrowed brows.

"Oh, sorry. Did you say something?" I ask, my cheeks colouring. I'd forgotten how much my concentration goes after a stint in my correction room.

Buckinghams never apologise, Aspen. How many times do I need to tell you that?

The Ambassador's words float through my mind, harsh and unforgiving, but I brush them aside for now. He's not here, and I've already said it now.

"Not to worry, I just said your student guide is here. He's one of our scholarship students, Rhett Butler, and it seems he's brought the other two scholarship students with him. You're in good hands, they've been here since Freshman year so they know the campus inside out."

Confused as to why a nineteen-forties Hollywood actor is showing me around my new school, I slowly turn only to come face to grinning face with Forest. Blaine and Landon are just slightly behind him, all three of them looking far too gorgeous to comprehend.

"Well, good mornin' Little Lady," Forest purrs, but I can barely hear it over the buzzing in my ears, my face tingling as blackness consumes me just like it did when I was locked away all those days ago.

CHAPTER 6

"BAD BOYS" BY AZEE

LANDON

Forest leaps forward and catches the Ambassador's daughter just as her eyes roll and her knees give way. Sally gives a startled cry behind the desk, leaping to her feet and quickly coming around as Forest scoops her up into his arms.

She looks too fucking pale, her dark eyebrows stark against her milky skin, her blonde waves tumbling around her face as Forest pulls her close. Blaine clenches his hands into fists next to me, and I know he wants to rip her from Forest, because as much as I want to deny it, a part of me does too, just to see that she's okay. To feel her breathing when she's just so fucking still.

"Bring her this way, Mr. Butler," Sally urges, opening the door across from her desk and ushering us into a quiet room with the blinds half closed and a hospital-style bed against one wall, open white curtains around it. "Place her there. Will you wait with her while I go call the nurse?"

"Of course," I state, my heart thudding painfully in my chest as I watch Forest carefully lay her down on the white sheets. Sally doesn't even question the decision of leaving an unconscious girl with three guys from the wrong side of the tracks unsupervised in a room. This confirms why I like her, whilst also making me glad it wasn't anyone else who had been tasked with showing her around. A lot of the rich dickheads here wouldn't stop to think of a pesky thing like consent if they were in the same situation.

"I knew I could trust you, Landon," Sally states, squeezing my arm briefly before she rushes out of the door, closing it behind her.

"She's too thin, she practically weighs nothing," Forest comments in a low voice from the bedside, and I go over to the other side, Blaine standing next to Forest and immediately taking her hand in his. Both their brows are deeply furrowed, and I can feel mine emulating them as I look down at her.

She is beauty fucking personified; tumbling, wheat blonde waves frame a delicate face, her lips painted a shade of red that has dirty thoughts running amok around my head. Maybe I am no better than those rich bastards out there.

"Her mom has her on some kind of fucked up diet," Blaine tells us, his eyes not leaving her face. "She regularly makes her fast and miss meals."

My nostrils flare as Forest actually growls like one of the strays that end up in his aunt's pound. I can sympathise. Why would she need to fast? There's fucking nothing to her as it is.

Do not get attached. My uncle's words float to my mind, and I have to clench my teeth, my hands tightening on the bars of the bed as I fight the war that rages inside me. She's a rich bitch that steals for fun, no matter that Blaine tried to deny it, he wouldn't give us a good enough reason to justify her actions, just saying that it was not his secret to tell. We never keep anything from each other, so another thing against her, plus the fact that her dad is into some seriously shady shit, hence us being tasked by my uncle to watch her and see if we can learn anything that way, as he's struggling to get an in.

Aeron Taylor, of the infamous Colorado Taylors, also asked us to keep an eye on her. Apparently, our fathers knew each other, and there was something about the way she reacted around her father at their party, the fucking British Ambassador, like she was scared of him. This got Blaine all riled up as, after his mom, he can't stand a woman being hurt by a man.

Basically, it's a fucking shitshow, all wrapped up in an irresistible package known as Aspen Buckingham.

"Forest?" Her breathy voice croaks and my gaze snaps to her, seeing her brows knitted together as colour returns to her cheeks. "Blaine? What are you doing here?"

She goes to sit up and, before I can stop myself, my hand gently pushes her back down. Shit, Forest was right, she's practically skin and bone.

"You passed out, Duchess," I tell her, my fingers pushing a lock of hair from her face and tucking it behind her ear.

"And I caught you in true Hollywood hero fashion," Forest interjects smugly, and I roll my eyes at him, my fingers lingering along her jawline. She closes her eyes briefly, and I snatch my hand back as if the touch burned. *Fuck, it did, the nerves all up my arm firing, which is bad. Yep, definitely bad, and I don't crave her touch one small bit.*

Her eyes open, and I'm drowning in a sea of green glass, my breath stolen out of my lungs before she looks to Forest and gives him a tiny, hardly there smile. The room fucking lights up like the fourth of July, and it takes everything I possess not to force her to look at me like that.

"Your name is Rhett Butler? Like, *Gone with the Wind*?" she asks, and Forest grins like he's not heard it all before.

"Yes, ma'am, though I most definitely do give a damn," he flirts, thickly laying on the Southern charm that has opened legs for him all across campus. The color on her cheeks deepens and she looks away, pausing at Blaine.

"I still have your jacket, if I'd known—" Her eyes are a little wide, like she's worried he'll be angry, and I don't like that is her initial reaction.

"It's okay, *mi princesa linda*. I can get it another time," Blaine reassures her in his deep rumble. I know that it's the only jacket he possesses and Blaine is very careful of his belongings, as we all are, as we have to be, given what little we have, so it surprises me how dismissive he is of it.

"I–I can get it to you after school. I'm sorry I had it so long. I..." she trails off, her eyes going unfocused for a moment, a flash of soul-shredding terror making my heart leap in my chest before she blinks and is looking at Blaine again. "I'm sorry." The sheets rustle as she fidgets on the bed, like she wants the floor to swallow her whole, her thin shoulders hunching inwards.

"Nothing to apologise for," he whispers, bringing her hand up to his lips and placing a kiss on her knuckles. Her eyes go wide, her chest hitching as if she didn't realise he had a hold of her this whole time. I've never seen him like this before. He's usually the last one to speak, let alone show any kind of affection, outside of our group of course.

The door opens and I look up to see Sally striding in, her heels clicking on the wooden floor as Nurse Jo follows behind her.

"Out of my way, boys. She doesn't need you fussing around like mother hens," Jo shoos us in her thick, Scottish accent. She's an older woman, and I like her, because like Sally, she treats us the same as everyone else, not less because we aren't worth the same as a small country.

I don't move, Forest and Blaine giving me the stink eye as they step back to allow Jo to take a look at Aspen.

"Now, lass, tell me what happened," Jo demands, strapping a band around Aspen's forearm and pumping it up to take her blood pressure.

"Um, well, I just fainted. I'm fine really, it happens sometimes," Aspen tells the older woman while not looking at any of us, instead, focusing on a spot on the wall opposite.

"I see," Jo states, her gaze sweeping over Aspen and a frown furrowing her brow. "And when was the last time you ate, lass?"

Aspen's eyes widen slightly, and I can't help feeling the way she nibbles her lower lip is because of panic, but why?

"I, um, well, just came out of a seven-day f–fast two days ago, so had half an avocado for breakfast," she tells Jo, looking down at her hands which are clenched tightly in her lap.

My gaze snaps up to Blaine's, seeing that he has come to the same conclusion as I have. Seven days ago was when they were both released from county jail. That's too much of a coincidence, but what the fuck is going on. *Surely the Ambassador, with all his riches and resources, isn't starving his daughter, is he?*

The metal creaks beneath my hands, and I ease up my grip, looking back down at Aspen, her forehead dotted in sweat and her breathing shallow as she looks like she's on the verge of a panic attack. I've seen it enough in Forest to know the signs, and without thinking, I reach out and grasp her hand in mine.

"Hey, Duchess," I say softly, and it's enough to have her whipping her head around to look at me, her eyes wild, the green vibrant and sparkling. "Breathe with me, okay?" I place her hand on my chest, taking an exaggerated inhale and not looking away from her as she starts to copy me. "That's right, just like that."

Her breathing deepens, my own muscles relaxing as her shakes subside, and soon she's back to normal, colour in her cheeks once more.

"Thank you, Landon," she whispers, sinking back into the pillows as if she doesn't have the energy to hold herself up anymore and her hand slipping from my chest to lie limply at her side. My brows wrinkle at the sight of her looking so weak and fragile, my inner caveman wanting to take over and care for her, the hand that held her clenching into a fist at my side as I try to stop myself from reaching for her once more.

Shit, no getting fucking attached, Lan.

"You back with us, lass?" Jo questions gently, and I can see concern written all over her face.

"Yes, I'm so s—" she cuts herself off, taking a shaky inhale. "I'm fine."

Blaine growls from the end of the bed, and I agree with him. She is clearly not fucking fine.

"Well, lass. I think it would be best if you went home and got some rest, and some more to eat. Such a long time fasting takes its toll," Jo states, her tone mildly scolding, and that pisses me off a little. I don't want her telling off Aspen, that's my job.

Wait, fuck, no. Not my job.

"No, I'm fine, honestly. I don't need to go home," Aspen pleads with Jo, her mouth in a tight line and her eyes watery. Why doesn't she want to go home? Unease slithers through me, leaving a sharp, bitter taste in my mouth.

"We'll take care of her today," I say, her head turning to look at me, eyes shining and lips parted. Fuck, she's too damn beautiful, even vulnerable and grateful, maybe more so. "Forest was meant to show her around anyway, so we can stay with her. I think, for the most part, our schedules match up."

Aspen tilts her head at me, the look of relief placed with one of consideration, like she's wondering how I know that. *Oh, Duchess, I know so much more about you, sweetheart.* But clearly, not everything, if my suspicions about the way her parents treat her are correct, and that has anger flooding through my veins once more.

She turns to look back at Jo and Sally. "See? I'll be well taken care of, and I have some nuts in my bag so I will eat those straight away, scout's honour."

Forest huffs a small chuckle, and my lips twitch upwards. I doubt our Duchess has ever been camping, let alone become a scout.

"Fine," Nurse Jo relents after a few moments. "Eat before you leave this room, lass, and take it easy. The first sign of another fainting fit and you will be going home. Understood?"

Aspen nods. "Yes, thank you for your care, nurse."

The old lady blushes, which has my eyebrows raising as I've never seen that before and we've been in here a few times over the years when one of those rich assholes thought they could take us down a peg or two. Backfired on them, and luckily for us, we were never the ones who started it so our scholarships were safe.

"Well, that's settled then. I'm heading back to my biology class, those kids don't know their arse from their elbow, let alone the intricacies of the female reproductive system," she tuts, turning away and striding from the room. I know from experience that she assists Mr. Greenford in biology and it can be an uncomfortable experience.

"You're sure you're okay, Miss Buckingham?" Sally asks, stepping forward, her face creased in concern.

"Absolutely fine," Aspen replies, biting her lip as if she were going to say something else. "Thank you for your concern and help."

Sally looks up at me. "You make sure she's okay, Mr. Capaldi, any sign of another fainting episode and you bring her straight back here."

"Yes, ma'am. Scout's honor," I reply, and am rewarded with a twitch of Aspen's lips in my peripheral vision.

"Good. I need to get back, take all the time you need, okay?" she says, looking back at Aspen and squeezing her arm gently, waiting for a nod before she, too, leaves us.

A moment of silence passes, and I stare down at Aspen, at the way she won't look at any of us.

"So, Duchess," I say, watching as her body stiffens. I don't like that reaction, but I continue anyway. "You going to tell us why the fuck you haven't eaten in seven days?"

CHAPTER 7

"WICKED GAME" BY GRACE CARTER

ASPEN

His voice is a low, rumbling growl as he asks the question that I can't—won't— answer. I swallow hard, licking my dry lips, and then risk a glance at Blaine. His huge arms are crossed over his vast chest, his jaw set in a hard, unforgiving line as he stares back at me from the end of the bed.

With a shaky inhale, I turn to look at Forest, finding his dark emerald eyes full of pain, like he knows exactly what I've been through over the past week or so, and it leaves sweat breaking out all across my skin. *He can't possibly know about the correction room, can he?*

Finally, I tear my gaze away to look up at Landon, and this close it's almost unbearable, his harsh beauty too much. Swallowing, I have to take another breath before I can even form a sentence.

"I'm on a special diet—"

"Bullshit," he snaps, the sound making me flinch, and his hands that are clenched tightly around the sidebar of the bed relax slightly. "Don't feed me those lies that you tell everyone else. Why haven't you been eating? Is it some rich bitch thing to stay thin?"

My mouth drops open, tears rushing to my eyes at the venom in his tone, at the judgement in his words.

"Lan," Blaine's deep voice barks, but I can barely hear it over the rapid pounding of my heart, the walls feeling like they're closing in as black dots spot my vision. *He knows, he somehow knows about the forced fasts, the correction room, everything.* I can't bear the way he's looking at me like I'm some kind of pathetic—

"Little Lady!" Forest's panicked tone sounds right next to me, and then my face is turned so all I can see is a sea of dark green, like a forest at dusk. "That's it sugar, ignore Lan. He thinks the sun comes up just to hear him crow." It calms me, my face held in his strong hands, the smooth cadence of his Southern accent soothing, even if I'm not entirely sure what a crow has to do with any of it.

"Forest," I hear Landon warn, but Forest just gives me a wink.

"Oh hush, Daddy. You know I love you, but she don't need your interrogation right now, do you, sugar?" His eyes never leave mine, and I can feel my body relaxing, my breathing slowing. I shake my head. "See, she needs a gentle touch is all, so stop pitching a hissy fit." His thumbs stroke my cheeks in a featherlight touch that has me wanting to rub my face against his palms like a cat. "Big Daddy? You got that protein shake you made this mornin'?"

I hear rustling in a bag, then Forest removes his hands from my face and a small sound of protest escapes my lips before I can stop it. He grins back at me, taking my hand in his and bringing it up to his lips, pressing a light kiss to my knuckles.

"Drink this, *mi princesa*," Blaine commands in a deep voice, and I break away from Forest's captive stare to find Blaine standing next to him, holding out a large, silver, insulated sports cup. "It's milk and protein powder, with some peanut butter and flax seeds."

Reaching out a shaky hand, I take the cup from him, bringing it to my lips and taking a sip. A small moan falls from my lips at the cold, rich, nutty taste, and I take another longer drink, licking my lips when Blaine places a finger on the cup and gently pushes it down.

"Slowly. You don't want to make yourself sick," he tells me, and I know he's right. It took me a while to stop gorging myself after time spent in the correction room, and I had to suffer through lots of stomachaches until I was old enough to search online about breaking fasts. Slow and little amounts until your body is used to eating again.

"It's delicious, thank you, Blaine," I tell him, one side of his lips kicking up in a half grin that has butterflies threatening to undo all the hard work I've put into not feeling too queasy. I take another small sip, then close the lid and go to hand it back.

"A little more, *mi tesoro*," he urges, so I open the lid again and take another slow drink, my cheeks heating knowing that all three men are watching me.

"I'm done," I declare after I've had about half. "I can always have more later?" I ask, and Blaine nods his head in confirmation, his fingers brushing mine as he takes the cup back. Like in the jail, electricity shoots up my arm at just that small touch, my breath stalling in my chest. I want more of the feeling, of the heady lightning that encases me anytime he touches me, but he pulls away before I can do anything stupid like grab his hand in mine.

"You think you can get up, Little Lady?" Forest asks, and I dip my head as I shuffle to the side of the bed where he and Blaine are. The metal side is down, so I'm able to swing my legs around and ease myself up. Both guys hover close to either side of me, ready to help if I need it, but after a small wave of dizziness passes, I straighten up.

"Thank you for catching me earlier, Forest," I murmur, looking once again into his beautiful, dark green eyes. He gives me a smile that's panty-melting, his dirty-blond hair falling into one of his eyes.

"Just call me your regular prince charming," he teases, taking my hand and placing it in the crook of his elbow. "Now, you ready for your tour of this fine establishment?" I can't help it, a laugh bursts out of me at his old-world Southern charm, and I don't know how it's possible but his eyes sparkle like the rarest of jewels. "Somethin' funny with the way I speak, sugar?"

"No! I love it," I rush out, worried that I've offended him. "*Gone with the Wind* was my favourite film growing up. I adored Rhett Butler—" I cut off, heat filling my cheeks as his grin gets as wide as the Cheshire Cat's. *His* name is Rhett Butler too, cue facepalm.

"Well, it seems like my namesake laid a good foundation for me to build on," he teases, his hand reaching out and tucking some hair behind my ear. My breath stalls at the light caress he gives my cheek as he pulls his hand back. "Shall we?"

It takes me a moment to remember what we are meant to be doing. *The tour, right.*

"Um, yes, I, uh, just need my bag," I stammer like a fucking idiot, but Forest has a way of scrambling my brain until I can't think straight. Looking around, I pause when I see Landon coming around the end of the bed, my leather satchel slung over his shoulder.

"Let's go," he commands in his savage tone while striding past, carrying my bag, and opening the door before walking out.

"Best do what he says, Little Lady. He can get real antsy if we push too much," Forest whispers conspiratorially as he starts to lead me out of the room. "It's not his fault, o' course. It's just that big, Dom dick energy he's got swinging around the place."

Blaine catches my other arm as I stumble and trip over my own fucking feet, my face flaming. *Did he just tell me that Landon is a Dom and has a big dick?* My brain short-circuits when the Dom himself comes into view, and my gaze immediately dips down to his crotch. Jesus, I can see the bulge pressing against his fitted black jeans, his black shirt tucked into the waist, leaving nothing to the imagination. Why does that make my mouth water?

"Anything I can help you with, Duchess?" Landon's deep voice caresses my ears, and my gaze snaps up to meet his dark eyes. There's definitely an air of amusement about his face, the hard lines softened and a single, black eyebrow raised.

"N–no," I squeak out, quickly looking away. My body screams *fuck yes you can—starting with that big dick of yours*, which is all kinds of messed up, given the mixed signals I'm getting from him. First, he's mean as hell at the jail, calling me a toy—*definitely not hot, nope*—and then he helps me out of my panic attack only to send me into another one with his brutal questioning.

Plus, your parents would never approve...

My heart sinks, a lump forming in my throat as the logical side of my brain makes itself known. She's right, the Ambassador and my mother would never approve of these three guys. I'm to marry well, make the family proud and, if the way my father informed me that I'll be dating Albert Pennington the Third—*who the fuck needs a number in their name?*—is any sign, I won't have a choice when it comes to my future husband.

"You good, Little Lady?" Forest asks softly from next to me, and blinking, I automatically nod, pushing down all my worries for now. There's little I can do to change things right now, so I may as well enjoy this tour of my new school with three guys who make me feel more comfortable than I have felt in a long time.

"Yes," I answer, surprised to find that with my hand tucked in his, Blaine on my other side, and Landon in front of us, I am good. More than good, if I'm being honest.

"Well, alright then. Buckle up, buttercup, it's time for the tour of your life!" Forest declares with a flourish, and a giggle escapes my lips again at his silliness.

It's a breath of fresh air, having someone just be playful and fun for once, not stuck up and serious like the crowd I'm usually around wherever I go. Being the Ambassador's daughter attracts a certain kind of person, usually entitled brats and sycophants, and I can't stand them but am forced to act as though they are my friends, even when I know they will stab me in the back the first opportunity they get.

Forest takes his time showing me the extensive campus; each department seems to have its own building. Some are old looking like the main building, others futuristic constructions of glass and metal. The music building is one such place, and I pause at the door, looking longingly up at the full windows where students can just be seen, various instruments in their hands.

"Do you play as well as sing, *mi princesa linda?*" Blaine asks quietly from behind me, his body so close that I can feel the warmth of it vibrating along my skin through my winter clothes.

"No, I wish I could, but alas, it's not my talent to play an instrument," I answer softly, physically having to hold myself in check so I don't lean back into him.

"You sing, do you?" Forest enquires, and I turn my gaze away from the building to look at him. He's wearing a thick grey hoodie underneath a denim jacket and stonewash jeans, the denim on denim look is really fucking working on him, but then again, I get the feeling any kind of look would work on Forest.

"A–a little, I guess. Mostly in choirs really," I say, biting my lower lip, suppressing my need to fidget under his scrutiny.

Buckinghams don't fidget, Aspen. We don't get nervous.

The Ambassador's lessons are never far away, and I hate that I can't just be myself, even when he's nowhere nearby.

"She sings like an angel," Blaine states, and my cheeks flare with heat at the praise.

"Makes sense since you fell from heaven," Forest says, that damn smile of his making me ache to feel his lips against my own. "Sings like an angel, looks like an angel."

I can't look away from him, can't take my eyes off his sincere green gaze as he speaks words that no one has ever said to me before. It's always about what I need to do to improve my appearance, and sure, past boyfriends—carefully chosen by my parents—have told me that I'm pretty, but never in a way that makes me almost believe them.

The bell rings then, and suddenly, doors are flung open as students pour out of the building like ants. Fairview Academy is an exclusive school, so it's not as crowded as I imagine a public school to be, but there's still enough rich kids needing an education in the surrounding area to have over six hundred on roll.

"Aspen Buckingham?" a feminine voice questions, an Irish lilt to her words. I peer around Forest to see a stunning girl with raven-black hair wearing delicate glasses looking expectantly at me.

"Yes," I answer, stepping away from the three guys so I don't have to keep looking around Forest.

"I'm Aoife," she tells me, taking another small step towards me, casting nervous glances at the boys who I can feel at my back. "The Irish Ambassador's daughter. Me mam told me to keep an eye out for you today, seeing as it's your first day and all."

"Oh, how kind," I say, used to embassy kids being stuck up pricks. "The guys were just showing me around, but I think we were just finished?" I twist and look behind me, catching Landon's look of annoyance before his mask falls back into place.

"We're all done with the tour, sugar. Just need to take you to the dining hall for lunch," Forest informs me, his eyebrows raised in a way that I think means they are going to make sure I eat.

"Perhaps, Aoife could join us?" I don't know why I'm asking, it goes against everything the Ambassador has ever taught me. I should take what I want, demand it. But I don't want to upset Forest or the others, and I would like to see if Aoife might be good friend material because god knows I'll need one if I'm to survive the rest of the year here. *You already have three hot-as-sin friends...*

"We have somewhere to be," Landon cuts in, and my attention darts to him again as he strides closer and hands me my bag. "Go to lunch with your new friend, Duchess, and we'll meet you after." His harsh features soften when I'm not quick enough to school the disappointment from my face, his hand coming out to trace the edge of my jaw. "We won't be gone long, then I'll take you to your English class. Make sure you eat."

"O–okay, Lan," I say in a breathy voice, his nostrils flaring at the nickname that falls from my lips. I'm unable to tear my gaze away from his dark eyes because they remind me of a starless sky, and something tickles at the corners of my mind, but I'm unable to grasp it enough to work out what it is.

He leans down, placing a light kiss on my cheek, and I'm engulfed in lavender, suede, and leather, his scent making my head spin with its deliciousness. "Good girl," he rumbles in my ear, and all the breath whooshes out of my lungs at the praise. Fucking hell, I want him to say it again as I'm on my knees in front of him and—

Blinking, I realise he's taken a step back, and Blaine is now in front of me, his woodsy smell mixing with Landon's to create an intoxicating fragrance. "See you soon, *mi princesa linda*," he murmurs before he, too, bends down and places a chaste kiss on my cheek, right over Landon's. He wraps my hand around his metal cup, giving me a pointed look, commanding me to drink the rest of the protein shake without a word spoken.

Before I know what's happening, I'm drowning in Forest's green gaze, his rose, gin, and leather scent overwhelming me until I wonder how I will ever choose which is my favourite. "You make sure you eat something, okay, sugar? Promise me." There's a demand to his tone, and I cannot deny him.

"I promise, Forest." There's no hesitation, and I'm rewarded with a huge grin.

He leans down, his lips a hair's breadth away from my cheek. "You can be a good girl for us all, Little Lady. You don't need to choose, we're used to sharing our belongings."

And with that heart-stopping information, he places his lips where the other two left their mark, and kisses over them, laying his caress on top. Pulling away, he gives me a wink, then turns and they all walk away, the crowds parting to let them through.

"I don't know what magic you wove over the Saints, but I need to learn it like yesterday," Aoife comments from my side, and I look down at her in a daze, my brows furrowed.

"The Saints?"

"Yes, the Tainted Saints? One of the most powerful gangs on the east side of Fairview, run by Landon Capaldi, Forest Butler, and

Blaine Garcia." She looks at me expectantly, and I just bite my lip before shrugging. "Jesus, Mary, Joseph, and John, you've got a lot to learn, girl. Lucky for you, I'm here to tell you all the gossip."

She links her arm with mine and turns us towards the main building, presumably where the dining hall is. I can't resist a look behind me, my steps faltering slightly when eyes as dark as a moonless sky catch my own and suddenly I remember.

The mall. The stranger watching from the shadows. Was that Landon? And if so, why was he, the leader of what sounds like a pretty infamous gang, watching me as if I was somehow important to him?

CHAPTER 8

"ANYONE ELSE" BY PVRIS

BLAINE

"What the fuck, Daddy?" Forest hisses as we walk towards the woodland trail at the back of the school. His arms sweep out back to where we've just left Aspen, his chin high. "I thought we were taking care of her all day? You know, like you promised we would?"

I've not seen Forest angry like this for a long time, especially at Landon. He's usually the most chilled of us, taking things in his stride, but I can't say that I blame him. I'm pissed too. I didn't want to leave her, let alone with someone she's just met too. I'm also still worried about the fact that she didn't eat for seven fucking days.

"She needs to mix with her own people," Landon grits out, his hands flexing at his sides as he leads us deeper into the woods. I growl, hating that a part of me agrees with him. We are not on the same level as Aspen Buckingham, the British Ambassador's daughter. "And, we have a meeting with Gio."

My pulse stutters. Gio is a runner for Landon's uncle, Alfonso Capaldi, a made man for the Italian mafia in these parts and who's been trying to get Landon, and therefore all of us, to join the ranks since forever. Lan won't though, not after what happened to his dad. He's never forgiven them for not protecting their own.

Guilt leaves a sour taste in my mouth, knowing that I am partly to blame for our current situation, for the debt we have owed Lan's uncle ever since he helped remove my cunt of a father from the picture and get me a home with Lan's aunt and uncle.

"What does he want?" I ask, my voice deep as the sounds of the students fade behind us, replaced with the cracking of leaves and twigs beneath our feet.

"An update on Buckingham," Lan states but doesn't elaborate as we come to the clearing that we've used before to meet Gio. The debt we owe isn't small, a favour in exchange for kickback to Alfonso with no end in sight. Well, the end would be the Tainted Saints also becoming made men, which is not going to happen. I can't protect the only family I have if we're part of the Family.

"Landon! Nice to see you again, *fratello!*" Gio greets, striding towards Lan and gripping his face before placing a kiss on either cheek as is the mafia way. Lan is stock-still, his teeth gritted. He hates this and wants nothing to do with that side of the family, but, because of me, he has to endure it.

"Gio," Lan grinds out, no emotion on his face, and it worries me that he's become so cold to anyone who is not us or his mother. He used to be so full of life, always smiling and joking as a kid, but since the day his father was murdered right before his eyes and he assumed the role of man of the house, he's turned into an ice prince.

"Come, no need to be like that. We're practically family," Gio scolds, releasing Lan to look at Forest and I. He's in the typical mafia attire of a black-on-black suit, complete with shiny loafers and so at odds with the forest that surrounds us. He's a wiry *bastardo*, thin and looks like a weasel. "Blaine. Rhett." We both just nod, letting Lan take the lead on this. "So, your uncle wants to know what progress you've made with the girl. What have you learnt?"

My jaw tightens until I hear my teeth creak. I don't want him knowing anything about Aspen. She's ours, even though I know that she could never truly be mine, our backgrounds are too different. My soul doesn't give a shit though.

"She got arrested for stealing, disappeared for nine days, and then turned up today. We were taking her for a tour when I got your message," Lan states blandly, and I want to punch *ese maldito* in his perfect face for giving Gio even that much.

"*Si*, we saw the police report before it disappeared when her father paid the cops off," Gio grumbles, and my brows start to lift before I gain control over them, holding my neutral mask so the fucker doesn't know what I'm thinking. It doesn't surprise me that they were able to gain access to the report. What does surprise me is that Aspen's dad was able to pay them off, enough so that even the mafia couldn't keep access. It does explain why we are involved, the Ambassador's reach must be extensive.

"Well, we've done what Alfonso asked, and I'm bored of trailing after rich bitches, so we're done," Lan states, and I glare at him, my brows lowering when his eyes dart to the side, a sure sign that he's lying. It's almost like he wants to keep Aspen out of this, which I am one hundred percent behind.

"Alfonso wants you to get close to her, gain her trust, and see if she knows anything about what her father is up to. Fuck her if you have to, she's a fine piece of ass so that shouldn't be too much of a hard—"

Gio's words are cut off as Lan slams him into a tree, his broad forearm pressing against Gio's scrawny neck. Rage fills my veins and my hands fist at my sides as I wish it was me squeezing the life out of the *ese maldito bastardo*.

"You don't say shit like that, got it?" Lan spits out, his face a mask of wrathful hate as he gets right into Gio's personal space, forcing the smaller man up on his tiptoes as Lan presses harder against his neck. "You don't even think shit like that."

"S–sorry–Landon–*fratello!*" Gio splutters, making a gurgling sound when Lan presses harder for a moment before he abruptly releases Gio, who falls in a crumpled heap on his ass in the dirt.

"Tell Alfonso that we'll be in touch when we know more," Lan sneers, turning his back on the fallen man and striding towards us. The click of a gun has us all pausing and my pulse pounds in my ears as my lips pull back into a snarl when I see the handgun aimed at Landon.

He dares to pull a gun on my brother! I will rip him limb from limb and beat him bloody with them.

Lan turns before I can take a step, then he's laughing, a bitter, painful sound that I fucking loathe coming from him. He saunters towards Gio like he doesn't have a fucking gun trained on his skull, and I want to shoot him myself for being so fucking careless of his own life.

"You going to shoot me, Gio?" he questions in a low, amused tone, stepping right back into Gio's space, the gun pressed to his forehead. "Well, go on then. Pull the fucking trigger. Or do you not have the balls to do it?"

The gun trembles, and I can't breathe as I wait to see what happens next. Gio's jaw is set, but his eyes are wide, the whites showing, and his body is full of tremors. Like Lan, I'm pretty sure Gio isn't man enough to kill him, and not just because of who Landon's uncle is, but because Gio isn't made of the same stuff as Lan. It's why his uncle wants him to join the Family.

"Didn't think so," Lan sneers, giving Gio a scathing look. "Be sure to pass my message on to your master like a good little dog."

A growl leaves my clenched teeth at the sheer stupidity of baiting a man with a loaded gun pointed to your head. Even if he's too weak to use it.

With a final curl of his lip, Lan turns on his booted heel and heads back towards us, giving no fucks that Gio still has the gun aimed at the back of his head.

"One day you're gonna poke the wrong hornet's nest, Daddy," Forest scolds as we leave the clearing, following the path back to school. Glancing at my watch, we have just enough time to check that Aspen ate something before we have to head to class.

Lan scoffs. "Doubtful."

His arrogance is one of his most frustrating features. It's also one of his most attractive qualities, but I won't tell *ese pendejo* that.

I catch Forest rolling his eyes, but see the smile playing on his lips and know that he's about to poke his own hornet's nest.

"You sure defended our Little Lady's honor quickly back there, Daddy," he teases, and I chuckle when Lan's jaw goes tight, his breath huffing from his nostrils like a bull.

"Looks like you two have the go-ahead to get inside that undoubtedly pretty cunt of hers," Lan retorts, and both Forest and I growl at him.

"Watch it, *bastardo*," I mumble, his lips lifting in a half-smirk. "And don't pretend that you don't want her too. You may be able to hide it from her, but we're your brothers and we know you, Lan."

His smile drops, and he pauses, rubbing the back of his neck with a large palm. We stop too, waiting just on the edge of the treeline.

"We can't get too close, she's not for us," he states, and a shot of pain hits my chest at his words. He's right. There is no world where Aspen Buckingham can belong to us. It doesn't change the fact that my soul is screaming at me that she does. That she's our very own angel, coming to join her saints and be tainted just like we are.

"So what do we do?" Forest asks softly. *Coño*, I think to myself when I look at him and see that wounded puppy look on his face. I want to say fuck the world and steal her away like a dragon would it's treasure.

Lan sighs and then shakes his head, his hand dropping at his side. "We get close to her, try to discover what shit her father is involved in, but we don't allow feelings to come into it. We have to remember the end goal; we do this and Alfonso will cancel our debt."

I'm not sure even he believes that, knowing that there will always be something that Alfonso will want from us. We're too much of a threat for him not to try and keep us under his thumb, our gang growing each year, despite the fact that none of us wanted a life of crime. But when life gives you lemons, you best learn how to make damn fine lemonade. That, or swap them for a kilo of coke and start selling it to rich kids.

"Sure, close but not too close. Clear as mud, Daddy," Forest states wryly as we continue to make our way through the campus and back to our girl.

I don't give a shit what Landon says, she belongs to us, even if the world tries to deny it. But fuck the world. I will burn it down if it means we get to keep her.

CHAPTER 9

"FRIENDS" BY CHASE ATLANTIC

ASPEN

Aoife talks nonstop as we make our way to the dining room, and although I thought it would feel overwhelming, it's actually refreshing after spending so much time in silence the past week or so.

"Tell me about the Saints," I ask as we make our way to the lunch hall. Curiosity has made me forget my manners, but she did offer so I'm going to make sure I get all the information she has.

"Keen, ain't you?" She giggles, and I flush. "Well, they've been here for their whole high school time, though there were rumours that it was Landon's mafia connections that got them the scholarships in the first place." Her voice is a low whisper, like they could hear, which makes me laugh as they just walked in the opposite direction.

"What about the gang? What do they do?" I question, my mind

coming up with all sorts of unsavoury things that I've heard about gangs in the past.

"No one is one hundred percent sure, but I think it's mostly protection for east side businesses," she tells me, and my brows quirk up.

"Protection? What kind?" I must admit, I only know what I've seen in films and sometimes the news about gangs and the mafia, never having known anyone involved directly.

"You know, people pay them money and they make sure no one targets that business, at least, I think that's what it is. My da knows a bit from back home and the Irish gangs," she answers as we approach the dining hall building.

"That doesn't sound too bad," I muse as we push open the doors and enter. The noise staggers me for a moment, and I have to take a deep inhale to ground myself before following Aoife.

"Well, there's also talk of them stealing from the west side, then giving all the spoils to people in need on the east side," she tells me, her tone wistful with a dreamy look on her face.

"What, like Robin Hood?" I laugh, but she just nods.

"Exactly! Isn't that just the most romantic thing, to steal from the rich and give to the poor?" She sighs again, and I can't help another laugh bursting from me, even if my heart skips a beat. "But the Saints aren't the only group to be aware of on campus," she continues, heading over to one of the counters that has food options. "There's Justine and the bitch squad, and Albert Pennington the Third and his jock cronies," Aoife tells me as she grabs some food and then we sit at our table in the large dining hall. It's a stunning space, high, wooden-clad ceilings with exposed beams and large, arched windows showcasing the extensive grounds and woodland that surrounds the Academy. There are also several wrought iron chandeliers hanging from chains, giving a faux mediaeval vibe that's kind of cute despite the building being no more than fifty years old.

We're sitting in one of the booths that are tucked down the side of the vast space, and I'm grateful for the hidden space away from the rest of the student body. I may crave noise after being locked away in the darkness, but the reality of it can be a little overwhelming.

"Wait," I interject, setting Blaine's steel cup on the table. "Did you say Albert Pennington the Third?" I feel like my eyes bug out of my face, my skin tingling as she casually mentions the guy the Ambassador wants me to date.

"Yep, the one and only," she agrees, then frowns. "Or I guess third seeing as there must be two before him. I mean, who even has a number in their name? That's weird, right?"

I laugh, knowing that I was right to trust my instincts with Aoife. "Really fucking weird."

"Oh, thank fuck you swear! Mam always says I curse like a sailor, and I was worried that I'd have to keep a lid on it for the rest of lunch."

We both laugh at that, and something warms in my chest at having found a kindred spirit.

"So, aside from swearing, what do you like to do with your spare time?" I ask her, popping the lid off the shake and taking a sip. Still cold and yummy. Aoife eyes it suspiciously, then looks down at her burger and fries and I can see the grimace on her face. "I would usually bite your arm off for some chips because they are life," I tell her, and her deep-blue gaze snaps back up to me. "But Mum put me on a special diet that includes lots of fasting and well..." I trail off, not knowing quite how to explain the fucked up situation I have at home where every calorie I eat is accounted for.

"Oh," she replies, looking relieved and a little sympathetic. "Mam says we're from good farming stock and men like something to grab a hold of, if you know what I mean, so I've never worried too much about all of that."

"I like the sound of your mum," I tell her with a soft smile, wondering, not for the first time, what it would be like to have a parent who actually cared about me for a change and not just what I can bring to the family. "She has some fab advice, and I wish I had more to grab hold of." I look down at my small chest, slim hips, and know that underneath my thick cardigan, the last couple of my ribs are showing.

"Maybe for a Saint or three to grab hold of?" she teases, then squeaks when a shadow falls across our table.

"Well hello, Aspen," the male voice greets, and I crane my neck to see a guy standing at the edge of our booth. He's handsome in that all-American, jock kind of way with sandy-brown hair and bright blue eyes. He's pretty muscular, though nowhere near as built as any of the Saints.

"Um, hello?" I answer, wondering who the hell this is and why they know my name.

"Forgive me, gorgeous," he croons, and there's just something about it that makes my skin prickle. "When they told me about you, well, I wasn't sure I wanted to be told who to date, but I am pleasantly surprised. You are pretty hot." His eyes trail over me and I squirm, not liking the fact that this must be Albert Pennington the Third, the boy my father told me I was going to be dating. "And it's nice to see a woman who doesn't fill her body with junk food."

My nostrils flare as he cuts a scathing look Aoife's way, my hands clenching around Blaine's cup when I see the red on her cheeks and the glisten of unshed tears in her eyes.

"I don't see what business it is of yours what anyone decides to eat," I snap back, and for a moment his eyes flare brighter, anger making them shine. Then it's gone, replaced with his boy next door smile.

"I like a girl with spirit," he states, running his gaze over me as if he'd like nothing more than to break my spirit for his own amusement, just like the Ambassador. Now I see why Albert was chosen for me, he has all the makings of a controlling, manipulator narcissist. "I'll pick you up after school, a bunch of us are going to Fairview Country Club so you can meet everyone properly then."

He doesn't bother to wait for my acquiescence, just gives me a smouldering smile that is nowhere close to the level of Forest's, and then prowls away, back to a table full of jocks and what looks like cheerleaders. Fuck. My. Life.

"I assume that was the one and only Albert Pennington the Third?" I ask Aoife, tearing my gaze away from the group, who all cheer and catcall when he reaches their table.

"Yep." I glance at her when she lets out a sigh to find her poking at her fries.

"May I?" I ask, reaching out a hand and hovering it over her chips. Her lips tug up in a slow smile that steadily grows into a wide grin.

"Abso-fucking-lutely." She chuckles, grabbing her own and we eat them with smiles on her faces.

"I'm guessing the cheerleaders are Justine and her bitch squad?" I question after a few moments, risking a glance in their direction and blowing out a breath when I see a dark-haired girl glaring daggers at me.

"Right again, and Justine has a hard-on for Albert..." she trails off, then huffs a breath, and I look back at her, my brows raised. "What did he mean when he said he doesn't like being told who to date?"

Now it's my turn to huff a breath out. "Last week, about four days after we arrived I think, the Ambassador, my father, told me that I'd be dating Albert." I grimace. Just hearing it out loud sounds so fucked up.

Both of her dark brows are almost in her hairline, but she quickly schools her look of surprise. "Oh, um, that's..."

"Fucked up? Yeah, I know." I let out a sigh. Suddenly, the sunny, winter day starts feeling dark and gloomy.

I just wish I had some control over my life, just a small part that was mine, but every aspect is taken care of without any input from me. The itch that landed me in a jail cell for a night begins, but luckily we're not near any shops, so there's no way for me to scratch it by stealing. My eyes still look around the dining hall, but I grit my teeth and refuse to take from my fellow students, no matter what my brain is trying to tell me to do.

"Why so glum, Little Lady?" Forest asks as he slides into the booth next to me, his plate piled high with all kinds of yummy smelling foods.

All my negativity drains away as he tucks a strand of hair behind my ear, the soft caress of his fingers sending tingles all across my nerve endings.

"Did you eat?" Landon asks, pulling up a chair to the end of the table as Blaine scoots in next to Aoife who moves over with wide what-the-fuck-is-happening eyes. Completely oblivious to my new friend's discomfort and confusion, Blaine starts to eat the biggest club sandwich I've ever seen.

"Ummm," I nibble my lower lip, looking at Blaine's steel cup on the table in front of me.

Landon's jaw tightens as he stares at me. "I didn't think so," he says, his tone scolding, and my cheeks heat. He takes a bowl from his tray, leaning over to place it and a spoon in front of me. "Chicken soup, and we're not leaving until you eat it all up, Duchess."

"You got me soup?" I ask, my eyebrows squishing together as I look at his savage features. He really is too damn beautiful with those tattoos climbing up his jaw and down the back of his hands. "But I didn't see chicken soup on the menu."

"My cousin works in the kitchens, so I had them make it for you. Be a good girl and clean your plate," he orders, taking a bite of a chicken leg.

I look at the delicious smelling soup, a lump forming in my throat at the fact that he was worried enough about me to get the kitchen to make something specific.

"Hey now," Forest coos from beside me, and I turn to look at him. He has the spoon in his hand, and I watch as he scoops up some of the soup before blowing on it and bringing it to my lips. "Here."

I open my lips, letting him slide the spoon in between them, and I know the act of feeding me shouldn't be so fucking erotic, but the way his pupils go dark, the black swallowing up the green as the flavour of herby chicken bursts on my tongue has my thighs clenching.

"Such a good girl," he murmurs, and I swear to god that a small moan falls from my parted lips. "We'll have this soup all gone in no time, won't we, sugar?"

I find my head bobbing as he holds out another spoonful to feed me. He's right, and soon the bowl is empty and I feel full, but not uncomfortably so. A bell rings, and I look in dismay at Forest's still mostly full plate.

"Oh! You didn't get to finish yours," I whisper, the soup now swirling uncomfortably as guilt makes my chest tight.

"Hey, don't fuss, angel. I've got a free period so I will eat the rest then. No need for you to worry about me, I'm a big boy." He winks at the end, and there goes my cheeks again, the double meaning to his words registering. Laughing, he slides out of the booth and holds out his hand to me, the soup settling down now that I know he'll be able to finish his lunch.

He doesn't release my hand, instead, bringing it up to his lips and kissing the back like he's now done several times. I don't think I'll ever get used to it, to the way his touch sends fire racing through my veins.

Warmth hits my back, and by the lavender and leather scent, I know that it's Landon. He's standing so close that I can feel the outline of his hard body.

"Let's get you to English," he purrs in my ear, and being sandwiched between them both has my heart beating frantically in my chest, my blood practically singing at their nearness. Butterflies take flight in my stomach, and that damn soup seems to be haunting me as my stomach begins to twist at having them caging me with their hard bodies.

"See you later, Little Lady," Forest tells me, placing another soft kiss on my knuckles before sliding back into the booth.

My eyes catch on bright blue ones filled with anger as Albert casts a withering glance at the Saints from across the hall. My stomach swoops like I've gone over a steep bridge, and I have to swallow repeatedly to stop bile rising to my throat.

The press of a warm palm against my back forces me to take a shuddering breath, and blinking, I look to the side to see Landon stepping up next to me. His gaze is trained on Albert's, his chin high, and I turn back to see Albert's lip curl before his friends usher him out of the hall.

"Come on, Duchess," Landon says after a moment, his hand still on my lower back and burning through my thick cardigan. Twisting, I look back as Aoife exits the booth, Blaine standing aside to let her pass. I catch his eye and he gives me a small smile before he sits back down.

"What is your next class, Aoife?" I ask, realising that I completely forgot about her with the Saints around. I have to bite my bottom lip to stop the laugh that wants to burst free at her bright red face. She narrows her eyes in a mock-glare but then smiles to soften it. I'm sure she'll be questioning me the first moment we are alone, but I'm not sure I can tell her anything. I've no idea why the Saints are the way they are with me.

"English too," she states, lifting her bag onto her shoulder. I go to grab mine, frowning when I realise it's not where I left it on the floor. We don't have textbooks, everything we need is downloaded to our iPads, but I still need that.

"I've got your bag," Landon murmurs in my ear, the soft caress of his breath against my skin sending a shiver across my nerve endings. I turn to see my satchel once again hanging off his shoulder, his own rucksack on the other one, and then he's applying pressure on my back to get me to start moving. "We don't want you to be late on your first day."

My feet move, almost as though he has taken command of my body, and I find that I don't mind this loss of control. Some part of me trusts Landon and the other two Saints to keep me safe. To not abuse this power they seem to have over me. So I let him lead me out of the

ROSA LEE

hall, Aoife resuming her chatter as we make our way to my first class while I wonder what game fate is playing to allow me three protectors and a new friend all in one day.

CHAPTER 10

"SMELLS LIKE TEEN SPIRIT" BY SAINT MESA

ASPEN

The rest of the day passes in a bit of a blur, and my concentration is not what it ought to be. I'm not sure if that's due to the fasting or the fact that one of the Saints is in three of my classes, sitting next to me like my own private protection.

I can't quite work out their place in the hierarchy here. The other students seem to look at them with a mix of grudging respect and loathing, probably on account of the fact that they are scholarship kids and not minted like the rest of the student body. The girls gaze at them with lust written all over their faces, and honestly, I can't blame them. There's nothing more alluring to a repressed rich bitch than a bad boy, I should know.

All in all, my day goes as expected, aside from my watchers, and soon the last bell is ringing and we're all heading out of the buildings into the crisp, winter sunshine. My stomach tightens when I remember my date with Albert, if it could even be called that. I mean, he didn't even ask me, just told me I was going with him. I guess when he's been informed that we are dating, why bother with pleasantries.

The Saints would...unless it's Landon of course, but the way he commands the world around him is kind of a turn-on. Not so much with Albert Pennington the Third. Urgh.

"So, you're going to the club?" Aoife asks from beside me as we walk out of our maths building, Forest next to me, my hand in the crook of his elbow again. It feels so natural walking like this, so close that our bodies brush against each other as we move.

"I guess so." I sigh, then pause when I spot Albert and the rest of the jocks waiting a few paces away, all laughing and messing around. My stomach churns at the look of anger on his face, and he strides over to us like there's a fire hot on his heels.

"You ready, gorgeous?" he asks tightly, his tone dark and commanding as he completely ignores Aoife and Forest, who tenses next to me.

"You offering to take us on a date, son? I'm afraid you're not my type," Forest says, his tone sharp with a cruel edge to it. I watch as Albert's face reddens, his jaw tightly clenched. Then a savage smile pulls his lips upwards.

"Thanks for taking care of my girl, *Butler*, but we really have to be going. Can't have her turning up with the stench of dog all over her, her father wouldn't approve." Albert's face is twisted into something monstrous, something that I recognise all too well from time spent with the Ambassador, and then I'm being tugged sharply away from Forest, Albert's hand like a vice around my bicep. Pain shoots up my arm, but I mask it before this situation gets out of hand, though it's the loss of my connection with Forest that leaves me feeling cold and empty.

"I–I'll see you tomorrow, okay?" I tell Forest, begging with my eyes not to make this into a big deal, even as Albert releases me only to tuck me under his arm. An overwhelming cologne makes me almost gag, I can't even identify the smell properly. It's so strong, something sharp and caustic.

Forest's nostrils flare, his teeth clearly grinding together as he takes deep inhales. "Alright, sugar. I'll see you then."

Albert doesn't waste any more time to let me say goodbye, just turns us around and all but drags me away, his arm a band around my shoulders.

"You shouldn't hang around with the Saints, Aspen. They are below you, criminals too, and they're not suitable for a girl of your standing," Albert grits out as he takes me past his group of friends and towards the student car park.

"Below me?" I ask, knowing full well what he means but wanting him to say it out loud, the elitist prick.

"Oh, sweet thing, don't worry. I'm here to guide you, just like our fathers told me to," he tells me in the most condescending tone I've ever heard. I want to punch him in the family jewels, but years of conditioning by the Ambassador holds me back. I've learned that it's easier to just stay quiet and not cause trouble.

He stops in front of an orange sports car, a Lamborghini I think, and all I can see as I look at it is the pretence that I'm so sick to death of. I don't want to be here with Albert *fucking* Pennington the Third. I want to be with Forest, Blaine, Landon, and Aoife. Hanging out like a regular high school girl and seeing where the chemistry between the Saints and I goes.

But I learned young that what I want doesn't matter. Hell, what I need barely factors into it so, with a sigh, I slide into the low car, Albert slamming the door just as the rumble of motorbikes fills the air. My heart rate picks up when I look through the window to see the three of them, the Saints, each on a metal beast that leaves me breathless. They're not wearing helmets—arrogant bastards—and they've turned to face me, watching as Albert gets in and switches the engine on.

The purr is nice, but it's nothing compared to the sound of the bikes as they idle there, waiting.

"Fucking sons of bitches," Albert hisses as he peers around me and sees what I'm looking at. "I'll make them eat my dust, show them their place."

His words leave me feeling nauseous, and I turn away from the Saints, not wanting to draw any more of Albert's attention their way. With a squeal of tires, we peel out of the lot, just missing several other students who are trying to leave. My hand clutches the oh shit handle, my grip white-knuckled as I rush to do my seat belt when Albert accelerates away, leaving the Saints behind.

"So, um, you play sports?" I ask after a few minutes, Albert still driving too fast like a twat, my training to be polite kicking in. A part of me also still wants to take his focus away from the three men, even though they are long gone. I can't have my father finding out about them, Albert is right in guessing that he'd be displeased. He'd be fucking livid, taking out his wrath not just on me but them too.

"I'm star quarterback of the football team," Albert preens, his hand landing on my thigh and squeezing hard. I freeze, my heart pounding. I don't want this, don't want him touching me like this, regardless of what our fathers have agreed. "It would be good if you joined the cheerleaders. Makes sense for me to be dating one."

I snort, and his grip tightens, pain making me gasp.

"I–I am not cheerleader material. Totally uncoordinated," I rush out, tears stinging my eyes at the pain of his touch. It lessens slightly, the spots where his fingers dug in throbbing and I know that I'll have bruises there.

"Well, you can always learn," he states, ignoring the fact that I basically told him I'm not interested in joining those bunch of bitches. His hand squeezes again, as if he knew a protest was about to fall from my lips, so I snap them shut and remain silent, like the dutiful little woman he and my father want. His grip eases and I breathe a soft sigh of relief.

We spend the rest of the car ride with Albert telling me all about himself, what he likes and doesn't like, in all things including women. Not once does he ask about me, but then, why should I be surprised? If he has my father's approval, he must be of a similar calibre of man.

I can feel my shoulders caving in, a sensation of falling spreading over me like a mist, coating my insides until I can clearly picture the life that lies ahead. Trading one controlling master for another, becoming exactly like my mother; cruel and uncaring because I am so unhappy that I have to take out my pain on those around me.

The car comes to a jerking stop, and I blink out of my grey haze, seeing that we've pulled up in front of a brick and wood building that looks like a typical country club. I barely notice when my door is opened, Albert helping me out and leading us into the club, his hand gripping mine tightly as the valet parks his car around the back. Too late I realise that I've left my bag and jacket in his car, but he tugs me along before I can say anything so I keep my mouth shut, figuring I'll get it later.

We're greeted by a middle-aged woman, who looks as though she's so full of filler she can hardly make a facial expression.

"Welcome, Mr. Pennington. So nice to see you again," she greets, her eyes raking over Albert in a way that she really shouldn't given their age differences. There's a flare of jealousy in her brown gaze as she turns to me, the skin around her eyes tightening slightly. "And you brought Miss Buckingham too. Welcome."

I don't even bat an eye at the fact she knows my name, I'm sure the Ambassador has been here already and told them all about Albert and I.

I give a quick fake smile, as is expected of me. *We don't talk to the staff, they are here to cater to us.*

"Good afternoon, Sarah," Albert replies, clearly not having been given the same lessons as I. "We'll go to the usual room." My stomach lurches for a moment, imagining some kind of private room where Albert plans to force himself on me. He wouldn't be the first to think that, because he has my father's approval, my consent is a given.

I push down the memories, enough to hear Sarah saying that some of the others are already here, and the relief that pours through me makes my knees weak.

Albert leads us down a wide corridor, and then into a room that has a panoramic view of the golf course that seems to be a must for any country club.

"Alby!" A girlish squeal makes me wince, and I see it's the brown-haired girl from the dining hall, the one who gave me the stink eye earlier.

"Hey, Justine. Have you met Aspen?" Albert asks, his arm around my waist giving me a squeeze that makes me feel sick. It's not like when Forest or one of the other Saints touches me, that's exciting and welcome. This is like having something sharp dragged across your skin; uncomfortable and just makes me want to step away. But I don't, I'm too well-trained for that, so instead, I give Justine my brightest smile, uncaring if I look fake as fuck.

"Pleased to meet you, Justine," I say, my tone so sweet that I want to throw up.

"Likewise, Aspen. We've all heard so much about you, and for the Saints to all have taken such an interest, you must be super special." Her smile is just as fake and brittle as mine, which falters when Albert's arm tightens.

"Yes, well, we've spoken about the kinds of friends Aspen will be making here, and the *Saints* do not make that cut, do they, gorgeous?" His lips are pulled up into a hard smile, and I quickly shake my head, my need to keep the peace and keep his mind off the three guys overriding my need to exert some kind of independence. "Now, let's get some drinks and introduce you around some more."

The fact that they are all drinking alcohol of some kind doesn't even phase me; money can and will get you what you want. I decide to join them, even though I know that with the small amount of food in my stomach I will feel the effects quickly, but one won't hurt, right?

The waitress brings over my long island iced tea, and I sip it gratefully as we take a seat on a sofa. There is a low table in front of us and other sofas surrounding it. All of them are full of what I imagine are the cool kids of Fairview, and I quickly forget names as I sip my drink and let the conversation flow around me, Albert's hand on my knee in a possessive gesture he hasn't earned the right to yet.

A little while later, the need to pee becomes overwhelming, so, excusing myself, I head to the bathrooms and take care of business. Washing up afterwards, I look in the mirror and see a girl who looks haunted staring back at me. Her cheeks are rosy on account of the alcohol creating a nice buzz, but her eyes are tormented, and I quickly turn away, unable to hold my own gaze any longer.

Is this all there is for me? Nothing of my own, always at the whim of others?

Shaking off the maudlin thoughts, and seeing that it's grown dark outside, I decide that it's time for me to head home. Albert has been drinking quite a bit, his glass of beer replenished and never left empty, so I'll have to see about ordering a cab.

I'm surprised to see that he's not in the main room when I return, and I curse when I remember my bag and jacket are still in his car so I have to find him.

"Has anyone seen Albert?" I ask, and Justine gives me a sweet smile.

"Oh, yeah, I think he went back out front to find Sarah. You'll probably find him in her office, the door just behind the welcome desk," she tells me, a genuine smile on her face which leaves me wondering why she's being so nice all of a sudden.

"Oh, thanks, Justine. See you later, I'm heading home after I find him," I reply, the alcohol making my words a little slurred.

"Anytime, Aspen," she coos, giving me a finger wave. Shaking my head, I turn to leave, hearing her and the other cheer bitches' tittering laughter as I walk away, but I've had enough bullshit for one evening so I just ignore them.

Making my way down the corridor, I come to the front desk and find it empty, so shrugging, I walk behind it and push open the door that I assume leads to Sarah's office.

Blinking, it takes a hot minute for my brain to process what it's seeing.

CHAPTER 11

"SHAMELESS" BY CAMILA CABELLO

ASPEN

Albert is sitting in an office chair, his face contorted in a mask of pleasure as Sarah's head bobs up and down in his lap, the loud slurping noise telling me exactly what she is doing. My supposed new boyfriend of only a few hours is having his dicked sucked by the receptionist. Hurt makes my chest ache. Not that I wanted him, but at the fact that he could treat me with such disregard, like I am less than nothing to him.

His eyes open and then widen when he catches me staring.

"Fuck!" he hisses, but Sarah clearly doesn't get that it's not a good fuck and goes harder. *Extra points for effort, girl.*

He goes to stand up, but I spin, my heart pounding as I sprint towards the glass doors which open automatically as I approach, thank fuck. The freezing night air is like a slap to the face, helping to sober me up a bit, my leather boots ringing as my feet pound the pavement and then the drive.

I have no fucking clue where I'm going, but lucky for me, my last school had a militant, ex-army physical education teacher who placed great stock in running, and I came to enjoy the forced ten-kilometre runs we had to take part in four times a week.

I can vaguely hear my name being shouted behind me, but I ignore it, my breath sawing out of my chest and sweat forming down my spine as I push myself to go faster, to get away. I've no idea what Albert will do if he catches me, but I don't intend to find out, all thoughts of my bad forgotten as I run.

The drive opens out onto the main street of Fairview and I keep going, the shops all around me closed and dark, shut for the night.

"Aspen! Slow the fuck down!" Albert roars behind me, and as much as I want to take a breather, I ignore him. My body is still weak from my enforced starvation however, and I can feel my pace slowing even as I try to push harder.

Tears prick my eyes at the thought of being caught, my flight instinct screaming at me to flee. Glancing back, I can see Albert catching up, but not even the shot of adrenaline can help me when I've been starved for the better part of a week.

All the breath whooshes out of me as I collide with something hard, strong hands gripping my biceps and steadying me before my face crashes into a firm chest.

"Easy there, sugar," a low voice sounds above me, and I look up, tears blurring my vision to see beautiful, green eyes staring back at me.

"F–Forest?" I stutter, my heart racing as my hands grip his soft, cotton hoodie tightly back. I sag in his arms, all the tension in my body leaving and his brows lower, his large hands holding my arms as he takes in my flushed cheeks and watery eyes.

"Aspen! Come back here right fucking now!" Albert's voice demands, and I sink further into Forest's grip, my fingers tightening in the front of his hoodie. Forest's head snaps up, a scowl on his beautiful face as he looks behind me, pulling me into his chest and wrapping his arms around me. I'm engulfed in his rose, gin, and leather scent, and it calms my racing heart, allowing me to breathe for the first time in what feels like hours. "Get your filthy east side hands off her," Albert snarls, and my eyes widen in shock as my body tenses. Did he just really say that? *Elitist pig.*

Forest just laughs, the vibrations making me shudder, the deep sound caressing my skin through my clothing as if he just ran a fingertip along it. I am definitely regretting my choice of stockings and a suspender belt rather than tights, I feel like it gives his voice too much access to my bare skin.

"I'd be mindful of what you say, son," he replies to Albert in a deep purr, pulling me even closer until our bodies are pressed so tightly together that there's not a sliver of air between us. God, he smells as amazing as I remember, like summer nights heady with the promise of a thunderstorm, and I bury my face in his chest, inhaling him into my lungs as I try to further calm my breathing and racing heart. "You're on our turf now."

I look up and around me, startled to see that he's right, the buildings around us have a dilapidated look, weeds growing in the cracks of the pavement, and a general air of neglect that tells me we're not on the west side anymore.

"Come over here, baby," Albert coos, and I twist my head to see he's talking to me, one hand out. Bile fills the back of my throat, remembering why I ran in the first place. "We can go back to my place and I'll explain."

I snort, turning in Forest's arms so that my back is pressed to his front, but not stepping away as I'm enjoying the feel of them around me far too much to give it up. There's something safe about him, even if he's in a gang from the wrong side of the tracks.

"Will it go something like 'She tripped and fell on my dick'?" I spit out, the alcohol making me bold as anger replaces the hurt and humiliation of catching him with his dick shoved down that woman's throat. Forest chuckles behind me, his head dipping as he brushes a light kiss on my neck. I have to release a slow breath as tingles race from the point where his lips meet my skin, the move turning some of my anger into pure, unadulterated lust.

Albert's face turns a mottled purple, his jaw clenching, and I'm not sure if it's a reaction to my words or to what Forest just did, but I find that I just don't give a shit right now.

"Your father should have told you the expectations of our world," he bites out, and I stiffen, all lust-filled thoughts for the man behind me disappearing.

"Expectations?" I ask coldly, ice filling my veins and knowing what he's getting at but daring him to boldly state it.

"Wives love their husbands, give them heirs, and look pretty on their arms when they go to important business functions," he informs me, his tone patronising, and I can feel every muscle in my body tighten. "And they don't ask questions if they smell someone else's perfume on their skin."

My jaw drops. Did he just tell me, his supposed girlfriend, that my lot in life is to have a husband who cheats on me? I mean, I'm not surprised given my parents' cold and fucked up relationship, but Jesus.

"Well, here's a newsflash, Albert," I scathe, sinking deeper into Forest's comforting embrace. His arms wrap tighter around me, his fingers tracing a pattern on my hip. "I deserve more than that shit. I deserve someone who won't even look at another woman because they can't take their eyes off me. I deserve someone who wants to spend every moment with me, wrapped in my arms. I deserve someone who wants to spend hours buried inside me, who can't get enough of me, who rushes home from work just to throw me up against the wall and fuck me hard and fast because he's so consumed by me he can't control himself." I'm panting, my chest heaving, my speech surprising even me with its ferocity, but it's all true, that's what I want. Not what Albert is offering and certainly not what the Ambassador is demanding.

"I volunteer as tribute," Forest whispers in my ear, and I would laugh but he thrusts his hips slightly so I can feel exactly how much my words have affected him. Then he straightens up behind me, his impressive hardness pushing into my lower back. *Damn tall boys!* "Well, Albert, baby," he drawls, his arms loosening only to have one hand slide possessively down my side, setting butterflies fluttering in my stomach. "The lady has spoken, and it seems to me you're not what she's looking for. So be a good little rich boy and run along out of my fucking territory."

Albert stares at us, his mouth opening and closing unattractively so that he looks like a fish. I bite my lip to hold the chuckle in, my chest warm with the fact that Forest just stood up for me. I'm not sure anyone ever has before, not until I met the Saints anyway.

"Fine," my now ex-boyfriend of a few hours snarls, an angry slant to his lips. "Stay here with your gangbanger, but don't come crying to me when he fucks you and leaves you like all the others! And don't think for one minute your father won't hear of this!"

I flinch at his yell but pull my lips back to bare my teeth. "I'm sure my father won't be too pleased when I explain that I found you, dick down the throat of a staff member in a public place. That kind of indiscretion is most definitely frowned upon," I volley back, my heart once again pounding as I will him not to tell the Ambassador about this. It won't only be me who is punished if he finds out that Forest has his hands on me like this.

His upper lip curls unattractively, and with another snarl, I watch as he spins on his heel and storms off. My body slumps against Forest, and I let him hold me as the adrenaline leaves my system. It's not until Albert has completely disappeared from view that I speak.

"Thank you, Forest." My shoulders droop as my breath huffs out of me in an audible sigh.

"I will always take care of you, Little Lady," he breathes in my ear. "I've craved you from the first moment I saw you holding Blaine's hand in county jail, sugar," he confesses, spinning me in his arms so fast that I gasp as the world spins around me. "And that little speech, well shit."

He pushes me backwards, my spine slamming into the wall of the building behind us with such force that plaster dust fills the air, a sharp tingle racing up my spine as my heart thuds in my chest. It's not fear that makes my pulse thud, it's anticipation and a need that leaves my knees weak.

His large hand cups the back of my head, cushioning the blow before it can make contact as his eyes bore into mine, lust making the green as dark as a nighttime forest. My hands automatically come up, grabbing his muscled arms which flex under my grip. What is it about a man's biceps that's so fucking hot?

"And this prim and proper outfit," he comments huskily, raking his eyes over me and the pleated wool skirt, shirt, and cardigan I'm wearing, my jacket also in that fucktard Albert's car. The skirt ends just below my knees, quite modest really considering what some of the girls here wear, but it seems to be Forest's cup of tea if the fire in his green eyes is anything to go by. "It would tempt a damn Saint," he tells me, smirking at his own joke. "And we all know that I'm a Tainted Saint."

His fingers tease down between my breasts, popping the buttons of my cardigan, and then making quick work of my blouse, my lace-covered breasts exposed to the cold night air. I'm aware that it's the middle of fucking winter, but I couldn't swear to it with the way my body is burning under his touch.

"So beautiful," he murmurs, leaning down to place a soft kiss on the swell of breast that's just above the lace edge. My nipples pebble, my hands sliding to his shoulders as he moves his lips over one peak, sucking it and the lace into his hot mouth.

"Forest," I moan, unable to tear my gaze away from his dark-blond head as he teases my nipple with his tongue, his teeth scraping the sensitive bud. He moves to the other side, giving my other breast the same attention, and I couldn't stop him even if I wanted to. He feels too fucking good, worshipping me in a way that I've never experienced before, and I want more. "Please, Forest." I don't care why Forest was there, or how I managed to bump into him just when I needed him. I couldn't give a shit if anyone is around, in fact, the idea of being seen has lightning tingling up my spine. All I know is that right now, I need him more than I need to breathe.

I watch the smile play on his lush lips, his palms gliding down my thighs. My breath comes in fast pants as he lifts the soft fabric of my skirt, bringing it up with him as he straightens to his impressive height to expose my stockings, suspenders, and lace underwear.

"Lan's gonna lose his shit when he realises you wear thigh highs and garters every day," he murmurs in a husky whisper, a deep groan sounding in his chest as his fingertips brush across the front of my core. A needy whimper falls from my lips, my fists clenching in his hoodie. We're not exactly hidden. Sure, this side of the building is shrouded in darkness, but we're still on the street where anyone could walk past and see what's happening, and bloody hell, that just makes me hotter, wetter. It's even more of a rush than when I steal something, and I have a suspicion that guilt will not follow this high like it does then.

"I'd apologise for this, sugar, but I ain't fucking sorry," Forest rasps out, and there's no time for my confusion as to what on earth he's talking about because his hand wraps around the front of my lace panties and rips them clean from my body, placing them in his back pocket. I squeak at the sharp sting of the fabric pulling against my skin, but before the pain can fully register, he's sinking two thick fingers into my wet channel.

"Forest–" I gasp, his fingers sliding in easily given how slick I am from his teasing moments ago. My fingers dig into his shoulders, and I wish he wasn't wearing this damn hoodie so I could get at his hot skin.

"You're so fucking wet for me," he groans, pulling his fingers out a little just to sink them in deeper, making me cry out. "So tight too."

His free hand grabs under my thigh, pulling my leg up to wrap around his hip as his fingers continue to fuck me. I can't help it, I move my hips, fucking them back, lost to the pleasure that I've been desperate for ever since I met Blaine and then Forest and Landon in county jail.

"That's it, sugar. Be a good girl and come all over Daddy's fingers."

Oh. Shit.

My orgasm rips through me, and I coat his hand in my release as my body flushes hot then cold, my nails digging into his large shoulders. The waves of pleasure are still rolling through me when I hear a zipper being undone, and I crack my lids to look down and see him lining himself up with my drenched opening.

"You're gonna let Daddy fuck you out here on the street like a good little whore, aren't you?" he grits out, sinking the thick head of him inside my opening.

"Y–yes," I whine, my eyes glued to his thick cock as it spears me in half.

"Yes what, sugar?" he asks in a firm voice, grabbing my chin with fingers drenched in my own release. I look into his eyes, the green the colour of a forest at night, full of dark promises and blissful nightmares.

"Y–yes, Daddy," I breathe out, my whole body trembling as he pauses, a smirk on his kissable lips.

"Good girl," he praises, then slams his lips against mine as he thrusts the rest of the way in, swallowing my scream. He's just so bloody big. There's a blinding pain followed by an exquisite pleasure as he moves his hips in a sensual rhythm, his mouth devouring mine in a kiss that fulfils all the depraved promises of his eyes.

His hand leaves my chin, grabbing my other thigh and hauling me up, using his body to press me back against the rough wall as he fucks me harder, faster, just like I asked. And oh my giddy aunt, it's exactly what I've been craving. None of my other sexual partners would lose control like this, too afraid that my small petite frame couldn't handle roughness. Too consumed with chasing their own pleasure to worry about mine. Not surprising since they'd all been carefully vetted by the Ambassador, chosen for what they could bring to my family and not because I particularly wanted them.

But Forest fucks me like he's about to die and the key to life is between my legs. The sounds coming from us would be embarrassing if it didn't feel so mind-blowing that I can barely think straight. My hands move up into his hair, tangling in the longer blond locks at the top as he continues to pound into me, sending waves of electrical heat with each thrust of his hips.

I pull back from his mouth with a gasp, his head burying in my neck and latching on as he sucks and nips at the sensitive skin there, tingles racing from his touch to join the molten heat at my core.

"Forest–shit–I'm so close," I mumble incoherently, my eyes opening briefly and immediately getting trapped in a gaze as dark as the night that surrounds us. *Landon.* Another set of eyes catches my attention, these I know are a chocolate-brown, although in the shadows of the alley, they, too, look pitch-black. *Blaine.* I should have known where one Saint is, the others are not far away.

I must tense a little, as Forest slows his ferocious pace, bringing his head up to look into my eyes. Seeing the direction of my stare, he twists his head to glance over his shoulder, then turns back to me with a devious smile that has my inner walls clenching around his still-moving cock.

"Oh, sugar," he coos, his eyes taking in my parted lips and no doubt flushed cheeks. I look away from the two other Saints and get lost in the heat of his stare. "You gonna show them how you come all over Daddy's dick like a good little fuck toy?" I whimper again as one of his hands leaves my thigh, snaking between us and circling my engorged clit. "Well?"

"Y–yes, Daddy," I reply barely above a whisper, my gaze going back to the men behind Forest as they watch their friend, their chosen brother, fuck me against the wall of some run-down building on the east side for all to see.

It doesn't take long for my climax to build to an overwhelming pressure, my eyes locked on Landon as it explodes across my skin like liquid fire, and I scream into the night air. My nails dig into Forest's scalp, but I can't pull back, the pleasure is too intense, too consuming. Forest doesn't even pause, pounding me into the wall as his fingers dance over my sensitive bud, and I want to beg him to stop and keep going all at once.

I tear my gaze from Landon's only to find Blaine standing there, still partly hidden in the shadows, his arm moving up and down in a firm grip that tells me he's pleasuring himself while watching us. Another rush of pleasure hits me hard as he braces his free hand on the wall beside him, his head thrown back in ecstasy. My mouth waters at the thought of licking him clean, swallowing every last drop until he's empty.

"Fuck, you're like a vise around me," Forest moans, thrusting harder several times before he joins us and roars out his release as his dick plunges deep inside me.

I look back at Landon, finding him out of the shadows, my eyes heavy-lidded as Forest continues these little thrusts, filling me with his cum. Landon doesn't have his dick in his hand, but a quick glance down shows me the large bulge in his trousers.

"We best get you back to the house to clean up," Landon states into the quiet night, and I shiver at his voice. It's so deep, like the sound of the depths of the ocean, washing over me in soothing waves.

Forest chuckles, making me groan as his semi-hard cock jostles inside me.

"Looks like you're coming home with me tonight, sugar," he says, pulling out of my body and a small noise comes out of my mouth at the loss of him, at the way his cum slides down my inner thighs. "Don't worry, sweetness, Daddy will take care of you."

My knees wobble as he takes my face in his hands, both now sticky with my release, and places a gentle, lingering kiss on my swollen lips. Tears sting my eyes at the softness in the gesture. Until Blaine at the jail, no one had ever held me like I'm something precious, kissed me like I'm something to treasure. Blaine was the first, and now Forest.

It's then that I realise how dangerous the Saints really are. It's not their frightening reputations, the tattoos, or the gang vibes. It's the way that they look after the things that belong to them, that are important to them.

And I'm wondering if I've just fallen into that category.

CHAPTER 12

"CEILINGS" BY LIZZIE MCALPINE

ASPEN

I follow Landon as Forest grips my hand tightly in his, Blaine's dark presence behind us as we make our way through the pitch-black streets of the east side. The cum that coats my inner thighs cools, drying slightly and making my skin tacky as I walk, but a part of me likes that he's marked me, that Forest is still inside me and on my skin.

I've never been to this part of Fairview before, and I can't help looking around with a tension in my shoulders. It's so...broken. There's no trees, no greenery at all really, and even though it's winter, I get the feeling that even in the height of summer it's barren.

We pass buildings that look like they've seen better days, the fronts cracked and some windows boarded up. It's a place that has been forgotten, the people who call it home left to fend for themselves, and a lump forms in my throat, my hand squeezing

Forest's tightly at the thought of how much he and the others must have struggled over the years.

My parents may be controlling, may withhold food from me as a punishment and correction, but I've never had to worry about money, about having a roof over my head. No matter how much I wished it was a different roof.

"Everything okay, Little Lady?" Forest asks as we approach a building that's separate from the others, and I turn to look at him, his brows furrowed as he pulls us to a stop.

"Yes...I..." I'm not sure what to say, looking at the run-down building in front of us and the rough dirt patch that's in front of it. A weathered sign reads 'Fairview Pound.' I catch Landon's gaze and his jaw tightens.

"Getting a dose of how real people live is hard, isn't it, Duchess?" he grits out, and heat flashes throughout my body at the venom that laces his tone.

"No, that is, I...I didn't know," I offer weakly, and he scoffs, then turns, heading to the side of the building where a metal staircase leads up to a door. I huff a breath, pissed at being so tongue-tied around him and hating that he thinks I pity them. I don't, though I am sorry for all the hardships I'm guessing they suffered over the years.

"Come on. Let's get you inside and I'll give you the grand tour," Forest offers gently, tugging my hand as he pulls us in the direction of the stairs. I grimace when more slick wetness slides down my inner thighs, but I follow him nonetheless. Blaine comes up behind us, his footsteps quiet, which is surprising given how large the guy is.

I gasp a small breath when his hand lands on my lower back, the heat of his palm against my clothes making me realise how cold I am now that the rush of sex with Forest is leaving me.

Fuck. I had the best sex of my life with someone I barely know out in the open after running away from the man the Ambassador chose for me. I'm not sure how to process all of that. So, taking a measured inhale, I push it to the back of my mind and focus on the metal stairs that will lead to someplace I can clean up at least.

The door is open when we reach it, and then we're stepping into a space that's small yet cosy, and feels more like a home than all of the mansions I've ever lived in.

"Close the door, Big Daddy, you're letting all the good air out," Forest chides, letting go of my hand as a huge furry dog strides up to him, tail wagging when Forest grabs his face and gives him scratches. "Now, you're gonna be a gentleman to our guest, ain't you, Bolt?" he asks the beast of a dog.

Intelligent, ice-blue eyes hone in on me, and then the huge creature is striding towards me.

"Careful, he's not good with strangers," Landon cautions as I crouch down with my hand out so Bolt can sniff it. He looks like a husky, beautiful, and so fluffy he's like a teddy bear.

"You're just a big softie, aren't you, gorgeous boy?" I coo at the dog, my hand sinking into the fur at his ear when he pushes his face into my touch. "Yes, you are, beautiful boy."

"Talk like that will make me hard again, sugar," Forest groans, and a giggle falls from my lips as my other hand comes up and scratches Bolt's other ear.

Soon he's panting, and then rolling over so I can give him some belly rubs. I look up to see all three guys watching with raised brows and wide eyes.

"What?" I question, Bolt licking my hand as I get back up to my feet.

"He doesn't usually like strangers, *mi princesa linda*," Blaine tells me, taking my hand and using it to pull me to him. I'm engulfed in his woodsy scent, and it relaxes my body when I didn't even know I'd tensed up. "But I'm not surprised you've tamed him."

My arms come up automatically and wrap around his huge frame, my head resting on his chest and his heartbeat pounding in my ear. My eyes drift shut and I let my muscles release all the pent-up tension they'd been holding from the past few hours before I found Forest who just about rocked my world.

"You should probably get cleaned up, Duchess. Then I can take you home," Lan states casually, and my eyes snap open as my stomach drops. The idea of washing Forest off me has a small whimper slipping past my lips, never mind the dread at the thought of going back to the cold hell I call home.

Blain's arms tighten around me, one large palm coming up to stroke soothing circles on my back as tears prick my eyes. I shouldn't be here, I don't belong in this small home with these guys, but my body craves it, craves them more than I've ever needed anything before. Nothing is my own at home, if the place where I live can even be called that. It's never been a place of comfort, never a place where I can relax. It's full of demons that I have no hope of escaping and of terror that is not confined to my nightmares.

"FAHRENHEIT" BY AZEE

LANDON

I watch as her breathing becomes shallow, her eyes open but not seeing the room she's in. Blaine notices too, pulling her even closer but it doesn't seem to register as her eyes water, her body shaking as a look of pure fucking terror crosses her beautiful face.

Bolt whines, pressing his body against her legs, but I ignore him, striding over to her and her face is in my hands before I've even realised what I'm doing.

"Hey, Duchess, it's okay. You're safe here," I tell her in a soothing tone, trying to pull her back from the panic attack that's she becoming lost in. *What did I say to set it off this time?* It was about her cleaning up and going home. Wasn't it the mention of home that made her spiral last time? My stomach tightens at the thought that something is happening to her behind those mansion doors. Something that would leave that fearful gleam in her eyes.

"Lan?" she questions softly as she blinks, her voice a cracked rasp that has me wanting to rage at the world. Her body relaxes a little against Blaine, the shakes just trembles now, and something inside me loosens as well.

"I'm here, baby. Forest and Blaine too," I tell her, aware of Forest at her back, his hand rubbing up and down as Blaine holds her close. Her eyes close, her face pressing into my palms even as she presses her body into Blaine's.

"I don't want to go back, Lan. Not yet," she confesses in a breath. "I—" She bites her lower lip, a shuddering breath easing past them. "I don't want to wash him off. I need him with me a little longer."

Her lids open and I'm struck speechless by the pleading look in her stunning, green eyes. They're the colour of leaves in spring, when everything is full of promise and the cold of winter is behind you, and I lose myself to their promise of something new.

"Okay, Duchess. We can do that," I assure her, her body releasing more of its tension. "Forest, go run her a bath."

He presses a soft kiss to her head, then does as I say, quickly striding towards our tiny bathroom.

"But—" she protests, pulling away from Blaine slightly as panic flashes in her eyes again. I shush her again, my thumbs stroking her cheeks.

"He'll get in with you, baby," I tell her, not even questioning my need to assure her, to make her happy. Her features soften, and she turns her face, pressing a light kiss to my palm that has tingles racing up and down my arm.

"Thank you, Lan," she murmurs, her stare on me, unwavering.

We stay that way for the time it takes to run the bath, Blaine holding her tight as I keep her face in my hands like she's beyond precious.

"It's ready, Lan," Forest says as he pads back into the room, his eyebrows drawn together when he sees Aspen still clutching Blaine.

"Get undressed, you're getting in with her," I order, and one of his brows goes up, but he doesn't argue, just starts to strip, laying his discarded clothes on the couch. He really is fucking stunning, and the little shit knows it, a smirk teasing his lips as I stare at him. Shaking my head, I release my hold on Aspen's face. "You too, Duchess."

Blaine releases her too, and the slight hitch in her breath tells me she's not happy, but we need to get her in a hot bath and give her the comfort that she's craving right now. My fingers make quick work of the buttons on her cardigan, sliding the garment off her arms and passing it to Blaine who carefully places it on the back of one of our chairs. She holds still, her chest rising and falling deeply as I start on the buttons of her blouse.

A delicate, pink lace bra is exposed as the material parts, and suddenly, she's not the only one breathing hard as I spot the outline of her nipples. Fuck, she's so beautiful. Sliding the shirt off her, my jaw clenches hard as I spot her protruding lower ribs.

"Don't hide from me," I snap out when she wraps her arms around herself. I take a steadying breath when she flinches at my harsh tone, my hand reaching out and my fingers brushing the bones that are visible. "Do you starve yourself on purpose?"

My eyes dart to her face and the way the skin bunches around her eyes as they fill with tears.

"No." It's barely a whisper, but it packs as much force as a punch to the gut. My fingers still on her skin, and although the words hurt, I force them through.

"Did your parents refuse to give you food last week after you came home from jail?" I watch every tiny movement her body makes, the way her muscles jump under the skin, her throat moving as she swallows.

"Yes." The word is a broken sound, but before the first tear can run down her cheek, she's in my arms and I'm pulling her fragile body so close that there's no space between us. Her body shudders with the force of her anguish, and my jaw is clenched so tightly that pain shoots up the sides of my face.

What kind of fucked up rich people bullshit is this? Starving your daughter for what purpose?

I look up to find Blaine, his hands clenched into fists at his sides as his own jaw works. Forest steps into my line of sight, still with his boxer briefs on, and there's the glisten of tears in his eyes. Out of all of us, he knows what it's like to go hungry. Though in his case, the starvation was a consequence of living in poverty and not the purposeful abuse she seems to be experiencing, for him that came in other forms. I don't know what's worse.

I don't have it in me to ask how many times her parents have starved her, withholding food that they clearly have in the house. From how thin she is, I'm betting this wasn't the first time.

After several moments, her sobs subside, and placing a kiss on the top of her head, I pull away a little. "Let's get you in the bath, Duchess."

She nods, her eyes red and the wet line of tears running down her cheeks, but I could swear there's a lightness to her that wasn't there before. I wonder if she's ever told anyone else of her parents' abuse? The thought of what they've done to her, what they continue to do to her, has rage threatening to overwhelm me, and I want to focus on her, not on them, so I take a deep breath, and then reach around to unzip her skirt.

My breath hisses out of my lips when I see her thigh highs and garters, her short, brown ankle boots just adding to the sexy vintage vibe she has going on. I help her to step away out of the pool of material, Blaine swooping down to pick it up and fold it with the rest of her clothes.

"I told you he'd go crazy for these," Forest says from behind her, stepping close and trailing a finger down the strap that holds up her thigh highs. Her chest trembles, and I don't miss the way her nipples harden under the lace of her bra at his words.

Not saying a word, not trusting my voice, I kneel down to take off her boots. I can't stop my fingers from sliding down her stocking-clad legs, and I'm so close to her centre that I can smell her arousal combined with Forest's musk. Her skin twitches under my touch, matching the movement of my dick which is a steel rod in my pants, regardless of my anger moments before.

Grasping her booted foot in one hand, I bring it up to my bent knee, her hands coming out to rest on my shoulders as she balances on one foot. Licking my lips, I focus on unlacing her leather boot, sliding her foot out of it and carefully placing it back on the bare wood floor. A gasp makes me pause as I take her other boot and place it on my thigh, the soft pink lace of her bra fluttering down to land on my hand.

Shuddering an exhale, I lift my eyes upwards, my entire body stilling when I see her bare breasts in Forest's hands, her heavy-lidded gaze fixed on me as he nibbles her neck.

"Forest," I grit out between clenched teeth, my fingers wrapped around her boot in a death grip.

"She needs to feel worshipped, Daddy. Don't you, sugar?" he replies in a husky tone, one that tells me he's just as fucking turned on as I am.

My nostrils flare, but that only draws in more of her intoxicating scent. "Bolt, bed." I don't have to look to know that he's left the room, going to his bed in Forest's room down the hall. We've trained him well. "Do you want this, Duchess?" I ask the golden-haired beauty above me, my pulse thundering as she arches into Forest's touch.

"Yes," she answers in a breathy voice, no hesitation, and fuck if my dick doesn't pulse with need.

I won't do anything about it though. Forest is right, I can see the concern in her eyes, the worry that we don't want her because she's not enough, because she's been rejected by the people who should love her. I won't add to that, and I need to prove to her that she is wanted, even if it's just by three men who have fucking nothing but a criminal gang to their names. Fuck the fact we're not meant to get attached. I can't fight this pull no more than the stars can refuse to shine.

Tearing my gaze away, I focus back on her boot, unlacing it and placing it beside us. Instead of placing her foot on the floor, I lift her leg higher and hitch it over my shoulder, opening her up to me. Fuck, she's a mess, her pussy slick and trails of Forest's cum leaking down her thighs.

Leaning in, I take a deep inhale of her musk, the sweet smell making me drunk with need for her on my tongue, but I rein it in, licking up the stickiness coating her inner thighs first.

"Lan..." My name is a breathy moan, a prayer from her lips and I am helpless to resist its plea. I lick a long line up her slit, a deep groan from my lips vibrating across her folds as her sweet taste bursts across my tongue, the sweetness only heightened by the saltiness of Forest's cum.

"How does she taste, Lan?" Forest asks, his voice a low, husky whisper.

"Fucking exquisite," I tell him, diving back in for more. Her hips buck and her hands tangle in my hair as she pulls me closer. Greedy little thing.

Wasting no more time when there is a feast before me, I get to work tasting every inch of her sweet cunt, dipping my tongue inside her and fucking her with it as my fingers dig into her thighs and keep them open when she tries to close them.

Rolling my eyes upward, I see Blaine has captured her lips, his huge hand squeezing and playing with her breast and nipple. Forest is still behind her, sucking and kissing her neck, his hand on her other breast, and something primal stirs inside me at all of us taking care of her. A rush of wetness coats my tongue, letting me know that she's close, so I turn my attention back to her dripping pussy and suck and flick her clit with my tongue at the same moment I thrust two fingers inside her.

Her muffled cry is followed by the tightening of her inner walls as she comes, soaking my chin and the front of my T-shirt with her release. It spurs me on, and I finger fuck her through her orgasm, relishing every twitch of her muscles and the small whimpers she makes.

When her thighs try to close again, I decide that she's had

enough, so I pull back, sitting back on my heels and looking up at her. Gone is the pallor of before, which is replaced by flushed cheeks and a heavy-lidded gaze that makes me want to preen like a fucking peacock.

She's slumped in the arms of my chosen brothers, and we share a look that feels like a mantle laid on my shoulders. It doesn't matter who wants us to watch her and for what reason. She belongs to us, our very own angel, and we will watch over her like guard dogs because we protect what's ours.

CHAPTER 13

"STICK AROUND" BY ENVYYOU

ASPEN

My muscles are like jelly, and I provide no resistance as Landon unhooks my suspenders and pulls my stockings off, standing up and passing them to Blaine who places them with the rest of my things.

Lan brushes the lightest of kisses against my lips, a teasing caress that has me chasing after him. Bastard just smirks, leaving me with a hint of a taste of myself and an ache for more.

A part of me knows that I should feel something about being naked in front of them, these almost strangers, but the shame just won't come, not after the way they worshipped me just now.

"Let's get you in the bath before it gets too cold," he tells me, tangling our fingers together and pulling me away from Forest and down their tiny hallway.

There are pictures tacked up on the unpainted walls, no frames, but the joy of the young men in them makes my heart hurt. I'm not sure I have any pictures like this, of me as a goofy youth, smiling and covered in mud. All the pictures from my childhood are staged, my smile fake-looking and tension around my young eyes.

"I know it's not much, Little Lady," Forest comments softly from behind me as we step into the small bathroom, his tone hesitant and unsure.

I look up at Landon, a flush high on his sharp cheekbones as he takes in the space around us like he's embarrassed. His gaze snags on mine and I give him a small smile.

"It's everything," I say, staring into his dark eyes, willing him to believe that I would give up all the riches in the world for this; a true home. A place to feel safe and belong.

He gives me a grin in return that takes my breath away, my heart thudding painfully in my chest at the pleasure and approval on his face. Breaking our stare, he leans down and dips his hand into the bubbly water.

"Still hot. Good call on the bubbles, Forest," he says, straightening up and reaching out to glide his fingers around my nipple, leaving a trail of bubbles in his wake. My brain short-circuits, my breath hitching, and he smirks again as if he knows the effect his touch has on me.

"Our girl deserves the best," Forest replies, his fingers teasing down my side, tingles racing from his touch and the fact he called me their girl. My chest tightens with the seemingly ordinary claiming. I want to be theirs, to belong to these Tainted Saints.

He places a kiss on my shoulder as he steps past, naked like me, and climbs into the tub. His whole body is covered in ink, beautiful designs in a riot of colour with no rhyme or reason to them. I love the chaos, it epitomises Forest, and when he turns to face me, hand held out with a devilish smile on his kissable lips, I know that I want to fall into this madness more than anything.

Taking his warm hand in mine, I reluctantly let go of Landon's grip, letting Forest help me into the tub. Releasing my hand, he sits down, spreading his legs with his hard cock jutting out of the water and stealing all of my focus.

"Awww, ignore him, sugar. He's just excited to have you here is all," he says with a laugh, and I giggle, my cheeks heating as I look away and turn, catching the dark, heated gazes of Blaine and Landon.

Taking a deep breath, I sit too, Forest encouraging me to lie back against him, and my body sinks into his and the hot water, my head resting back on his chest as each of my muscles lose tension and relax.

"Have you eaten?" Landon questions, and I blink open my eyes, not realising I'd closed them in my bliss.

"Um..." I trail off, nibbling my lower lip when his jaw tightens.

"I'll take that as a no, that fuck boy didn't think to make sure you ate," he growls out, baring his teeth for a split second. "I'll go make you something now. Any allergies?"

"Oh, y–you don't have—"

"Allergies, Duchess?" he asks again in a firm tone, talking over my protest. My mouth snaps shut as he closes the distance between us, bending low to get in my personal space, hands braced either side of the tub.

"No, Lan. No allergies," I breathe out, my chest stilling when one hand dips into the water between my legs.

"Good," he states, bringing his hand up and swiping over his chin, my cheeks burning when I realise that he's cleaning off my release.

Straightening up, he pulls off his T-shirt to expose a torso covered in black ink that's chiselled to perfection. I only get a single moment to stare in awe before he's turning around to show me his back, which has a stunning design of an angel with fiery hands, horses, and waves at his feet with beams of light behind him. Then he's dropping the garment into the laundry basket by the door and striding out.

"Beautiful, ain't he?" Forest murmurs in my ear, his hand coming up to glide water over my breast in a move that leaves me shivering and arching into his touch.

"Yes," I agree in a breathy whisper, pausing when Blaine crouches down, a washcloth and some soap in his hand.

"Let's get you clean and then fed, *mi tesoro*," he suggests, rubbing the soap over the cloth and then dipping his hand under the water to grasp my ankle. Lifting it out of the water, I watch, mesmerised, as he swipes the cloth over my skin with a touch that shouldn't be as gentle as it is coming from such a giant of a man.

He repeats the move with my other leg, then takes the washcloth up higher, my breath stalling when he swipes over the apex of my thighs. My legs widen without conscious thought, inviting him to touch the place he's teasing.

"Would you like Blaine to touch you too, Little Lady?" Forest breathes in my ear, and Blaine's chocolate gaze snaps to mine, his pupils widening with what my face must be showing him.

"Yes," I beg, holding Blaine's heated stare as I feel the brush of his fingers against my folds. My body arches, heart pounding as he parts my lips, sliding a finger around my clit. "Blaine...please..."

I'm lost to this wanton version of myself, the need to have had all of them touch me in some way is almost overwhelming, and for once in my life, I embrace it. I decide to be selfish and do this thing that I want with every cell in my body.

"I've got you, *mi princesa*," he rumbles, gliding his hand lower and sliding two thick fingers into my heated core.

"Fuck," I hiss, his digits stretching me in the most delicious way.

"Now you see why I call him Big Daddy," Forest jokes, both his hands on my breasts, teasing and flicking my nipples. "Well, his large fingers aren't the only reason."

A deep groan leaves my lips when Blaine thrusts his fingers hard inside me and the image that Forest is hinting at; that they play with each other. It has my hips bucking.

"W–will you show me, one day?" I ask in a breathless tone, Blaine not pausing in his movements, the water lapping at the underside of my breasts. Sparks tingle and fizzle up my skin, setting my nerves alight with every thrust of his hand.

"Whatcha say, Big Daddy? Wanna come over here and give me some sugar?" Forest challenges, and Blaine lifts a dark brow.

"It's cute when you try to top from the bottom, Pup," Blaine growls, but leans forward anyway, his fingers still pumping inside me as his other hand comes up to grab the back of Forest's neck.

My breath punches out of my chest when he slams his lips down on the other man's, trapping me between them as he continues to finger fuck me. My hands land on Forest's large thighs, my nails digging in which elicits a deep moan that Blaine swallows as he devours Forest.

It's brutal and hard, like both of these men, and my inner walls begin to tighten around Blaine's fingers as he fucks me harder, in time with the clashing of their tongues.

Heat lights up my body, all my muscles going rigid as my orgasm tears through me, leaving me shattered and boneless once the pulses subside. I blink open eyes I hadn't realised I'd closed to find Blaine looking down at me with kiss-swollen lips, his fingers tracing lazy circles around my clit that have me twitching with how oversensitive I am.

"You are beautiful when you come, *mi tesoro*," he murmurs, his hand stopping its torture and coming out of the water to cup my cheek. Leaning over, he places his lips against mine, and my hands immediately come up to grab his face, bringing him closer, having learnt my lesson with Landon earlier. He huffs a laugh against my lips but follows my lead and kisses me back, his tongue demanding entry which I give him.

Fuck, he tastes like Forest, a mixture of comfort and exhilaration, of feeling safe as you freefall, and I'm instantly addicted. I whimper when he pulls away, and I feel his smile before I see it, my eyelids fluttering open.

"The water is getting cold, sugar," Forest tells me gently, holding the washcloth in his hand and then swiping it over my upper body. "Can't have you catching your death, Lan would have my hide."

I love the way Forest speaks. I could happily lie here with him all night just to hear him talk, but a small shiver lets me know that yes, the water is getting chilly. So, with a sigh, I let him finish up and then get out of the tub with Blaine's help.

He wraps a thin but warm towel around me that smells a lot like him, which has me relaxing even more. He watches me practically rub my face all over it with a considering stare, then pulls his T-shirt off in that one-handed, sexy man way and holds it out for me.

My lips part, my body suddenly flooded with warmth as I take in every toned muscle that makes up Blaine Garcia. His skin is a rich, sandy-brown covered in swirls of dark ink that my tongue wants to taste, each ab chiselled to perfection and leading to a deep V that disappears underneath the waistband of his dark jeans.

"Another reason for his Big Daddy status," Forest comments in a husky murmur behind me, and all I can do is nod, rendered stupid by the god of a man before me.

Rolling his eyes, Blaine tugs the towel away from me, but before even a small squeak can leave my lips, darkness covers my eyes as his still-warm T-shirt is pulled over my head. My arms glide through the sleeves and as soon as it's on, I give in to my instincts and wrap my arms around the man himself, pressing my cheek against his hot skin.

His huge arms engulf me, wrapping me up so tightly that I can barely breathe, but I don't care. I need him to hold me together, to keep me from fading away into someone I don't know anymore. Tears sting my eyes, a painful lump forming in the back of my throat at the realisation that someone I met just nine days ago holds me with more care than either of my parents ever have, and that he knows more about me, the real me, than they do.

"Thank you, Blaine," I whisper thickly against his skin, willing the tears not to fall. I know that this can't last, that sooner rather than later I'll have to go back there, to that cold, unforgiving mansion, but just for a little while, I'd like to pretend that I get to keep the Saints.

"You're welcome," he rumbles back, and I feel the light press of his lips against the top of my head. "Let's get you something to eat."

Nodding, I pull away, missing the comfort of his embrace like I'd just stepped out into a winter storm. Grabbing my hand, my chest loosening the moment our skin makes contact, he gently leads me towards the hall, and we walk back the way we came, Forest behind us. I shiver slightly in the cool air, the apartment isn't that warm but I don't want to make a fuss because maybe they can't afford the heating.

Bolt pads over as soon as we enter, heading straight for me, and I sink my fingers into his soft fur, not even having to bend down to reach.

"Arms up, sugar," Forest demands from behind me, and I twist to see the hoodie he had on earlier bunched in his hands. Giving him a grateful smile—and not just because of the extra layer but because it's his—I do as he says, Blaine releasing my hand so Forest can slip the garment over my head. Like Blaine's shirt, it falls to my knees, and before I can thank Forest, Lan is handing me a pair of sweats and thick socks.

"Now you have something from each of us, Duchess," he tells me, swiping some of my damp hair behind my ear, then helping me to get into the sweats. We all laugh when they fall down straight away, but by tightening the string and folding them over at the waist a couple of times, we manage to get them to stay up.

He kneels, helping me into the thick socks, and I flush when he glances up at me, a knowing smirk on his face when he catches my blush. Not only am I now warm, but Lan was right, having something of each of theirs settles something deep within me that I can't examine too closely.

They're not yours to keep, Aspen...

Pushing that thought aside, I shake my head and look at each of them.

"Thank you," I tell them in a soft tone, unable to voice all the reasons for my gratitude.

"Let's eat," Landon says after a moment, taking my hand and leading me to the small table that has four chairs around it.

"I knew it was a good idea to keep all the chairs," Forest beams, and I find my lips tipping up to match his infectious smile.

My mouth waters at the bowls of spaghetti, the scent of parmesan, pancetta, and garlic leaving me practically drooling.

"Take it slow, Duchess," Landon cautions as I sit down. "Your stomach might not be able to handle too much, but the egg and pancetta are a good source of protein."

"You made this? From scratch?" I ask, gazing up at the gangster who's now sitting across from me, Forest and Blaine sitting down either side of me.

"There are some benefits to having a mom who owns the best Italian restaurant in town, not least the fact we get free groceries," he remarks, a half smile tilting up his lips. "Don't look so surprised. You shouldn't believe everything they say about us, you know."

I flush, shame washing over me at how rude I just sounded. "I didn't mean—" Looking away, I take an inhale. "I don't know how to cook, and well, I'm impressed that anyone can, never mind make something that smells so delicious." Sneaking a glance upwards through my lashes, I don't see censure in his face, only a sort of softness that makes the back of my eyes sting.

"I can teach you, if you want?" Lan asks, and my head shoots up.

"Really? You would? I would love that," I rush out, excitement making my pulse sing.

"Well, eat your dinner like a good girl and we'll see," he says back, his intense, dark stare never leaving mine, and my pulse races with the command in his tone. Unlike with the Ambassador, I want to please Landon, if nothing else to hear him call me a good girl again.

"Yes, sir," I whisper, biting my lips to hide the smile that tries to break free when his nostrils flare. Two can play that game.

"Just don't touch his knives without permission," Forest states from next to me as I swirl my fork in the pasta and bring it up to my lips. "He's mighty protective of those blades."

"Forest," Landon snaps out, and I wonder why he's warning him for a brief moment, but then the flavours of the dish bursts on my tongue and a loud moan falls from my lips.

"Oh my god, Landon," I gush after chewing and swallowing, glancing over at him to find his fork halfway to his mouth, his jaw clenched tightly and heat making his dark eyes shine as he licks his lips. "Um, this is really good."

"Fuck, sugar. You can't make noises like that at dinner. You'll have us all panting like dogs before we've even taken a bite," Forest groans, adjusting himself in his sweats. I didn't notice him getting dressed, but like Blaine and Landon, he's forgone the T-shirt, and all of his glorious muscles are on display.

I narrow my eyes at him. "It's only fair and serves you all right, sitting at dinner half naked like that. It's enough to make my poor kitty kat roll over and beg." I snap my mouth shut, blaming my utter fucking lack of filter on everything that has happened tonight.

Stunned silence fills the room, and then Bolt rests his head on my thigh, looking up at me with soulful blue eyes.

"I am here to stroke your kitty kat anytime. You just say the word and I'll be there, sho' nuff," Forest murmurs into my ear, and I look away from Bolt to see them all studying me with heat and amusement in their eyes.

"Eat your dinner, Duchess," Landon commands after a few moments, and I do as he says, taking another mouthwatering bite full of deliciousness. I don't bother to keep my noises of appreciation down, tit for tat after all.

CHAPTER 14

"ALL MINE" BY PLAZA

FOREST

Her presence in our home, at our table, just feels fucking right, and I know by the soft glances that the other two give her they feel the same way. She's ours. She belongs to us, just like we belong to each other. I learnt long ago to trust my instincts, and they are screaming *mine* at me whenever I look at her.

When she told us what her family does, that her parents starve her on purpose, I wanted to head on over there and give them exactly what they deserve. We're not called the Tainted Saints for nothing. We have a great many tools in our arsenal, learnt over many years, and I can think of a few choice ones to use on the British Ambassador and his wife.

My parents were shitty, beyond shitty, and it pains me that she has the same thing; a house that is no home. A place that feels more like a prison and a punishment than a retreat. I didn't truly feel safe until I came to live with my aunt and uncle when I was seven, and even then, it wasn't until I met Lan and Blaine that I knew what it meant to belong.

Her head rests on my shoulder, her soft breaths fanning against my chest. Her plate is still half full but we're not pushing it, knowing that her poor stomach can't eat too much after the way food has been withheld recently.

Lan catches my eye, his jaw set in a grim line as he looks at the sleeping beauty, then he flashes his phone screen at me. Midnight. The time for coaches to turn back into pumpkins, and my stomach sinks with the knowledge that we have to take her back.

We spoke earlier about her, about the power that her father seems to hold already in our small part of the world, and I know that he wouldn't want her anywhere near us. If he finds out...fuck, I can't even think about how long her punishment will be.

"Hey, Little Lady," I whisper gently, stroking her cheek. She huffs out a breath, her dark lashes fluttering open as she gazes sleepily up at me.

"Hmmmm?" she mumbles, blinking and then lifting her head to stretch her arms above her head. I don't think I've ever met anyone more beautiful, even sleep-mussed and drowning in our clothes. "What's the time?" Her voice is thick with sleep, and my dick perks up at the sound but that boy will have to wait.

"Midnight, beautiful," I tell her, standing from the dining chair and stretching my back. It's not the most comfortable place to sit for a long time, but I'd be damned if I was going to move her once she'd drifted off.

"Oh." There's a world of heartbreak in her voice, her face a mask of desolation that makes me want to burn the fucking world down to stop that look from ever coming across her features again. "I should go." She nibbles her lower lip, her delicate fingers toying with a paper napkin that was left from dinner.

"I can take you, sugar," I offer, and she gives me a sad smile.

"If anyone sees..." she trails off, begging with her sorrow-filled eyes for me to understand, and a part of me does, but it still stings, the rejection of her not wanting to be seen with any of us in her rich neighbourhood. "He would hurt you too," she adds in a cracking voice, her eyes filling with tears as her lips tremble. "He has so much power, Forest, and none of it is used for good."

Leaning towards her, I take her face in my palms, my soul soothed by her worry, not rejection. "He's not the only one with power, baby," I tell her, looking between her eyes, then at the tears that trails down her cheeks. Fuck, she's pretty when she cries. "We can take care of ourselves."

"Not against him," she breathes out, her chest stuttering with her ragged inhales as her hands drop the shredded napkin and clench into fists. "No one can."

I hate that I know what she's feeling. I've been there, thinking that this is it. That all the shit and pain and terror is all there is to life. But I got out, and I'll be damned if I don't get her out too. Kneeling down so my face is more level with hers, I hold her gaze.

"I will take you where he can't reach you, even if the whole of Fairview has to burn to the fucking ground. I will get you away from him," I swear, not letting her look away for a moment, my hands tightening on her face when she tries to pull away. I don't give a shit that I've known her for such a short time or that Lan's uncle wants us to use her for whatever shit he's got going on.

She. Is. Mine. She's ours, and I *will* bring her home.

"You'll have to kill him first, he'll never let me go, Forest. I'm his property, to do with as he wills, just a pawn in his fucked up game, but one he will never let go," she tells me, her body tense as her hands come up to try and prise mine away, but I refuse to let her go.

"Then we'll kill him too," Lan states, and her eyes widen, her lips parting, and I allow my grip to loosen so she can twist her head to stare at him. "We've killed for less, Duchess, and you don't belong to him anymore. You are ours, and we take care of our own."

"Y–you don't know me," she stutters out, leaping to her feet, the chair clattering to the floor and forcing me to let her go as she strides around the table to get right up into Lan's space, her small body trembling. Bolt whines and my hand goes to the top of his head to reassure him. "You can't say shit like that!" She smacks his chest with both palms, but the pain in her voice has my eyes stinging, my soul raging at the knowledge that no one has ever shown her what she's worth.

"I can say shit like that, and more," he grits back, grabbing her wrists and pulling her to him, her soft body falling into his. "The Saints take care of what belongs to us, and you, Aspen Buckingham, fall into that category." And before she can deny it, he slams his lips against hers.

She tries to pull away, but his grip is too tight, and he just hauls her closer until not a sliver of air is between them. Fuck, it's quite possibly the hottest fucking thing I've ever seen, and I can't tear my gaze away as he claims her until she sags against him. I watch as all the tension leaves her body, and with a sob, she kisses him back, her fingers clenching against the bare skin of his chest, digging in as if she is desperate to keep him.

After a moment, he finally pulls away, his eyes glazed and both their chests heaving as they stare at each other.

"You. Belong. To. Us," he states again, panting. "And nothing, fucking no one, will stand in our way."

They stay locked, staring at each other for several long moments, and my heart races, waiting to hear what she says.

Her chest rises with a deep inhale, the exhale loud in the silent room.

"Regardless, I have to go back. Tonight, and you can't be seen," she tells him as a smile tilts my lips. She didn't deny it, that's a fucking win in my books. "If only I had my phone, I could call Bobby," she muses, breaking their stare, her hands still resting on Lan's chest, like she can't bear to pull away just yet.

"I know Bobby's number," Blaine confesses in that quiet way of his, and her head whips around to him.

"How?" A chuckle escapes me at the look of confusion across her pretty features.

"He's a cousin of my mama's," Blaine admits, his jaw tensing at the mention of his mom. Fuck, the wound he has for not being able to save her is still raw and bleeding, even when it wasn't his job as he was only a fucking kid.

"Oh," she remarks, her brows still furrowed, and I pray that she doesn't find out we put him in the position of her family's driver in the hope of gathering intel about her shit of a father. Not sure how well that would go down. "Can you get him to pick me up please? I don't think he would tell the Ambassador..." Lan lets go of one of her hands to smooth the deep lines between her brows as she trails off.

"We'll make sure he doesn't," he assures her, and although I can see the question in her face as she gazes at him, she doesn't ask.

The low rumble of Blaine on the phone is quick, then he turns back to us. "He's on his way."

I hate the way her body tightens, the way she straightens up as if preparing for a battle that she knows she will lose. Striding over to her and Lan, I push the still damp hair away from her neck, not resisting my urge to kiss her soft skin. Fuck, she smells good. It's a mixture of us and her own floral scent that makes me feel like anything is possible.

"Let's get you dressed again, sugar," I murmur against her skin, wanting nothing more than to get her in one of our beds and keep her all night, sandwiched between the three of us as we worship her stunning body.

"Okay," she answers in a voice so small that my heart aches with the sadness buried in it.

Lan releases his grip, and I lead her to the pile of clothes that Blaine carefully folded on the back of the old armchair. He took more care than he usually does, but she's worth the extra effort.

I help her take off my hoodie, then Blaine's T-shirt, and finally, Lan's sweats and socks. Jesus fucking Christ, I will never get used to seeing her naked, thin as she is. I hate the way her bones jut out, but with Lan's cooking, we'll have her curves back in no time.

It's a lesson in self-control that I'm sure I will fail every fucking second, getting her dressed in her own clothes, minus panties of course. Those are in my pocket and I'll be keeping them for later, which only makes me think of being balls deep inside her wet heat, and the desire that runs through my veins makes me feel as though I'm on fucking fire.

All too soon she's covered up, and Blaine gets a message from Bobby telling him that he's waiting downstairs.

"We'll see you tomorrow, okay?" I tell her, cupping her face in my palms and kissing those lush lips of hers before she can answer. I hate the fact I can taste salt, that her sorrow is nothing I can fix. Although, a part of me loves that she doesn't want to leave us, that given the choice, she would stay. I never said I wasn't a bastard sometimes.

"See you tomorrow, Forest," she breathes out when I release her, and there's a catch in her voice that has my soul screaming to not let her go. With a final, small peck on her lips, I use every ounce of willpower to step away, hands fisted at my sides to stop from snatching her back and keeping her here.

Blaine pulls her to him next, not saying a single word but the way he holds her like she's the most precious thing he's ever been allowed to touch speaks volumes. I watch as he kisses her deeply, her hands clutching his face like it's her lifeline. My chest warms at the sight, at the fact that my chosen brothers, my soulmates, feel the same way I do about this beautiful creature that we don't deserve but get to touch anyway.

They pull away, her eyes sparkling with the tears that she refuses to let fall. Then Blaine forces himself away, coming to stand by me as Lan takes his place in front of her.

"We will see you tomorrow, Duchess," he tells her, and although his words are so simple, they are full of a promise that is deeper than their meaning. We will be there for her, no matter what.

He presses a light kiss to her lips, the bastard leaving her wanting more. Then he takes her hand and opens the door. With a command to Bolt to stay, he walks out, taking our heart with him.

CHAPTER 15

"365" BY MOTHER'S DAUGHTER

ASPEN

Lan leads me down to the car, our usual black Rolls that is idling next to the pavement, looking completely out of place in this run-down neighbourhood.

"When you get your phone back, I'll put our numbers in so you have a way to contact us if anything happens," he tells me as we approach the vehicle, and my hand grips his tighter, my body refusing to acknowledge that it's almost time to let go. "But until then, get in touch through Bobby if you need us, okay?"

His dark eyes bore into mine, and I'm reminded of the day of my arrest, when he watched me from the shadows. I desperately want to ask him why he was watching me, how long he'd been there, but the words won't come, some part of me not wanting to ruin the moment.

"Okay, Lan," I answer instead in a soft voice, stopping by the passenger side of the car. Bobby is there, door open and waiting for me, so I give him a small smile of thanks before Landon grips my chin to turn my face back to his.

"See you in the morning, Duchess," he tells me, his gaze travelling over my face as if he's memorising every line.

I just nod, unable to speak for fear that my anguish will pour out. I'm not sure I can still blame the alcohol from my drinks earlier at the club for my odd behaviour. I feel like these boys have opened a dam that will be almost impossible to shut again. They've shown me what it's like to be wanted, to belong to someone in a way that doesn't hurt but just brings comfort and pleasure beyond my wildest dreams.

He brushes another light kiss on my lips, leaving them tingling in memory of his consuming earlier, then he's helping me into the back passenger seat and shutting the door. He stays by the door, talking to Bobby in a low tone that I can't make out, and I watch as he places a hand on the other man's shoulder before spinning and walking back towards the Pound and their apartment.

Shivers make my body tremble, even though the car is warm, and I wrap my arms around myself, wishing with every atom, every cell that it was one of my Saints holding me.

Not yours, Aspen. They can't be yours...

The driver's door opens with a blast of freezing air, and soon we're making our way along the dilapidated east side.

"Your parents think that you spent the evening with Mr. Pennington," Bobby murmurs into the silence. My heart thuds painfully, nausea swirling in my stomach at the mention of Albert and what he's meant to be to me. "I will tell them that I picked you up from his house, if they ask, Miss Aspen."

My eyes fill at the kindness of his words, at the fact that he's willing to lie for me.

"T–thank you, Bobby," I rasp out, the words a struggle to get past the lump in my throat.

We sit in silence for a while, the streets becoming more cared for, trees beginning to line them as we enter my neighbourhood. It makes something twist inside me, the fact that only a few minutes away people are living in such hardship with no green spaces for their kids to play in, and yet wealth is in everything around me.

"They're good boys," Bobby says quietly as we pull up to the wrought iron gates that lead to the Ambassador's residence, my new house that will never be a home like the apartment I just left. "They do a lot to protect the people of the east side."

My head tilts to the side as I look at his profile in front of me.

"What do they do, Bobby? The Saints, I mean?" I ask, focusing on the way he swallows, his eyes unblinking as the guard lets us in.

"It's not my place to say, Miss," he replies, and disappointment makes me slump back. I can't deny that I'm desperate to know what it means to be a Tainted Saint. I've never even met anyone in a gang before, let alone someone, or someones, who run one. And for it to be so well-known, as Aoife suggested when she told me about them, I can't help wondering what they do to earn that kind of notoriety.

Plus the casual way Landon told me they'd killed people, that they would kill the Ambassador if he tries to hurt me...

It left me not frightened as I would have expected, or horrified, but instead, I feel protected and want to find out everything there is to know about them.

Bobby doesn't say anything more, and even though questions pile up on my tongue, I don't want to make him uncomfortable. Especially as he's helping me to keep my whereabouts tonight a secret, so I don't push the subject.

No one is waiting for me at the front steps, a good sign I hope, and after Bobby lets me out, I quickly dart to the door as it opens, Gerrard, our butler, letting me in.

"I'm so sorry it's so late, Gerrard," I tell the older gentleman, wincing when I see that he's still in full uniform and no doubt will be up with the crow in a couple of hours.

"Quite alright, Miss," he assures me, his slightly wrinkled face giving me a reassuring smile. "Did you have a good evening?"

My steps come up short, my cheeks flushing as I recall all the events of the evening; running from Albert after seeing him with

Sarah. Letting Forest fuck me against a wall with Landon and Blaine watching. Landon going down on me and eating me like I was his last meal. The bath with Blaine touching me so that I had all of them in one way or another tonight. The meal Lan cooked for us. His kiss.

"Yes, Gerrard. I had a lovely evening," I tell him, my voice soft as a smile plays around my lips. "Good night. Thank you again for waiting up."

"Good night, Miss Aspen," he says back, and I hear the locks behind me as I head up the stairs in a sort of dream, glad that I don't meet my parents as I make my way to my part of the house.

I shut the door quietly behind me, pressing my heated forehead against the cool wood as I let my smile tug my lips upwards and try not to burst into giggles.

"Thinking about me, sugar?" a deep voice drawls from right behind me, a hand coming up to cover my mouth and stifling my scream. "Shhhh, it's just me, beautiful."

My body sags against his hard frame, and he releases me enough so I can turn to face him, my heart still racing.

"Fucking hell, Forest," I gasp in a whisper-shout, leaning back against the door, his body pressing against me. Heat flares across my skin, my nerve endings tingling at his nearness.

"I wanted to make sure you got home okay," he whispers, his hand coming up to trail against my cheek, the leather of his jacket creaking in the quiet room. My breathing stutters as he makes contact, my body singing with his featherlight touch.

Licking my dry lips, I try to clear the lust from my mind. "H–how did you get in?"

"Oh, baby, a little old thing like security can't stop me. Not when you're on the other side," he tells me, closing the minuscule distance between us and running his nose up my neck, causing small explosions to erupt in my core.

"You got past our security?" I ask breathlessly, arching my head to one side to give him better access.

"It was child's play for someone with my…skills," he murmurs back, peppering my neck with kisses as he presses closer to me, trapping me between the solid door and his firm body. I can feel his hardness against my lower stomach, and my thighs clench with the memory of him inside me up against that wall. "Plus, earlier was just a warm-up. I plan to take hours devouring you this time, Little Lady"

The sound of the lock on the door engaging is as loud as a shot, and I shudder, want for the man in front of me setting my nerves alight.

"This time?" My fingers dig into the wood behind me, in a futile bid to stop myself from reaching for him. I should send him away, this is too risky, but I can't seem to make the words leave my mouth, I can't force my hands to push him away rather than pull him closer.

"The first of many," he purrs, his hands coming to the cardigan he helped me put back on less than half an hour ago. He takes his time popping open each button, making my heart thud with each move. Then his large palms slide it off me, pulling me away from the door enough to let it drop to the floor.

Giving up on my plan to stop this—my kitty kat threatening to strike action if I do—I bring my hands up to his jacket, pushing it off his shoulders and letting it fall to the floor in a heap.

My heart is like a thousand hooves thundering, the chance that we might get caught just adding another layer of excitement to the mix. His lids are hooded as my fingers go to the hem of his T-shirt, tugging that up and over his head, letting it join his jacket on the floor.

Fuck, he's pretty, and his body is something that I didn't know existed in real life. My fingers trail over the ridges and furrows of each muscle, his skin burning hot and twitching underneath my touch.

"Fuck, sugar, I need to feel you against me," he rasps, yanking me to him and tearing my blouse open, practically ripping it off me, the small pearl buttons flying across the room with little pinging sounds as they hit the wall and various bits of furniture. A gasp falls from my lips as he unhooks my bra, pulling that off and bringing our bodies together, his skin burning into mine. "That bath earlier was the best kind of torture, baby," he moans, his lips slamming down onto mine with enough force to almost bend me in half.

Our hands are a flurry of desperate movements, my fingers fumbling with his jeans as he unzips my skirt, letting it pool at my feet. He spins us as he kisses me, his hands cupping my face and caressing my cheeks as he claims me with his lips and tongue. All I can feel is him. He's consuming me completely and nothing on this earth could stop this storm we're creating.

I don't even realise that I've been moving backwards until he gives me a little shove. I squeak as he pushes me onto my bed, then looks down at me with eyes dark with lust, his jeans around his thighs and his huge cock grasped in his fist. My bare pussy pulses in return, my skin feeling hot and tight as he gazes down at me.

"You are so fucking beautiful, you know that?" he breathes out in a low tone, pushing his jeans the rest of the way off and stepping out of them. I wonder for a moment where his boots are, but then he's on top of me, his hard length pressed against my core. "I wanted to take my time, baby, but you make it too fucking hard not to lose control."

We both groan as he pushes himself inside of me, all of his hot skin touching mine. I still have my stockings and suspenders on, plus my boots, but he doesn't seem to care as he thrusts forward until he's fully seated inside me.

"Forest," I gasp, my fingers digging into his shoulders, nails leaving half-moon crescents as I mark him. He is so big, and it's so fucking good that I can already feel an orgasm hovering at the edges of my vision. "Please, fuck, you feel so good."

"So do you, darlin'," he grits out, his large palm gliding along my stocking-clad leg and hitching it higher on his hips. "I never want to leave this sweet fucking pussy." The moonlight highlights him in its glow as he pauses and just takes us in, looking down at the place where we join. "Fuck, Aspen."

My breathing hitches as he lowers himself down and presses his lips to mine, moving his hips at the same time, pulling out just to slam back in, and swallowing my cry of pleasure. He takes my hands from his shoulders, tangling our fingers then bringing them over my head, pinning me down in a way that has wetness flooding between us.

"Shit, you're so wet for me," he growls, fucking me harder and sending shock waves racing across my entire body, inside and out. "As much as I want to hear you scream my name, baby girl, you're going to have to keep quiet for Daddy," he instructs, his lips pressing against mine again to swallow every whine and whimper as he fucks me so hard I know I'll be sore tomorrow.

Taking my wrists in one hand, he brings his other arm down to hitch my leg over his elbow, and the deeper angle has us both groaning.

"Fuck, Forest! I'm so close," I pant against his kiss-swollen lips, my hands clenched tightly into fists as my body arches into him. Our skin is sweat-soaked, the sound of our fucking loud and obscene in the quiet room, everything forgotten apart from this man and how he makes my body sing.

"Then come for your Daddy," he commands in a harsh tone. "Show me you can be a good fucking girl and take Daddy's dick."

His hips piston into me in hard and brutal thrusts, and I bite my lip hard to stop the scream that wants to escape as my climax drags me under, my body going rigid and clamping down on him as I come even harder than I have all evening. I soak him with my release, and he grunts, burying himself so deep that it sends a sharp judder of pain through me which only heightens and prolongs my orgasm.

"Fuck, baby, that's it," he grits out, making shallow thrusts and pumping me full of his cum.

My body goes boneless, weightless as I come down from my high, Forest pressing light kisses all over my neck and lips.

"Shit, Forest," I murmur, his arm releasing my leg. My thighs come around his hips, my ankles crossing at his back as I pull him closer, and his hand lets go of my wrists, his palms cupping my face.

"I know, sugar," he breathes against my lips. "Fuck, I know."

He kisses me sweetly, reverently, our tongues exploring each other in a way that has tears pricking behind my closed eyelids.

"Will you stay? Just a little bit?" I ask in a choked voice, knowing that I shouldn't have, but the idea of him leaving now makes me feel sick to my stomach, panic clawing at my throat.

"I wouldn't wanna be anywhere else, Little Lady," he tells me, pulling out and leaving me gasping at the sudden emptiness. "Let's get cleaned up."

Curling up, he holds out a hand to help me up, my legs a little wobbly which only makes him laugh softly when I fall into his naked body.

Going into my en-suite bathroom, I try not to worry about him comparing the huge, luxurious space to the small room back at their apartment. We quickly clean up, and then he helps me to change the bed with fresh linen from the closet.

"Not sure how I'll explain this," I mumble, balling up the wet sheets into the laundry hamper in the bathroom.

"Just tell them you got a new toy," he suggests with a deep chuckle as we get under the covers.

"I can't say that!" I burst out, then cover my mouth at the loud sound. Not that my parents will be able to hear it as they're on the other side of this enormous mansion, far enough away that I doubt they'd have heard me screaming Forest's name as he fucked me.

"Sure you can," he teases while climbing into bed, my bed. My chest tightens at the sight, wishing that he could always be there to hold me in the night. Maybe the nightmares wouldn't be so bad then. I hate the dark and usually sleep with at least the curtains open, if not a side light. "What's wrong, sugar?" His face is full of concern, his eyebrows lowered as he sits up.

"N–nothing," I whisper, my voice thick as I climb in next to him, scooting over. He lies down, pulling me to him until my head rests on his chest, his heartbeat loud in my ear. My entire body relaxes into his, sinking into his hold like we belong here.

"I'll let that one slide for now," he tells me, kissing the top of my head. "But I don't want you to lie to me, okay?"

"Okay, Forest," I say after a beat, thinking about the reason for my hatred of the dark. I can't admit that to him, to them. It feels shameful somehow, that my parents hate me so much that they've locked me in a dark room ever since I can remember whenever I did something to displease them.

"Sleep now, baby. I'll keep you safe," he whispers, pulling me impossibly closer, and it's as if my body already knows to obey his command because soon my eyes are closing and sleep drags me under.

CHAPTER 16

"LAVENDER HAZE - ACOUSTIC VERSION" BY TAYLOR SWIFT

ASPEN

Morning light brushes over my eyes, and I stretch, my body expecting to make contact with another, only my bed is empty. Opening my eyes, I confirm that Forest is no longer next to me. He's gone, and I have to bite my lip to stop the tears from gathering in the corners of my eyes as my chest aches at the rush of loneliness.

"He doesn't belong to you, Aspen," I whisper to myself, sitting up and getting out of bed. The place between my thighs throbs, and I get a flash of Forest pounding into me not once but twice yesterday. I wonder what it would be like for Blaine to take his place? Or Landon?

Maybe all three together...

My entire body feels as though it's been doused in a hot bath, which doesn't fucking help as it only reminds me of the bath I took with Forest, Blaine's expert fingers bringing me such mind-blowing pleasure.

Shaking my head at my own wantonness, I make my way to the bathroom and have a quick shower before getting ready for the day. I've always loved the quiet of the early morning, unless it's winter and then the dark makes me fearful. Unsurprising given my history of being confined in dark spaces, I didn't need Google to tell me that one.

Opening my wardrobe, I pause, thinking about what to wear today. *What would they like to see me dressed in?* Forest liked the demure skirt and boots, and I want to look sexy today, given that I embraced that side of myself last night.

Reaching in, I take out a green, wool circle skirt, the same colour as Forest's eyes, and pair it with a burnt orange blouse and cable knit cardigan in the same colour. I place the clothes on the bed and head to my underwear drawer, where I pull out an emerald-coloured, lace bra and knicker set with matching suspenders and some nude thigh highs. My cheeks flush when I remember how feral Landon looked when he saw me in them, just like Forest predicted he would.

After getting dressed, I take some extra time to style my hair in tumbling waves and apply a light coat of makeup, looking at myself in the mirror and wondering what they'll think when they see me at school.

*Still too thin...*I sigh, hating that other girls have gorgeous curves and I'm like a stick, not allowed to put on any weight.

The Saints didn't seem to mind...

Why does my inner voice keep trying to convince me that they are mine? This thing between us can never go anywhere, not unless I stand up to the Ambassador and I just don't know if I can.

But if not now, when?

With my mind whirling, I head downstairs, my muscles tensing the closer I get to the formal dining room where I know my parents are. Just as I pass by the Ambassador's study, his raised voice pulls me up short.

"I don't give a shit if you have to go out and steal some fucking pets, you promised me you could fulfil our needs and currently you aren't doing that." His voice is a menacing growl that has me shrinking back, but curiosity roots me to the spot. I've never heard him so angry before.

He waits a beat, like maybe he's listening to someone on the phone. "And we need something with a bit more of a backbone than the spineless whelps you've delivered so far. It's no fun if they don't put up a fight."

Dread pools in my stomach, my senses heightened as I wonder what the fuck he's talking about. Some part of me knows that it's not the annual charity gala or the coronation celebration he's planning.

"Just remember, your position at the Poundis only guaranteed so long as you please me and my associates. We can withdraw our support very quickly, and if anyone were to find out about your extra side hustle...well..."

My heart pounds with the threat, and it's that which finally unfreezes me and gets my feet moving silently again. I can't be caught eavesdropping, I daren't imagine what my punishment would be if I got caught.

Who was he talking to? Someone at the pound? Forest maybe? But I can't imagine how he'd be involved in the clearly shady business the Ambassador was talking about.

You don't know him, or the others, so how can you be sure?

God I hate that bitch known as anxiety, she colours everything in shades of uncertainty and makes me question my gut and heart all too often.

"Stop frowning, Aspen. You'll get wrinkles and it's not an attractive look on you." My mother's harsh voice cuts through my racing thoughts, and I realise with a start that I'm in the dining room, sitting at the table. Fuck, I really must have been thinking too hard.

"Apologies, Mother," I mumble, seeing the way her light blue gaze cuts across me, assessing me, weighing me up, and no doubt finding me wanting. Something she confirms a moment later.

"I've hired you that personal trainer I got you for Christmas, dear. You need to tone up," she remarks as a member of staff places what my mother has decided I'll have for breakfast today. A plate with half a grapefruit sliced into segments and a glass filled with a green juice that no doubt is disgusting is put in front of me. I fucking hate grapefruit—it's too bitter—but like the dutiful daughter I try to be, I use my small fruit fork and pick a piece up. "He'll be here after you finish school, so come straight home."

"Yes, Mother," I reply softly, my hand clutched around the handle of the fork, tightening until the metal bites into my skin. I'm staring at the grapefruit, trying to control my breathing enough not to snap at her that it's *my* life and I can do as I please. Though, that would be a lie, and I don't know where it comes from, because it's been drilled into me over the past few years that I most certainly *cannot* do as I please.

"How was your time with Albert? You came back late," she throws out, and my eyes dart up to hers to see a gleam in her eyes. "His father is a senator, a very important man, Aspen. Don't mess this up for your father."

"W–we went to the country club and hung out with some people from school," I carefully inform her, my heart pounding in my chest as I prepare to tell the lie that Bobby gave me. "And then we went back to his house."

She gives me a maniacal grin. "Excellent. Well, I hope you left him satisfied, dear. It's important to keep men like that happy, and there is one surefire way to do that."

My cheeks flush as I feel my eyes go wide at her words. She's telling me to fuck him because the Ambassador wants to keep Albert's father on his side...Jesus fucking Christ.

"Oh, don't look at me like that, Aspen. Us women have to do what we can to get on in life, and often that involves some sacrifices, but it doesn't have to be all bad, just think of being set up for life with a future senator," she instructs me, and my mind flashes to the way

Forest made me feel, the way Landon and Blaine made me come so hard that I saw fucking stars.

"Of course, Mother," I answer, dipping my head so she can't see that my eyes must reflect the way my blood currently burns in my veins.

The Ambassador joins us a few minutes later, ignoring me completely as he sits down with his mound of newspapers as he does every morning. I wouldn't be surprised if someone on the staff has to iron them for him so they are crease-free.

I finish up quickly, bidding them both goodbye as I rush from the room and into the waiting car.

"Good morning, Miss Aspen," Bobby greets me as soon as the door is shut.

"Good morning, Bobby," I reply, still thinking about the conversation I overheard and what it means. *Who was he talking to? And what did it have to do with the pound, the place that Forest's aunt and uncle own?*

Again, time seems to slip away from me and before I know it we're pulling up outside the impressive gates of Fairview Academy. Just like yesterday, I can appreciate the beauty of the buildings as I pass through the gates. The way the modern buildings seem to blend with the old ones shouldn't look so good side by side given how different they are, but it works.

"Aspen!" an Irish voice calls out, and I turn, the first genuine smile I've had since last night splitting my face into a wide grin.

"Good morning, Aoife. How are you?" I question, appreciating her quirky dress sense. She's wearing head to toe black, chunky Doc Martens on her feet with a soft, jersey-style dress printed in a tarot card pattern covering her gorgeous curvy figure, all topped off with a fitted wool coat, also in black. With her sleek hair, she's got the Wednesday Adams vibe going for her.

"Urgh, you know, fucking hate getting up early, like who actually enjoys the morning?" she answers, sipping from a travel mug, then pausing at no doubt the look on my face. "You do, don't you? You're one of those morning people me da always bangs on about, aren't you?"

"Guilty," I say, chuckling as we make our way towards the art building for our first class of the day.

"Just my luck," she teases, nudging my shoulder with hers.

"Hey!" I hear a voice call, and turning around, my stomach drops when Albert storms towards me.

"He looks pissed..." Aoife muses, stepping closer to me until our arms brush.

"You left your shit in my car," Albert spits out, throwing my bag and jacket on the ground with a look of disgust.

My body just freezes in the face of his anger, all of the bravado from the previous night disappearing as my body screams at me to run from the danger.

"Is there a problem here?" a deep voice sounds just behind me, and my muscles release all their tension as Landon, Forest, and Blaine come up on my other side.

Albert's lip curls. "Your whore left her shit in my car," he sneers, his face set in ugly lines of distaste.

"I'd watch what you call her, Pennington," Landon grits out, and I glance at him to see his body tense, his jaw clenched. "Wouldn't want Daddy to find out about that coke habit of yours."

Albert splutters, but before he can say anything, Forest cuts in. "And I bet you wouldn't want all your dealers to cut you off, right? I hear sudden withdrawal can be a real mind fuck."

My eyes widen as I look from the Saints to Albert, who is grinding his jaw and fisting his hands like he really wants to launch himself at them. There's a small crowd forming around us, but my attention is on the men around me and the standoff they seem to be in.

With a noise of frustration, Albert spins and storms away, taking most of the tension with him.

"You okay, *mi princesa linda*?" Blaine whispers softly to me, and I automatically nod my head, then after a few moments shake it.

"M–my mother told me I needed to keep Albert satisfied, his father and the Ambassador, they're in some kind of business together I think," I tell them in a rush, twisting in time to catch the look they share between each other. I narrow my eyes. "Do you know something?"

Landon's dark gaze darts to me, then Aoife, and the crowd behind us.

"Not here, meet us after class, you have a free period and we'll talk then," he tells me in a low tone, and my brows furrow.

"How do you know I have a free period?" I question him, and he just gives me a half smirk that has butterflies dancing around in my stomach.

"See you later, Duchess," he replies, his fingers brushing mine at my side in an all too brief caress before he turns to head in the opposite direction. The small crowd has dispersed, clearly deciding that nothing more exciting was going to happen, for which I am grateful because I can't let this get back to my parents. I need them to believe that I am with Albert.

"I wish I could kiss you," Forest murmurs hotly as he leans into me a little, his eyes raking over my skin and leaving fireworks in their wake. His fingers caress mine, just like Lan did, then he, too, is leaving.

"Later, *mi tesoro*," Blaine breathes out before he copies the others and leaves my fingers twitching to grab hold of him. When he walks away, I have to bite my lip to stop from calling them back, my stomach knotting and heart screaming at me not to let them go.

"Oh, girl, you guys have got it bad," Aoife comments from next to me, and I blink, realising that I'd completely forgotten about her. I'll collect my terrible friend of the year award on the way out.

"Got what bad?" I ask, tearing my gaze away from the rapidly emptying courtyard.

"I was hoping you'd confess all," she teases, a hopeful gleam in her eyes. "The tension between you, shit! I've never seen them with another girl at school, much to the rich bitch crew's annoyance."

"They don't date?" I question as we turn to head inside.

"Not from Fairview Academy," she tells me, holding the door open so we can walk inside. The English building is one of the older ones, and there's a hush even as students make their way to their classes.

"Huh," I muse. "Aoife, do you know what they do? I mean, as the Saints?" My heart pounds after the question leaves my lips, anticipation making me feel jittery.

"Nice subject change," she drawls, winking at me when I blush. "I'm not sure. I heard they offer protection to businesses on the east side, and that Landon's uncle is in the mafia."

"What?" I hiss, pulling up short just before we enter our classroom.

"Yeah, rumour has it that his uncle isn't the Don but is quite high up and the Saints work for him sometimes," she tells me quietly. "I mean, they help out at the pound, but that's just a front, or so people say."

Well, shit.

The bell rings, jolting me out of my stupor, and we rush into a classroom, sitting down next to each other.

"What happened last night?" she whispers to me as we get our tablets out, our teacher bringing up something on the screen before us.

"Quiet, class, we've a lot to get through today," our teacher, Mrs. Sinclair, announces, saving me from having to try and explain the craziness of the past twenty-four hours.

CHAPTER 17

"I'M YOURS" BY ISABEL LAROSA

ASPEN

My brain is mush two hours later when we emerge, bleary-eyed into the winter sunshine, but I soon get my focus back when I see Landon waiting for me.

"I've got bio, but you best be prepared to catch me up on every-fucking-thing later!" Aoife whisper-yells at me before she rushes off.

"Where are the others?" I ask Lan as he comes to a stop before me. His eyes blaze heat as he looks me up and down, and I feel the flush creep up my cheeks at the look of approval in them.

"They're waiting somewhere else. We didn't want it to be too obvious," he tells me, darting his gaze around us before he takes hold of my hand and tangles our fingers together.

I blow out a slow, measured breath as the tingles from his touch race up and down my arm. I've never reacted this way to anyone before, my body suddenly aching for him in the most primal way.

Get a fucking grip, Aspen. You've known him for like a week or so. This isn't real.

"Come," he orders, and I swear my core pulses at the command which immediately makes me think of the way he made me explode last night without so much as a word.

I follow him, our hands wrapped around each other, and we head into the woods that surround the school. The sound of nature takes over, the birds singing in the trees calming me as our footsteps break twigs and rustle leaves. The path is well-worn, and I wonder how many times Landon has come this way before.

Soon, we reach a clearing, and I spot Forest resting on a fallen tree while Blaine has his huge arms folded in a pose as he takes in his surroundings. They look gorgeous, Forest wearing his hoodie and denim jacket combo, his dark jeans hugging his thick legs and tucked into brown cowboy boots that make me smile. Blaine is also wearing black jeans, black boots, and has a black hoodie on, no coat. I inwardly curse myself for forgetting his leather jacket that's hidden in the closet in my room.

Forest glances up at our approach, and before I know what's happening, he's sweeping me up in his arms as his lips crash down on mine.

My hands come up to tangle in his hair as I sink into his kiss, my mouth opening for him when he demands entry with his tongue. He pulls me so close that I can feel the heat of his body all along the front of mine, and I have a vision of us last night in my room, naked, our skin touching everywhere. Heat flares across my body, and I whimper when he starts to pull away.

"Fuck, I missed you, sugar," he breathes against my lips. "Leaving you this morning was one of the hardest things I've had to do in a long while."

No matter how much my mind screams at me that I shouldn't be kissing him, not in public where anyone could see and report back to the Ambassador, I pull him towards me again, fusing our lips together. My body tells me I'm full of shit, and we kiss until someone clears their throat.

Forest pulls back but keeps his arms around me as he looks over his shoulder.

"If you're quite done?" Lan's sardonic drawl fills the space, and I blush even as a giggle slips past my kiss-swollen lips.

"Only because you made her laugh, Daddy," Forest replies, giving me a quick kiss on the tip of my nose. Releasing one arm and keeping one around my shoulders, he leads me to the fallen tree trunk. He settles me down on it, sitting so close that the whole side of our bodies touch, and then wraps an arm around my shoulders again, like he just can't bear to be apart for too long. I allow myself to melt into him, my entire body relaxing. Then Blaine is in front of me, holding out a travel thermos.

"I made you another protein shake," he tells me, bending down and placing a soft kiss on my lips as he hands me the cup. "Make sure you drink all of it, *mi princesa*. It's got added nutrients and vitamins."

My chest feels like it expands a thousandfold at his words. "Thank you, Blaine." My voice is thick, but I can't help it. No one has ever taken care of me the way these guys have, and it makes me feel all warm inside knowing that Blaine made this nutritious shake just for me. Taking a sip, I moan in appreciation. "So much nicer than the one my mother made me drink this morning." His face splits into a wide smile that steals my breath away for a moment, he's just so damn beautiful, even more so with the imperfection of the scar down his cheek.

Reaching out, I trace my fingers down the length of it, and although his stare intensifies, he doesn't flinch. "What happened?"

He heaves a breath, his chocolate eyes boring into mine as a flash of pain makes them darken. "My father." He doesn't expand, but my eyes fill with tears at how cruel the world can be, when we're given parents who never deserved the joy of children.

"I'm so sorry, Blaine. You didn't deserve that," I whisper, my fingers falling away from his scar to cup his cheek. His eyes close briefly, his face leaning into the touch before he straightens up.

"We don't often get what we deserve in this life, *mi tesoro*," he tells me, then stands so that he's got a view of the clearing around us.

My brows dip as I think about his words, wishing with all my soul that they weren't true.

"We believe that your father is running some kind of illegal gambling ring," Lan states in the silence, and my gaze snaps to him, my eyes wide. Talk about ripping the Band-Aid off, Jesus.

"What? Why?" I ask, trying to figure out why he'd need to do something like that. "It's not like we need the money."

"Boredom, maybe," Lan suggests, shrugging his broad shoulders. "Either way, we have been trying to find out what it is and when it takes place, and it would make sense that Senator Pennington is involved, being one of your dad's closest friends."

My head shakes slightly, my eyebrows furrowing, then raising as my heart thuds painfully in my chest. I focus on Forest, the conversation I overheard earlier playing back in my mind. "Could it be something to do with the pound?"

Forest's spine snaps straight, his brows dipping. "What do you mean, sugar?"

Taking a deep inhale, deciding to trust my gut, I tell them the truth. "This morning when I walked past his study he was yelling at someone about stealing pets if need be, and that they needed to be able to fight." All three of them are laser-focused on me, poised like predators, and I shiver at the intensity. "Not the spineless whelps they'd been supplying apparently. Then he told the person that their position at the Pound wasn't guaranteed, he threatened them."

"Motherfucker!" Forest thunders, leaping to his feet and pacing the forest floor. "That spineless, no good piece of shit!"

"What?" I ask, my body quivering at the rage that pours off of him. Strong arms wrap themselves around me from behind, and I stiffen until the woody scent of Blaine surrounds me.

"You didn't do anything wrong, *mi princesa*," he assures me quietly, and Forest looks over, his mouth parting when he takes me in; a shaking mess in Blaine's arms.

"Oh, baby," he whispers, rushing over and cupping my face in his warm, albeit trembling palms. "I'm sorry, sugar. I lost my head, but I shouldn't have gotten so mad and scared you like that."

He places a soft kiss on my lips before releasing me when he sees that I'm no longer shaking.

"I knew there was something shifty about Wallace recently," he says to Landon, Blaine keeping me in his warm embrace, lifting me to settle me in his lap. My arms wrap around his, pulling him closer around me, and I swear a deep purr rumbles in his chest.

"Who's Wallace?" I question, snuggling back into Blaine and allowing myself his comfort, even if it's only for this short time.

"He's the assistant manager at the pound," Lan tells me, his face unreadable.

"My aunt and uncle hired him a while back so that they could take it a bit easier," Forest adds, his voice still low and full of anger. "I've never liked him, too quick to put a dog down, but they wanted me to focus on school so I could better myself or some shit."

"What could he be doing for the Ambassador?" I ask, my tone uncertain as I try to puzzle it out.

"I think that's pretty obvious, Duchess," Lan states with a frown, and I look up at him, my stomach churning, knowing that whatever he says is not going to be nice. "Your father is holding dog fights, and he needs his cannon fodder from somewhere."

It takes a minute, but when what he's saying clicks, it's like the woods around us no longer exist.

"You're saying that he's using the Poundto get dogs for the fights? That he's allowing innocent creatures to die for entertainment?" Tears spill over onto my cheeks, burning my skin as just how much of a monster the Ambassador really is hits me in the chest.

I should know, he's been tormenting me in the pursuit of perfection for years, starving me and locking me in pitch-black rooms.

But to hear that he could be so cruel to a defenceless creature like a dog, who doesn't even have a home to begin with...

"I–I d–didn't know," I stutter, Blaine's arms tightening around me. Forest sits down at my side, taking one of my hands in his and rubbing my knuckles. Landon crouches down in front of me, brushing the tears away from my face. "Why is he such a monster?" My tone breaks on the last word as I beg Landon for an answer I know he doesn't have.

"I don't know, Duchess. Fuck, I wish I did." He sighs, his brows deeply furrowed. "But we'll stop him."

"No one can stop him," I whisper in an echo of our conversation last night, but doubt creeps in. Maybe the Saints have what it takes with their gang and mafia connections.

"We can," he states, like it's a statement of fact, a given. "But we need your help, Duchess."

"Lan," Blaine rumbles behind me, but I squeeze his arm, letting him know that it's okay.

"I'll do it. Whatever you need," I promise, and Lan's lips tilt up into a feral smile.

"Good girl."

CHAPTER 18

"TIDAL WAVE" BY CHASE ATLANTIC

BLAINE

I know we're all reeling from the information Aspen just gave us, but her vow to help us has a warm glow running through my veins. It's been just the three of us for so long, but I must admit that she fits in seamlessly. If only she was a little less out of reach. She belongs in another world to ours, and I can't help worrying about what dragging her down in the mud with us will do to her.

"Good girl," Lan praises, and I feel the way her body responds; the way her thighs part ever so slightly and her chest hitches. My fingers stroke her hip, and I smile when her body shudders.

"Were you a good girl this morning and put on the thigh highs and garters that Lan likes so much, *mi princesa linda?*" I murmur into her ear, skimming my nose up the column of her neck. I catch Lan's heated gaze and know that he just overheard my question.

"Yes," she replies on a breath, and when I place a light kiss on her neck she shudders against me again.

"Show him," I command, and her whole body freezes. The silence is thick, the birdsong loud as I wait to see if she'll follow orders. I think she will, and she'll be rewarded and praised if she does as I command.

Her torso rises and falls with a deep inhale, and then I look over her shoulder when she places her hands in the fabric of her skirt and starts to lift it up. Her cute as fuck, brown leather boots are revealed first, and I've never found an item of footwear so fucking attractive before. Her shapely legs are next, and I can't even tear my gaze away to see Lan's reaction as I wait for the tops of her stockings to be shown.

"Goddamn, Duchess," Lan grits out as the top of her emerald garters and nude thigh highs come into view. *Coño*, she has gorgeous legs.

"Such a good girl for your Saints," I whisper, kissing her neck. She arches her head to the side, giving me more access, so I indulge in a little nibble which has her taking in a sharp breath. "Now, open your legs more for him, and I'm sure he'll give you your reward."

There's no hesitation this time, her thighs spreading wide, and if the curse Lan makes is anything to go by, he's enjoying the view. She gasps sharply, and I look down to see Forest has unbuttoned her coat, cardigan, and shirt, exposing her lace-covered breasts to the cold air.

"Such beautiful tits," he murmurs, echoing my thoughts as he leans down, and the way a moan slips from her parted lips, I can imagine he's taken one of her pert nipples into his mouth.

"Fuck," she breathes out, wiggling on my rock-fucking-solid dick as Lan disappears between her thighs. He loves eating girls like they're his last meal, and I imagine it's a feast between her legs.

"Let us take care of you, *mi princesa linda*," I tell her, kissing and sucking the elegant column of her neck. "You deserve a reward for giving us our first lead."

She jerks forward a little as Lan really sets to work, the sound of him licking and sucking her loud in the quiet forest. I know Forest will be getting off on us being outside, that boy is an exhibitionist if ever I met one. Her hands come up to grip my arms which are still wrapped tightly around her, holding her in place for my friends to give her pleasure.

"Lan, fuck," she rasps, totally lost to the way he's worshipping her. Deciding to test her limits a little, I uncurl one arm from around her, sliding my palm around the front of her throat and squeezing lightly.

"Shit, Blaine, she just gushed all over my tongue," Lan rasps, and I feel him pull her wider apart, feasting on her pussy like he really will die if he doesn't make her come in the next twenty seconds. I know the feeling, my dick hard and balls aching, desperate to be inside her.

But this is about her, about giving her a reason to forget how shitty her dad is. I couldn't stand her cries when she found out, my inner beast calling out for revenge on anyone who made her that sad.

Her breaths become laboured, her body squirming as she reaches closer to the release she is craving.

"Come for us now. Come for your Saints," I command her, then squeeze my palm until I can feel her pulse in my fingertips.

With a muffled cry that startles the birds from the trees, she climaxes, her body going rigid and nails digging into the sleeve of my hoodie. Lan groans, deep and low, but doesn't stop, Forest sucking and nipping at her breasts until she's slumping and whimpering in my arms.

I release her throat, promising myself that next time I have my hand around it I'll be deep inside her sweet cunt. Forest pulls away next, with Lan the last one to lean back, his lips and chin glistening with her release. I catch Forest looking at her half-lidded expression, then he gives her a wink and leans over to drag Lan towards him.

Their lips collide, and I groan at the sight but it's nothing compared to the noise she makes. We've shared women before, but never shown them the affection we have for each other, our true bond, for fear of judgement. She's not like that though, and the way her thighs press together tells me that, like when Forest and I kissed when they were in the bath, this sort of thing turns her the fuck on.

She's fucking perfect for us, and although we've not yet spoken about it, I'm pretty sure the others want to keep her just as much as I do.

"Shit, you taste like the sweetest nectar, sugar," Forest purrs when he pulls away, his lips red and glistening a little now. "I can't wait until we can all sample your honey."

Distantly, we hear a bell go off, our free period at an end.

"Let's get you cleaned up a little for your next class," I tell her, and she huffs a laugh.

"I think my knickers are ruined." She sighs, her voice husky and deep. I can't help but press a kiss to her neck, wishing we could spend so much longer worshipping her. Guess I'll have to wait until later.

"Give them to Lan as a keepsake," I whisper, and she stills. I watch as she nibbles her lip in the sexiest fucking way, and then lifting her hips, she pulls her panties off and holds them out to Lan.

His nostrils flare, a slow smile forming on his lips as he reaches out to take them, then tucks them into his pocket before holding out his own hand and helping her up.

"Thank you, Duchess," he purrs, placing a slow, lingering kiss on her lips. I love the way she sinks into him, her hands gripping the front of his black button-up shirt—you can take the boy out of the mafia but apparently, he can't leave the mob fashion sense behind.

"ONE WAY OR ANOTHER" BY UNTIL THE RIBBON BREAKS

ASPEN

The day drags a little after my time in the woods with the Saints. I catch glimpses of them, but they keep their distance which I'm grateful for and hate in equal measure. I know that we can't be seen too much together, but I loathe the separation all the same. And I have no more shared classes with any of them today, which leaves me feeling lonely and vulnerable.

I also manage to avoid Aoife, which I feel terrible about but can't say that I'm not a little bit relieved about too. I'm not sure where to start, or what to tell her. I mean, she knows that my parents are a little fucked up, but how can I tell her how bad they truly are?

I'm quiet and pensive when I get into the car at the end of the day, my anxiety about returning back to the house keeps me on edge as it always does.

"Good afternoon, Miss Aspen," Bobby greets as we pull away. "Mrs. Buckingham asked me to remind you about your personal trainer appointment today as her and the Ambassador have been called away for the next couple of days."

My eyes widen as my heart gives a little skip. "They're away?"

"Yes, Miss," he replies, and I catch the hint of a smile on his lips. "Until Sunday, I believe."

My entire body sinks back into the plush leather seat of the Bentley. Four days. Four blissful fucking days with no parents hovering me, criticising me, and the threat of correction looming over me.

"Thank you, Bobby," I whisper, my hands trembling slightly as I clasp them lightly in my lap.

The journey feels less oppressive than it usually does, and although I'm not looking forward to my PT appointment—it's hard to build muscle mass when you are regularly denied food—nothing can dampen my happy mood as we roll into the drive.

Bobby comes to open my door, and I step out into the weak sunshine, taking a deep lungful of the crisp air.

"Your trainer will be waiting in the gym, Miss," he tells me, a glint in his eye that I can't quite interpret.

"Okay, thanks," I hesitantly say, pursing my lips as I try to read him. He just gives me a wink that almost floors me before going back around to the driver's side and taking the car to the garage.

Shaking my head, I approach the door, Gerrard opening it before I even reach it and letting me in.

"I'm just going to get changed, can you let my trainer know that I'll be a couple of minutes please, Gerrard?" I ask, and he inclines his head, shutting the door and heading in the direction of the home gym.

Hurrying upstairs, I quickly change into workout gear, tie up my hair in a messy bun, then make my way downstairs and to the side of the house with our gym, indoor pool, and sauna.

Pausing in front of the door, I take a steadying breath. I've never been great with new people or new situations, my heart fluttering like a trapped bird, but after counting to ten, I place my hand on the door and push it open.

My steps falter when I catch sight of my trainer, all six-foot-something, tattoos covering every inch of skin on display as he wears a skintight vest and shorts. He has a nose ring and a scar bisecting his left brow and upper cheek that I traced with my finger only hours before.

"Blaine?"

CHAPTER 19

"TALK TO MY SKIN" BY STALGIA

ASPEN

"Hello, *mi tesoro*," he greets in that low, rumble of his as he saunters towards me. Gods, the man is fucking huge, muscles on muscles and all of them visible in that outfit he's wearing. Those vests with large armholes should be made illegal in my humble opinion. *How the fuck am I meant to function when he looks like that?*

"What are you doing here?" I squeak out, darting my gaze around the room as if the Ambassador is about to spring up and catch us.

"I'm your new trainer," he tells me, stopping just in front of me so I have to crane my neck back to keep eye contact.

"How?" I question, my body begging to close the distance between us, but I hold back. I don't know if there are cameras in here, plus one of the staff could walk in at any moment.

His hand comes up, his fingers toying with some strands of my hair that have escaped the bun. I swear each tug and pull is directly linked to my pussy, making it pulse as lust hazes my thoughts.

"My cousin owns a personal training company that caters to the bored housewives of the west side of Fairview and I work for him," he tells me, still playing with my hair as his chocolate-brown eyes drink me in. "And when I'd heard he'd secured this gig, I persuaded him to let me be your trainer."

"Oh," I reply, trying and fucking failing not to sound all breathy. "Wait, what do you mean cater to the bored housewives?" My eyes narrow as a blush creeps up his cheeks and my chest tightens at the thought that he may have fucked some of his previous female clients which leaves me feeling like I can't draw a deep enough breath. "Actually, don't answer that."

Stepping away, I spin and wrap my arms around my body, trying to blink back the sudden tears that fill my eyes. He's not mine, and I've had partners before the Saints, so it shouldn't bother me.

"*Mi princesa linda*," he says in a pleading tone right before his strong arms wrap around me which only makes me stiffen more.

"Let me go! There might be cameras," I all but yell, trying to wriggle out of his grip as my limbs tremble, but his arms just tighten around me, pulling me closer.

"No one is watching us," he whispers in a low hum. "There are no cameras here. We're safe." His words filter through my panic and my body slumps, hot tears tracking down my cheeks no matter how much I try to swallow them back. "The thought of you with someone else hurts me too." His confession is a whisper and a small sob falls from my lips.

"But it's not fair of me to feel mad at shit that's happened in the past. You didn't even know me, and I didn't know you," I reply in a choked voice, my arms wrapping over the tops of his as I pull him closer.

"We can't help what we feel, *mi tesoro*," he tells me, placing his lips against my neck. I arch, giving him better access which he takes as he kisses and nibbles the flesh. "But I can assure you that anyone before you is nothing to me. They don't exist."

His large hands glide over my body, my tight gym wear providing no resistance to his touch.

"Blaine," I moan as he palms one of my breasts through my sports bra and squeezes, shivers cascading over my body from his touch.

"You want me to fuck you right here? Prove that you are the only woman I'm interested in? Fuck you like a dirty little slut where anyone could walk in?" His voice is a delicious rumble that has my core clenching, and his words? Fuck. Me. Why does the idea of being caught turn me on as much as it terrifies me? "Well?"

I lick my lips, my fingers digging into the muscles of his arms.

"Yes." It leaves my lips on a breath, and I push back into him, the significant bulge in his shorts giving me pause. Shit, Forest did say he was a big guy, but Jesus.

"Go over to that bench and bend over it for me," he commands, releasing me.

On shaking steps I do as he says, watching him in the mirror as I walk. Fucking hell, the hard outline of his dick is huge. He must see my panicked face because a low, dark chuckle escapes him.

"Don't worry, beautiful. We'll make it fit," he assures me, not moving as I take the final few steps to the weights bench.

It's horizontal to the mirror, so when I lower my hands to the leather surface I can watch as he strolls towards me with a grace that shouldn't be possible given how huge the man is. He reminds me of a lion, all that restrained violence just waiting to spring free.

He doesn't say anything as he comes around to block my view of the mirror, giving me a front row seat to the monster that lives in his pants. His fingers stroke my jaw, and he uses his grip to tilt my face upwards so that I'm looking him in the eyes.

"You're going to get me nice and wet first, aren't you, *mi princesa?*" A shiver wracks over me, making my nipples harden to points under my bra.

Not able to make a sound I nod, watching as his pupils blow out at my answer.

"Good girl," he praises, his thumb brushing over my bottom lip and tugging it down. "Keep your hands on the bench for me."

Keeping hold of my chin, he lowers my face as his other hand reaches into his shorts and pulls his dick out.

Good. Fucking. Lord.

All the blood rushes to my pussy at the sight of his rock-hard cock in front of me. It's huge. Like, I didn't know they could come in this size. His large hand tilts it upwards and holy fucking shit my brain short-circuits at the glint of metal on the underside.

I count the metal bars with my eyes and come up with eight. He has a jacob's ladder piercing—thank you, smuggled steamy romance books for that knowledge—with eight. Fucking. Rungs.

My eyes dart back up to his, no doubt wide and terrified, and he gives me what can only be described as a smug smile.

"You can take me, *princesa*," he tells me softly, placing the tip of his dick against my lips. This is a fucking trust exercise if ever I saw one. With my hands on the bench, all the control is his, and with the monster that he's hiding—or not—in his pants, he could very well choke me to death if he's not careful.

I hold his stare as my tongue darts out, tasting the musky saltiness of him, my fingernails digging into the leather of the bench and making it creak. A small moan sounds in my throat at the taste, and then I'm wrapping my lips around him, giving an experimental suck.

"Fuck!" he exclaims, his thighs twitching as I use my tongue on his tip, working my way to take more of his length inside my mouth. I won't get it all in, but I refuse to be defeated by a monster peen.

His other hand grabs my bun, using it to help guide me lower until he hits the back of my throat and I gag.

"That's it, baby. Just like that," he moans, bringing me back up and then forcing my head down again. The metal of his piercing is strange in my mouth, and my tongue traces them which has his hips snapping forwards, his cock going deeper.

Tears fill my eyes, but for an entirely different reason than earlier, and I let them fall as I watch him, his brows wrinkled and jaw tight as he seeks pleasure from my mouth. Heat blooms between my thighs, which clench together as I try to seek some relief from the ache.

"You desperate for my fat cock, *mi tesoro*?" he grits out, pausing with his dick halfway in my mouth. I nod, tears dotting my eyelashes. "Good girl."

He pulls out and I suck in a breath, my jaw aching with how much he stretched it with his dick. I watch in the mirror as he walks around to the back of me, his large hands landing on the waistband of my shorts and easing them and my knickers down. The cool air hits my overheated flesh and I gasp.

"Such a beautiful pussy," he comments, swiping a finger through my folds which has me pushing back to seek more. "And so desperate to be filled." I watch his arm move as he brings his tip to my opening, then pauses. "I don't suppose Forest asked you whether you were on birth control before he fucked you bare?"

His dark eyes hold mine in the mirror.

"N–no, but I am," I stumble out, my cheeks flushing. I didn't think to ask if he was clean or anything at the time either. "And I'm clean."

"We all are too," he tells me, easing his tip inside me and my eyes roll. "And it wouldn't have stopped him or me if you weren't on birth control." He pushes in a little more and my fingers grip the bench even harder. The stretch is almost burning but is so damn delicious.

"S–stopped you?" I question, my brain slower on account of the huge dick trying to impale me.

"If putting a Saint's baby in that belly of yours will keep you with us, then I will flush all your pills, cut out any implant, take out any IUD myself, *mi tesoro*," he informs me as he pushes in more, my body breaking out in a fine layer of sweat.

Why does that idea turn me on more? And I can't hide the fact it does because wetness slicks from my already soaked folds.

"You like that idea? You like the idea of me filling you full of my cum and getting you pregnant?" I moan loudly as my pussy flutters around him, more of my juices easing his path even deeper inside me. "Answer me."

I hold his stare in the mirror, my body trembling as I don't speak. How can I admit that yes, it turns me on? I'm not even nineteen for fuck's sake, and don't exactly have great role models for parents. Plus, I'm not ready for a child yet.

But the idea of having his, or Forest or even Lan's baby?

"Yes," I say in barely a whisper, my heart thundering in my chest at my admission. His lips tilt up in a half smile.

"Good girl," he says, right before he slams the rest of the way inside me, his hands holding my hips so I don't fly off the bench with the force of the thrust.

I scream, no one has ever been this deep before, and my body shakes and shudders as he stays buried to the hilt, letting me adjust. After a few minutes, the need to move, to feel him move becomes overwhelming, and all it takes is a pleading look in the mirror before he's pulling out of me and thrusting back inside.

I can't hold in my cries and curses, my nails digging into the leather so hard that I'm surprised they don't break. Fire races across my body as he fucks me hard and fast, his grip bruising, and I relish all of it. I want his marks on my body. Want to feel claimed by him inside and out.

"*Coño*, you're strangling my dick, baby," he grits out, and I lift my lowered lids to watch his face in the mirror. It's twisted in a snarl, sweat beading his forehead as he keeps pounding into me, sending me closer and closer to an edge that I know will destroy me. "Play with your clit, *mi princesa*. Touch yourself while I fuck you."

Taking one hand off the bench, I place it between my legs, and the first brush of my fingers against my soaked nub has pleasure pulsing through me.

"Blaine," I pant, my fingers stroking and teasing my swollen clit, brushing against his massive dick every so often, and fuck, I love the feel of him pushing inside me.

"That's it, baby. Come all over my dick," he commands and I cannot disobey. My climax tears through me with such force that I clamp down around him like my body is refusing to let him go. "*Coño!*"

Electricity shoots up my spine, making my nerve endings tingle and pop like I have an entire fireworks show going off inside me. I'm still screaming when he surges deep inside me, a low, rumbling growl vibrating across my skin as he orgasms.

Only his strong grip is holding me up, my body feeling like liquid that's being shaken in a bottle, and my muscles tremble with the residue euphoria. Sweat coats my skin, and we stay connected for long moments, our breaths slowing eventually. I gasp when he pulls out, the rush of liquid that drips down my thighs should make me blush, but I'm too blissed out to care.

I slump down over the bench when he lets me go, and he walks away only to return moments later with a small towel, which he uses to clean me up before pulling my underwear and shorts back up. I'm less than helpful, and he chuckles when I just continue to lie there.

"Come, *mi princesa*, time to train," he coaxes gently, crouching down in front of me and brushing loose strands of hair off my sweaty forehead.

"W–what? Train?" I mumble, yawning as I get up on shaking legs, and he stands up until I have to tilt my head to look at him, the bench between us.

"That's what I'm here to do. Train you," he tells me, glancing at the watch he has on. "And we still have thirty minutes of our time left."

My mouth falls open. "You expect me to train? After that?" My muscles still tremble from the rush of endorphins that are coursing through me.

"I went easy on you, beautiful," he states with a sinful grin that has my toes curling. He's too damn pretty for his own good. Or maybe mine.

"Easy?" I all but screech. "I'd hate to see what going hard would be."

He steps around the bench and gets up into my space, tilting my chin so that I'm looking up at him from only a few centimetres away. It reminds me of the way he did similar when I sucked his dick, and a flush spreads across my overheated cheeks.

"When we have more time together, then I'll show you what hard is like." Leaning down, he places a gentle kiss on my swollen lips, then pulls away, grasping my hand in his. "Let's start slow and we can work up."

With a sigh, I let him tug me in the direction of the equipment that I've used before, the last time Mother got in PT to tone me up. They could never understand why I used to faint so frequently, and it wasn't like I was about to confess that my parents would starve me regularly. I guess that's not an issue with Blaine though since he knows some of my sordid home life.

CHAPTER 20

"NO MAN'S LAND" BY HANDS LIKE HOUSES

LANDON

I glance down at my phone screen, a slight chill racing up my spine when I see my uncle's name flash up as the caller ID.

"Good afternoon, Uncle," I greet, keeping my tone polite even as my jaw wants to clench. I fucking hate being in his debt, but I can't regret helping Blaine get out from under his abusive, deadbeat dad's fist either.

"Landon, my boy!" he greets enthusiastically, the sound of cutlery clinking against plates in the background letting me know he's probably at Mama's restaurant. My fingers grip my phone so hard that the plastic creaks. "How are you?"

"Well, Uncle, and you?" I enquire, not giving a shit but it's expected.

"Good, my boy, very good. Your mama is doing an excellent job of keeping us all fed, aren't you, Maria?" My teeth clench so hard I swear one of my molars cracks. I hate that my uncle visits Mama's restaurant so fucking often. I've tried so fucking hard to keep us away from mafia life. After my dad was murdered because of the Family, I wanted nothing to do with it.

"I try, Alfonso," I hear her answer softly, and the sound of her voice helps to calm me, even as my heart thuds at how much danger she's in with my uncle and his men so close. "Though you are determined to eat me out of house and home." She laughs, and it's the sound I remember from my childhood when Papa used to tease her.

"You are a good woman," my uncle replies, and I don't miss the softness in his tone. I swear he's been after my mama to marry him ever since Papa, his fucking brother, died, but she has always said that her heart belonged to Papa and that's the end of it. Still makes my hackles rise listening to him try though. "So, any news on our little mouse?"

The hair lifts on the back of my neck at the mention of Aspen. I don't like the way he refers to her as a mouse. It makes it sound like she's something to be trapped and caged, and I think she has enough of that with her home life. There's damage in her eyes that I wonder is due to more than just being starved regularly. Taking a deep breath before that train of thought can lead me down the path of rage, I take a moment before answering him.

"We think that the Ambassador has been running dog fights and has an in with the pound," I tell him in a measured tone, waiting to see how he reacts.

"Go on," he murmurs in a low voice that has the hair standing up on the back of my neck.

"It seems that Wallace, the assistant manager there, has been providing stock and they want something of a better calibre than what he's been giving them," I add, my body tensing as my blood boils at the mere thought of that fucking weasel.

"Hmmmm," my uncle muses aloud, and I hate that I don't know what he's thinking. "You need to find out when and where the next fight is taking place. Offer up that mutt of yours, he looks like he'd provide enough of a challenge to get you in."

My previously boiling blood freezes, turning to ice in my veins as he mentions Bolt. He's been with us since he was an abandoned pup, left behind when someone moved away, tied up to a tree with just a bowl of water and just as much anger at the world as us.

"I won't offer up Bolt to be slaughtered," I grit out, my body shaking as I race through options in my mind. It's never good to disagree with my uncle.

"Oh, you won't?" His voice is deadly calm, and my stomach clenches at the threat in there. "Need I remind you what you owe me, Landon? A life. I can easily arrange for you to pay that and join my men, like your father, if that's a better option?"

My throat bobs as I swallow hard. There was a price to be paid for getting Blaine away from his dad. I owe a life for the one they took, but if I kill someone for them, in front of them, I'm a made man, and joining the mafia is a life sentence with no way out. I don't want to be a fucking criminal for the rest of my life, always looking over my shoulder, my family and friends always at risk.

"I'll sort it," I murmur, the words burning as they leave my throat.

"Excellent. I knew I could rely on you, Landon." His voice is back to the jovial man who called me. It's always been this way, anger him and he's like an icicle, but agree to his demands and he's the doting uncle once more. "Keep me updated."

The line goes dead and I can't move for a moment.

How the fuck am I going to tell the others about this? That we have to use Bolt as bait? That he may have to fight—and possibly die —for my uncle's cause?

ROSA LEE

"COUNTING STARS" BY ONEREPUBLIC

ASPEN

I'm wrecked by the time Blaine finishes our workout session, my muscles tired and twitching, but I feel good, and not just from the incredible sex that we started our session with. He's an amazing trainer, knowing when to push me and when to give me breaks, and I did so much more than I ever thought I was capable of.

"You did well today, *mi princesa*," he says as I flop down on the mat, panting and covered in sweat. "Let's do some stretching while you're warmed up, then you need to have a hot bath to relax all the muscles you built."

He ignores my groan, grabbing my leg and getting me in a position, my foot against his shoulder to stretch it out.

"My parents are away all week," I tell him before we start on the next leg. He pauses, looking at me with those deep-brown eyes that feel like home. "Until Saturday or Sunday, I think."

"And what were you thinking to do while they are gone, beautiful? We have a session booked every day which you will not be missing," he tells me with a smirk, getting me to push against him until my thighs burn.

"I didn't mean that," I puff out as he pushes against my leg, making the stretch go deeper. "Fuck, Blaine!"

"I prefer to hear you say that when I'm inside you, *mi tesoro*." He chuckles, releasing my leg, and I just flop against the mat, chest heaving, face flaming. "Drink some water."

Sitting up with a groan, I take the bottle he hands me and have a long drink, the cool liquid refreshing. "Happy?" I ask, my brows raised.

"I will not hesitate to put you over my knee if you start behaving like a brat," he casually tells me, my eyes going wide even as my thighs clench together at the sudden pulse between them. Would I be into that? "Or maybe I'll tell Lan you need some correction, he's the master of doling out punishment."

I barely hear the end of his sentence, the word *correction* tightening my chest, my body curling in on itself as I struggle to breathe. The gym no longer surrounds me, just a long corridor with a nondescript door at the end that's full of all my nightmares.

"Aspen!" Blaine's panicked voice breaks through the black dots that were blotting my vision, and it's like the real world comes rushing back in, his face creased as he's kneeling before me, his chocolate eyes wide. "That's it, beautiful. Breathe with me, baby." One of my palms is on his broad chest, his hand holding it there, and I take a gasping inhale when he takes a deep breath. "Good girl, keep breathing."

His face blurs as tears fill my eyes, slipping beyond my lashes and down my hot cheeks. "I–I'm s–so s–sorry," I stutter, my voice choked.

"No, *mi princesa*. I'm sorry if what I said was too much, I thought...*coño!*" he curses softly, torment furrowing his brows.

"I–it wasn't the idea of Lan p–punishing me," I rush out, my breathing almost back to normal. "It was the word. C–c–correction." I have to take another inhale before I can continue. "I–The Ambassador uses it whenever I've done something to displease him. It has a bad effect on me." I drop my gaze to my lap, unable to confess the shame I feel at my treatment. I know that it's not my fault, that the extreme punishments aren't normal, but it's hard to believe that I'm not in some way to blame. That maybe if I was better I wouldn't have been locked away in the dark so much.

"Look at me, *mi tesoro*," Blaine pleads, and helpless to disobey, I lift my lashes and look into his soulful eyes. "You are perfect, and whatever that *bastardi* has done to you is on him. Not you. Understood?"

"I know it's just...it's all I've ever been told. Sometimes it's hard not to believe it," I confess, watching as a deep sigh leaves his lips.

"My father beat my mother to death in front of my eyes when I was a boy, then blamed me, saying that I made him so mad he couldn't stop," he tells me in a matter-of-fact tone, a wounded sound falling from my lips as more tears scald my cheeks. "He used to beat us both regularly. This scar is courtesy of him." I trace the scar over his eye with a fingertip and he shivers at the light touch. I wonder how old he was when his father gave it to him.

"W–where is he now?" I ask, my soul aching for the strong man in front of me who's been through so much. More than anyone should have.

"Dead." He doesn't elaborate, and although I feel there's so much more to his story than what he's told me. I don't pry.

"Good," I tell him, placing my free hand on his cheek and rubbing over the scar there with my thumb. "I'm glad he can no longer hurt you."

"But the Ambassador can still hurt you," he says with his jaw clenched, and his stare turns pained. I bite my lips, unable to say anything in response. He's right. For now, at least, the Ambassador can still hurt me. Until I turn nineteen in a few weeks, then maybe I can finally get out from under his thumb.

"There are showers down here. Will a hot shower be okay rather than a bath?" I ask him, my eyes begging that he drops the subject of my shitty home life which I am unable to get out of.

"Distracting me with that beautiful body will only get you so far, *mi amorsita*," he tells me but helps me get up anyway.

"What does *mi tesoro* and *mi amorsita* mean?" I ask, leading him to the shower facilities we have down here, which are just off the gym.

"They're Spanish for my treasure and my little love," he informs me, so casually like he didn't just almost confess that he loves me. Maybe.

"Oh," I breathe out, pausing in my steps. He chuckles, the sound caressing all over my skin.

"Come, *mi amorsita*. Let's get you clean and maybe a bit dirty again."

CHAPTER 21

"MORE THAN FRIENDS" BY ISABEL LAROSA

ASPEN

"Lil' Lady..." the deep, soothing voice infiltrates my dreams, dragging me from the darkness of sleep.

"Forest?" I ask sleepily, my lashes blinking open to see him crouched next to the bed, the planes of his face highlighted by the half-moon that shines through the open curtains. I blink, expecting this to be a dream, but he's still there when my eyes open again, looking too beautiful like a forest spirit ready to whisk me away.

"Not just me, sugar," he says, stroking some hair away from my face.

Twisting, I catch sight of two other shadows in my room, my heart giving a dull thud until they, too, step in the moonlight, and I see it's Blaine and Landon.

"What are you doing here?" I question as I sit up, the blankets pooling in my lap. Their eyes go to my chest, groans sounding in the quiet.

"I'm going to need you to put something on, Duchess," Lan growls, and I blink again, looking down and only then remembering that I'm naked.

"Oh, um, sorry. I hate pyjamas," I tell them, scooting to the edge of the bed, which Forest is standing next to, and slipping out.

"Fucking hell," Forest hisses, and a small giggle falls from my lips. "It's not funny, I'm now gonna be walking around with a hard-on."

"Walking around?" I ask, looking around the room for something to put on. The cool air of the room is like a soothing balm to my overheated skin. I always get so hot sleeping, my nightmares often leaving me a sweaty mess. "What are you guys doing here in the middle of the night?"

"Here," Landon says, offering me the hoodie that he was just wearing. I want to tell him I have plenty of clothes, but my feet are already taking me closer to him, my heart skipping a beat at having them all in my room.

"Thank you," I breathe out, reaching out to take the garment, but he shakes his head.

"Arms up, Duchess," he commands, and I do as he asks automatically, my body bypassing my brain as my arms lift of their own accord.

A shuttering gasp sounds from my lips when he pulls the hoodie over me, his fingers grazing my sides and leaving me burning. With my vision obscured by the material, the sensation is multiplied tenfold, and I sway towards him, a small sound escaping my throat.

"Later, baby. We need your help now, okay?" he asks me as his hands leave my skin to come and cup my face as I pull the hoodie down.

"With what?" I murmur, my brain still fogged with sleep and lust.

"My uncle wants us to find out when the next dog fight is, and Blaine said your parents are away for the rest of the week?" His voice is a low hum that does nothing to help clear my lust-addled brain, but eventually, his words penetrate.

"Yes, they're away, but I think there are cameras in the house." I suck my lower lip between my teeth and start to worry it. His thumb comes up and tugs my lip away.

"Only one of us gets to make these lips bleed, Duchess. Understood?" His tone is hard, yet also somehow coaxing, and I wish I could see into his eyes properly but it's too dark to make much out.

"Understood, Lan," I reply without thinking, and his thumb brushes over my abused flesh.

"Good girl," he praises, and Jesus fucking Christ if that doesn't get me wet. "The feeds have been looped, so as far as anyone can see, all is quiet."

My brows dip. "How did you manage that?"

"The same way we managed to bypass your security, sugar," Forest says, sauntering up to me. Lan allows me to turn my head, but his hands remain cupping my face, and I can't say I mind the contact. "Because we are the Saints, and things that may stop others don't stop us."

That information should scare me, make me fear for my safety, but it doesn't. I feel comforted that they can get in, that maybe they can keep an eye on me too. My body relaxes even more at the knowledge, my muscles losing all tension.

"I could take you to his study," I suggest, turning my face to look at Landon again. "There might be something there."

"Clever girl," Lan praises, and fuck me if I don't preen a little. "Perhaps put some panties on first?"

My cheeks heat, my thighs clenching as I remember that I am only wearing his hoodie, which although long, would still not hide much if I were to bend over.

"Right, knickers first," I mumble, Lan releasing my face so I can grab one out of the drawer.

"I don't find the term knickers that sexy," Forest states, his voice light and teasing as I hunt in the drawer. A smile splits my lips when I spot a bright red lacy pair.

"I guess you won't be distracted if I put these *knickers* on then?" I ask, turning around and holding them up. I watch as his nostrils flare, unable to hold my smirk in. "I thought not."

Bending down, I step into them, looking back up to see all three of them facing me, watching as I pull them up my legs and then over my hips, flashing bare pussy as I do.

"I take it back, sugar. You can call them whatever the fuck you like and they'll always be sexy," Forest rasps, and my breathing hitches, my core pulsing. His hands are clenched into fists at his sides, and although I can't see his face, I can feel the tension thrumming in the room. They're right fucking here. My bed is right fucking there. My body sways towards them, overriding my brain which is telling me we have more important things to do.

"Duchess," Lan's warning tone cuts through the haze of lust that's trying to take me over. I've never felt so desperate before, like if they don't touch me I'll fade away. "Take us to the study."

He comes forward and takes my hand in his, rubbing my knuckles with his thumb to soften his commanding tone. I dip my head, then pull him in the direction of the door, using my other hand to open it a crack and pausing to listen. My parents might be away, and the cameras won't show what we're doing, but someone on the staff might catch us.

Not hearing anything other than the usual sounds of a house at night, I open the door wider and lead them down the corridor to the staircase. Pausing again, I listen, only hearing the pounding of my heart. Landon squeezes my hand in encouragement, and then we head down the stairs to the ground floor where the Ambassador's office is.

My hand trembles as I reach out to clutch the handle, and I can't seem to make myself grasp it, sweat beading on my forehead. Warmth at my back has my tense muscles relaxing, and then a tattooed hand is grabbing the handle and opening the door.

"We're right here, Duchess," Lan whispers into my ear, and as much as I want to sink into him, I take a step away and into the dark study.

The rich, cloying cologne that the Ambassador wears assaults me first, rooting me to the spot as my entire body trembles. My breathing becomes shallow, panic leaving my body ready for flight as the door closes behind me, cutting off what little light was being let in from the hallway. I can't see anything, and it's just like being in the many correction rooms I've had throughout my life.

"Breathe, Duchess," Lan says in my ear, wrapping his larger body around mine from behind, his lavender, suede, and leather scent overpowering that of the man who torments me. It's enough to have my body calming, my breathing deepening. "That's it, baby. Good girl."

Movement in front of me has me tensing again, then Blaine's woodsy scent combines with Forest's rose and gin and the mix of all three smells makes my body almost relax completely.

"We're all here, sugar," Forest whispers, a large palm gliding up my side under the hoodie, his hot touch distracting me.

"We won't leave you, *mi tesoro*," Blaine adds, another hand cupping the side of my neck, a thumb massaging my tight jaw.

"They don't j–just starve me," I confess in a hushed, choked voice, as if the words are being dragged from me. I feel them all go still, waiting. Tears fill my eyes as the truth comes spilling from my lips. "They lock me in a dark room, no light, no windows, and only bottled water." The tears spill down my cheeks, burning a path of anguish over my skin. "When I was little, it was only a day or two, but it's getting longer with every year that passes."

"How long after you got out of jail?" Blaine asks, his own voice low and tight.

I swallow, my arms coming up to wrap around myself only to find Lan's already there. He pulls me closer. "Seven days."

"Fuck!" Forest hisses under his breath.

"I was so weak Bobby had to carry me upstairs. They put me on a drip after, but I was asleep for the two days before school started," I tell them, unable to stop now that it's finally come out. There's a relief in telling someone your darkest secrets, and my breathing returns to normal, leaving me feeling drained but like a weight has been lifted.

"We will get you out of here, Aspen. I fucking swear to you," Lan grits out, pulling me closer when he feels me sag in his arms a little. I'm shaking my head before he's even finished.

"You can't, Lan. He will find me, and hurt you to get to me," I tell them, hopelessness leaving me exhausted. "Maybe when I'm nineteen, but even then, he has too much power. I'd have to disappear, always looking over my shoulder."

"Or we make him disappear," Forest says darkly, and although my stomach lurches, it's not with horror at what he's proposing. It's with fear of what would happen to them if they followed through.

"It's too dangerous," I whisper, as if the Ambassador can hear us. Hell, for all I know he may have the house bugged and knows exactly what we're doing.

"We're dangerous too, *mi princesa*," Blaine murmurs softly, his thumb caressing my face and sending shivers down my spine.

Before I can speak again, Lan interrupts. "Let's focus on the next dog fight. We can discuss everything else later." His voice is commanding, but his grip on me doesn't loosen, even as the others step away and turn on small torches, sending beams of light across the room.

"Aren't you going to help them?" I ask quietly, snuggling back into him regardless of my words.

"They know what they're doing," he says, his lips brushing my ear as the sounds of rustling papers and drawers being opened fills the space. "And I think you need a reminder that your father is not the only powerful man you know."

"Lan," I breathe out as he brushes a soft kiss on my neck, his arms loosening so that one of his hands glides down the front of my borrowed hoodie, pulling it up until my lace-clad pussy is exposed.

"You will be quiet as I finger fuck your cunt in his office," Lan commands, a full-body shiver making my nipples peak. "And you will come when I tell you to. Understood, Duchess?"

I have to lick my dry lips before I can reply, my words just above a breath. "Yes, Landon."

"Try again," he growls in my ear, his fingers dipping below the waistband of my underwear then stopping just short of where I need him.

I wrack my brain, trying to think through the desperation that is setting my veins alight. "Yes...Sir?"

A deep rumble vibrates across my back and I know that I got it right. "Good fucking girl."

A gasp falls from my lips when his fingers make contact with my clit, and then I remember his decree; to be quiet. I have to suck my lips between my teeth to stop the moan that wants to escape.

"Does that feel good, Duchess?" he asks in a low tone, swirling his finger around my slick clit, sending spirals of pleasure shooting through me. "You're so wet for me already, I bet my cock would just slide inside you and you'd take it like my good little slut, wouldn't you?"

Fuck. Me.

His dirty talk, the way he calls me his slut? I did not know that was a kink for me but I can't help the way my head nods in agreement, my hips moving as I try to seek more friction.

"Nothing here yet, Lan," Forest whispers in the dark room, and I'm not sure if he knows what's going on between Lan and I, but hearing his voice, knowing that he's in the room has heat thrumming through me, sending me higher.

"Keep looking," Lan orders, dipping his fingers lower and thrusting two deep inside me. "That's it, baby. Take them like a dirty little whore."

My breath stutters in my chest, my nails digging into the arm that's wrapped around me like a vice. The sound of his fingers pumping in and out of my soaked pussy is all I can hear, and each thrust is driving me higher, pushing me closer to the edge that Lan is determined to throw me over.

"Now, you're going to come for your master, aren't you, little doll?" he rasps in my ear, his hard length pushing against my lower back and driving me wild. I want him inside me. I need him inside me, but I also can no longer hold back my climax, not when he's ordering me to come.

A small sound falls past my closed lips as my walls clamp around his fingers and an orgasm rips through me, leaving my knees weak and unable to stop the groan from slipping past my lips.

"I see you've been having some fun without us, Daddy," Forest's teasing voice infiltrates my post-orgasm haze, and I blink my eyes open to find his shadow standing in front of me.

Lan pulls his fingers out of my drenched pussy, then holds them out in offering. My lips part as I watch Forest take Lan's hand and bring it up to his face, and although it's too dark for me to make out what he's doing, the sound of sucking lets me know that he's licking my release off of Lan's fingers.

"So fucking delicious, sugar," he groans, finally releasing Lan's hand and stepping closer so that the front of our bodies brush. I'm so sensitised from the orgasm I just experienced that it's the worst kind of torture having him so close, knowing what his exquisite body can do to mine, yet not being able to indulge right now.

"Did you find anything?" Lan questions just as Forest reaches a hand to brush his fingers against my cheek. He pauses, then heaves a sigh.

"Nothing, Daddy. Not a fuckin' thing," he huffs, his hand dropping away.

"Me neither," Blaine adds, and Lan curses behind me. His arm is still wrapped around me, and I snuggle closer, smoothing my hand down his arm.

"Then we have no choice," Lan states, and the defeated resignation in his tone has me pausing in my comfort, my skin going cold.

"No choice in what?" I ask and am met with silence. "In what, Lan?"

I try to spin but his grip tightens, keeping my back to his front and he takes in a deep inhale, his lips brushing my head.

"We can get Bolt into the fight, to find out where it's being held and when," he confesses through gritted teeth and my stomach sinks, my fingers going numb at his words.

"B–but you can't! He might get killed!" I stammer, heat flushing through my body and making me tense. I can't bear the idea of anything happening to Bolt. Even though I only met him once, he's a part of their family.

"We know, Lil' Lady," Forest tries to soothe me, his own voice full of anger and distress. I bat away his hand as I struggle to get out of Lan's arms but he only holds me tighter.

"Let me go!" I hiss, only stopping when I feel large hands cupping my damp cheeks.

"We need to stop this, *mi amorsita*," Blaine whispers, and it's enough to make the fight drain out of me, his gentle, calming tone stealing the sharp edges of my anger enough so I'm actually listening. "Not just because Lan's uncle has told us to. They're taking dogs from the pound, dogs that might be able to have a life and family one day, and offering them up for slaughter. How long until dogs aren't enough?"

It's the most I've ever heard him say in one go, and his words have the same effect as ice-cold water drenching my body. The Ambassador is a monster of the worst kind and I've no doubt his friends are just as bad. And he's right. How long before they start using prey that is more interesting? Before they start using people for their entertainment?

"We won't let anything bad happen to Bolt, Duchess," Lan says behind me, brushing a soft kiss to my temple. "But we need to use him to get in. We have nothing else."

My head drops forward as I see this for what it is. A last resort, and one that they don't take lightly. Blaine's warm palms are a comfort against my skin, Lan at my back, and Forest slips a hand under my hoodie to wrap around my waist.

"Why is the world so cruel?" I breathe out, my chest aching as my limbs feel too heavy to hold me up.

"Because bad people live in it, Duchess," Lan states simply. "And all we can do is try to stop the worst of them, however we can."

His words ring in the silence, all the euphoria of my orgasm replaced with the despair that knowing the worst the world has to offer lives in your very house. I wish that things were different, that I didn't come from a world that is so corrupt and hateful. That the Ambassador wasn't a heartless man who will do anything in his quest for power, even hurt innocent children and animals.

But wishes are like dreams, nice while they last but fading quickly in the light of day, and I learned long ago that both will not change the nightmares and demons that plague my life.

Maybe, just maybe, all I needed was some Tainted Saints to even the odds. Perhaps these three broken men full of their own brand of darkness are going to be the ones to finally enable me to break free from my shackles and step into the light.

CHAPTER 22

"PICTURES" BY ECÂF

ASPEN

We head back upstairs, the silence thick and heavy in the air, and it only grows when my bedroom door is closed, sealing us in the moonlit room.

"I'm going to wash up, I guess," I say quietly, heading over to my bathroom. My chest aches, partly because of the whole Bolt situation and partly because I know that they can't stay all night. There are too many people around in the morning to risk it, no matter how much I crave the comfort they can give.

After using the loo and a quick freshen-up, I throw my ruined lace panties in the laundry basket and put Lan's hoodie back on, not quite ready to give it up yet. Exiting the bathroom, I come to a stop when I see Lan and Forest in my bed, chests bare and looking all too beautiful in the moonlight. I drag my eyes away to find Blaine sitting in a chair by the window. It's my comfy reading chair, huge and plush, but he makes it look a little like dollhouse furniture.

"You're staying?" I ask tentatively, my heart skipping a beat as I step towards the bed, eyeing up the two beautiful men currently occupying it.

"Of course we're staying, sugar," Forest says into the dark, folding back the covers and showing me that he's only in plain, black boxer shorts. "As long as you don't mind?"

"No," I rush out, blushing at the quickness of my answer. "I just thought that it would be too..." I trail off, biting my lower lip as I try to think of how to finish my sentence. I don't want to make them feel like they're a dirty secret...but that kind of is exactly what they are at the moment, for their own safety as well as mine.

"We'll be gone before anyone is awake, Duchess," Lan assures me, not even needing me to voice my concerns. "You need some sleep, and you looked like you might find that difficult on your own."

It astounds me how well he can read me. I've known him for such a short time, yet he knew that I wanted them to stay but didn't feel like I could ask.

"What about, Blaine?" I ask, casting a glance in his direction again.

"I'm fine, *mi tesoro*. I don't sleep much anyway," he tells me, and I get the feeling that he wants to keep watch over us, which is too sweet for words.

"Come to bed, Little Lady," Forest encourages, patting the space between Lan and him. "Just to sleep though."

"And if I'm not tired?" I ask in a whisper as I make my way to the bed, my heart thudding in my chest. This is so new to me, having two men in my bed, one of whom I've fucked while the other has made me orgasm more times than I can count, and not forgetting their friend by the window who I literally had sex with a few hours ago. I shake my head, wondering how this is my life now.

"Just sleep, Duchess," Lan decrees in a firm voice, and as much as

I want to argue, a yawn practically cracks my jaw in half a moment later.

I get in, having to climb over Forest to do so, and a deep chuckle sounds behind me.

"What's so funny, Big Daddy?" Forest asks, his hand skimming up my leg and then pausing when it reaches my naked backside. "Oh, fuck."

Giggling, I settle between them, my muscles completely relaxing as I snuggle down. Lan immediately pulls me against him, my back to his front, spooning me from behind, and it's the best fucking feeling in the world. A small contented sigh leaves me as my eyelids grow heavy, even when I don't want them to.

His hand reaches around, palming my bare pussy, and I groan.

"Two can play that game, Duchess," he breathes in my ear. "Now, go to sleep."

Fucking. Bastard.

Forest chuckles as he settles down in front of me, stroking my cheek with the back of his knuckles.

"Good night, sugar," he whispers, leaning in to press a soft kiss to my lips.

"Good night," I murmur back, resigned to having Lan tease me all night. I do give a little arse wiggle, pressing against his hardness. At least I'm not the only one desperate.

"Sleep, Duchess," he growls, and like when he ordered me to come earlier, my body obeys his command as my eyes grow heavy and sleep overtakes me.

ONCE AGAIN I WAKE UP ALONE, BUT MY BED SMELLS LIKE THEM and I just spend a moment luxuriating in the combined scents of Landon and Forest. Sudden tears sting my eyes when the thought of having this every day flits through my mind, but I blink that pipe dream away. I just can't see how I could make it work, not while the Ambassador still lives.

They offered to kill him...

My breathing stills as I really think about that fact. I could have him out of my life forever, never be subjected to his awful corrections and punishments again. Finally be free.

But could I live with the blood of his death on my hands? Sure, I've wished so many times to be free of him, but am I the type of person to be able to live with a death on my conscience?

Huffing out a frustrated sigh, I get up and start getting ready for the day, opting for tight wool, high-waisted trousers and a cream blouse with embroidery on it. A deep-red knitted cardigan and my brown leather boots completes the look, and with a brush of lip gloss over my lips and a couple of pins holding my blonde waves in place, I'm ready.

There's a lightness to the house as I make my way down the stairs, and it takes some effort not to allow the grin that wants to break free slip over my face. I can't have people, even the staff, suspecting that anything has changed. The Saints need to be my secret, for now at least.

"Good morning, Miss Aspen," Gerrard greets as I enter the dining room. It's so much calmer without my parents here, and I guess I'm lucky that they are often away for business because at least then I can breathe without the threat of correction hanging over my head every minute.

"Good morning, Gerrard," I reply, taking my usual seat. He places a covered plate in front of me, and when he lifts the lid, my breath stills in my chest.

There's a full English breakfast, with a side of pancakes and syrup, and it all smells incredible.

"Cook prepared you something special this morning," he tells me, and I lift my suddenly watery gaze up to his. His creased face softens, his eyes full of a compassion that I rarely see inside these walls.

"P–please pass on my thanks," I whisper, blinking furiously to stop the tears from falling. I've not had any of the staff in our previous houses treat me this way, even when my parents are away. They're kind of course, but none have ever gone against the express opinions of the Ambassador and my mother, even though they knew what was happening. It's a kindness that I didn't expect here, on the other side of the world, but it is one that makes my heart feel like it's too big for my chest.

"I will Miss," he says gently, straightening up and placing a hand gently on my shoulder. "Best eat it before it goes cold."

Shuddering an exhale, it takes me a few moments and a sip of fresh orange juice to gather myself enough to be able to eat. Every bite is delicious, and even though I can only manage half, it's one of the best meals I've ever had. Second only to the pasta that Lan made me that night at the Pound.

Before my wayward mind can take me down that path and all that transpired that night, I get up, grabbing Blaine's jacket from my room before heading to the front door where the car is waiting for me, like it is every night.

"Good morning, Miss Aspen," Bobby greets as he holds the door open for me.

"Good morning, Bobby," I return, getting into the back and buckling in as he goes around to the driver's side.

We drive in easy silence, and I watch the winter scenery pass by the window, a lightness in my heart that I wish could stay with me always. I'm going to take this reprieve, my parents being away, and just have fun like a normal teenager would, leaving all the other shit for when they come back.

Arriving at school I see all three Saints idly waiting by the three motorcycles that I spotted on my first day, and I can't say that the sight of them dressed in leather and leaning on their bikes doesn't do things to me that really should be illegal. Their heads all turn in my direction as the car pulls up, and my heart starts beating faster as I grab my bag and Blaine's jacket off the seat.

Bobby opens the door for me, and exiting the car, I cast a glance around us, noticing that, as it's still early, there is hardly anyone else here yet. Taking a trembling breath, I walk towards them, my skin tingling the closer I get. *What would it feel like to be able to kiss them, touch them without having to worry about it getting back to my father?*

Going up to Blaine, I hold out the jacket. "You left this last night after our training session," I state, just in case anyone does overhear or is watching. He gives me a smouldering smirk, his fingers brushing mine as he takes the jacket and shrugs it on.

"Not feeling too stiff?" he asks, and I can feel my cheeks heating at the insinuation.

"No, a bit sore but not too bad." Forest's deep chuckle has my nipples pebbling under my clothes, and the need to be in their arms is almost overwhelming.

Sliding the jacket on, his hands slip into the pockets, and I see the moment when he freezes. Then I watch as he draws out the envelope of cash that Bobby tried to give him at the jail two weeks ago.

"What's this?" he questions while opening it, and his eyes widen briefly at the quantity of bills in there. His jaw tightens and he looks back up at me with a hint of anger in his brown eyes.

"Please, Blaine," I rush out quietly, glancing around us. "The Ambassador will be offended if you don't take it. You'll be a loose end." I beg him with my eyes to understand that he has to take the bribe, otherwise they all might be watched, and if my parents find out he was the one in jail with me, he won't be allowed to train me anymore either.

I watch him grind his jaw, then he gives me a terse nod, relief making my muscles loosen.

"Thank you," I breathe out, fighting my instinct to go to him, to wrap my arms around him and let myself get lost in his touch. In their touch. "I'll see you later?"

He gives me a nod, and yet I still can't make my feet walk away from them. My fingers clench around the strap of my bag, my eyes closing as I let the cold winter breeze brush my face.

Why is it so hard to walk away from them?

"We'll see you later, Duchess," Lan's serious voice has me swallowing hard past a lump in my throat, my eyes opening to find him standing closer. "Now get to class, you don't want to be late."

Taking another deep inhale, I nod before spinning around to catch the narrowed blue gaze of Albert, my heart stilling in my chest as he looks beyond me, and then gives a cold, cruel smile that reminds me all too much of the Ambassador.

Shit.

THE REST OF THE WEEK PASSES BY IN A BLUR OF CATCHING UP TO speed with schoolwork, hanging out with Aofie at lunch, and answering all her questions regarding the Saints—and yep, I'm always bright red by the end of that as she has no shortage of suggestions of how to manage three men. I also have training sessions with Blaine which are the highlight of each day. Each one starts with blinding pleasure, followed by making me sweat as he helps me to tone what little muscle I have, building my strength up.

I don't spend a single night alone, Forest joining me and making me see stars again until I pass out in his arms. It's always a shock to wake up alone though, and I do wonder why Lan is keeping his distance. He's the only one I haven't had sex with, and I wonder why he's holding back.

Friday rolls around, and when I get in the car to go home, Bobby eases some of the tension that was building in my shoulders.

"Your parents wanted me to inform you that their trip has been extended and they won't be back until Monday," he says as I buckle my seat belt.

I catch his smiling gaze in the rearview mirror, and my lips tug up into a grin of my own.

"Will you take me home to grab something and then to the Pound?" I ask, my heart beating wildly as I take out my phone and open up my messages, selecting the thread I have with Aoife.

"Yes, Miss Aspen," he says with a nod and smile.

ASPEN:
> Can I say that I'm staying with you this weekend? Xxx

I wait as the three dots appear.

AOIFE:
> I got you, babe. But in exchange I want all the gory details! Xxx

I have to actively control my breathing as excitement runs through me. A whole weekend to pretend that I'm free, even if it is risky, but I'm only eighteen, why shouldn't I take risks?

ASPEN:
> Done xxx

I barely register the rest of the journey, excitement thrumming through my veins and making everything around me seem sharper, more vibrant. Once we get back, I don't even wait for Bobby to open the door, flinging it wide and bounding up the steps, the door to the house opening as I approach.

"Good afternoon, Miss Aspen," Gerrard greets as I whizz past.

"Good afternoon. I'm staying at my friend, Aoife's, this weekend, so I'll be back on Sunday at some point," I tell him in my rush upstairs, not waiting to hear his reply as I hurry to my room and start to pack a bag.

Apparently, Friday is my day off from training, so Blaine isn't waiting for me in the gym, but I can't wait to see his face when I turn up at the pound.

I'm not even aware of what I'm grabbing as I stuff it into my leather overnight bag and then rush back out of the room and down the stairs.

"Have a lovely time, Miss Aspen," Gerrard calls out as I practically run to the car. I wave over my shoulder, butterflies dancing in my stomach as I get in the still-open door.

I bounce in my seat the whole drive over, then we're there, pulling up in front of the pound.

"I'll come and get you on Sunday, Miss Aspen," Bobby tells me, and I catch his eye in the mirror, giving him a nod, sudden nerves making it impossible to speak.

Exiting the car, I slowly make my way up the metal stairs, my steps quiet and timid. Then I'm in front of the door and raising my trembling fist.

"RUNAWAY" BY AURORA

FOREST

We're just shooting shit in the living room when a knock on the door sounds. Frowning, we glance at each other, uneasy looks on Lan's and Blaine's faces. Bolt sits up and walks over to the door, whining low and scratching at the wood which is not how he'd usually react to an unexpected knock.

"Who the fuck is that?" Lan asks as I get up to get it.

With furrowed brows, I open the door and all the breath leaves my lungs when I see her, standing there with wide, beautiful green eyes and a large bag slung over her shoulder.

"My parents are away until Monday," she blurts out, her cheeks colouring as I just stand there, drinking her in. "Aoife is saying I'm at hers and I thought..." She swallows, shifting from foot to foot.

"You want to stay with us, here, for the weekend, sugar?" I

question, a moment before I'm being pushed to the side and Blaine is dragging her inside and slamming the door closed.

"If that's okay?" she asks, looking at each of us as we surround her, Blaine still holding her arm.

Fuck, the idea of having her here, all to ourselves, to touch and hold anytime we want to...well, shit. It damn near short-circuits my brain, but luckily, some part of me knows what the fuck to do, and I'm pulling the bag off her shoulder before pulling her away from Blaine and into my arms.

"It's so much more than okay, Little Lady," I whisper, wrapping her in my arms and just breathing her in. She smells so fucking good, like everything I've been missing in my life.

"You sure it'll be okay for you?" Lan questions like the dick he is, and I feel her stiffen in my arms.

"As okay as it can be," she mumbles, her hand gripping the back of my shirt. "I want to be normal, just for a couple of days."

"Then that's exactly what will happen," I tell her, pressing a kiss to the top of her head and giving Lan the stink eye. His jaw works, then I watch him take a breath and visibly relax his shoulders. "What do you want to do first?"

I pull back, just enough so I can look into her beautiful face, and like always, I'm fucking blown away. I don't care that we barely know each other. That she's so much higher than me in society's eyes. She feels right, like she was always meant to be ours, and I will fight anyone who tries to take her away from us.

"I don't mind," she answers, her beautiful smile making my heart skip several fucking beats. "What do you usually do on a Friday night?"

My heart stills as her words register, and Lan curses. Then Blaine grinds his jaw as we share a loaded look.

"Friday is Saint's night at Lan's mom's restaurant," I tell her, watching her brows scrunch in the cutest way.

"Saint's night?" she asks, tilting her head to the side, studying me, and I fucking love having her attention.

"It's when we meet with the rest of the Saints, discuss business, and touch base," Lan tells her, coming up to stand next to me, running his hand through his hair. "After Mama closes up for the night, we use it."

She twists in my arms to look up at him, nibbling her lower lip. "Is anyone from school going to be there?"

I laugh. "No, sugar. These kids don't have scholarships to fancy schools like we do."

"And they're all loyal to you?" she questions, and I can't help but love the way her eyes light up as she thinks.

"Every last one, without a doubt," Blaine states, drawn to her like we all are, cupping her cheek in his huge palm as she turns her face to him. She closes her eyes and nuzzles into his touch, breathing out a contented sigh that I want to hear from her lips always.

"Then I don't see the issue with me tagging along, right, Lan?" She opens her eyes, looking straight at him, and I think I just fell for her. No one challenges Lan, and boy does he need it.

I tear my gaze from her to see his lip almost quirking up into a smile while he also attempts to keep that stern look on his face. He fails.

"One of us will be at your side all night, Duchess. That's non-negotiable," he warns, and I flit my gaze back to her to see those plump lips lifting in a coy smile.

"Yes, sir," she agrees, looking at him from underneath her lashes, and fuck me seven ways til Sunday. My dick springs to attention in my pants, and by the growls that rumble either side of me, I know my brothers feel the same.

"Until then," I start after clearing my throat and tugging her away from the others. "How about a movie? Are you hungry? We usually eat with the others. Lan makes something fucking delicious and we share it like one big family meal."

"A movie sounds perfect," she beams, and my goodness it's like the sun is suddenly in our apartment, making everything seem brighter. "And I can wait to eat."

Lan scoffs as I get her settled on our threadbare couch, letting her snuggle into my side. "You will not fucking wait to eat, Duchess. I'll make you something now and you can have more later," Lan states, heading over to our kitchen to prepare some food for our Little Lady. He's a feeder, and whether she wants to or not, she's become a new outlet for him. Someone to take care of, even though he already shoulders so much.

Bolt walks up to us, knowing better than to jump on the couch, and then rests his head in her lap, the sound of his tail thumping against the coffee table loud.

"Looks like you've got an admirer," I murmur, chuckling as she scratches behind his ear and his tongue lolls out. "Well, another one anyway."

I love the way her cheeks flush, the colour deepening as Blaine comes to sit on her other side, squashing her between us. If anything, rather than protesting, her body relaxes more, telling me that she's as at ease with us as we are with her.

"Will you come to the Pound with me tomorrow?" I ask as I find us something to stream. "I usually work there on Saturdays and it's Wallace's day off so he won't be around to see you." Her brows smooth out when I tell her the last part, and I hate that we have to keep our connection a secret but understand that it's for her safety more than anything. After what she told us about how her dad locks her in a dark room for days on end with nothing but water, I know none of us want to put her in his sights any more than she is.

"That would be lovely," she tells me, pausing, and then a bright smile tugs her lips upwards. "The Pound is a charity, right?" I nod. "Then if I become one of its benefactors, it won't be strange at all for me to be there."

"Benefactors?" I ask, my forehead creasing.

"Yes, rich people are always encouraged to give to charity, some kind of tax avoidance thing, I think. Mother is on the board of several charitable organisations across the globe and says it looks good, so I can make the Pound one of my charities." Scooching forward, she grabs her phone out of her back pocket. "Do you have the bank details of the Pound?"

She blinks at me and my brows dip. "Why would you need those, sugar?"

"To make a donation, silly." She giggles, her cheeks flushed and eyes bright. "So if anyone questions me being there tomorrow we have a reason."

Blinking, I get my phone out of my jeans and grab the details.

"Would fifty be reasonable?" she asks, looking up at me, her brows furrowed.

"Fifty dollars? Sure, that would be amazing," I tell her, thinking of the new bedding that we could get. Her mouth opens and her cheeks colour. "What? That's not what you meant?"

"Um, no, I meant fifty thousand?" She licks her lips, flinching when the sound of a pan being dropped comes from the kitchen. I freeze, unable to look away as shock renders me speechless.

"We are not charity cases, Duchess," Lan growls out, storming over and pointing a finger in her face. Bolt growls at him, but Lan just ignores it as she shrinks back, her face pale as tears spring into her eyes.

"I–I didn't mean—"

"Didn't mean what, Duchess? To point out just how much better you are than us? How fucking poor we are, that we can't even get new bedding for the dogs that are abandoned on the streets?" He's shaking, anger pouring off him in waves that hit like a punch to the gut. I know it's a sore subject for him. That kind of money would see us set for life, and the fact that she thinks nothing of it and just giving it away highlights the stark difference between us.

"Better than you? You think that's what I believe?" she questions, her voice thick with the tears that tremble on her lashes. It guts me to see them, and I want to growl at Lan for making her hurt. "You have more than I ever will, Landon. Look around you. How can you believe that being locked away in a basement with no food for days on end is better than this? Of having no freedom, no choice in who I see or where I go? Who I'll spend the rest of my life with? Tell me, which life would you rather have?" Her body vibrates with the force of her desolation, her jaw tight as she calls Lan out.

I watch as the fight drains from him, his throat bobbing as he swallows, and I feel the pain of her statement in my very soul.

"Fuck, Duchess," he breathes out, dropping to his knees in front of her. Bolt scoots out of the way as Lan takes her face in his hands. "I'm a bastard, I shouldn't have said that shit. It's just a fuck-ton of money, baby. It took me by surprise."

"I would give you every fucking penny, drain my account dry if it would free me from him," she whispers, and tears sting my eyes at the confession and the hopelessness lacing her tone. "Being rich has never bought me anything but misery."

"You will be free," he vows, bringing their foreheads together, and I watch, my chest tight as they both close their eyes and breathe each other in for a moment. "We will free you from him. I swear it, Aspen."

A shiver cascades across her body, and I grasp her closer to me, nuzzling against her neck.

"You have our word, sugar. He will not rule over your life forever," I tell her, my lips brushing against her ear.

"Trust us," Blaine's deep rumble sounds from the other side of her.

We hold her between us, and I know that the promise we just made is set in stone, sacred. We will get her free from her father, whatever it takes. We are her Saints now, at her disposal to do with as she sees fit. To avenge her and protect her.

CHAPTER 23

"BELLA NOTTE" BY PEGGY LEE

ASPEN

We spend the rest of the afternoon and early evening watching Marvel films because apparently, Forest is obsessed with superhero movies. Lan made me a delicious early dinner of chicken salad and some of the yummiest, homemade focaccia I've ever had. The man has a gift and I am more than okay with being a part of it.

After our little hiccup earlier, Forest said my donation would be more than perfect, if that's what I wanted to do. Apparently, they've been wanting to add an extra area to hold more animals and revamp the outside area, plus about a million other things, so the money would enable all of that to happen.

It felt amazing knowing that something which has never helped me get what I want is actually going to make such a difference, and a satisfied glow filled me as I snuggled between Forest and Blaine on the sofa.

The hours seemed to go past too quickly, and then all too soon, it was time to meet the others in their gang.

Butterflies flutter around my stomach as they lead me out into the cool night and down the steps. We walk around the back, and in a small lot are the three black motorbikes that I've seen the guys with at school.

I come to a standstill when realisation hits me.

"I get to ride on one?" I ask, a wide grin tugging my lips upward.

"You get to ride on the back of mine," Lan states, walking over to me and holding out a helmet.

"You guys don't wear helmets," I pout, my eyes narrowing as I watch Forest and Blaine get on the backs of their bikes, no helmets in sight.

"That's different. Put the helmet on, Duchess," Lan commands, not even giving me a chance to do it myself. *Overbearing arse.* "And you'll need this too." He shrugs out of his leather jacket, leaving him in just a hoodie.

"It's freezing out!" I complain, but again he just bypasses me and drapes it over my shoulders. The heat of his body seeps into me, even over my own wool jacket. I feed my arms through the sleeves even though I don't want him to be cold. I can't help it, I love wearing their clothes, being utterly surrounded by them.

"Good girl," he murmurs, his eyes almost feral as he takes me in. I shiver, but not from the cold. No, this is all due to the animal magnetism Landon Capaldi exudes. Threading our fingers together, he leads me over to the last motorbike, letting go of my hand to swing his leg over and settle onto the seat. "Hop on, baby."

With excitement making my pulse quicken, I do as he orders, glad I wore trousers as I copy his move, sitting down behind him. His arm immediately comes back, pulling me closer, and I gasp when I feel something hard pressing into my stomach as I wrap my arms around him.

"Why do you have a gun?" I breathe out, the reality of who exactly the Saints are hitting me all of a sudden. They are leaders of a gang. A gang who clearly needs guns.

He sighs, his back moving as he releases a heavy breath. "Anytime we're not at school we have guns, Duchess. In our line of work, we have no choice."

Taking a shuddering inhale, I press closer to his back, breathing in his leather and lavender scent, letting it calm me. The gun doesn't bother me per se, there's a comfort in knowing that he can protect himself and the rest of us. What bothers me is that they're in enough danger to warrant carrying one at all.

"I hate that you're in danger sometimes," I whisper, and I feel him still underneath me.

"I hate that I don't know if you're safer at home or with us," he replies, not giving me a chance to answer as he starts the engine and the bike roars to life.

My breath catches when he guns the throttle and then takes off into the night, the sound of the other two following loud causing my heart to beat even faster. I bite my lip at the way the vibrations between my thighs affect me, the man in front of me not helping as I hug his powerful body to mine.

We haven't gone further than him making me come and I haven't felt him inside me, the need becoming desperate the more he denies me. I don't care that we've only really known each other for a couple of weeks, I want him. Badly. And I know that he wants me, so I'm not sure why he's holding back.

It doesn't take long to get to the restaurant, which is situated downtown in the east side. It's on the end of the line of shops, and the outside is covered in plant pots, full of evergreen plants that give the whole place a homely feel.

Lan and the guys pull up outside the front, and I spot a woman with the same dark eyes as Lan waiting in the doorway, a huge smile on her face.

"Landon!" she calls out as he kills the engine, and I get off, my legs trembling slightly while Forest comes up behind me to wrap an arm around my waist. "Forest, Blaine, so lovely to see you boys." She's stunning, her hair falling in chestnut waves around her shoulders, her curvy figure highlighted by the fitted skirt and blouse she's wearing. Her dark eyes are fixed on me, sparkling with curiosity like she doesn't often meet Lan's girl friends, and my heart skips a beat. "You brought a friend?"

"Mama, this is Aspen," Lan says, taking my hand and tugging me away from Forest, striding up to his mother and placing a kiss on each cheek. "She goes to school with us. Aspen, this is Maria Capaldi, my mama."

I nibble my lower lip as she takes me in, her gaze catching on Lan's hand still in mine, and I swear her smile kicks up a notch. "Beautiful," she whispers as she reaches out to palm one of my cheeks, bringing her lips to my other and placing a light kiss there. "Make sure you keep them on their toes, don't let them give you shit," she murmurs, and a giggle falls from my lips as she draws back.

"I will," I tell her, and she gives my cheek a small squeeze.

"Good," she answers, letting me go to kiss Forest and then Blaine on their cheeks. "You come by anytime, Aspen dear. I want the chance to meet you properly." There's censure in her tone and Lan's cheeks colour in a blush that has me biting my lips to stop the laugh from pouring out.

"I'll bring her by the house soon, Mama," he agrees, and it's my turn to blush. It feels like things are moving quickly between us if I'm meeting their family. My stomach sinks when I think of introducing them to the Ambassador and my mother.

"You ready, Duchess?" Lan asks, and blinking, I realise that I was so lost in my thoughts that I didn't even register his mother leaving.

"Sure," I say, shaking my head and smiling up at him.

"Remember, stick with us at all times," he cautions, waiting for my agreement before he turns and pushes the door to the restaurant open.

The sound of chatter filters out into the night, and I have to squint for a minute at the warm glow of lights that fills the space. Cheers ring out as we enter, and I instinctively shrink back, Landon's hand in mine tightening as he pulls me closer, wrapping his arm around me.

I look up to see that all the tables have been pushed together, to create a huge table with chairs all around it. They're all full, bar three at the head of the table, a mix of young men and women, maybe ten or so sitting in them.

The chatter dies down as they catch sight of me, and panic speeds up my breathing, my anxiety rearing its ugly head. I hate being on display, and my throat goes dry as my flight instinct tries to kick in.

"Hey, sugar, we're here," Forest breathes out under his breath, coming up on my other side and taking my cold, clammy hand in his. "Nothing will happen."

His soft voice and touch helps to soothe me a little, my body relaxing further when Blaine comes up behind me and presses his body into my back. It's enough that I can take a deeper breath, enough to let me push aside the usual worry that being the focus in a crowd gives me.

A large guy stands up, making his way towards us, and it takes everything in me not to bolt back out the door. He stops before me, holding out a hand that's covered in ink. Like the guys, he has tattoos on all his visible skin, including his head and face.

"Name's Reg, nice to meet you," he says, and I hear a few chuckles in the background.

"Aspen, and lovely to meet you too, Reg," I reply, willing my hand not to shake as I let go of Forest's and place it in his.

"A posh girl, eh? You been hiding her at that rich school of yours, Landon?" a voice teases in the background, and my eyes widen, my hand frozen in Reg's as the implication that they could easily find out who I am and it gets back to my parents that I'm here hits me.

Reg's brows furrow, his jaw clenching as my guys rumble growls.

"Don't be salty just because they walked in with the most

beautiful girl in Fairview, Snake." He chuckles over his shoulder, then turns back to me and gives me a wink. Letting go of my hand, he makes his way back to his seat.

"Come on, Little lady, you get to sit with Blaine and me while Lan does all the cooking," Forest tells me, pulling me by my hand and away from Lan. He gets stopped countless times as we walk towards our seats and introduces me to everyone, who on the whole seems really nice and friendly.

There are a group of girls on the other side that keep giving me the stink eye, but I've met their kind in every school I've ever attended. Doesn't matter if you're rich or not, mean girls exist everywhere, so I just ignore them.

When we reach the head of the table, I see the three empty chairs and as I go to sit in one, Forest *tsks* me.

"These are for us," he tells me, a sly grin on his face.

"So where will I sit?" I ask, just as he settles himself in his chair. He gives me an answer by patting his knee, and I roll my eyes before doing as commanded and sitting in his lap.

His arms wrap around me and he pulls me closer, his lips against my ear. "Don't make me have to show all these fine folk who your Daddy is, sugar. I'm not above making you come in front of this whole damn room."

All my nerve endings tingle, my breath shuddering out of my lungs as his words penetrate my brain. Fucking hell. How does he know that exhibitionism is a kink I never knew I had until I met him? His low chuckle when I clench my thighs together lets me know that he is well aware of the effect of his words.

He toys with the top of my thigh, drawing circles with his fingers as he chats to the various members of the Saints gang who grab his or Blaine's attention. Even through my wool trousers, it sends tingles racing up and down my body, and I can barely concentrate on what they're talking about. There are tumblers with what looks like red wine in them, and when I reach out to Forest's and take a sip, the full-bodied flavour of a pretty decent vintage makes my taste buds tingle.

"Diana's been having some trouble," I hear Reg say to the guys, the name one I recognise. It takes a second, but I realise that was the name of the place where Officer Anne bought me a sandwich when I was with Blaine in the county jail. "With the Ravens."

"Those fucking assholes are getting too big for their boots," Forest hisses under his breath. "You and Snake hang out there this week, show them that Diana's is under our protection and if they keep fucking with her we're gonna have a problem."

"Yes, boss." Reg nods, turning to a guy on his other side and relaying the instructions. I assume that's Snake, especially given the snake tattoo that winds its way around his neck and up the side of his head.

"Can I ask you something?" I whisper, twisting so I can look at both Forest and Blaine.

"Sure, sugar," Forest replies, taking a sip of his wine, his lips over the place that mine were.

"I heard that you guys do protection," I start, my gaze darting between them as I try to formulate my question. "And I wondered, what does it cost the people who you protect?"

"Cost them?" Blaine rumbles, tilting his head to the side.

Forest barks out a laugh, drawing eyes to us, and my cheeks heat as I fidget on his lap. "You've been watching too many Godfather reruns, sugar." He chuckles, and I narrow my eyes at him. Then his face softens, his fingers squeezing my thigh. "It don't cost them nothin'. Well, Diana feeds our guys when they're staking the place out, but we do it because we like to take care of our community, Little Lady. Make everyone feel that bit safer."

My mouth opens a little, surprise scrambling my filter. "But, how do you make money?"

Forest chuckles, and Blaine joins him, his laugh a deep rumble that does bad things to me.

"We have jobs, like normal people, *mi tesoro*," Blaine answers. "Forest helps out at the Pound on the weekends, and Lan and I fix up motorbikes in a garage a couple blocks away."

"Everyone here works when they can and helps when they can," Forest tells me, pride shining in his eyes. "It's a family, angel. We look out for each other, and anyone else that needs it, because most here don't have anyone else on their side. Don't get me wrong, we have the odd job that sits on the line of the law, but we try not to make that kind of work a habit."

"Oh," I say weakly, my mind spinning with the information they've given me. I thought their infamy was because of being like every gang I've ever heard of, into all sorts of illegal shit, but it really does sound like they are one big family, looking out for each other and taking care of their own.

"Food's ready!" Lan calls out as he walks in carrying a huge bowl of steaming pasta sauce with what looks like meatballs in it while several other guys bring in spaghetti and other bits and pieces for our meal. It smells delicious, as Lan's food always does, and my stomach rumbles even though I only ate a few hours ago.

People pass the dishes around, and my throat goes tight seeing just how much of a family they have here, everyone smiling and chatting with ease.

"Duchess?" I twist to look and see Lan sitting next to me, holding out a fork with spaghetti covered in sauce wrapped around it.

"Thank you," I whisper, the rest of the room disappearing as I lean forward. My mouth opens and he slides the fork in, the sweet, tangy tomato and herb sauce bursting on my tongue. "Oh my god, Lan," I moan, blushing when ruckus laughter and lewd comments follow from the rest of the gang. Blaine silences them with a death glare and Lan scowls at his gang who quickly shuts up. Forest's lips twitch up in a smirk, and I can't help wondering if a part of him enjoys the attention of his gang admiring me.

He continues to feed me from his plate, Forest giving me sips of wine, and Blaine leaning over to feed me small morsels of bread. It's the best meal I think I've ever had, and when I lean back into Forest's chest, too full to eat another bite, the song that's just beginning to play filters in past all the noise.

Closing my eyes I sing along to Peggy Lee's version of "Bella Notte," allowing the wine and music to relax me enough to forget about everyone else here and just enjoy the moment.

When the final note leaves my lips, I blink my eyes open to find silence, every eye on me, and the bubble bursts as I squirm under their shocked gazes.

"Duchess..." Lan breathes out, and I tear my eyes away from the people around us to get lost in his midnight gaze. His lips are parted, his eyes wide and sparkling.

Before I can say anything, he pulls my mouth to his, his large palms holding my face as he devastates me with his kiss. It's beautiful, everything a girl could ever dream of in a kiss from a stunning man. He worships me with his lips and tongue, telling me that our souls have belonged together for aeons, and tears spring behind my lids at the sweet perfection of the embrace.

Words race to my mind, three words that shouldn't be there after only such a short time, but denying them is like trying to stop the tide. A small sob falls between us, which he swallows, kissing me deeper in return, claiming me with no words spoken.

"You're perfect, Little Lady," Forest whispers in my ear, his lips skimming the column of my neck. "And you belong to us as surely as the sun belongs to the sky."

My breath hitches, my hands clutching the front of Lan's shirt as our kiss slows.

"Lan," I breathe out against his lips in a choked whisper, a maelstrom of feelings raging inside me and making it hard to speak properly.

"I know, Duchess. Fuck, I know," he answers back in a hushed whisper, his own voice just as thick as mine.

Neither of us say it, those words that sit on the tip of my tongue, begging for release regardless of the short time I've known them. Because no matter what Forest says, what they all vow to me, I can't be theirs.

CHAPTER 24

"YOU'RE SPECIAL" BY NF

ASPEN

When we finally break apart, the room is near empty, save for Reg who stands near what looks like the back door. He's looking off to the side, giving us privacy but also watching out for us. I like knowing that my guys have someone so loyal, someone who'll look out for them no matter what.

"Looked like you needed a moment, boss," he states, and I'm guessing he ushered everyone out of the room sometime during the kiss that I will never forget.

"Appreciated, Reg," Lan says in a husky voice, his hands leaving my face. Before I can miss his touch too much, he grasps my hand in his and pulls me from Forest's lap. "Let's get some air, Duchess."

Nodding, I follow him, the other two Saints behind us and Reg watching our backs. I pause when we pass a short corridor where I can see signs for bathrooms.

"I just need the bathroom, I'll meet you outside?" I say, tugging my hand out of his. I don't give him time to argue, my bladder making it clear the urgency is needed.

After finishing, I open the stall door and come to a stop when I see the three girls from earlier waiting for me, arms crossed under their full breasts and matching scowls on their faces.

"You need to back the fuck off, rich girl," the one in the lead snarls. Her dark hair is thick and falls in waves around her face, her jeans and tiny top tight-fitting to show off her curvy body. She'd be pretty if she wasn't wearing so much make-up, her foundation making her look orange in the glaring white light.

"Excuse me?" I say, a sharp edge to my tone as my heart thuds in my chest. How dare she try to claim them! I look beyond them to where the door is. They're blocking the exit, bloody bitches.

"You heard her," the blonde one sneers. "The Saints are ours, they don't need some rich slut who wants a tumble with a bad boy."

Heat flashes through my body, my teeth grinding together as her words ring in my ears. I may not be able to have them forever, but it's not out of choice. If I could choose...I take a deep inhale through my nose and let it out of my mouth in a measured exhale.

"They don't belong to anyone, they're not fucking objects to collect," I tell them, trying to keep my tone even as I step closer to the lead bitch, my hands clenched into fists at my sides. "I will have them for as long as I can, and you should be the one backing the fuck off."

I've never been confrontational before, and a part of me is screaming to run, but a bigger part wants to slap her silly for daring to even think of my Saints, even consider them as hers. They are mine, even if it's just for now.

"You coming, Little Lady?" Forest says from behind the girls as he swings the door open. "Don't want to keep Lan waiting."

The three of them whirl, plastering flirtatious looks on their faces as they walk towards him. My pulse speeds as they get closer, but he just steps aside, allowing them to pass without so much as taking his bright green eyes off me.

Taking a steadying breath, I go to walk towards the door, but Forest steps in, letting it shut behind him.

"You got one thing wrong there, sugar," he tells me, advancing until he's backing me up against the counter, a predatory gleam in his deep green eyes and his nostrils flaring. Heat pools in my core, desire searing my insides as his hard body presses into mine. "We belong to you, simple as that."

Before I can speak, his lips are on mine, a deep, panty-melting moan falling between us as he kisses me like I'm the answer to a question he's had his whole life.

"If Lan wouldn't kill me, I'd bend you over this counter right now and fuck you so hard they'd all hear your screams," he murmurs against my lips, and white-hot lava fills my body. Fuck, I'm like a bitch in heat around Forest, desperate for him at every opportunity. "Come on, sugar."

My chest heaves as I try to scramble enough thought to follow him out of the bathroom, his hand holding mine in a firm grip. He leads me down a corridor, through a back exit, and then we're in a beautiful garden. Most of the plants haven't grown fully yet, but there are heaters and arches covered in vines that will be green once spring rolls around.

Taking me further into the garden, I jump when a shot rings out and he chuckles.

"They're just practising, Little Lady," he assures me as we come out of a gate and into some fields, which is crazy as we were just in what I thought was the centre of the east side.

Sure enough, there's a metal bin with a raging fire in it and lots of chairs around it. Off to one side are a few guys, Lan and Blaine included, and they seem to be shooting at targets down the field. Forest leads me to that area, passing by the trio of bitches who all glare daggers at me. *Twats.*

A sense of breathlessness comes over me as we get closer, a rush of adrenaline making my nerves tingle. I don't jump at the next shot that goes off, and there's some back slapping as Lan hits the glass bottle across the field which shatters into a thousand tiny fragments.

"Can I have a go?" I ask as he catches my eye. One eyebrow raises, a smirk on his lips.

"You know how to shoot, Duchess?" he asks as everyone goes silent around us.

"Well, they had to teach us something at the boarding school I was at last," I tell him, letting go of Forest's hand and stepping closer. "So, may I?"

I hold his intense gaze as I hold out my hand, and he gives a dark chuckle. "Line them up, Reg."

I bite my lip as I grin, Lan placing his gun in my hand. It's still warm from his touch, and there's something intimate about that which makes my core heat. It feels heavy in my hand, and I take a moment to feel the weight of it against my palm. There's power to holding a gun, a safety that comes from knowing that you can pull the trigger and stop the monsters.

"Ready, Duchess?" Lan asks, and smiling, I give him a nod, then walk to the line scratched in the dirt.

Closing my eyes, I take a couple of deep breaths, allowing my mind to settle in the place of stillness that our shooting master used to tell us to find. Once my racing heart has calmed, I open my eyes and raise the gun, firing off three shots in quick succession. The sound of glass smashing fills the night, followed by stunned silence.

Turning around, a fissure of anxiety races through me at the shocked faces.

"Well, you're just full of surprises ain't you, sugar?" Forest comments, blinking and then giving me a naughty grin. "And that was hot as fuck."

I shrug. "I was top of my class."

"Damn, *mi tesoro*," Blaine whispers, and I look over to see his smiling face taking me in as if for the first time. A blush steals across my cheeks, then my gaze lands on Landon, stalling at the fire raging in his dark eyes.

"Top of your class?" he questions, sauntering over to me like a jungle cat. My heart flutters wildly in my chest the closer he gets, my body humming when he's just before me. "Let's see how good you really are, shall we?"

My brows dip as he presses a chaste kiss on my cheek, then bends down and grabs something before walking towards the target area. Spinning, my stomach tightens when he stops and places a tin can on his head.

"What's going on, Lan?" I ask, my voice trembling as he grins back at me. Fuck, he's pretty like this, all wild and mischievous.

"Take your shot, Duchess," he says, arms open at his sides, and my eyes go wide. There's a challenge in his, and I think of the girls who told me to back off, like I didn't belong here. I mean, maybe I don't, but I want to.

Raising the handgun, I calm my mind again, letting everything float away and focus on the can. There's a zen place you need to find to shoot, I've no idea how anyone does it effectively in a warzone or battle, but this I can do.

Releasing the breath I just took, I pull the trigger and the shot rings out, the can flying off Lan's head and landing in the grass. My shoulders slump, my breath panting as adrenaline rushes through me.

Before I can take another full breath, Lan is hoisting me up in his arms, my legs wrapping around his waist as he palms my arse and strides back towards the restaurant.

"Lan—" I cut off when he kicks the door open, the sound of it bouncing off the wall loud as he takes me into the main room, the low lights making the space feel intimate.

The table has been cleared, but they are still pushed together and he strides over to the end of it where we were sitting not so long ago before lowering me to the ground. Taking the gun, he lays it on the table top with a thud.

"You're fucking perfect, you know that?" he asks in a raspy voice, his palms gliding over my shoulders and pushing my wool jacket off, letting it fall to the floor. "Fuck, I've tried to hold back, Duchess." His chest heaves as he unbuttons my cardigan, pushing that off my shoulders too. "But it's like you were made for us, regardless of what this fucked up world says."

"Lan…" I moan when his head dips and he kisses the column of my neck, his fingers working the buttons of my blouse and then tugging that off my body, leaving me in just my lacy bra and trousers. The room is warm, but my nipples still pebble, my skin breaking out in goosebumps.

His fingers move to the waistband of my trousers, popping the button and lowering the zip. They are wide-legged, so they drop to the floor in a swish of fabric, and then he's pulling back, his gaze devouring me like I'm the thing that will save him.

"So fucking beautiful," he whispers reverently, his fingers trailing a line of fire down my skin. A pleasurable shiver cascades over me, my fingers desperate to get him undressed, to feel his hot skin pressed against mine.

"Lan, please," I beg, reaching out to push his leather jacket off his shoulders. His chest rises and falls rapidly with his breathing as I reach for the zip on his hoodie and unfasten that, my hands trembling as that joins the piles on the floor. Gripping the hem of his long-sleeved T-shirt, he raises his arms, his gaze never leaving my face as I tug upwards.

The heat of him hits me like a furnace, his lavender and leather scent washing over me, drowning me until I'm dizzy with it. His body is stunning, every inch covered in artwork, and my fingers are reaching out to trace an image of a dragon before I've even given it any thought. He shudders, then he's pressing up against me and I want to weep at how fucking perfect it feels to have him touching me like this.

He brings a finger up under my chin, lifting my face as he plants his soft lips onto mine. It's no less destroying than our previous kiss, maybe even more so because he's pressed against me, all of his warmth and vitality seeping into me like a balm that will heal me of all my trauma.

His hands cup my arse, pulling me towards him even closer before he picks me up, placing me on the edge of the table. My legs open for him, and he fills the space between my thighs, his hard length pushing against my core in a way that has my knickers a mess in seconds. I can't stop running my hands all over his skin, tracing the lines and furrows of his muscles, pausing at a puckered scar on his lower abdomen.

"I wanted our first time to be slow and take hours making love to you," he whispers against my lips, then his hands are on the crotch of my panties and he yanks, tearing the fabric. A pained gasp leaves my lips at the sting of the fabric pulling against my soft flesh, but a stroke of his fingers soothes the hurt. "But if I don't have you right fucking now, Duchess..."

He doesn't finish his sentence, but I look down between us to find him undoing his jeans, his thick length springing free, a glint of silver at the tip flashing in the low lights. The breath leaves my lips at the sight, at his tattooed hand wrapped around his large dick.

"Look at me, beautiful," he commands, and my gaze snaps to him, widening when I see the gun in his other hand.

"Lan?" I question, my heart pounding in my chest as a thread of fear races through me.

"If you're pointing a gun at me, Duchess, my cock will be inside you," he growls, pressing the firearm into my hand, then bringing it up to press the barrel against his temple.

I open my mouth to protest, but his hips surge forward and I groan as he stretches me wide for him.

"Shit, Duchess. So. Fucking. Tight," he purrs through gritted teeth, pushing forward until he's fully seated inside me. He still has my hand around the gun, my other hand is braced against his shoulder, my nails digging into his skin. I can barely breathe with just how fucking incredible he feels.

He pauses for a moment, his forehead dipping down to meet mine as we share the same breath.

"Lan, please, I need…" He shifts his hips, dragging his dick out, his piercing massaging my inner walls before he slams back inside me and gives me exactly what I need. "Fuck! Yes!" My eyes roll as I close them, the pleasure of having him finally inside me too intense to keep them open.

He doesn't hesitate, and like he's finally loosened the reins, he fucks into me so hard that he has to hold onto my hip to keep me in place. The sound of our bodies meeting is obscene, my cries and his curses filling the room as he keeps the barrel of his gun pressed to his temple.

"Do you know why you're holding this gun to my head, baby?" he asks in a husky voice, never pausing fucking me into oblivion.

"N–no," I pant, opening my eyes to stare at him. Sweat coats both our skin, his body tense and glistening.

"Because you fucking own me, Duchess," he snarls, tugging me towards the edge of the table so he can go deeper. I gasp at the new angle, my entire body thrumming with how close my orgasm is. "Every part of me doesn't exist without you. My life is yours to do with as you will."

He kisses me before I can protest, slamming into me over and over again, and I'm helpless to stop the orgasm from tearing me into pieces, shattering me just like his shots did to the glass bottle earlier. I scream into his mouth, my nails raking down his chest as my grip tightens on the gun and I lose the ability to think. Waves of pleasure drown me, and he doesn't stop, fucking me harder, faster, until he's thrusting deep and roaring out his release as he fills me with his cum.

He holds me, our chests heaving as we lie connected in the most primal way and just breathe. He finally lets go of my hand and takes the gun away from me, my arms wrapping around him and pulling him closer as tears sting my eyes.

"I don't want to give you up, any of you," I confess, my voice thick with the tears that threaten to spill. "But I think one day I'll have to, and it will break me beyond repair."

He pulls me even closer, his arms banded around me as if that will stop the inevitable.

"We will never stop fighting for you, Aspen," he murmurs into my hair as my tears drip onto his chest. "I don't give a fuck who we have to kill. I will set this entire world on fire if it means we can keep you."

"You don't know me," I argue weakly, and he pulls back slightly, cupping my face in his palms, his dick still buried inside me.

"I've known you my whole goddamn life, Duchess. I just needed to find you."

His lips are against mine in the next moment, swallowing my cries and drinking my tears as he kisses me like it's the easiest thing in the world. Like we can spend an eternity together because that's what was always meant to happen.

CHAPTER 25

"GANGSTA" BY KEHLANI

BLAINE

Forest, Reg, and I make sure everyone leaves out the side gate, knowing that Lan and Aspen will want some privacy. I smirk when I think back to the look of feral hunger on his face when he grabbed her and carried her into the restaurant like he needed to be inside her now. Lan is always so controlled, it's nice to see him ruffled.

"Think we can go in yet, Big Daddy?" Forest asks, shifting from foot to foot as we wait by the bikes. I feel his impatience.

"No need," I tell him, nodding in the direction of the front where Lan and our *princesa* are just stepping out of the door.

Of course, Forest goes bounding up to her like one of his puppies at the Pound. That kid is just too lovable.

"Missed you, Little Lady," he breathes out before slamming his lips against hers and claiming her like I want to. Lan refuses to let go of her hand, but her other one tangles into Forest's dark-blond hair, using it to pull him closer.

I catch Landon's stare, and I tilt my head in a 'you good?' gesture. He gives me a feline grin, his eyes sated and his face relaxed. Incredible sex will do that to even the most wound up of us.

"Let's go, Forest," I call out, and he pulls back, a deep flush staining Aspen's beautiful cheeks. "It's late."

She gives me a coy smile which does nothing to diminish the raging fucking hard-on in my jeans, and chuckling to myself, I adjust my dick, her eyes darting down and nostrils flaring as she catches sight of me doing it.

Shaking my head at the thrall she has us all under—willingly I might add—I mount my bike, waiting for the others to do the same, and then we're heading back to the Pound.

We make good time, and I'm not the only one who notices her sluggish movements and yawns as we make our way up the stairs. Bolt greets us as soon as we enter, and clearly, her draw is for all males regardless of species because he basically ignores us in favour of her cuddles. Can't blame him.

"Come, *mi amorsita*. Let's get you to bed," I say softly when she yawns again, rubbing her eyes.

"B–but I'm not sleepy," she mumbles, another yawn practically cracking her jaw. Taking her hand, I help her up from the crouch she was in while hugging Bolt.

Lan and Forest give me matching glares as I lead her down the small hallway, but I just raise my eyebrows at them. They got her all to themselves the other night, it's my turn and then we'll share her tomorrow night. Maybe Lan and I could push two of the beds together for more space while she's at the Pound with Forest.

She follows me, her eyes heavy with tiredness, and as much as I want to sink into her, especially with her pussy full of Lan's cum, she needs to sleep more. She looks around my small room—none of our bedrooms are even close to the size of hers—but there's no judgement in her eyes, just curiosity.

"How did you all end up living together?" she asks as I help her out of her clothes, clenching my jaw tight when she's stripped completely naked.

"Do you want something to sleep in? I remember you saying you didn't like pyjamas," I ask gruffly, my body shouting at me to throw her on the bed and fuck her hard. Her sleepy blink and another yawn gives me just enough strength to resist.

"Can I have your T-shirt?" she asks, her eyes tracing the worn cotton black shirt that I'm currently wearing. Some primal part of me preens and shakes his mane as I strip it off and help her into it. Her entire body relaxes when the fabric falls around her, stopping mid-thigh and teasing me with what I know is underneath.

Coño. This is going to be harder than I thought.

Stripping my jeans off, leaving them in a pile on the floor, and ignoring my semi-erect cock, I take her hand and lead her to the bed, pulling back the covers and helping her into it. Hitting the light, I climb in beside her, and she immediately snuggles into my side before throwing a smooth thigh over mine.

"You didn't answer my question," she states sleepily, taking a deep inhale like she's trying to breathe me in. *Coño*, I love that.

My arms tighten around her. "It's not a pleasant story, *mi tesoro*."

"Will you tell me anyway?" she asks, sounding more alert, and I curse inwardly. It's late and I don't want her exhausted for tomorrow. "Please, Blaine?"

I sigh, pulling her even closer. "I told you what a waste of fucking space my dad was." She nods against my chest, her breath tickling my skin. "Well, after he...died, Forest's aunt and uncle managed to get custody of me." I remember the relief of it finally being over, of having a space that I knew was safe. I press a kiss to the top of her head, my mind thinking back to what she told us about her home, about the many times that she has been locked away in the dark. Anger makes my blood boil in my veins, and I have to breathe in deeply several times to calm my racing heart. "So, they took me in, and I lived in a home full of love and laughter. It took some getting used to."

She sighs, like my words are a fairytale she could only dream of. I'm struck again by how, on the surface, she may have everything, but scratch that and you see the rot of her cunt of a father and selfish mother.

"And then what happened?" She asks quietly, snuggling in closer. I wrap my arm around her tighter, as if that'll keep her here with us forever.

"When we finished junior year, Susan and Stan, Forest's aunt and uncle, gave us this apartment above the Pound. Helped us to do it up a little bit too." I chuckle, remembering the mess we made painting the walls for the first time. "And we've lived here ever since."

She hums. "Is it true that Lan's uncle helped you get the scholarships to Fairview?" My stomach plummets with her question, the option of lying not one I'd consider with her, but I don't know how she'll take my answer.

"Yes," I answer in a low voice after several moments, bracing, waiting for her to pull away. She's quiet for a few moments, then snuggles closer, brushing a kiss against my pec that sends heat shooting all the way to my dick.

"Well, I'm glad at least he's done one good thing, mafia boss notwithstanding," she comments, and a feather could knock me down at this moment, shock rendering me speechless. Usually, when people find out about our mafia connections, they run a fucking mile or look at us with a mixture of disgust and fear.

"It doesn't bother you?" I ask into the dark, curious, as I hold my breath, waiting for what she says next.

"I don't like that it puts you in danger," she whispers, and I squeeze her to me, wondering what the fuck I did in my life to deserve someone like her in it. "But it doesn't scare me. I've known the monsters of this world, and you, Lan, and Forest aren't among them, regardless of your connections."

Swallowing hard, I have to blink a few times to fight the moisture that is threatening to spill over. No one has ever given us their faith the way she just has. We may be feared and respected, may be the leaders of the Tainted Saints, but no one has ever really believed in us just because of us, not what we can give them.

"You may not think we're monsters, *mi amorsita*," I tell her, my voice thick. "But we can do terrible things, have done terrible things, and we would do all those and more for you, to set you free and keep you safe."

"Blaine..." she starts, but I hush her.

"Sleep now, *mi princesa linda*," I instruct, brushing a kiss across her soft hair. "We'll talk more in the morning."

She huffs a little which is just too adorable, and my lips press together to keep in the smile at her bratty antics, but soon her deep, even breathing tells me she's fallen asleep.

I lie awake for a while longer, just holding her, this small slip of a thing that has come into our lives like a wrecking ball. I can't even be mad about it. She is already bringing out the best in each of us, making us want to be better for her.

Finally, just as the sky outside my window begins to lighten, I drift off, our girl clutched in my arms. I fall into a dreamless sleep, the likes of which I'm not sure I've ever had before.

"WAKE ME UP" BY TOMMEE PROFITT, FLEURIE

ASPEN

"Wakey, wakey, sleeping beauty," Forest's gentle voice filters into my dreams, and blinking open my eyelids, I'm greeted by his beautiful green eyes, sparkling like dappled sunlight through leaves. "Good morning, sugar."

"Good morning," I mumble, stretching and encountering the

hard body of Blaine behind me. He grumbles, pulling me closer and nuzzling into my neck. I chuckle lightly, trying to gently peel his arm from around me, but he just clings on tighter. "Blaine? Big Daddy? I have to go."

Forest groans at the same time Blaine does.

"Don't call me that unless you want me inside you, *mi tesoro*," he grumbles in the sexiest fucking voice I've ever heard. Heat sears my insides, and I clamp my teeth down on my lower lip to resist telling him that's exactly what I want, but then my bladder decides to remind me that I need to pee, and as Blaine finally lifts his arm, I scoot out of the bed into the cool room.

"Damn, that is a mighty fine look on you," Forest says, his eyes lazily trailing up and down my body, pausing on my exposed thighs. My cheeks heat, but I can't help doing the same to him, my mouth going dry at the fitted, chequered shirt, jeans, and cowboy boots he's wearing. Boy is fucking gorgeous and he knows it if the smirk he's currently giving me is any indicator. "Now get that fine ass ready for a day with puppies!"

I squeak when he smacks my arse as I pass by, my hand rubbing the sore spot even as my core pulses.

After using the bathroom, I head towards the delicious smell coming from the kitchen to find Lan shirtless, standing by the cooker and making something for breakfast. I watch as the muscles of his back bunch and move as he works, the sight of all his inked-up skin doing something to my lady parts that I seem to have no control over when I'm near these guys.

Bolt nudges my hand with his wet nose, and his tail thumps against the old wooden floor as I scratch behind his ear.

"Morning, Duchess," Lan greets, not even looking away from his task. There's a definite hint of amusement in his tone, and when I convince my feet to move again and start to walk around to the table, his lips are pulled up in a smirk. *Smug bastard.*

"Good morning," I reply, my cheeks heating when the image of holding a gun to his temple while he fucked me last night flashes into my mind. "That smells delicious." I slowly sink into my seat, my pussy aching when it touches the hard wood of the seat. I'll blame that on Lan.

He turns with a plate in his hand, wafts of steam coming off the omelette as he brings it over to me. I'm once again struck dumb as he gives me a beatific smile while presenting my breakfast to me.

"Eat up, beautiful. You've a busy day today," he informs me, pausing and watching as I blink out of my stupor and pick up my cutlery, cutting a piece of the fluffy goodness and placing it in my mouth. The buttery, salty flavour of ham and cheese bursts on my tongue and I moan aloud.

"Jesus, you have talented hands, Lan."

"Among other appendages," he comments, and I almost choke on my next bite, taking a gulp of the orange juice that he hands me next, freshly squeezed of course.

Forest comes bounding into the room just as I'm finishing up, looking a little flushed, his lips red and puffy. I tilt my head, my brows lowered.

"Everything okay, Forest? You're not getting poorly?" I reach out as he flops on the chair next to mine, and place my palm on his hot forehead just as Lan sets down an omelette in front of him. Lan tries to hide a smile, and when I switch back to Forest, his cheeks are a deep pink.

"Just had to lend Big Daddy a hand with something," he tells me, and Lan outright barks a laugh.

"You mean a mouth," Lan mumbles loud enough for me to catch, and my confusion grows until the penny drops and my eyes widen.

"You gave him a blow job?!" I yell, a bolt of molten heat making my thighs clench. His face is pretty much the colour of a tomato, and I don't know whether to laugh or slam my lips against his just so I can taste Blaine on his tongue.

"Is that okay, Duchess?" Lan asks, his tone serious, and I swing my gaze to his. His dark eyes are intense, like my answer will change something important.

"I—" I cut myself off, a blush stealing across my cheeks as I try to get my words out.

"Be honest, Duchess. We've not shared this side of our relationship before, but we are all more than friends and I'm not sure any of us can give that up." I can't look away from those bottomless depths of his, his soul is in his eyes if you only look hard enough.

"I'd like to watch next time, if that's okay with you guys?" I ask, not looking away even as my chest heats at the same time my pussy clenches.

"We can put on the best show for our girl," Forest tells me, grabbing my hot face and placing his lips against mine. I immediately demand entry with my tongue, moaning low and deep when I taste Blaine's saltiness on his tongue. I lap at his mouth, chasing the taste, my hands clutching his shirt and pulling him as close as we can get sitting on two separate chairs. "Shit, sugar," he moans when we part, both of us breathing heavily. "If I'd realised you wanted to watch more than just us kissing, I'd have dragged you back in with us."

"Maybe later you can show me what Lan likes and we can make him feel good together?" I ask, my core like molten lava at this point.

"Fuck, Duchess," Lan groans, and I slide my gaze his way to see him adjusting his hard cock in his sweatpants. Now that is a good look.

"Puppies first," I tell them, getting up on shaky legs and deciding that Lan can have some of his own medicine. He did leave me with an aching pussy the other night, cupping me all night with no relief. I saunter over to him, feeling Forest's burning stare on my bare legs. "Then Forest and I will suck you so good, swallowing that big, beautiful cock until we gag, that you'll forget your own name, Landon Capaldi."

Wrapping my arms around his neck, I go up on my tiptoes and lick at his lips until he parts them so I can slide my tongue inside. He lets me lead the kiss, allowing me the chance to explore his mouth and lips, and even though it's not the heat-filled desperation of my kiss with Forest moments ago, it's no less destroying.

Lan kisses me like I already belong to him, like we were meant to be together and have the rest of our lives to kiss just like this. His hands come up, cupping my face, and my knees threaten to buckle with the tenderness of the gesture. He takes over the kiss, angling my face to his liking, and I melt into him, my heart skipping a beat when his thumb brushes my cheek.

"You are some kind of special, Duchess," he murmurs against my lips before pressing our foreheads together while I catch my breath.

"You are some kind of special too, Lan," I whisper back, and suddenly this weekend with them feels too short, the idea of leaving on Sunday making every cell in my body rebel.

"Now, get dressed and go with Forest, and we'll see you later." Placing one final kiss on my lips, he reluctantly pulls away as if it takes a gargantuan effort to do so. I can sympathise, my arms taking some convincing to let him go as all I want to do is hold him close and breathe him in for as long as I can.

"Come on, sugar. Your bag is in my room," Forest tells me, taking my hand and guiding me down the short hallway, Bolt's claws clicking on the floorboards behind us.

When he opens his door, it doesn't surprise me that his room is a bit of a mess, clothes strewn on the chair that sits in front of a small desk, his bed a tangle of dark sheets, and Bolt's bed in the corner. The dog in question trots over to it, turning around in a couple of circles before curling up, head lolling out the side.

Sat by the side of his bed is my bag, and I let go of his hand to walk over to it, picking it up and placing it on the bed. Glancing over my shoulder, I smile at Forest leaning against the doorjamb, his arms crossed and looking like a wet dream.

Turning back to my bag, I smile to myself as I grab the hem of Blaine's shirt, tugging it off and dropping it onto the end of the bed.

"Jesus fucking Christ, woman," Forest rasps as I bend down to look into my bag, biting my lower lip when I feel him behind me, his large palms gliding up my naked sides. "What did I tell you about tempting saints?"

One hand comes around the front of me, gliding down my stomach to the apex of my thighs.

"Forest..." I don't know whether I'm telling him to stop or urging him to continue, but all speech disappears when his fingers slide through my admittedly damp folds.

"You're always so wet for Daddy, such a good fucking girl," he purrs in my ear, and I straighten up, leaning back into his hard body, one hand coming up to grab the hair at the nape of his neck. He chuckles when I pull him closer, begging him with my body. "Bolt, out." I hear the click of Bolt's claws at the same moment that Forest slams two fingers inside me, making my back arch and a moan hiss between my teeth.

He finger fucks me hard and fast, whispering dirty words in my ear until I'm screaming his name, an orgasm rushing through me and all over his hand. The waves of pleasure leave me boneless, slumped in his arms as he tells me what a good girl I am for my Daddy, coming all over his hand like that.

Finally, he pulls his fingers out of me, and I blink open my eyes to see him offer his hand up at the side. I watch as Blaine takes a finger into his mouth, his eyes on me as he sucks it clean, then moves onto the second finger.

"Fucking delicious, *mi tesoro*," he rumbles, his voice sending shivers across my body. "Now you really do need to get ready and go or you'll be late."

"O–okay," I mumble, trying to get my brain to reboot enough to figure out what I need to do to enable that to happen.

They both chuckle, the deep vibration of Forest's laugh making me shudder.

"Shower first, sugar. I'll choose something for you to wear while you wash up." Forest's voice is an octave lower than it usually is, his pupils blown so wide that the green is almost swallowed whole.

Forest steps away, Blaine taking my hand and leading me to the bathroom. He grabs a fresh towel off the shelf and turns on the showerhead that rests over the bath.

"It's not what you're used to," he gruffly says, rubbing the back of his neck as his cheeks flush, but I put my hand over his heart, loving the feel of the firm muscle beneath it.

"It's exactly what I need," I tell him softly, giving him a smile that he returns with one of his own which almost makes my heart stop beating.

"I'll leave you to get sorted, use whatever you need, it's all yours, *mi amorsita*," he murmurs, placing a brief kiss on my head and then leaving, shutting the door behind him.

Closing my eyes, I take a deep inhale, blowing out the breath through my lips. Tears try to prick my eyes, and my fists clench at my sides. Why can't my life always be like this? So full of...everything good and amazing rather than horror and despair?

Taking a few shuddering breaths, I pull my non-existent knickers up and open my eyes to a room full of steam.

"Not today, Satan," I whisper to myself as I climb into the tub. Today is a day for love and laughter, nothing that my family knows anything about, and I refuse to let them ruin it when they're not here. I'll worry about that tomorrow.

CHAPTER 26

"EAT YOUR YOUNG" BY HOZIER

ASPEN

Forest and I head down the metal stairs to the Pound entrance at the side of the building, Forest opening the door with a key and ushering me inside. I'm immediately assaulted by the smell of dog, and not in an unpleasant way, more of a comfort. Butterflies flutter in my stomach as he walks us down a bright corridor, through a door, and then we're in a large space with barred sections on either side of a walkway. It reminds me of the jail, and my brows dip as I take in the bare but necessary space.

Excited barks and yaps fill the room as we enter, and Forest turns back to me with a huge grin on his face, his green eyes sparkling. I can't help but smile back, his happiness is just so infectious.

"Welcome to the best place in town, sugar," he beams, and my lips tug up into an even bigger smile. "Let me introduce you around."

He takes me by my hand, intertwining our fingers as he leads us to a cage at the far end, where a beautiful, blonde cocker spaniel waits for us, tail wagging and tongue hanging out. He grabs some leads that hang on the wall as we pass, draping them over his neck.

"This is Lola," Forest tells me as he opens the door, herding Lola back in as he lets me inside and I shut the bars with a clang. "She's eight years old, rules the pound, and loves fireworks." He chuckles as he crouches down and she wraps her front legs around his shoulders, licking his face all over. "And she gives the best kisses and cuddles."

I laugh as I bend down too, holding my hand out when she gets off Forest. She sniffs my fingers, gives them a lick, and then she's pressing up against me too, trying to lick my face.

"Pleased to make your acquaintance, Lola." I chuckle, burying my face in her fur and hugging her to me. My muscles relax, heat radiating through my chest as she shows me all the love that only a dog can give.

"Come on, let's take her out and you can meet some of the others too," Forest gently coaxes after a while.

He takes me to several of the other cells, introducing me to Barli; a six-and-a-half-year-old miniature schnauzer who oozes mischief. We take him and then I meet Winnie; a beautiful, chocolate labrador who apparently is a bit of a princess, and also grab Cooper, an adorable chihuahua who seems super chilled and laid back.

We take them all out of another side door that I discover leads out into a large yard-type space, the winter sunshine beating down on us. It's pretty barren, but there are a couple of leafless trees and what looks like obstacles.

"Let's give them a run around," Forest suggests, bending down to let them off their leads. He grabs a ball he'd stashed in his pocket, throwing it, and they all chase after it, barking with their tails wagging.

"You love it here," I observe, and he turns to me, his smile firmly in place.

"That I do, sugar. Dogs can't hurt you the way a person can," he sighs softly, bending down and grabbing the ball that Lola drops at his feet. He throws it again, looking after the dogs that chase it once more. "All they want to do is love you and be loved in return. Nothin' else. There's no meanness to them, no hatefulness that some people seem to be born with."

My eyes fill with tears as a small sound falls from my throat.

"Ah shit, sweetness," he exclaims, closing the small distance between us and wrapping his arms around me. His rose, gin, and leather scent surrounds me, and my hands clutch at his shirt as I cry quietly into his chest. I wanted to keep the pain at bay, wanted to not let the darkness that has been my life infect this day, but his words hit too hard, too close to home for me to ignore the despair that I didn't even acknowledge I lived with. "My parents were bad too, rotten to the core." He takes a shuddering inhale, not releasing me as my cries quieten so I can listen to his story. "They were addicts and would do anything to get their next fix. Including selling their little boy to whoever would pay."

"No, Forest," I whisper, horrified. My soul breaks for him, for the terror he must have experienced as a child. "Why are people so monstrous?"

"I wish I knew, angel." He sighs, pulling me closer and brushing a kiss on top of my head. "But there is always a silver lining, sometimes you just have to look real hard to find it. If they'd never overdosed that night in our trailer, I never would have come here and met Lan and Blaine. Never would have known you."

I pull back a little, enough so that I can look deep into his beautiful eyes.

"I'm not mad for being locked away after being arrested," I confess, watching as his jaw tightens. "I might not have ever met you all if I hadn't been caught, and I'd do it all again in a heartbeat."

"We will get you out of there, I swear, they won't ever lock you away again." His words are strong, unwavering as the breeze lifts some of my hair around us.

"I don't want you to get hurt, any of you," I tell him, wishing I could believe his promise, but sometimes hope is more dangerous than even the biggest monsters. "And he's capable of so much, I—" His lips press against mine, silencing my protests with a sweet kiss.

"Trust us, Little Lady," he breathes against my parted lips, his words sinking into the very centre of my being. "We will keep you safe, and he will pay for all the hurt that he's caused you."

Fresh tears spill down my cheeks, and I'm so sick of crying but I can't seem to stop now that they've opened the floodgates.

"O–okay," I agree, my breath fluttering against his lips. A small weight lifts from my shoulders, as if placing my trust in them has allowed me some respite.

"Good girl," he praises, kissing me again with a smile on his lips as the dogs bark around us and the wind brushes its cool fingertips over us, taking our sordid pasts away with it and only leaving our futures behind.

WE SPEND THE REST OF THE MORNING TAKING THE DOGS OUT OF their cages for some time in the yard, and Forest explains their plans for expansion, including having lockable dog flaps in each of the cells so that the dogs who are okay to mix can head out whenever they like.

He's so enthusiastic about the Pound, it's clearly a place that he loves and wants to make into a career. I'm not sure how it fits with his Tainted Saints commitment, but I'm sure this is what he was meant to do. Look after the waifs and strays of the world.

Forest finds me just before lunch, sitting on the floor with Lucy, a fifteen-year-old poodle mix who is a total princess diva and is currently in my lap receiving homage as is her due as I sing "La La Lu" softly to her.

"Seems you made lots of friends today, angel," Forest comments, and I look up to find him leaning against the doorway, arms crossed and looking too delicious with a smirk on his beautiful face. "You know, you should sing professionally. The world should hear your voice."

My cheeks heat at the compliment, and finishing the song, I set a now sleepy Lucy in her bed and get up, padding slowly towards him.

"I don't think a career on stage is befitting the daughter of the British Ambassador," I tell him with a sigh, pausing in front of him. He unfolds, brushing a strand of my hair from my face.

"Well, how about next Saturday at Maria's?" he asks with a challenging lift of one of his brows.

"Landon's mother's restaurant?" My forehead wrinkles, my mouth going dry at the thought of singing in public. I used to sing all the time at my old school, but that was with the choir and carefully selected classical pieces. Not the music that makes my heart soar.

"The very same," he replies, his eyes intense as he holds my gaze. "Big Daddy can even accompany you."

My mouth drops, my eyes widening. "Blaine sings?"

"Guess you'll need to say yes to find out, won't you, sugar?" His lips twitch, and my eyes narrow. He's bloody playing me, and it's working.

"Fine, I'll do it," I huff out, adrenaline rushing through me the moment the words leave my lips. "But only if Blaine is on stage with me."

"Deal." He holds out his hand, and then another idea springs to mind. Reaching out, I clasp my palm to his.

"And you all have to come to the coronation party the Ambassador is holding the following Sunday." His brows raise, but a devilish grin spreads across his face.

"Deal."

CHAPTER 27

"MOONLIGHT" BY CHASE ATLANTIC

LANDON

Blaine and I spend the morning shuffling my room around to make space for his bed, and I chuckle when we are finally finished.

"Well, I think it's big enough," I state, noting how the sides practically touch the walls. My dick twitches in my sweatpants, still semi-hard from this morning and just having her here, wearing practically nothing. He huffs a laugh, then pushes me onto the bed, pinning me beneath him. "Get off me, you big fuck!"

"You need to take the edge off, Lan. Otherwise, you won't last long enough to satisfy her later," he grunts, flipping me onto my back.

"Fuck you, I can take care of our girl," I snarl, but I don't stop him as he moves down my body, roughly pulling my sweats and boxer briefs down.

My now hard cock springs between us, the Prince Albert piercing glinting with precum that almost drips from my tip.

"Told you you need this, boss," he grumbles, wrapping his huge hand around my shaft and pumping.

"Fuck, Blaine," I moan, my back arching as the pleasure rockets through me. He's fucking right, I would have busted my load as soon as she touched me with how wound up I am right now.

"That's it, Lan. Let me take care of you," he murmurs, and I open my lids to see him bend over me, his hand guiding my dick between his parted lips.

I hiss a curse as he wastes no time and swallows me whole, my dick nudging the back of his throat as his hand squeezes my base hard. My fingers grip the messy bed sheets, my head tipping back as I let Blaine work me over with his mouth, his tongue massaging the underside of my shaft in a way that has my hips bucking up and thrusting deeper into his throat.

"Shit, Blaine, that's fucking it, right there," I rasp, my fingers tangling into his hair as I shamelessly fuck his mouth.

We are both naturally dominant, so I rarely have him at my mercy like this, and I intend to make the most of it. He doesn't stop, just lets me pump my dick in and out of his mouth, his eyes watering as saliva drips down my shaft.

My balls tighten, and then I'm coming down his throat, roaring my release into the quiet room as I force him to swallow every drop. My body liquifies, and slumping down onto the bed in a sweaty heap, I pant out my breaths as tingles race across my skin.

"Feel better, Lan?" Blaine asks, his voice scratchy and deeper than usual. Guess I did throat fuck him pretty hard.

"Yes," I breathe out, cracking one eye open to watch him swipe the back of his hand over his swollen lips. "Thank you."

"Anytime." He chuckles, getting off the bed and adjusting his hard-on.

"I'll make them some lunch while you finish up," I tell him, getting up but not bothering to pull up my pants. I'll freshen up first.

TAINTED SAINTS

"Yes, boss," Blaine teases, and I punch his arm as I pass, a grin on both of our lips.

I'm just putting the finishing touches to our lunch; steak with a side of bruschetta, when Forest and Aspen walk in, giggling about something. Her laughter fills the space like a sunbeam, and I almost burn my hand plating up the steak, my eyes drawn to her like a moth to a fucking flame.

"That smells divine, Lan," she breathes out, coming to help me take the plates to the small table, but Forest beats her to it and grabs them before she can. "Forest." Her tone is censorious, even as she smiles.

"You are our guest, sugar, so sit that beautiful ass down and let us wait on you like the queen you clearly are," he teases, but I know that he means every damn word. She is a queen, our queen, and I intend to worship at her feet for as long as she'll let me. Even after that. I'm not above strapping her down.

"I am no such thing," she protests, but we just ignore her, Forest ushering her into a seat.

"Here's your steak, Duchess," I tell her, setting her plate in front of her and then gripping her chin with my thumb and finger, tilting her face upwards before placing a lingering kiss on her plump lips. God, she's so fucking addictive, I could spend eternity kissing her and it wouldn't be enough.

"T–thank you." She shivers when I finally release her, claiming the seat next to hers.

"I want to see you eat it all. You need the protein," I instruct her, admiring the flush to her cheeks and the way her pupils widen at my commands.

She licks her lips, looking through her lashes at me. "Yes, sir."

My nostrils flare and my dick instantly hardens.

"Fuck me, sugar," Forest rasps, and I couldn't agree more.

"She eats first," Blaine growls as he comes striding into the room, his lips still a little puffy. He heads straight for her, even though the spare seat is between Forest and I. "*Hola, mi amorsita.*" His voice is a deep rumble that has blood rushing down to my already painfully hard cock.

Bending down, he kisses her like she's the air he needs to breathe and I can't even be pissed at the steaks getting cold. There's something about them that's mesmerising, and I'm unable to look away as she sinks into the kiss, her tongue chasing his. His large palms engulf her petite face, her hands clutching the front of his tee as if it's the only thing tethering her to this world.

Slowly, reluctantly, he pulls away, and I watch as she takes a shuddering inhale, like she's trying to commit his kiss to memory because she may not get more. I'll make damn sure she never goes without though.

"Hello, Blaine," she whispers, her blonde lashes fluttering as her eyes open.

"Now eat your lunch, *mi tesoro*. It's getting cold." He places a light kiss to her nose, then straightens up and walks around the table to his seat opposite her.

Taking a deep inhale, she grabs hold of her cutlery and cuts a sliver of steak off, bringing it up to her lips, and her eyelids flutter as soon as it's in her mouth. Jesus fucking Christ.

"That good, huh?" I tease, and her cheeks flush even as she nods.

"If you keep feeding me, I'll soon be the size of a house." She laughs, taking a sip of water before cutting another bite.

"Good, all the more to grab hold of," Forest tells her, and I can't stifle my chuckle when her eyes widen and she almost chokes on her food.

The rest of lunch passes with her telling us all about her morning at the Pound, and of Forest's plans now that he has some capital behind him. Although I was against her donating that much to start with, I can't deny how much pleasure Forest will get finally being able to change the Pound and make it into a happy place for any strays. It's not lost on me that's how he's always felt, Blaine too. Like unloved strays, dumped and forgotten by the people who should have loved them.

"And our angel here has agreed to sing at Maria's next Saturday," Forest states, and I blink.

"What about your parents?" I ask, hating the way she starts to curl in on herself at the mere mention of them.

"They'll never find out, how would they? They don't come to this side of the tracks," Forest reasons, placing a hand on her thigh and rubbing it while giving me a dirty look.

"Forest says Blaine will be there too," she says, her fingers toying with the hem of her sweater. Blaine raises a single brow. "We'll need to practice." She looks at him, her eyes wide and hopeful, and I feel even more like an asshole for mentioning her folks.

"*Si, mi tesoro.*" Blaine inclines his head. I don't blame him though, I wouldn't be able to resist her doe eyes either.

Her smile is like fucking starlight, and when she turns to me, I'm captivated in a way that I know I will never forget.

"As Forest says, my parents will never find out, and I'd love to sing for myself, just once. Please, Lan?" Fucking hell, I knew those bright eyes would be irresistible.

"Of course, Duchess," I cave, laughing and catching her as she launches herself at me.

"Thank you, Lan," she whispers against my ear, and I pull her tighter to me, just for a moment.

"You don't need to thank me, Duchess. You didn't need my permission," I tell her as she pulls away to look into my eyes.

"But I wanted it. It's important to me that you approve." She nibbles her lip, releasing me and sitting back down in her seat, her blush deepening the longer I remain silent.

But I'm speechless. Rendered fucking mute by her confession. No one has ever given me that sort of power over them and trusted me to look out for them in such an innocent way before. It's a heady rush, and a responsibility that I will gladly take on, my dominant and controlling nature craving someone to fully take care of. Someone who needs me above all others, who knows that I will keep them safe, no matter what.

"Then you have it, Duchess. Always, if it makes you happy," I choke out, my hand trembling as I reach for my glass of whiskey and bring it to my lips.

"Forest said that you'll come to the Ambassador's coronation celebration the Sunday after too, as my guests," she casually says as she cuts another piece of steak.

"He did?" I question, managing not to choke on my mouthful of alcohol as I hurriedly set my glass down.

"I can invite you as I'm now a patron of the Pound, and it would mean so much to have you there, even if we can't be open about..." she trails off, and I automatically reach for her hand, tangling our fingers together and giving it a reassuring squeeze.

"Of course we'll be there. We wouldn't want to be anywhere else," I assure her. "Now, let's finish up as we still have dessert."

Her eyes light up, and I know it's partly because she's not usually allowed sweet things, her mom keeping her on a strict diet when they do feed her.

"I'm ready for pudding," she states, practically bouncing in her seat and I frown at her.

"I think I could rustle up something a bit more exciting than pudding," I scoff, standing up to collect plates and walking to the kitchen area.

"Oh, no." She giggles and the sound stops me in my tracks. It's so light and carefree, I need to make her do that more. "I meant dessert. We call it pudding back home."

"Huh," Forest murmurs, helping me to clear the plates. "You guys say the strangest things."

"Excuse me!" she exclaims, laughing when she passes Blaine and he pulls her into his lap, Forest grabbing the glass she was trying to clear away. "I'll have you know that we speak the King's English unlike you barbarians." I chuckle at the way she makes her voice even more British, sounding like those stuck up assholes we get at school sometimes.

"You hear that, fellas. She thinks we're barbarians," Forest states, a dangerous gleam in his eyes that has my heart racing. "I say we show her exactly how barbaric we can be."

CHAPTER 28

"WE GO DOWN TOGETHER" BY DOVE CAMERON, KHALID

ASPEN

"I say we show her exactly how barbaric we can be."

Forest stalks towards me, his green gaze predatory, and my heart races, the sound of my pulse loud in my ears the closer he gets. It's not fear that makes me feel a little lightheaded. No, it's anticipation of finally having them all. I may have known them for only a short while, only properly known Lan and Forest for a handful of days, but my soul knows that we belong to each other, no matter what my head tries to tell me.

Blaine strokes a soothing palm down my side, his touch sending goosebumps all over my skin even through my clothes. His other hand comes around to the front of my trousers, his deft fingers popping open the button and pulling down the zipper.

"Up, angel," Forest quietly commands, taking my hand in his and helping me to my feet. Blaine pushes my trousers over my hips, and they land on the floor with a swish of fabric. "Goddamn, sugar. I fucking love your lacy underwear." He bites his lower lip in the sexiest way, heat pooling in my core at the look of adoration and want in his green eyes.

My entire body flushes hot at his words, at the way I can feel all three of their heated stares on me, burning me from the inside out. Letting go of my hand, he reaches out, his fingers undoing my cardigan one button at a time. I'm breathless by the time he's done, my fingers aching to touch him, but I keep my arms at my sides, letting him undress me until I'm just in the lacy underwear he loves so much.

"Fucking stunning, Duchess," Lan admires, and I turn my gaze to see him leaning on the kitchen island, his large arms crossed and his ink on display, the outline of his hard dick visible through his grey sweatpants. I lick my lips at the sight, and when I tear my eyes away to meet his, he's grinning like the Cheshire Cat.

"Come," Forest orders, drawing my attention back to him as he tangles our fingers together and leads me down the short hallway to what I assume is Lan's room as it's the only room I've not seen yet.

My breath stutters out of my chest when I step through the open door, seeing the two beds filling the space, suddenly making what we're about to do, what I'm desperately hoping we're about to do, all the more real.

"Trust us," Lan whispers in my ear, and I shiver, my nipples pebbling inside my bra.

"Always," I breathe back, and he brushes a light kiss on my cheek that leaves me tingling all over.

I freeze as something that feels soft as silk is placed over my eyes.

"Shhhh, *mi amorsita*," Blaine soothes as my vision goes dark, panic threatening to overwhelm me.

"Let us teach you to love the darkness, Duchess," Lan adds, his palm skating down my arm, his touch comforting and restarting my breath. I take a steadying breath through my nose, centering myself in this moment, not in my past.

I gasp when the clasp of my bra is undone, the straps tickling as they make their way down my arms. A warm, hot mouth sucks in my nipple, and I moan at how good it feels, at how much losing my sight has heightened the sensation.

"Some things feel better in the dark, angel," Forest utters against my breast, his breath making my nipples pucker even more.

Someone pushes my knickers down my hips, and as soon as I step out of them, I'm being held in strong arms from behind as one of my legs is thrown over a broad shoulder.

"Blaine is desperate for a taste, Duchess," Lan murmurs in my ear, my breath stuttering out of my lips, sweat dotting my spine as I wait for that first stroke of his tongue. "And you're going to come so beautifully all over his face, aren't you?"

"Yes, sir," I readily agree, one hand reaching down to trace through Blaine's thick hair as the other wraps around Landon's neck, pulling him down even closer.

"Good fucking girl," he praises just as Blaine licks from my opening to my clit and Forest sucks a nipple into his mouth, his tongue playing with it.

"Oh god," I breathe out, my head falling back on Lan's hard chest, their combined scents a heady mix that only sends me higher.

"There are no gods here, Duchess," Lan tells me in a husky whisper, nuzzling my neck before licking and biting his way along it. "Just Saints."

Blaine takes that as his cue to worship me with his tongue and lips, the most delicious noises of appreciation coming from his mouth that have me getting wetter by the second.

"You are such a good girl for your Saints, sugar," Forest rasps against my lips, capturing them and destroying me with his kiss, his tongue moving in time with Blaine's, building me higher towards a peak that I have a feeling they will throw me off with no remorse. "Now come for us, baby."

Blaine chooses that moment to suck my clit hard, thrusting two fingers inside me, and I explode, tearing my lips away from Forest as I scream my release, uncaring who can hear. My body trembles as waves of ecstasy flows over me, drowning me under their swell. Then I dig my fingers into Blaine's hair, not sure if I'm trying to bring him closer or push him away.

The noises Blaine makes as he laps my release are obscene. It's like the man has just found ambrosia and intends to drink it all up. I'd be embarrassed if I could give a fuck about anything other than the almost painful pleasure that holds me as captive as these three men do.

"That's it, Duchess," Lan whispers in my ear as his arms band around me. "Soak him in your release."

I'm a shaking, sweaty mess by the time Blaine decides he's tortured me enough, placing a final wet kiss against my mound. I never knew pleasure could feel almost painful, but it seems the Saints are determined to teach me that the line between pleasure and pain is a fine one.

Slumping, my legs unable to hold me any longer, Lan lifts me into his arms, and then I'm being gently placed on the bed. I shiver at the sudden loss of heat, which doesn't last long as a firm, naked body presses against me, the scent of summer nights and thunderstorms telling me it's Forest who wastes no time in sliding inside me as his body covers mine completely.

"Forest," I moan, the stretch so delicious that my toes curl even as my trembling legs wrap around his waist.

"Fuck, your pretty, tight pussy was made to take us, wasn't it, Little Lady?" he groans in my ear.

"Yes, Daddy," I rasp back, feeling his body shudder at the term.

"Shit, baby. You feel so fucking good wrapped around me, trying to milk me already, greedy little cunt." His dirty words have my limbs shaking even more, my nails clawing at his back as he fucks into me hard and fast, just the way I crave from him. "You make me so fucking wild, so desperate for you, angel."

A hand snakes around the front of my throat, my breath hissing out of me as the grip tightens to the point that only a sliver of air can get past.

"Time to come again, Duchess," Lan orders in a harsh, demanding tone.

I try to shake my head, tell him that it's too soon, but fingers find my swollen clit and start to strum it like I'm an instrument and they know how to make me sing for them.

Lightning races up my spine and across my skin, my nails digging into Forest as I shatter around him, my inner walls clenching around his dick as if I want to hold him inside me forever. A small cry leaves my lips, it's all that the grip around my throat allows, as my world rearranges itself into something I know will be brighter and shinier than ever before.

"Fuck, she's like a vise," Forest grunts, not stopping, fucking me through my orgasm.

"You're not allowed to come until Blaine is deep inside your ass, Pup," Lan snarls, and another wave of pleasure washes over me at the mental image he just gave, leaving me boneless and slumped on the bed, unable to even hold my legs up.

A kiss is pressed to my lips as the hand on my throat loosens, then a small whimper sounds in my throat as Forest pulls out, leaving me empty but so satisfied.

"We're not done yet, Duchess," Landon promises in a dark murmur, and a small shiver cascades over me. Slicked-up fingers glide over my soaked opening then venture lower, and I gasp when they trace my puckered hole. "Has anyone ever fucked you here?"

"N–no, s–sir," I stutter, my hips moving as he continues to play with the opening.

"Then I'll be your first, but I'll take it slow, beautiful, okay?" He pauses in his teasing, chuckling when I try to push down in a bid to get his finger to move again. "I need your words, Duchess."

"Yes, please, sir. I want you to fuck me in the arse," I shamelessly plead, knowing that this will be another way they will destroy me, and I am here for it.

"Such a filthy mouth," he chides, but his finger resumes its teasing strokes. "It suits you being our little cum slut, and we're going to fill you up until we leak down those pretty thighs for days."

A deep groan falls from my parted lips as he sinks the digit inside me, pumping it slowly in and out, letting me get used to the feel. Fingers play with my clit at the same moment that Lan sinks a second finger inside me and my body begins to tremble as they move together, forcing me closer to another orgasm.

"P–please," I beg, not sure whether I want them to stop or keep going.

Clearly they do, because their movements speed up, pushing me closer to the edge. My head is turned to the side, and something hard and yet soft as silk is pressed against my lips.

"Open up, *mi amorsita*," Blaine orders, and my body follows his command, my mouth stretching around his thick length.

My tongue plays with the metal bars on the underside, eliciting a deep, rumbling groan from him that only makes my pussy gush more.

"She likes you filling her mouth, Big Daddy," Forest states in a husky tone, and I shiver as Blaine's hand tangles in my hair, angling my head so he can slide deeper.

"You're going to scream around my dick as you cum like the filthy slut you are, aren't you, *mi tesoro*?" Blaine asks in a harsh whisper, and all I can do is groan as I can't even nod in agreement. "Good girl."

They double their efforts, Blaine never leaving the heat of my mouth as the others use their fingers until I'm doing exactly as Blaine ordered, screaming my release around his hard shaft.

He doesn't come, just pulls out with a loud pop as the others keep pushing me through my orgasm, leaving me shaking and almost begging for no more.

"You doing okay there, Duchess?" Lan asks softly in my ear, the sound of my panted breaths loud in the quiet.

"Y–yes," I answer, my body twitching and sweat coating my skin.

"Good girl." He strokes some strands of hair off my forehead, and a straw is pressed to my lips. "Drink, beautiful. We need to keep you hydrated, you're losing a lot of...fluid."

I try to chuckle, but the sound is more of a raspy cough, so I greedily drink the cool water they offer.

"Forest is going to help get you into position, your back to my front, okay, darling?" Lan asks, and I mumble an agreement, not sure if I'll be any help whatsoever.

The straw leaves my lips, then I'm being picked up again and placed on top of Lan's hot, firm body. I can feel his skin against my own and it's one of the best feelings in the world, and his scent is so much stronger this way than it usually is.

"That's it, sugar," Forest encourages, his hands stroking down my body. "Lie back and let us do all the work." I do as he suggests, relaxing against Lan, the fine tremble in my limbs having subsided since my last orgasm. My legs are lifted, then draped over Lan's arms, opening me up wide. "I'm going to help get him inside that sweet little ass of yours, angel. Just keep relaxing and let him in."

My body automatically tenses at his words. How the fuck will Lan fit? He's not exactly small in the dick department. In fact, he's more than just above average. Not to mention that piercing.

"I won't hurt you, Duchess," Lan assures me, his deep voice soothing and slightly strained as I feel the tip of him poke my entrance. "That's it, baby. Let me in."

A sharp hiss leaves my lips as he breaches that tight ring of muscle, and then a mouth is on my clit, turning my pain into pleasure. I begin to shake once more as Lan pushes deeper, the tongue lashing my clit easing the sting.

"*Coño*, you look so beautiful, *mi amorsita*," Blaine rasps from somewhere in front of me, and a deep moan leaves my lips as Lan finally bottoms out. My muscles tremble, the tongue on my clit pausing.

"Pretty as a peach speared on his dick and waiting for her pretty pink pussy to be filled by Daddy," Forest comments, and Jesus fucking Christ on a cross, that boy's mouth isn't just an expert at licking pussy. His words are just as deadly as his tongue.

"P–please," I gasp, not sure how long I can last with Lan buried so deep where no one else has ever been before. "Please, Daddy."

"As you ask so prettily, sugar," he replies, and I can hear the smirk in his voice.

"Oh, shhhhit," I hiss as he pushes inside my aching cunt, the stretch almost unbearable until fingers toy and tease my clit.

"Breathe, Duchess," Lan instructs, his voice strained as Forest continues to thrust slowly inside me.

"She's so fucking tight with you inside her too, Lan," Forest groans, and I can feel the strain in his body as he holds himself in check, not forcing before my body accepts him.

"I know, Pup, shit, I know. She's fucking perfect," Lan grits out, and their exchange sends tingles racing across my skin, their dicks twitching inside me as I clamp down around them. "You were made for us, baby. Our perfect Duchess."

"Our fucking queen," Forest grunts out as he fills me completely, pausing to let me feel just how full I am.

"I w–want to watch," I whisper in a strangled tone. "I want to see Blaine fuck you, Daddy. Please." I beg them with my tone to let me in on this part of their relationship.

"You're so beautiful when you beg, sugar," Forest praises huskily, then my blindfold is being untied and I'm blinking my eyes open. The room is dark, lit only by candles that dot many of the surfaces and cast their gentle glow across the space.

The plane of Forest's beautiful face are highlighted in the flickering lights, his green eyes dark and the muscles of his neck corded as he holds still.

"There she is, so stunning, our angel," he whispers, bending down to place his lips against mine. "And this way is better. I can look into those soulful eyes as I fuck you."

I shiver, both him and Lan groaning as I tighten around them.

"You ready, Pup?" Blaine asks from behind Forest, and I watch the man in front of me swallow.

"Stick it in me, Big Daddy," Forest jokes, an edge to his voice that is a mix of anticipation and perhaps a tinge of apprehension.

I gasp when Blaine pushes between Forest's shoulder blades, forcing him down on me, holding my gaze the entire time.

"You ready, *mi amorsita*?" he gently asks, and all I can do is nod, my mouth dry as I watch with rapt attention.

"Fuuuuck, Big Daddy," Forest groans when Blaine surges forward, and Forest's dick gets harder inside me, pushing deeper and leaving me reeling.

"Daddy..." I moan as he sinks even deeper with Blaine's next thrust, my nails sinking into Forest's biceps deep enough to leave crescents of blood.

I feel so fucking full, so consumed by them that it's almost too much. Especially with Blaine staring deep into my eyes as he pushes the last couple of inches inside Forest. The latter has sweat dotted all over his ink-covered, golden skin, his arms shaking as he holds himself up off me as much as Blaine allows.

"I always forget what a big bastard you are, Big Daddy," Forest grits out, hissing his breath when Blaine pulls out a little only to thrust hard back inside his friend's body. "Shit."

Lan chooses that moment to remind me of his presence, stroking in and out of my arse until I'm trembling and almost crying with how incredible it feels.

"Fuck, Duchess," he hisses, "you're perfection."

"Lan, please, it's too much," I plead, my body full of so many sensations that my brain can't keep up.

"You can take it, baby," he whispers, unrelenting in his movements. "You were made to take us."

I get lost in the dance our bodies do, all of us connected in a way that is as old as time. My body feels like it's full of stardust, sparks flying in all directions as they worship me and each other. Forest leans down to kiss Lan right next to my face, Blaine taking that opportunity to fuck into Forest even harder, and it's enough to make my body go supernova as I explode.

I scream a primal cry as waves of pleasure drags me under, the boys cursing around me as my body clamps down around them with such force that they have to fight to keep moving. But I can't focus on anything except the unrelenting pleasure that consumes me whole.

CHAPTER 29

"HEAVEN" BY FINNEAS

FOREST

I pull away from Lan's lips to watch as our beautiful angel comes so hard that her eyes roll. This is exactly as it should be, us worshipping her until she can't think straight.

"Shit, she's so fucking tight," Lan hisses out, his movements becoming jerky in that way which tells me he's about to explode too.

I feel the same, unable to speak as I fuck her tight cunt and Blaine fucks my ass like he's trying to get to our girl through me. Before I realise it, my balls are drawing up practically into my stomach and I'm crying her name as I fill her up with my release, electricity zapping through my limbs as I come harder than I ever have before.

God, she feels so fucking exquisite wrapped around me, my orgasm unrelenting in its ferocity, Blaine going even harder as he chases his climax. Lan roars out his release, deep in her ass, and I can feel his dick pulsing inside her, filling her up just as surely as I am.

I grunt when Blaine thrusts hard inside me, his teeth biting down on my shoulder as he comes with a deep groan that has my dick twitching inside our girl. She moans my name softly, blinking her eyes open and giving me a sated half-smile that makes my chest burn. This girl. Fuck. She's ours all right, and after today, I know that none of us will want to let her go.

We stay connected like that for several moments, Lan and I planting kisses on her sweat-soaked skin as our chests heave. Blaine pulls out first, leaning over me and crushing me into her as he kisses her mouth like she's the oxygen that he needs to stay alive. *I know the feeling, Big Daddy.*

I watch her lips chase his when he finally pulls back and it makes me smile. My damn heart feels so fucking full right now, all of my favourite people are right here with me. All safe, and it's as if nothing can touch us in here. The world outside doesn't exist, only us and our love.

I have no doubt that's exactly what this heat in my chest means, and looking into Lan and then Blaine's eyes, it's plain as fucking day they feel the same. She is our soulmate, the one person put on this earth to complete us.

"Let's get you cleaned up, Duchess," Lan says, his voice husky and full of emotion. She blinks slowly, half asleep already even though it's probably still daytime. Gotta love some afternoon delight.

She gasps when I pull out of her body, my own missing her heat instantly as I roll off her and lie next to Lan.

"I think you broke me." She sighs, nuzzling into my side when Lan pulls out of her and places her next to me on the bed. I can't help it, I pull her to me, wrapping her sweat-slicked body in my arms.

"In the best possible way, sugar," I croon in her ear, her breathing evening out as she falls asleep in my arms.

Blaine strides back into the room with a washcloth, and he gently wipes her between her sweet thighs. She stirs a little but doesn't open her eyes, and I'm content to hold her close while Blaine and Lan look after her.

"Let her rest," Blaine rumbles when they're done, leaning down and placing a kiss on her temple. A small sound of contentment falls from her lips against my chest, making my chest tight. God, I love having her here.

"I'll start prepping dinner," Lan mumbles, replacing Blaine's lips with his own, then pulling up some blankets over us both. "She'll be hungry when she wakes up. You stay with our girl, Forest."

"I wouldn't be anywhere else, Daddy," I tell him softly, not wanting to wake the sleeping beauty in my arms. The idea of ever letting her go sends my pulse skyrocketing, my soul rebelling at the thought. "She stays with us. Whatever it takes." I first hold Blaine's, then Lan's stares.

"She stays," Lan says after several moments, his brows deeply furrowed. "But it may take some time to organise. She'll have to go back for now."

My jaw clenches at the knowledge that he's right. At the fact we have to send her back into that house where she's abused so casually by the people who should love her.

"He'll pay for hurting her," I whisper, my voice darkness personified. My words are a vow of the most solemn kind. I will kill that man for hurting my angel, and have killed for far less. His death won't sit on my conscience.

"First, we get what Alfonso needs, then we take him out," Lan replies, Blaine growling in agreement.

We may be saints, but our hands are stained with blood and I will gladly add the British Ambassador's to the mix.

"DON'T BLAME ME" BY TAYLOR SWIFT

ASPEN

I wake to warmth surrounding me and the delicious smell of Italian cooking.

"Welcome back, sleeping beauty," Forest's teasing voice caresses over me just as surely as his palms now do.

"How long was I asleep for?" I mumble, stretching and feeling every delicious hard inch of him pressed up against me. My core pulses, a deep ache letting me know that they fucked me good and proper earlier.

"A few hours, but you've woken up just in time for dinner," he tells me, kissing and nuzzling my neck. Tingles race from every point of contact his lips make, and I arch into him, giving him more access to my skin. "You are so fucking addictive, sugar, you know that?"

My fingers grip his shoulder, pulling him into me as I wrap my leg around his hips, his solid shaft teasing my slick opening.

"Forest," I pant as he pushes the tip inside and my entire body shudders, already on the brink of an orgasm. It's like my body is so attuned to him, so starved of his touches that a single caress will have me exploding.

Clearly hearing my pleading tone, his thrusts all the way in, his hand coming up to cover my mouth.

"Shhhh, baby. Don't want them knowing and interrupting us before you've come," he murmurs, pounding into me so hard and fast that I shatter around his cock moments later, even without any clit stimulation.

"That's it, angel, come for your Daddy," he commands in a low voice, fucking me until I'm trembling and almost crying for him to stop. "Such a good, perfect, Daddy's girl."

His dirty words only prolong my pleasure, leaving me a twitching, hot mess.

"Fuck, Forest," I gasp once I come down, and he pulls out, still hard. "You're not...?"

"Oh, Little Lady, Daddy can wait." He kisses the tip of my nose. "Now go clean up and let's eat."

I get up on wobbly legs, Forest steadying me with a shit-eating grin on his perfect face when my knees almost buckle. I do the mature thing of sticking my tongue out at him, which earns a laugh and an arse slap as I leave, causing me to yelp and rub the sore patch.

I make my way to the bathroom, taking care of business and hopping into the shower as a warm flannel won't cut the amount of cum dripping from me. Once I'm done, I grab one of the large towels, wrap it around my body, and then head in the direction of the main room where I find Lan putting the finishing touches to a pasta dish and Blaine playing tug of war with Bolt.

Bolt spots me first, letting go of the rope toy and trotting over to me, nuzzling my hand with his soft face. My fingers disappear into his thick fur as I scratch him behind the ear and his tail thumps on the ground.

"Evening, *mi tesoro*," Blaine greets, striding up to me and taking my chin in his fingers, placing his lips on mine and making my toes curl with the pleasure that zaps through me.

"Good evening, Blaine," I whisper back once he releases my lips. "Do you have a shirt I could borrow?"

He answers by stripping out of his T-shirt, leaving all of his glorious muscles on display. My mouth practically waters, his smirk telling me he knows exactly the effect he has on me. Arching a brow, I undo the towel, letting it drop to the floor. His eyes turn molten, his nostrils flaring as he traces my body, burning a path with his gaze.

"Touché," he murmurs, taking his shirt and helping me into it, his fingers ghosting down the bare skin at my sides. I shiver, my nipples pebbling and pressing against the fabric, my core pulsing when I glance beyond Blaine to see Lan staring at me with lust filling his dark eyes.

"Let's eat," he states in a somewhat strained tone, placing a steaming bowl onto the table in front of the chair that they always sit me in.

"Thank you, Lan," I say, walking over to him and kissing his cheek. His leather and lavender scent engulfs me, and I pause with my hand on his forearm, just breathing him in. My cheeks heat when I think about what he did to me earlier, the way he fucked my arse and how much I loved it.

"You're welcome, Duchess," he whispers into my ear, giving me a light kiss on my cheek before he steps away to get the rest of the food. Goddamn, that man is the master of making me crave him with a single, innocent touch.

We eat a delicious pasta pesto dish, the creamy flavours bursting on my tongue and leaving me moaning while the guys growl at me to stop otherwise none of us will finish our food. Obviously, that just makes me do it more, laughing at them all until they each stand up, hard cocks clear as day pressing against their sweatpants—which should be illegal by the way.

"So, what do you guys usually do on a Saturday night?" I ask as once again they refuse to let me clear away the plates. Lan returns with what looks like a glass full of Tiramisu. "Oh my fucking god, is this Tiramisu?" I squeal as it's one of my favourite desserts.

"It is, Duchess." Lan smirks, practically preening as I grab the spoon from his fingers and dive in.

"Oh lord, that's so fucking good, Lan," I moan, closing my eyes and licking the spoon clean.

"Right, that's it. Get up on the fucking table, Duchess," Lan orders, and my eyes pop open at his harsh tone, seeing his face set in hard lines. "Now, beautiful."

"Yes, sir," I reply in a whisper, pushing my chair back and climbing up onto the table, hissing when the cool wood touches my bare arse.

"Shirt off," he commands, and reaching down to the hem, I pull it upwards and let it fall to the floor. "Good girl. Now lie back." I pout at him and he laughs. "Don't worry, you'll still get your dessert, beautiful."

Placated that I'm not missing out on the most delicious Tiramisu I've ever eaten, I lie down, my spine arching when it hits the surface.

"Perfect, sugar," Forest murmurs, and I watch as he takes a spoon of his own dessert and dollops it onto my nipple. The cold has me gasping, my breasts rising when Blaine does the same to the other side.

"Best way to eat such a delicious treat," Lan whispers, and I look down my body to see his spoon poised over my pussy. I watch as he tips the spoon, giving it a little shake, and the Tiramisu falls, landing on my clit and sending a bolt of fire racing up my body. "Let's tuck in, boys."

As one, they converge on my body, warm lips and tongues tracing the cool dessert until I'm writhing, my limbs trembling on the edge of a release.

"Please," I beg, needing something extra to send me over that edge. "Please, Lan."

I gasp as another cool spoonful lands on my heated cunt, followed immediately by Lan's mouth as he sucks my bud hard enough for an edge of pain to shoot through me and push me off the cliff.

I come while screaming their names, my fingers clawing at the wooden surface of the table, no doubt scratching it but I have no fucks to give as I'm rolled over and under the waves of pleasure. Every nerve ending tingles, pulsing as if a current is running through me, and I need them to mark me as theirs right the fuck now.

Blinking, I open my eyes to find them all watching me. "Cover me with your cum," I beg in a hoarse voice. "Please, mark me as yours."

"As you wish, Duchess," Lan growls, dropping the spoon to the table top with a loud clatter and then pulling his impressive length out. He lines it up with my clit, then wraps his fist around it and starts pumping hard and fast, his thick head nudging me and building me up again.

I tear my gaze away from the erotic sight to watch Blaine pull his dick from his sweats, stroking it as he looks at my sticky body. I reach out with my hand, covering his, and he groans, his eyelids fluttering as we both jerk him off.

"Don't forget about me, Little Lady," Forest rumbles, and I twist to reach for him, doing the same as I am with Blaine, and wrapping my palm around his fist as we both stroke him up and down.

My gaze flits between the three of them, the sight alone enough to have my thighs trembling as another climax approaches.

"Come for me," I demand, squeezing my hands tighter and having both Forest and Blaine hissing my name. "Mark me as yours."

I watch as the orgasm takes over Lan's face, his body thrumming with tension as he growls out his release. Spurts of his hot cum cover my pussy, and he uses his tip to rub it all over my cunt, sending me into another orgasm that hits like a fucking freight train.

My back arches just as I feel cum splash across my breasts, and the thought of them all marking me makes me come that much harder.

"Fuck, sugar," Forest grits out, slamming his lips on mine once I finally start to come down from my high. I kiss him back languidly, my body utterly spent and satisfied. "You are so fucking hot covered in our cum."

I hum, unable to form words, and I crack my lids open and grin at him.

"Looks like you need another shower, *mi amorsita*." Blaine chuckles, and I huff a laugh, my nose wrinkling when I feel how sticky I am.

A warm washcloth swiping across my folds has me looking down to see Lan cleaning me up, just enough so that cum isn't dripping down my skin.

"Dessert first," I say, and he gives me a breathtaking smile.

"Shower first, then I'll feed you your Tiramisu," he counters and laughs when I pout at him. "I made you extra."

"Fine," I relent, letting Forest help me off the table, my legs once again jelly-like.

Once I've showered and am back in Blaine's T-shirt, we settle in front of the TV where Lan makes good on his promise, feeding me Tiramisu until I can't eat anymore. I fall asleep with my head on his shoulder, my feet in Blaine's lap, and I can't help but wish that this was my life always.

CHAPTER 30

"WHEN THE PARTY'S OVER" BY BILLIE EILISH

ASPEN

I wake up with a sense of dread pooling in the pit of my stomach, regardless of the warmth of the men that surround me.

"What is it, Duchess?" Lan asks sleepily from in front of me, clearly having sensed the sudden tension in my body. Unbidden tears fill my eyes, his palm coming to cup my cheek in such a tender way that they spill over my lashes.

"I have to go home today, and..." I trail off, not sure if I can say the words that are stuck in my throat.

"And what, beautiful?" he whispers, his gaze intense but haunted too. Like he's feeling the exact same way.

I lick my lips. "And it feels like I'm leaving a part of my soul behind." My words are whispered, quiet in the dim light of what I suspect is very close to dawn. His jaw clenches, his thumb stroking my cheek.

"We'll lose our heart when you leave, Duchess," he confesses, and my own heart soars and cracks at the same time. This can't be a forever thing, this thing between us. My life isn't my own, and as much as I wish it were, I know that I will always be under the heel of the Ambassador. "But you will come back. We will make sure that this separation is temporary. You belong to us, Aspen. You're a part of us just like we're a part of you, and that can't easily be taken away."

I want to believe him, and am desperate to have faith in them, but how can I when the Ambassador is just too powerful. I want to confess my love for them, fuck the fact that it's only been such a short time, but the reality of my situation comes crashing down around me, holding my tongue.

"I should get ready. I need to be back before they are, just in case," I tell him, my voice cracked and broken, just like my heart will be when I have to put a stop to this fantasy life.

Just a little while longer. I'll end it after the performance at Maria's, just give me until then.

With a sigh, he places a light kiss on my lips, then rolls out of bed, helping me out. Forest and Blaine remain asleep, snuggled together in the cutest way that has my heart threatening to explode from my chest.

I shower quickly, going through the motions yet hardly feeling the warm water that traces down my skin. I hate that I'm already so distant, that I'm pulling away even before I've left.

Emerging into the main room, I find just Lan, his palms resting on the work surface, his jaw set into a hard line. He looks up, dark eyes full of torment as he takes me in, dressed with my bag at my side.

"Fuck, Duchess. This is…" He lets out a sigh, scrubbing a hand down his face, and my eyes fill with useless tears once more.

"Horrible," I whisper, and then he's there, pulling me into his arms as I shed silent tears into his chest.

"It'll be okay, beautiful. I swear we will get you out of there and with us, whatever it takes," he murmurs, but it only makes me cry harder.

"I–I don't want any of you to get h–hurt," I stutter, my fingers tracing the lines of his chest as if this is more than just a farewell.

"We can look after ourselves, Duchess. He can't get to us," he assures me, and I want to believe him, I really do, but how can I when all my life I've witnessed the destruction the Ambassador leaves in his wake?

The sound of a car pulling up has me sniffing, wiping my damp cheeks with the back of my hand.

"Is that Bobby?" I ask quietly, pulling back a little but not completely. I need his strength a little longer.

"I called him, thought it would be easier if the others aren't awake," he tells me, his voice husky and eyes pained. "We'll see you tomorrow at school?"

I nod. "And no doubt Forest will try to sneak into my room tonight." I chuckle, but it's an empty sound, like leaves rustling against the ground. Lifeless and full of desolation.

"No doubt," he agrees, leaning down and hovering his lips above mine. "I love you, Aspen."

Not giving me a chance to answer, leaving my heart pounding and butterflies erupting in my stomach, he closes the small gap and kisses me like he's trying to save me. I open to him, desperate for the comfort and love that radiates from his entire being. Telling him with my lips that I love him, love all of them too.

All too soon he pulls away, and I blink my eyes open to see the small smile playing on his gorgeous lips.

"I love you too, Landon," I whisper, and my breathing stops altogether at the beaming smile he gives me. It lights up the dull room, radiating warmth and the kind of thing only poets can dream of.

"Let's get you home," he whispers, taking my bag and one of my hands in his as he steps towards the door, Bolt on our heels. "Bolt, stay."

The dog whines, so I pause, ducking down to press a kiss to his soft nose before straightening up, letting Lan lead me out into the wintery light, to where Bobby is waiting.

"Good to see you, Miss Aspen," he greets warmly, taking my bag from Landon and giving him a nod. "Your parents are due back later this morning so you should be all settled when they get in."

"Thank you, Bobby," I reply, giving him a grateful smile even though my stomach is in knots at the mere mention of them. Turning to Lan, I take a deep inhale. "I guess I'll see you tomorrow?"

"See you tomorrow, Duchess," he murmurs, swiping his thumb across my lips and then taking a step back, shoving his hands in his pockets as if it's the only way to stop from clutching me to him.

"Goodbye, Lan," I whisper, turning to the open door and getting into the car, forcing my watery eyes to not look back, otherwise I won't be able to leave.

The door slams behind me just as the first tear falls, and I cry silently all the way back to the Ambassador's residence.

"RUNNING UP THAT HILL (A DEAL WITH GOD)" BY LOVELESS

LANDON

We don't see Aspen properly for the rest of the following week, Forest even unable to sneak into her room as it seems her dad has upped the security around the house. All we get are glimpses of her at school, and it's fucking driving me crazy to be so close to her yet feel so far away.

I get that we can't run the risk of her father finding out about us and then punishing her for it, but it still grates on me, and I know Forest is feeling the strain too. Blaine, lucky bastard, is still her PT, so gets to spend every day after school for an hour or so with her. He's kept it strictly professional after her mother joined them on Monday, so I guess that in itself is a type of punishment.

Forest manages to speak to Wallace, securing a spot for Bolt at the next fight which happens to be the week following Aspen's scheduled performance. I feel sick about the whole thing, hating that we have to put our loyal friend in such danger, but it's the only way to get in and discover what is really going on. I spend the week trying to come up with a plan to stop him from getting hurt too badly, or even from having to fight at all, but come up fucking empty.

An invitation for the coronation party arrives at the Pound, all our names on it, including Susan and Stan who are beyond excited about their new patron and going to such an exclusive event. Initially, they gave Forest an earful for having Aspen there on Saturday without them, as they're dying to meet her, their words, but as always, he charmed them—like he does all of us—and they forgave him like they always do, only after he assured them he'd introduce them to her at the party.

"I need to see her," Forest grits out from his seat on the couch, the room dark with only a single lamp on. Blaine got back from his session with her a couple of hours ago and has been silently fuming ever since. Something about the way her mother criticises her constantly, telling her she's not good enough has understandably made him see red, but kudos to the big guy, he kept it in check which is more than I could do if I was in his place.

Bolt gives a happy bark just as there's a knock at the door. I don't think, my soul knows it's her even before I wrench the door open and she's standing there, soaked from the rain that started falling an hour ago.

I pull her to me, uncaring that now I'm getting wet, as my entire body relaxes the instant she's in my arms.

"They're gone for the night," she whispers against my chest, her arms around my neck as she snuggles closer. "I told everyone I was staying at Aoife's and had Bobby bring me over." I barely let her finish before my lips are on hers, tasting her as if for the first time.

"Fuck, Duchess. It's been too long," I rasp against her cold lips, kissing her again even though I know the others are waiting.

She giggles. "I saw you at lunch." Her eyes sparkle when she looks up at me, and I press my forehead against hers, unable to let her go just yet.

"It's not the same, and even if it was, every minute we're apart is too fucking long," I breathe out, my chest loosening the longer she's here, in my arms, safe and sound.

"I know, Lan. I wish..." she trails off, and I know what she wishes because fucking hell, so do I. I would give up so much just to have her with us always.

"Quit hogging our girl, Daddy," Forest whines, and she laughs again, the room so much brighter than it was moments ago.

I let him tug her from me, watching as he wastes no time in kissing her senseless. My brows dip when I notice the slight tremor in her limbs, obviously cold from being soaked through, but before I can do anything about it, Blaine is there with a towel, one of his huge hoodies, and some of Forest's sweats.

"Let her get changed, she's freezing," he grumbles, and Forest immediately lets her go, frowning.

"Why didn't you say anything, sugar?" he asks, helping her take her wet things off and drying her skin with the towel before letting Blaine get her dressed.

The restraint we show is fucking admirable given how long we've been without her, but she needs care right now. The fucking can come later.

"Are you hungry, Duchess?" I ask, drawing her attention back to me, and fuck if it's not like having the sun shine down on your face after a long, cold winter.

"Yes, always if you're offering to make me something," she answers, tucked under Blaine's arm as he finally gets his turn with her.

"You guys sit down, I'll make us some food," I tell them, my mind already on what I can make her to feed her back up. From what I've seen and what Blaine tells us, her mother barely lets her eat when she's at home.

I start making some pizza, having made up a batch of dough this morning before we left, and I can feel her eyes on me as I spin it out into the right shape. Moments later there's a warmth at my back as her slender arms wrap me in a hug from behind, her intoxicating scent of spring woods easing my soul in a way that nothing before ever has.

"What do you like on your pizza, Duchess?" I ask her, spreading some homemade sauce on the first base.

"Just cheese and tomato please, with some basil?" she replies, and I smile at how simple her tastes are. She gets enjoyment from the basics of life, which is something not many people can say. Often they are too concerned with making shit complicated, unable to see the beauty right in front of them.

"One margarita coming up," I joke, leaning back into her hold as I place the rest of the ingredients onto the pizza and then get to making one each for the guys and myself.

Placing them in the pizza oven that I saved up for and installed last year, I twist and grab her before she can go back to sitting with the others.

"Have you been practising for tomorrow night?" I ask as I gaze down at her. God, she's so beautiful it almost hurts to look at her sometimes.

"A little," she confesses, biting her lower lip that has a small growl leaving my throat. I tug it out with my thumb, soothing over the small wound.

"Only I'm allowed to bite this lip," I tell her, and the way her pupils dilate lets me know exactly how much my orders turn her on. Fuck, she really is perfect for me, for us.

"Yes, sir," she answers, keeping those beautiful green eyes on me. I love how she makes me feel like I hung the moon for her, and I would. Or burn down the world, whichever she desired. Either way, it would happen.

"Good girl," I praise, watching the shiver that takes over her body. God, the effect I have on her is intoxicating in and of itself.

The smell of cooked pizza starts to waft around us, so I let her go, taking them out of the oven and knowing that they're cooked to perfection. I have a sixth sense about cooking, or so Mama says, always have. And I love to feed others, watching them enjoy my food is one of life's greatest pleasures.

"God that smells so fucking good," she groans, hovering by me as I cut hers into slices. Something in me preens at her praise, at the way that I can feed her like no other, take care of her in the way I know how.

"Glad you approve, beautiful," I tell her, plating up hers first with a side salad and then taking it over to the table even though she keeps trying to snatch it out of my hands.

"I can carry my own food, you know," she huffs but sits down anyway, and then looks down with a small smile when I arch a brow at her. Brat.

After we've eaten, she sits back, patting her still very flat stomach—I make a note to myself to feed her at least five more times before she leaves tomorrow—then she sits up with a jerk.

"What about family dinner?" she gasps, looking up at the clock and seeing that it's close to the time that we'd need to leave.

"We can skip tonight, sugar," Forest says, and Blaine and I readily agree. It would be a first, but I'm sure they'll cope.

"Not a chance!" she scolds, and I can't even hide my smile at how damn adorable she is when she tells us off. "It's family dinner, we have to go."

"Okay, Duchess. As you wish." I chuckle, grabbing her half-full plate and taking it over to the counter with mine. "Let's go eat again."

CHAPTER 31

"HE'S A TRAMP" BY PEGGY LEE

ASPEN

We spend the rest of the evening with the Tainted Saints crew, and I once again marvel at how much of a family they are. Sure, they're not related by blood, but sometimes chosen family is the strongest kind, an unbreakable bond that stands firm against all kinds of storms.

We get back late, and my body is exhausted even if my mind wants to stay awake and enjoy my guys. It's like my body knows we can rest easy here, that we are finally safe and protected from all the monsters that plague my life back at the Ambassador's residence.

"Sleep, *mi tesoro*." Blaine chuckles when I yawn for what feels like the twentieth time.

"But—"

"No buts, beautiful," Lan interrupts, taking my hand and leading me down to his room. "You need to rest."

"But we have such little time together," I whisper, smiling when I see the two beds as they were last week, pushed together and waiting for us all to pile in.

"We have the rest of our lives together, sugar," Forest interjects, unbuttoning his shirt and pushing his jeans to the floor. "Plenty of time to explore." He winks and I giggle, another yawn practically cracking my jaw in half.

Lan helps me out of my clothes, giving me one of his T-shirts to sleep in, and I crawl in beside Forest, snuggling into his hot body, my eyes closing before my head has even hit the pillow.

I WAKE UP SURROUNDED BY WARMTH, MY BODY UTTERLY relaxed, and the soft light of morning filtering around the edges of the curtains.

"Good morning, sleeping beauty," Forest whispers huskily, and I look up at him, his hair all sleep-mussed and looking far too gorgeous for this early in the day.

"Good morning," I reply, snuggling into his chest when he pulls me close, the entire line of our bodies touching. I can feel the hard length of him pressed against my thigh, and suddenly I'm wide awake, desperate for him.

"Little Lady..." he hisses as my hand dips under his boxer shorts, wrapping around his hard, silky length. "Fuck."

"Let me wake you up properly, Daddy," I breathe out, scooting down the bed until my face hovers over his crotch. My mouth waters when I bring his cock out of his underwear, and I waste no time in closing my lips over the tip, licking and sucking it until his thighs tremble.

I gasp, taking Forest deeper when my knickers are pulled down, a tongue swiping across my damp folds.

"Good morning, Duchess," Lan breathes against my core, leaving me shivering, then moaning as he thrusts his hard length inside me in one smooth move. His piercing drags against my inner walls in the most delicious way, and it becomes increasingly more difficult to focus on Forest when Lan is giving me such pleasure. "You don't come until Blaine has had his turn, Pup."

Forest moans, his hands digging into the sheets at his sides as I continue to work up and down his length with my mouth and tongue. "Do you know how fucking hard that's gonna be, Daddy?" He groans again when I swallow him, his tip nudging the back of my throat and making me gag a little.

The sound makes both men growl, and I look to the side to see Blaine, his huge hand wrapped around his equally impressive dick, slowly pumping it up and down as he looks at us, his own personal porno.

"You look so beautiful with your lips stretched over him, *mi amorsita*," he murmurs, his gaze fixed on the way I move Forest in and out of my mouth.

Lan reaches around, his fingers finding my clit and making me scream and writhe around him as a sudden orgasm hits me. My body tenses, Forest slowly fucking my open mouth as Lan fucks my pussy hard and fast, prolonging the pleasure until I'm whimpering as he thrusts hard inside me, filling me up with his cum.

No sooner has he pulled out that Blaine is forcing his way inside me, grunting when my still pulsing pussy clamps down on him.

"That's it, *mi princesa linda*, let me into that beautiful pink pussy," he growls, and then a loud slap echoes across the room, leaving me gasping and clenching as the pain adds to the pleasure. "You like that?"

I nod, making an incoherent moan and pushing my arse back for more. I don't know who this wanton version of myself is, but I am here for it and will be the Saints slut any day.

He does it again, forcing Forest's cock deeper in my throat.

"Fuck, Big Daddy. She really likes that," he groans, grabbing my hair in his fist and using it to fuck my face. "That's it, sugar. Take all of me in that beautiful throat."

"Make sure she can still sing later, Pup," Lan chides, and I open watery eyes to see him lounging back, watching us with heavy-lidded eyes.

Blaine slaps my arse again and I hum around Forest's cock in my mouth, hollowing out my cheeks and sucking him deeper.

"Fuuuck, sugar!" he yells, thrusting to the back of my throat as his shaft goes rock-solid in my mouth. His dick pulses as he comes down my throat, holding me in place and giving me no choice but to swallow his release down.

Blaine keeps fucking me, his thrusts becoming erratic and jerky as he nears his own climax. I gasp when Forest finally releases me, his semi-hard cock popping free and leaving me room to scream as Blaine's piercings massage my inner walls and send me crashing headfirst into another earth-shattering climax. My body stiffens and lights up like there's a fire raging inside me, and then Blaine is roaring his own release, settling deep inside me that an edge of pain flares as I'm sure he touches my cervix, big dicked bastard.

I'm gasping for breath, my skin tingling as I flop on top of Forest, my chest heaving. My lids are closed and I bask in the afterglow, my mind quiet as I just feel the way Forest wraps his arms around me, pulling my spent body against his own.

"You are so fucking perfect, Little Lady," he breathes out, kissing the top of my head.

My lips pull up in a grin but I'm still too blissed out to form a coherent sentence. We lie for several moments like that, the others on either side of us, all touching me in some way, and it's the most perfect way to wake up.

I must have drifted off, waking up again some time later to an empty bed, the smell of delicious cooking making my stomach rumble. Getting up, I smile when I realise that someone cleaned me up before I fell asleep because I'm not as sticky and gross as I should be. Still could do with a wash, so I make my way to the bathroom, taking a quick shower and throwing Lan's T-shirt back on. I normally would only wear my vintage-style clothes, they're such a fundamental part of who I am, but there's something about being enveloped in these guys completely, even when I'm not in their arms, that makes me want to wear their clothes any chance I can.

"Good morning," I say as I walk into the room, glancing at the clock and seeing that it's actually just gone midday. "Afternoon, I guess."

Lan chuckles from the kitchen, that boy is always in there making food. "Glad you slept well, Duchess, but you missed a meal and now must eat."

He indicates that I sit, placing a plate full of traditional breakfast foods; bacon, fluffy scrambled eggs, and a stack of pancakes with butter and drizzled with syrup.

"Yum," I say, licking my lips and grabbing my cutlery.

"Yes, I will say that Americans do breakfast better than Italians." He laughs, setting his own plate down next to mine, then grabbing two glasses of fresh orange juice. "My mother's family just have coffee and cigarettes in the morning."

I wrinkle my nose. I dislike both of those things though at least coffee smells good. "Where are the others?"

"They're downstairs, sorting out the dogs, but I'm sure they'll be back up once that's done," he tells me, clearly getting fed up with my slow speed and using his fork to cut a piece of his pancake off before holding it to my lips. "I want to see most of this gone, Duchess."

Opening up, I let him place the bite in my mouth, releasing a contented sigh when the sweet, buttery goodness explodes on my tongue. We eat the rest in much the same way, though at least he lets me feed myself half of the time. I can't quite manage the full plate, years of forced starvation have left me with a small stomach that can't cope with too much at once.

I've just placed my knife and fork on the plate when the door opens and Forest comes storming in. Immediately, I know that something is up, his shoulders are tense, his brows lowered, and there's an air of rage rolling off him.

"What's happened?" I ask, getting to my feet and rushing over to him, my heart racing.

"Fucking Wallace!" he seethes, his entire body trembling with rage. "I caught him taking some dogs, ready for next week."

"Next week?" I ask, frowning as a flutter in my stomach threatens to bring back all the yummy food I just ate. "What's happening next week?" Forest clamps his jaw shut, Blaine stepping in behind him and shutting the door. "What's going on?"

He looks to Lan, so I turn and find him standing, his hands clenched in fists at his sides. He huffs out a breath, his shoulders dropping.

"Next Saturday is the dog fight." I'm surprised they didn't tell me sooner, my stomach sinks remembering Landon's confession in the Ambassador's office.

"And Bolt is still going to fight?" I ask, not missing when his gaze darts to Bolt who's pressed against Forest's side, Lan's entire face tensing. He looks back up at me, pain in the depths of his dark eyes.

"Duchess..." he starts, his hand reaching out as he steps towards me, but I step to the side, away from them all, a sense of betrayal churning my stomach.

"You said you'd find another way, that he wouldn't get hurt," I plead through clenched teeth, their silence speaking volumes. "He'll be killed, Lan."

"I won't let that happen, Duchess," he vows, taking another step towards me. This time I don't move away, wanting so desperately to believe his words, but even I know how these things usually go.

"You won't be able to stop them, Lan," I whisper as he closes the gap between us, his warm palms cupping my face. My shoulders sag, my body feeling like it's caving in on itself as the realisation that there is no other way settles like a weight on my chest.

"I will not let anything happen to him, I swear. It's the only way we can get in, Duchess." He sounds just as frustrated as I feel. I hate this feeling of uselessness that the Ambassador always gives me, like he's the one always in control and I have no choice but to follow along like an obedient slave.

Sighing, knowing that they're stuck between a rock and a hard place, aka Lan's uncle and the Ambassador, I drop the subject.

"What time do we need to leave for the performance?" I ask, my bright tone falling flat. Lan smiles at me anyway, brushing a soft kiss on my lips.

"We have about a few hours. I said to Mama we'd be there at seven," he tells me. "Let's relax until then, okay?"

"Okay," I agree, my stomach churning with a mix of trepidation for the dog fight and nerves and excitement over singing in front of strangers.

"You'll be amazing, Little Lady," Forest states, the tension in his shoulders still there even if his face is all smiles. I hate this, that we have to pretend it's all okay when it's not. "Now, The Flash has just come online and I hear it's a good one."

We spend the rest of the afternoon watching Marvel films, again, the guys laughing at me when I cry at the sad bits. I'm too nervous to eat more than a little bread and a selection of dried meats that Lan feeds me with his fingers, persistent bastard.

"I need to change," I tell them when we only have half an hour until we have to leave. Grabbing my bag, I head into Forest's room and take out the deep-red velvet dress I bought to wear. It's pretty simple, a low crossover V-neck that shows plenty of cleavage and falling to the floor in soft waves.

Leaving just my lace knickers and stockings on, I slip the dress over my head, taking out my make-up and applying a wicked flick and bright red lips. I also take out my heels, red sequin ones from my favourite British designer, and slip those on too.

"Fuck me, sugar," Forest whispers from the doorway, and I look up to see his gaze devouring me. "You look…well prettier than a peach."

"Thank you," I reply softly, walking over to him and placing my hand on his flannel shirt. "You look pretty hot yourself, cowboy."

"Why, thank you, ma'am." He smirks, dipping down to place a kiss on my cheek. "You ready?"

"As I'll ever be." I huff a laugh, wondering when I got so nervous about singing in public.

"You'll be incredible," he murmurs in my ear as we walk down the short hallway to meet the others.

Two sets of eyes are on me as soon as I walk in, the intensity of their attention has me instantly flushing.

"You look beautiful, *mi amorsita*," Blaine rumbles, striding towards me and kissing my cheek in the same place Forest just did. "I'm not sure how I'll concentrate on the keys." I giggle, feeling giddy with all the praise. Earlier in the week, Blaine asked me for my song choices so he could practise accompanying me on the piano—apparently, he can sing but also plays piano and wanted this to be my night—and tonight will be the first time we actually perform together.

"You are breathtaking," Lan tells me, Blaine stepping aside so Lan can take his place. He takes my hand and presses his lips to the back of my knuckles, sending tingles racing all up my arm. "You're riding with me."

I bite my lip. Obviously, I forgot about our transportation when I made my outfit choice. Figuring I'll wing it, I let the guys lead me out into the cool night, the promise of spring in the chill air, and we head to the bikes.

Like before, Lan places the helmet on my head and I pray to the gods of styling that it doesn't fuck up my hair. He gets on the bike first, and then deciding the only way to do this is to lift my skirt and flash my stockings. I get on behind him, hearing the whistle Forest gives me ringing out in the quiet night.

Lan's palm caresses down my stocking-clad thigh, using his grip to pull me closer to his body.

"Fuck, you really do try a Saint, don't you, Duchess?" he asks, not giving me a chance to answer as suddenly the engine roars to life and then we're racing down the road, the wind freezing on my legs.

We get a few honks along the way, each one making Lan's body tense underneath my grip, but soon we're pulling up outside the restaurant. There's a warm glow coming from inside it, the place looks packed, and as Forest pulls in beside us, leaping off his bike in order to help me get off Lan's, my stomach roils again.

"You'll be fine, angel," Forest tells me, clearly seeing my terrified face.

"What if someone recognises me and tells him?" I ask, voicing my main concern.

"No one who knows the Ambassador comes here, *mi tesoro*," Blaine assures me, taking my smaller hand in his large one and leading me towards the doors. "You're safe here."

Taking a deep inhale, I stand taller and make the decision to fuck it. This is something that I want to do, and I won't let that man ruin it for me.

The loud noise of chatter hits us when Blaine opens the door, along with the warmth of bodies and the smell of delicious food.

"Blaine!" I hear the feminine voice of Maria, Lan's mum, shout over the din. Then Blaine is being wrapped in her arms, a kiss planted on each of his cheeks. "Oh, don't you look beautiful, bella!" she exclaims when she catches sight of me behind him.

My cheeks heat, and then I'm in her arms, being pulled into a hug that feels like home and smells like all my favourite foods. My body relaxes after a tense second, my arms going around her as I marvel that this is what it must be like to have your mother hug you. Tears sting my eyes at the thought of all I should have had but didn't. I refuse to let them fall, blinking furiously to dispel them.

"Thank you, Mrs. Capaldi," I say when she pulls away, cupping my face in her hands.

"Please, bella. Call me Maria," she beseeches, her face lined in smiles and love shining from her eyes.

"Thank you, Maria, and for letting me sing tonight. I appreciate it," I reply earnestly, and her gaze softens even more.

"When my boy told me that you sing like an angel, who was I to say no?" She brushes my cheek with her thumb before leaning in to place a soft kiss there that warms me like a roaring fire.

She releases me, giving Lan, then Forest a hug as Blaine leads me to the corner where there's an upright piano and a small space around it. There's an old-fashioned microphone gleaming under the lights, and I smile, even as butterflies erupt in my stomach. This is it. My time to show the world that I am more than just the daughter of the British Ambassador, more than his pawn in a game I don't know the rules to.

"Quiet!" Maria calls out, not even bothering with the microphone as she shushes everyone. "Tonight we have a special treat for you. The beautiful Aspen will sing for us, accompanied by Blaine on the piano, so give them a warm Maria welcome!"

The patrons burst into applause and I step away from Blaine and up to the microphone, my fingers trembling as I grasp hold of it.

"Good evening," I say, and Forest wolf-whistles at me, my lips quivering with a smile. "This first song is from one of my favourite childhood films and reminds me of a certain person or two that I've come to know since moving here a few weeks ago."

They clap again, and then Blaine plays the intro to "He's a Tramp" by Peggy Lee, and I see Forest burst into delighted laughter as I start to sing, Lan beaming too. After that, I lose myself to the song as I always do, everything else melting away as I sing and let the music flow through me.

Singing the final notes, I come back into the room, the patrons standing and clapping wildly after the last note fills the air.

"That's our girl!" Forest hollers before whistling, and I laugh, giving Blaine a nod to start the next song.

My blood hums as I launch into another couple of my favourites, ending with "Bella Notte," some of the audience singing along. I feel like I'm sparkling, happiness filling me up until my skin feels too tight as I take a small curtsey and step away from the microphone.

Lan and Forest surround me, pulling me into their arms and kissing me soundly, uncaring of our audience.

"You were perfect, Duchess," Lan tells me, his voice deep and husky as he stares into my eyes.

"Shit, sugar, you were meant to be on a stage!" Forest laughs, tugging me away from Lan and twirling me around.

"Forest!" I gasp, laughing as he sets me back on my feet but doesn't let me go.

"It was an honor to play with you, *mi princesa linda*," Blaine murmurs into my ear, sending goosebumps all over my skin as his hand glides down my arm.

"You were amazing, Blaine," I whisper, twisting so that I can face him. "Thank you for playing for me."

"Anytime," he replies, bending down and kissing me too. The noise of the crowd disappears as his tongue seeks entrance, his hands pulling me closer until not a millimetre of space is between us.

"Wonderful show, bella!" Maria exclaims once Blaine releases me. "You must come back and sing for us again, you have such a gift." Her eyes are watery, her hands pulling me into another hug which this time I sink into and return straight away.

"Thank you, Maria. I would love that," I say, my cheeks aching with how wide my smile is.

"Let's have a drink to celebrate!" she exclaims, tucking her arm in mine and leading me to the bar area.

"Wonderful performance, Miss Buckingham," a deep voice croons, making me freeze.

"T–thank you," I stutter, looking at the dark-haired man. His eyes remind me of Lan's, but they're cold, sending a shiver down my spine. He's handsome for an older man, with slicked back, almost black hair, and is wearing a perfectly tailored suit.

"Uncle," Lan greets from behind me, his hand landing on my waist and pulling me into his body as Maria lets go of me to head behind the bar. Mine relaxes at his closeness, my hand covering his and intertwining our fingers together. He squeezes my hand, letting me know that I'm okay, that I'm safe.

"Good to see you, Landon," his uncle replies. "And apologies, how rude of me. Alfonso Capaldi, a pleasure to finally meet you." He takes my hand, pressing the back of it to his lips, and my mind screams at me to run and hide from such a predator. For this man exudes danger, not unlike the vibe the Ambassador gives, regardless of his smiling face.

"Good to meet you too," I answer politely, withdrawing my hand. Forest immediately takes it in his, rubbing the place where Alfonso just had his lips.

"I'm pleased to see my nephew and his friends have taken you under their wing, I hope they're treating you well?" he comments, bringing a glass full of amber liquid up to his lips, and my eyebrows dip as I wonder what this is all about. How does he know me? Perhaps because he's keeping an eye on the Ambassador? And why would he be interested in my relationship with the Saints?

"You know we do, uncle," Lan answers before I can, an edge of warning to his tone that seems strange considering he's talking to a member of his family.

"Wonderful," Alfonso comments, placing his empty glass down on the marble countertop. "I must be going, but I do hope we see each other again, Aspen."

My mouth opens but I'm not sure what to say, the whole encounter leaving me uneasy and the hair standing on my arms. Alfonso leaves with a sharp nod to the guys, who also remain silent until he's made his way to the door, stopping and warmly greeting several people along the way.

"How did he know who I was?" I ask aloud once the man in question has left, a black car pulling up at the curb which he gets into.

"He knows everything that goes on in Fairview, Duchess," Lan states in a quiet voice.

"Sounds like him and the Ambassador would get along," I wryly comment, and Forest huffs a laugh.

"Keep your enemies close, I guess," he says, reaching for a bottle of limoncello. "Now let's forget about him and celebrate your success, sugar!"

I giggle at his exuberance, raising my brows when he hands me a shot glass full of it. "You trying to get me drunk, Daddy?" I ask, my voice lowered so only he and the guys hear, Maria having gone off to chat with someone across the room.

"Perhaps," he answers with a grin, clinking his glass with mine, then downing it in one go, hissing as it clearly burns its way down his throat.

"Bottoms up." I laugh, tipping my head back as I place the glass to my lips and swallow the liquid. "Fuck!" I gasp, feeling my taste buds practically shrivelling at the tart flavour.

"Limoncello should be savoured," Lan comments, taking a sip and not even flinching.

"I think you're just being a coward, Daddy," Forest teases, and my eyes widen.

"Oh, that's fighting talk." I laugh, watching as Lan's lips tip up in a smirk. Placing his shot glass down on the counter, he takes the bottle from Forest and holding eye contact, he takes several large gulps before placing the bottle back on the countertop.

"Never get into a drinking contest with an Italian," he states, cool as a cucumber while I just gape at him.

"I reckon I could give you a run for your money, seeing as I'm a redneck and all," Forest counters, taking the bottle and also drinking down several swigs. My mouth hurts from watching him, his own pulled back into a grimace, no doubt at the sour taste. "Damn, that's rough."

"Come, *mi tesoro*," Blaine whispers, pulling me from between them and tucking me under his arms. "Leave the boys to their games."

"Are you not drinking too?" I ask as Lan and Forest both glare at him, their drinking competition forgotten.

"I don't drink, *mi amorsita*. I've seen what it can do to a man firsthand and I like to keep my wits about me." There's a haunted look in his eyes that I hate, but one I have seen all too often in the mirror, telling me this is about his childhood, and not a nice part of it.

"We can celebrate in another way then," I tell him, the shot relaxing me and giving me the confidence to run my hand down his hard chest.

Taking his hand in mine, I lead him out of the restaurant, our progress slow as everyone wants to congratulate us on our performance. The other two guys follow us, also chatting with people as we pass, and I see that they have earned a great deal of respect in the way that people treat them. The cool night air hits my face when we finally open the door, and it's refreshing after the stuffy heat of Maria's.

"Where are we going?" Blaine asks, his hand trailing down my back.

"Do you know somewhere quiet?" I ask, looking at his bike and tilting my head as I wonder if my idea will work.

"Yes, there's a lake not far from here. I go there often to think," he tells me as Lan hands me the helmet.

"Perfect. Let's go there then," I reply, putting the helmet on, then waiting for Blaine to get on his bike, climbing on behind him. "You guys coming?"

Forest and Lan give me matching grins, then Blaine is taking off, and I squeak as I wrap my arms tighter around him. I let the night breeze wash over me, snuggling close to Blaine as we weave through the streets until nature surrounds us and we're pulling down a dirt track.

He stops just as we reach a lake bathed in moonlight, and my pulse races at the thought of enacting my plan.

"Stay there," I tell him, his low chuckle at my order giving me goosebumps.

Getting off the bike, I take the helmet off, then lift my skirt and shimmy out of my underwear. Walking around to his side, I place them in the pocket of his hoodie, his lips pulling up into a panty-melting smile. Well, if I had any on that is. Lifting my skirt again, I move his arm out of the way and straddle his lap, his legs bracing either side of us.

"*Mi amorsita*," he moans as I tangle my fingers into his hair and tilt his face to mine.

"Will you fuck me on your bike, Blaine?" I whisper against his lips, his deep growl answer enough.

I'm wet enough not to need any foreplay, and honestly, I prefer the burn of a hard dick being thrust inside me before I'm quite ready, forcing me to take it anyway. Letting go of his hair, I reach between us and unbuckle his jeans just as the roar of two motorcycles sounds down the track.

My hand wraps around his already hard length, my fingertips tracing the piercings on the underside, and I relish the deep groan he gives me. I lift myself up, my pulse racing as I position him at my entrance and begin to slide down, one of his hands coming to grasp my hip and steady me as I take his huge dick into my body.

"*Coño, mi princesa*," he rasps as I go lower, my limbs shaking at the delicious stretch he gives me. "You're such a perfect little slut for me, aren't you?"

"Yes," I gasp, seating him fully inside me and just holding there for a moment, relishing the way he feels so right buried to the hilt.

"Then ride me like one," he commands, using his grip to encourage me upwards, then pulling me down hard and fast. The breath is punched out of me, my core already tingling at just how fucking good he feels inside me.

Bracing my hands on his broad shoulders, I repeat the movement, vaguely hearing the bikes pull up either side of us. The idea that they'll be watching me fuck Blaine just encourages me to go harder, my hips swirling the next time he's fully inside me and making us both groan.

"Fuck me, that's a pretty sight," Forest exclaims, and I look over with heavy-lidded eyes to find him leaning against his bike, his dick in his palm as he pleasures himself watching us.

"Beautiful, Duchess," Lan rasps from the other side, and I twist to look at him, my hips moving up and down and sending tendrils of pleasure all across my body. He, too, has his cock in his hand, stroking it up and down as he watches us with an intensity that has me gasping and clenching around Blaine.

"Eyes on me, *princesa*," Blaine growls out, and my attention immediately snaps back to him.

His gaze burns into me, his chocolate eyes molten as he guides me up and down his shaft, taking control in just the way I like him to.

"Blaine, I'm so close," I moan, sparks flying up and down my spine as he fucks me hard.

"Come for me, *mi tesoro*," he orders, one hand leaving my hip and finding my clit, strumming and playing with it as expertly as he did the piano keys earlier.

I shatter, my cries filling the night as exquisite pleasure fills me up like the best kind of fireworks. My nails dig into the back of his neck, my inner walls clenching around his giant cock as my release coats us both.

"Good fucking girl," he grits out between clenched teeth, thrusting up into me so hard that I scream, his dick pulsing as he comes inside me with a roar of pleasure.

He holds me to him, filling me up until I'm slumped in his lap, my eyes closed as I try to relearn how to breathe again. His palms run over my heated back, the chill breeze a welcome relief from the fire that is slowing to embers inside my skin.

I hear the others groan either side of us, and I smile into Blaine's heaving chest knowing that they found their releases too. I love how wanton they make me feel, the fact that they can orgasm just watching me is one hell of a turn-on.

"I have to go home soon," I tell Blaine quietly, my life outside of the Saints always coming in to taint my time with them.

He hugs me tighter. "Let's get you back and cleaned up then, *mi princesa linda*." His voice is deep, huskier than usual, and it sends shivers down my spine.

Breathing out a sigh, Blaine helps me off him, and Forest is there behind me to steady me as I wobble on my heels in the soft earth next to the lake.

"You are so beautiful," Forest whispers in my ear, placing a small kiss on my cheek that I wish I could turn into more.

"I have to get back tonight so I'm up early for the party tomorrow," I tell him, straightening my dress. "You are all still coming, right?" My neck suddenly feels stiff as I think about the party. The itch to find a shop and take something flares like a beacon, but I quash it down, knowing that nowhere will be open now anyway even if I did give into the urge.

"We wouldn't be anywhere else, Duchess," Lan tells me, striding over and taking my face in his palms. "You won't be alone there, we will be with you however you want us."

I close my eyes and let his lavender and leather scent wash over me, let it calm my racing heart and lend me the strength that he always gives me without even knowing.

"Thank you, Lan," I whisper, opening my eyes and looking into his. They really are dark like the sky above us, fathomless and never-ending, but I find comfort in them too, like he will always be there, always fight for me and keep me safe, no matter what.

CHAPTER 32

"IN THE STARS" BY SAMI ROSE

ASPEN

I wake up in my bed, alone, and it feels as though my heartbeat is sluggish, like there's a weight on my chest that I thought I'd shed the moment I met Blaine in that cell.

A knock on the door has me sitting up, my heavy heart thudding painfully as the door opens.

"Good morning, Miss Aspen," Rosie, one of our maids, greets. "Mrs. Buckingham says you need to start getting ready for the party."

"Oh, thank you, Rosie," I reply to the young girl, wondering briefly what her life must be like, working for us and then being able to go home at night. Does she live with her parents? Does she have siblings? A partner?

"It's no trouble, Miss," she tells me, walking into my room and hanging up the floral dress that I'll be wearing today. It's forties-style, flowing in a wide skirt that cuts off mid-calf, and is an original piece that is one of my favourites.

I've often wondered why my mother lets me wear the clothes that I adore. I'm always expecting her to take that small independence away, but I think that her friends once commented how unique and beautiful the style was on me so perhaps that's the reason I'm allowed.

Just a few weeks until you're nineteen and then you might be able to leave.

I cling onto that small hope, that I may be able to get out of here when I've reached what the world considers adulthood. I come out of my musings when Rosie stops by my bed, a small smile on her lips. My brows dip as she reaches into her pocket, looking around before handing me a small envelope with **'Duchess'** written on it.

"Holler if you need anything, Miss," she says after placing it into my hand with a wink and then leaving the room.

I tingle all over as I gaze at the envelope, feeling something more than a piece of paper in there. With trembling hands, I open it, a small gasp leaving my lips as I tip out a beautiful pearl necklace. I fumble for the piece of paper inside, my eyes burning as I read the message.

Duchess,
This was my grandmother's, but it's yours now. Wear it at the party and know that we will always be with you, even if for now, we can't be next to you.
Lan xxx

P.S. We will give you more pearl necklaces later. Forest xxx

A choked laugh escapes me at Forest's comment, dirty bastard. My spirit somehow feels lighter, and carefully setting the pearls on my dresser and the note in my underwear drawer, I head to the bathroom to shower and start getting ready, knowing that mother will have hair and makeup here soon.

After my shower, I get dressed, just putting the necklace on as a knock sounds on the door and then two women are walking in.

"Hello, beautiful!" Bruna, my makeup artist says, pulling me into a hug, and something in me just relaxes at her casual affection. She's done my makeup a few times now and I love her, she's so happy and chatty and I love hearing tales of her childhood in Brazil. Jenna, my hair stylist also gives me a hug, and I wonder if this is what it's like to have sisters. How different would my life be if my parents hadn't stopped at just me but had another child? Then I shiver, thinking that I'm glad it's just me so no one else has to go through what I've had to endure my whole life.

"Let's make you even more beautiful than you are," Bruna beams, ushering me to a high chair that someone must have put in here whilst I was showering.

They set to work, and in an hour, after much laughter and chatter that has lightened my soul, I'm ready. Looking into the mirror, I can safely say that they have done an excellent job. My hair falls in soft waves around my shoulders, pinned back on one side with a pearl clasp that matches my necklace perfectly. My face is understated, but with a perfect flick at the corners of my eyes that I can never quite manage on my own, and my signature red lip completes the look until I feel like I've stepped out of the nineteen-forties.

"Thank you, it's perfect." I sigh, turning to hug them again.

"It helps to have such a pretty canvas to start with," Bruna compliments me, and I can feel the blush staining my cheeks. "Now go and wow all those stuffy people!"

"Bruna!" Jenna exclaims, looking around but giggling anyway. I join in, and for just a moment, I know what it would have been like to have somewhat of a normal life, with friends to laugh with.

"Time to go, Miss. The guests are arriving," Rosie says from the doorway, giving me a look that feels too close to sympathy. It wouldn't surprise me if she knew about my corrections, but my throat goes tight at the thought of my punishments being common knowledge. Her eyes dart to the necklace, and a small smile tilts her lips upwards as I walk towards the door. "They just arrived," she whispers when I reach her, and butterflies erupt in my stomach.

I know who they are, my Saints. I can no longer deny that they are mine, just as I am theirs, and that kernel of hope flares brightly inside me. Maybe once I'm nineteen I can truly be with them, no more hiding or sneaking around.

We make our way down the stairs and towards the large drawing room that is bright with sunlight filtering in from the French doors that lead to the garden. There are already several people milling about, and I spot my guys immediately, their eyes tracing every step I take as I enter the room.

It's like the world around me disappears, the only thing that exists is them, each dressed in a suit that makes them explosively hot. None are wearing ties, and I love that small rebellion, not to mention the peek at inked-up skin that their slightly open shirts give. I have to bite my lip when I spot Forest wearing his cowboy boots, and when I look back up, his face is full of smiles.

"Aspen, dear." My mother's voice breaks the spell, and I see Forest's brows dip before I turn away. "Come and say hello to Albert."

I swallow hard as bile rushes up my throat and I turn to see Albert fucking Pennington the Third standing next to the Ambassador and another man who I assume is his father. Albert looks handsome, in that boy next door kind of way, and when he glances over to see me coming his way, he gives me a wide, feline grin.

"You look beautiful, Aspen," he says, placing his hand on my waist and leaning in to kiss my cheek. "Shame about the stench of dog that clings to you, but no worry, we'll soon have that taken care of." My jaw clenches, my body strung tight, and I swear I hear growls somewhere behind me. "Let me introduce you to my father."

I give him a tight smile, hating the feel of his hand at the small of my back as he guides me to where his father is standing next to the

Ambassador. I'd try to wiggle out of his touch, but all eyes are on us and I daren't risk the Ambassador suspecting my dislike of Albert.

"Well, so here she is. The beautiful English rose my son keeps talking about," the man exclaims. He's like an older version of his son, handsome but with a definite coldness just like the Ambassador, and I have to suppress a shiver that runs down my spine. "And what a beautiful couple. I'm so glad our families will be aligned."

My brows furrow, not quite understanding his words.

"I suppose now is as good a time as any to make the announcement, Albie," the Ambassador says with a rueful chuckle. "Everybody, we have some wonderful news, and it's not just that there is a new king on the throne of England." Chuckles ring out around the room but they all sound sinister to my ears, my pulse almost drowning them out as I break out into a sweat. "Although we've only been here a short while, it seems that our daughter, Aspen, has found someone she wants to spend the rest of her life with." My eyes dart to the Saints, all of whom have matching furrowed brows and clenched jaws. "And, indulgent father that I am, I can't deny my little girl the happiness she desires." He turns to me, a look of love and joy on his face that stops my heart because it's such a convincing lie. He doesn't give a shit about my happiness, only my obedience. "I'd like to announce her engagement to Albert Pennington the Third. A toast to the happy couple."

Blood rushes in my ears, my gaze locked on his cold eyes that dare me to defy him in front of all these people. I'm barely breathing, the edges of the room swimming, but then I'm wrapped in my mother's arms, again something that never happens, and the spell the Ambassador had me under is broken, the room rushing back in.

"Smile, dear," she hisses in my ear, and my lips respond even as my heart shatters, my soul screaming that the men I want to be tied to are standing across the room. As if they are my north, my eyes find them over my mother's shoulder to see Forest deathly pale, his sparkling green eyes dull and his fists clenched. Blaine looks thunderous, his nostrils flared and shoulders tense as he stands frozen, like if he moves even a muscle he'll explode. My gaze then finds Lan, his dark eyes narrowed not on me, but on Albert who is next to me, his hand being pumped enthusiastically by the Ambassador. His neck is corded, his fists clenching and unclenching as his eyes swing to the Ambassador.

"Welcome to the family, daughter-in-law," Albert's father says, taking the place of my mother and pressing a wet kiss to my cheek. "I can't wait for you to join us."

Bile fills my throat, my smile wavering as I have to swallow it down or risk throwing up all over him. I guess there wouldn't be much, not having been allowed breakfast this morning has left my stomach empty and aching.

I lose sight of my Saints as more people come to congratulate me, Albert slipping the most gaudy diamond ring on my finger to a round of applause. The rest of the party passes in a blur, one that I'm mostly silent for. After all, my opinion means nothing at this point, so why bother speaking at all. Plus, I'm not sure I could talk past the lump that fills my throat, which only grows every time I get a glimpse of one of the Saints. I feel their eyes on me the entire time, the comforting weight of their gazes never leaving me alone.

I stroke the pearls at my throat more than once, allowing it to bring me some relief from the situation that I'm in. I should have known, my triumph last night was never going to last. I just thought that I had more time. More time to work on a way out.

"So, when's the big day?" a voice asks, breaking me out of my pity party.

"Well, it seems that these two can't wait to get hitched." The Ambassador chuckles, the sound slithering over my skin like a snake trying to find the perfect place to choke me. "So next Sunday is the plan. It'll be an intimate affair, just close friends and family..."

The rest of his words are lost to me as I stumble a little even though I haven't moved. A strong grip steadies my elbow, the scent of lavender and leather almost undoing the mask that slammed down into place the moment the announcement was made.

"Careful, Duchess," Lan whispers in my ear from behind, the warmth of his body so close that I can feel it along my back. "I've got you."

It takes a gargantuan effort not to sag back into him or burst into tears, and for the first time, I'm grateful for the Ambassador's training. The touch is gone as fast as it came, and when the Ambassador's eyes find mine, I breathe a sigh of relief knowing that Lan is gone, even if my soul screams and rages at a world that would take him away from me.

I'm exhausted by the time the party ends, and can barely hold my smile in place as the guests leave, Albert's parents hugging me and his mother gushing about the plans she and my mother have for our nuptials.

I'm just about to head to my room, needing the sanctuary to finally drop the mask and break down, when the Ambassador calls to me.

"In my office, Aspen," he commands in a tone that sends shivers down my spine.

My feet follow him without thought, my body knowing the best way to avoid his anger is to obey without question. I enter the room behind him, my stomach in knots and heart racing as I look at the ground, not wanting to invoke any kind of anger.

The scent of lavender and leather washes over me, snapping my head up, and my stomach drops, my heart ceasing to beat altogether when I see Lan waiting by the large desk. I flinch as the door clicks shut behind me, my eyes never leaving the leader of the Saints.

"I'm not sure if it's more insulting that you snuck behind my back, or that you thought I wouldn't discover your deception," the Ambassador says into the silence, and I swallow hard, tearing my eyes from Lan to look back at the man who sired me. He chuckles, but it's a horrible sound, like the scratch of branches against a window in the dead of night. "Now, you both have a choice to make. You stop this foolishness and get on with your lives as if you'd never met, or I give my friends at the police department all the evidence I've gathered of the Tainted Saints criminal activity and you and your *brothers* go down for a very, very long time."

Pain lances my chest at his words that paint an all too vivid picture of Lan, Forest, and Blaine behind bars for the rest of their lives. Caged like beautiful beasts, never to be free, for I have no doubt that is what will happen. My legs feel weak, every breath I take like a rasp in my chest, burning and unable to really reach my lungs.

"You're not the most powerful player on the board," Lan grits out, and I swing my gaze to him, the skin on his face mottled, his lips pulled back, teeth barred as if he's about to rip the throat of the Ambassador clean off.

The older man just chuckles again, goosebumps peppering my flesh. "Oh, you mean your mob ties? The federal government is very interested in those, having been after your uncle and his goons for years. What my team has on them will ensure swift and brutal punishment, not unlike what happened to your father." My eyes widen, my heart cracking as Lan's jaw clenches even more. "I'll leave you to make the right choice; this childish infatuation or your future."

I'm frozen as the Ambassador leaves, shutting the door behind us. I don't trust it, the space he's given us, but I guess being faced with an impossible decision is punishment in itself. Just the sort of game he enjoys.

"We'll run." Lan's voice is deeper than I've ever heard it, and he turns to look at me, his midnight eyes fierce.

"He'll find us," I breathe out, tears stinging my eyes, my entire world collapsing when the realisation hits me that there's only one choice.

"I don't fucking care, I'll keep running, Aspen." His chest heaves, his voice choked with emotion as he steps closer.

"And Forest? Blaine? What happens when he catches them?" His jaw tightens once again, his fists clenching at his sides.

"So what? We just give up? We just let him win?" He throws his arms wide, his head shaking in denial, the whites of his eyes showing the panic that I feel to my very bones.

I can't fight it anymore, the need to be held by him is too strong. I go to him, pressing myself against his trembling body, and his arms immediately cage me to him, pulling me so close until there's no space between us. The devastation I've been holding back washes over me, drowning me, and for a few moments, I just sob as he holds me.

Somehow, I find the strength to rein it in enough to look up at him, finding his cheeks damp with his own sorrow.

"Tell them it was just a fling for me, just a rebellion against my father." My voice is a broken whisper, the words cutting me and making me bleed as they leave my lips, hot tears trailing down my face.

"They won't believe me," he tells me, his voice thick and broken. He knows that this is the only way, and I know he'll do anything to protect his chosen brothers, his family.

"They will when they learn that I was engaged all along to Albert." He rears back, but I grip the front of his T-shirt in my fists. "You have to make them believe it, Lan. It's the only way to keep them safe." His jaw works, then he gives a nod, but his arms tighten around me to the point of pain. I don't care though, it's nothing compared to the fracturing of my soul right now.

"I will always fucking love you, Aspen Buckingham." Fresh tears fall down his cheeks, and I have to force the words past the lump in my throat which threatens to choke me.

"I will always fucking love you, Landon."

Then he leans down, placing his lips against my own and I taste the salt of our despair, coating us like a black mist that clings to your very bones and chills you to the core. All too soon, our kiss ends and he lets me go, taking one step, then another, turning around and striding from the room, leaving me more alone than I've ever been.

Then I shatter into a thousand tiny pieces as I crumple to the floor and wish my heart would stop beating.

CHAPTER 33

"THE GOOD DIE YOUNG" BY ELLEY DUHÉ

FOREST

She won't even look at us. Every fucking day this week I've tried to gain her attention and it's like we don't exist, Albert's hands all fucking over her as she hangs around with his crew, even ignoring her friend, the Irish one.

When Lan came back from that party, his eyes red, and told us what the Ambassador had said, what she'd tried to convince him to tell us, I was all for ending her father right now.

I wasn't angry at our girl, she was doing what she thought it took to protect us, but how many fucking times did I tell her that we can take care of ourselves? I guess we just have to show her.

My phone pings as I sit on our couch, knowing that this Friday evening no knock will sound on the door.

Wallace: Sacromant County Park. This Saturday, 9pm.

"Are those details for the fight?" Lan asks, his glance pained as it darts to Bolt lying next to me.

"Yeah." I sigh, feeling a hollow in my chest where a blonde beauty should be. It hurts to see her with that dumbass every day. Not to mention the urge to go and rip his fucking hands off for daring to touch her was almost overwhelming. "Sacromant County Park, 9pm tomorrow."

Lan nods, Blaine doing the same. The big guy has barely spoken since the weekend, just working out like crazy. I know he feels just as frustrated as the rest of us, but we will get her back. No other option is acceptable.

"Okay, it's going to be cutting it fine but we can do it," Lan states aloud, looking from me to Blaine. "We do the dog fight, get the intel for Alfonso, and then we kidnap Duchess and get the fuck out of here."

I watch as a grim smile crosses Blaine's face, and I'm sure I'm wearing a matching one.

"We can get the security down around her home for about fifteen, maybe twenty minutes max," I tell them, going over the plan that we came up with last Sunday. There was no way we were ever going to let her marry that fucktard, or leave her with her family. I glance at Bolt, a pang going through me at the danger we're putting him in. He used to be aggressive to other dogs and people, was almost put down before I took his training on and showed him another way. I just have to hope that he remembers his survival instincts. It still cuts like a knife to think about even putting him in that ring, like I'm betraying one of my best friends.

"He'll be fine, we've got Roger on standby," Lan tells me, clearly seeing where my mind just went. Roger is the Pound's vet, and a good man to boot. We've not told him what he's on standby for, he'd chew our hides if he knew, but it's reassuring to know that he'll be able to patch Bolt up if need be.

"So now we wait," I huff, glancing between my brothers who both look as antsy as I feel.

SATURDAY DRAGS, ESPECIALLY WITHOUT MY BEAUTIFUL HELPER as I see to all the dogs. It's not the same without her, there's no laughter and her angelic voice singing to them floating through the space.

But, soon, after a sombre dinner of pasta that Lan made us choke down, it's time to go. With a heavy sigh, I clip a leash to Bolt's collar, barely able to look at him as I lead him from our apartment.

A car idles next to the sidewalk, and Bobby hops out, pulling Blaine into a hug.

"Stay safe, cuz," he murmurs, loud enough that I hear.

"It's not us that you need to worry about, son," I utter as Blaine gets into the driver's side, Bobby lending us his car as we can't exactly take Bolt on the bikes.

"Just keep your wits about you. Those rich pricks are slimy fuckers and I don't trust the Ambassador to not have something planned for you guys," Bobby tells me, clapping me on the shoulder and then going to shake Lan's hand.

He hands Lan something metal, and my brows furrow when I realise it's a knife. We were warned not to bring guns or weapons of any kind, but it seems that Bobby is serious about not trusting the Ambassador. Lan tucks the blade down the back of his pants, giving Bobby a firm handshake and then getting into the passenger side.

With a heart that's made of fucking lead, I get Bolt into the back, climbing in beside him and resting my head back as Blaine takes off down the road with the purr of the engine.

It takes a little over an hour and a half to get to the woods, and it's completely dark when we pull up in a lot filled with Bentleys and other million-dollar cars.

My lip curls as I take in the wealth surrounding us as we leave Bobby's old Mustang and head into the trees. Bolt growls low as we approach a clearing. I want to reassure him, but I can't. My voice is trapped behind a lump so fucking big that I'm surprised I can still breathe. This feels wrong, so fucking wrong.

All the hair rises on my arms as we approach a small clearing, a circle of men filling it. The circle opens up and we see several dogs, all standing and eyes locked on us and Bolt. My brows dip as I take them in. They're not the usual fighting breeds. No, these dogs look like bloodhounds, tracking dogs that are often used to find people. The stamp and whinny of hooves has my head snapping to the side, my chest tingling as I take in the horses that are being held on tight reins. They paw at the ground, chomping at the bit, and I know that something definitely isn't right here.

"Boys, so glad you decided to join us," a voice calls out, and it takes every ounce of control I didn't know I possessed not to launch myself at Aspen's sperm donor, the Ambassador. His grin is wide in the moonlight, and he looks ridiculous dressed in a bright red tailcoat. "It would have been disappointing indeed if you'd not showed up."

"What the fuck is going on?" Lan grits out, clearly sensing the same wrongness about the situation as I do.

"Ah, I suppose we should let the cat out of the bag so to speak." The older man chuckles, and there are low rasps of laughter from the other five men that have formed a semicircle in front of us. "We do run dog fights, as you know, but sometimes we like a little something more challenging to entertain ourselves with. You see, back in England, they banned fox hunting, a poor show indeed," he tells us with a hint of irritation in his tone, and my stomach sinks. "But, we are not in England, and apparently, there aren't many foxes around these parts." Again, low chuckles fill the space and I want to shoot each and every one of them. Bolt growls again, the other dogs responding in kind until their handlers hush them. "So, we moved on to a more...stimulating quarry."

"If you think we will let you hunt us, old man, you are more fucking stupid than you look," Lan sneers, and I smile. I love it when Daddy gets all arrogant. My grin grows when the Ambassador's smile falters, his cheek twitching.

"So you have no interest in my daughter then?" We all go still, my chest barely moving as I wait for him to continue. "I have a deal of sorts for you boys. You play along with our little game, and if you evade capture until midnight, you can have her. I shall leave her on your doorstep like one of those abandoned mutts you take in. We'll even give you an hour's head start."

A low rumble sounds from Blaine next to me, and I'm inclined to agree with Big Daddy. I want to rip out his tongue for daring to speak of her like that.

"And if you catch us?" Lan asks, and I can't fault him for contemplating the devil's bargain. I would have taken it without even asking, because there's no way we will lose.

"You never see her again, you leave Fairview and set up your little enterprise somewhere far, far away," the Ambassador offers, his tone even and oh so reasonable.

"A moment," Lan grits out, trusting Blaine to have his back as he faces us, ushering us closer. "Thoughts?"

"I say let's do it," I rush out, grabbing onto any chance to get our girl.

"And what about Alfonso's proof?" Lan asks, his brows lowered.

"This is something we can take to him. I doubt we're the first they've hunted. He practically told us they've done this before," Blaine growls out, and I have to agree. There must be a trail Alfonso and his people can follow.

"So we evade them for the next"—Lan checks his watch—"two and three-quarter hours." My heart thuds painfully. It's a long fucking time to be running, but you don't get to be the leaders of a pretty badass gang without learning about hiding from the feds. *This can't be too much harder, can it?*

"Nothing that was ever worth it was easy," I say, and they both nod. "Let's go earn our girl."

We break apart, facing the waiting men once more.

"We agree to your terms," Lan states in a hard voice, and I don't imagine the glee that lights up more than one face in the dark. They look like fucking ghouls, and shivers run across my skin at the deal we've just made with these creatures.

"Excellent," the Ambassador coos, and I swallow hard. Something still isn't right here, but I can't put my finger on it. "Your extra hour starts now."

A thrill runs down my spine as I unclip Bolt's lead, knowing that he'll follow us and it'll be easier if he's free to move.

We take off at a sprint into the dark woods that surround us, Lan in the lead as usual, and soon we can no longer hear the horses or dogs, just the silence of nature around us and our own footfalls and heavy breathing.

"It'll be harder for them to follow us if we stick to the trees," Blaine huffs, his chest heaving as we slow to a jog, pacing ourselves. Now that we've got ahead, we need to keep our energy for the next couple of hours ahead. "The dogs can sniff us out, but the horses won't be able to get to us as easily."

I shrug off my light hoodie. "Let's leave a false trail to confuse the dogs," I tell them, running in a random direction for a few seconds, throwing my hoodie and then doubling back to meet up with the other two who paused when I took off. We move on, lightly jogging, and then Blaine copies me, Lan doing the same when we've gone a bit further. Then we take a new direction, we can always do the same with our shirts if we need to, although it's fucking freezing out so I'd rather keep something to stave off the cold.

All the hair on my body stands on end when a hunting horn sounds in the distance, our eyes connecting for a second, then we pick up the pace, following a river that we came upon which takes us deeper into the park.

I know that this area is a mix of woods and open grassland, but as Blaine says, it's better to stick to the woods, although they may be able to see our trail through the broken undergrowth if they've got some decent trackers. The odds may be against us, but we have a determination that they lack. We know how to survive when it seems like that is impossible.

I jump when the sound of a shot rings out in the night.

"They've got fucking guns," Lan pants, his jaw clenching as we pick up speed again. "We have one knife between us."

"Well, luckily we're good at running, Daddy," I puff out, my chest starting to burn a little as we keep moving. The discomfort will have to wait, we can't afford to let our guard down.

Bolt is by my side, though Lan is up ahead, he's always been closer to me and it warms my soul to have him here, even if this is a fucking dangerous situation. The sounds of dogs barking fills the night air, and it's way too close for my liking.

"We have to split up," Blaine states, barely out of breath even though sweat dots his brows. The moon is both a blessing and a curse because it lights our way, but will also make our paths that much more obvious.

"No," Lan growls, his fists clenched as he jogs.

"It'll send them in different directions, confuse the dogs more," Blaine reasons, and although I don't want to separate from them, it does make the most sense. "We have our phones so we can call each other if need be. Just make sure they're on vibrate only."

Reaching into my pocket I do just that, cursing myself for not thinking about it sooner.

"He's right, Lan," I huff out, Bolt growling low in his chest but not barking, like he knows that would give us away in an instant. "We need all the advantages we can get."

"Fuck," Lan hisses, knowing that we're right but hating it as much as I do. "Fine, we split up, but I swear to fucking god if they catch either of you I will kill you myself."

"Love you too, Daddy," I tell him, veering off down a small deer track, Bolt at my side. I check my watch, we have an hour left. That's nothing really.

My heart races as I hear the sounds of crashing hooves from somewhere nearby, and I try to keep as quiet as possible while also going as fast as I can. The sound seems like it's getting closer, but looking around, I can't see anything so I go down another small pathway, jogging for several heart-stopping moments as it feels like whoever is chasing me is catching up.

A shot rings out, making my ears ring as I jerk and stumble, falling to the ground with a grunt. Rolling onto my back, I look down to see a flower of blood blooming on my pec, my brows dipping as I feel no pain. It takes a moment for the fact that I've been shot to register, my body so full of adrenaline that it doesn't even hurt, but as the flower grows and my head starts to swim, I know it must be a bit serious.

"Fuck," I say, only it's a bit garbled, like I've been drinking too much of my favourite whiskey. Bolt whines next to me, then growls low, his lips pulled back to expose sharp canines as the sound of hoofbeats slows and then stops.

"Gottcha," a voice I vaguely recognise says, and blinking, I watch as the figure dismounts, a shotgun slung over his arm, sauntering towards me. It's not until the moon hits his face that I know where I've seen him before. He's that asshole's father, Albert Pennington the Second, I assume. Dumbass name. "Time to finish the job."

I blink, but it feels slow, and although I try to get up, to move away or do fucking something, my limbs are too heavy and just won't obey. I blink again, the sound of a snarl and then a man's screams assaulting my ears, and slowly, I try to make sense of the image that is now before me.

The man, Albert, is writhing on the ground, Bolt with his jaws clamped around his neck, the shotgun lying on the ground. The horse is gone, but I know the sounds will draw the other hunters. I try to reach for the gun, but my fucking arms won't obey, and then a gurgling sound has my eyes darting back to watch as Bolt tears Albert's throat clean out, lifeless eyes looking at me as he dies.

"Forest!" a hiss sounds from my other side, then hands are cupping my face, Lan's dark eyes full of storms. He always had such beautiful eyes. "Don't you fucking dare die!"

I gasp as white-hot pain flares in my shoulder, seeing Blaine on my other side with his T-shirt balled into his fist as he plugs the wound, but the coldness spreading across my limbs tells me that they may just be too late.

"Take care of her, Lan," I say, my voice barely above a whisper. "Keep her safe."

"You will be there to help me do all of that," Lan chokes out, his head lowering as he presses a tender kiss to my lips. "You are not leaving us, we won. It's midnight."

I breathe a sigh of relief, knowing that Aspen is finally free. My Little Lady, our angel is ours and safe from the Ambassador. A frown dips my brows.

"Take him out, he can't be trusted, Daddy," I breathe out, hoping Lan knows who I'm talking about.

"You can help me, help us," Lan promises, but I know that it's hope speaking, not fact.

"We need to get him back to the car and to Howard right the fuck now," Blaine grits out, but the darkness around me is already closing in.

"Stay with us, please, Forest," Lan begs, and I hate the sob in his voice, but I'm helpless to say anything in response as I'm engulfed in black as dark as his eyes.

CHAPTER 34

"HANDS" BY ORKID

ASPEN

I wake up with a gasp, the most awful nightmare still fresh in my mind. It was so cold and dark, and I could hear Forest calling for me but I couldn't find him. I wipe my cheeks, my fingers coming away damp, the salt of my sadness staining them just as the door opens and Rosie walks in.

She looks away as soon as our eyes connect, but I don't miss the red rim around hers, the sympathy making them dull.

"What's wrong?" I breathe out, shards of glass lodging in my throat as I force the words out.

"Oh, Miss Aspen," she whispers, coming over to me and taking my cold hand in hers. "I'm so sorry."

"For what?" I can hardly get the words out, shivers making my hands tremble.

"Some of the others were saying there was a hunt last night," she chokes out, her voice thick and her eyes filling.

"A hunt? I don't know what that means." I shake my head, trying to work out what the fuck she's talking about.

"The Saints were offered a deal; if they could evade capture by the hunters, they could take you," she tells me, her eyes locked on mine, and all I see is sorrow and pain. "But they lost, Miss, and they were tricked because the hunters had guns."

A shuddered exhale leaves my chest, knowing what she's going to say before the words fall from her lips.

"They didn't win, Miss."

The world stops spinning, my lungs no longer taking in any oxygen as those terrible words sink in.

"Rosie." It's his voice, the sound of my tormentor, and it snaps me out of my desolation, white-hot rage pulsing through me. Rosie jumps as I leap out of the bed, launching myself at him. He catches me, his cruel hands burning when they grip my arms in a punishing hold.

"I did everything you asked! You didn't have to..." The anger drains out of me as the reality of the situation sinks in.

They're dead. He killed them and there is nothing I can do to bring them back.

It's all my fault. I fall to the floor when he releases me suddenly as my weight sags, but the pain of hitting the rug is nothing to the tearing of my soul. I look up at him, his lips curled and his eyes cold, flat, and dead-looking.

"Get her cleaned up," he orders, then strides out of the room as if he didn't just facilitate the death of three men, my soulmates.

"It's better this way," my mother says, gripping my arm and hauling me to my feet, pushing me onto the stool that sits in front of my dressing table. "It's easier to just give in to his demands. Why could you never see that? We all have to make the best of the hand that we're dealt with."

I look at her, really look at her, and for the first time, I wonder what she was like before she married a monster. Did she know what he was like before their wedding? Or was she sacrificed by her family too?

"Now, let's get you cleaned up and ready for your future husband. You will walk in on the arm of your father, smiling like all brides do on their wedding day." I sneer at her, uncaring of how ugly I must look at this moment.

"He. Is. Not. My. Father," I grit out between clenched teeth, that flare of rage like a candle burning in my heart. "And you have never earned the title of mother, not in any way that matters."

She recoils, her eyes tracing me before her trembling hands smooth down her outfit. Something befitting the mother of the bride, all lilac lace, and it fills my mouth with bile.

"Get her ready, Rosie," she commands, her demeanour straightening and back to the cold woman that I've known my entire life. Then she, too, is gone, and like she took all my bravado with her, I slump, silent, useless tears tracking down my cheeks.

"Come now, Miss. Let's get you sorted," Rosie cajoles gently, leaving me, and the sound of the shower comes on a few moments later. She's back by my side, helping me to stand and walking me over to the bathroom. "Best to do what they say for now, Miss."

It's as though time slows and speeds all at once, and the next time I look at myself, I'm in a white lace dress that flows around my body, in a style that I would have chosen if given a choice, and a long veil covering my face.

"You look stunning," Bruna compliments as she adjusts my veil, her usually happy eyes full of sadness.

I don't say anything back, no words will leave my mouth. What good will they do now? They're gone, the ones who my soul yearns for, and nothing will bring them back.

"Time to go, Aspen," my mother snaps from the door, and mutely, I follow her out and down the stairs to where the Ambassador waits. He gives me a callous once-over, nodding as if his approval means anything, and then we're heading outside into the early spring sunshine.

It's so at odds with how my morning has gone, how much has changed since I woke up, that I have to hold in a hysterical laugh. It's easy to do, just remembering the reason for my desolation has me retreating into the numbness that I'm hoping will get me through the day.

All too soon, we're pulling up outside a church that I've never even been to before today, so I guess money really can make the way smoother. My door is opened, the Ambassador there, placing my hand in the crook of his arm and it almost pulls me from my numbness.

Chills sweep over my body as we enter the cool building, the quiet murmur of the crowd drowned out by the playing of an organ. I've always hated organ music, but like with most things in my life, I wasn't given a choice.

They gave you a choice...

I shut that shit down fast. *This is not the place to break, Aspen.* I look straight ahead, paying no attention to the crowds of people sitting in the pews. If this is an intimate affair, I'd hate to see what a large wedding would be like.

Before I know it, we're at the front, Albert Pennington the Third waiting. He looks handsome in his suit, but there's something off about him, a redness to his eyes that has me wondering what sorrow he's facing today. A loud sniffle has me glancing to the front pew behind him, catching sight of his mother with a handkerchief to her eyes, but it doesn't look like joy written across her features. No, her eyes are puffy, her spine bowed as another woman wraps an arm around her.

My attention is drawn back to Albert as the Ambassador places my hand in his, giving the younger man a squeeze on his shoulder.

"He would be proud, son," the Ambassador says in a low voice to the younger man, Albert clenching his jaw and giving him a nod.

It's enough to penetrate the numb fog that surrounds me, making me wonder what is going on. Of course no one has told me, although, maybe they did and I just wasn't listening.

"Dearly beloved..." the vicar begins, drawing my gaze to the old man in his fancy embroidered robes. His words wash over me, my mind racing with what has happened this morning.

They're gone...

I take a sharp breath, drawing the attention of Albert, my fiancé, but I don't see him. All I can picture is Forest's laughing face, Lan's midnight eyes staring into my soul, and Blaine's steady presence, always protecting me from any threat. Only, he's not here. They're not here, and I am the only one who can make sure they're sacrifice isn't in vain.

"If anyone sees any reason why these two shall not be wed, speak now or forever hold your peace," the man continues, and like a tsunami, the words fall from my lips.

"No." I look up, registering the shock on the old man's face but it's done and the relief I feel almost brings me to tears. "I don't want this."

"Aspen," the Ambassador growls, but before he can take a step, the large doors at the entrance slam open, drawing everyone's gaze to them.

My heart skips a beat as three men enter the church, and I blink several times to ensure that they are not ghosts or figments of my imagination.

"I object," Lan's deep voice booms, bouncing off the walls as he walks towards the front, his eyes on me. He looks like hell, his shirt covered in blood that has me frantically trying to see where his injuries lie.

"I object," Blaine states next, and I look at him, seeing that he's in not much better condition, and is supporting Forest as he limps down the aisle.

"I object," Forest grits out, a sheen of sweat making his forehead glisten, his usually golden face pale and lined with pain. He's shirtless, the arm not slung over Blaine's shoulders is in a sling, and there's a bandage over his right pec, a hint of red in the centre.

"Stop them!" the Ambassador roars, but no one does, and then

Lan is before me, lifting my veil and cupping my face in hands that have dried blood underneath his nails.

"Y–you're n–not dead," I stutter, hardly able to take a breath as I trace his face with my gaze, my hands tentatively reaching up and brushing his cheeks. "They told me..." I can't finish, my eyes full of tears as he leans down and places his lips on mine, proving that he is very much alive and here.

A sob falls from my lips, my hands pulling him to me by his neck, pressing our bodies close. I vaguely hear gasps and murmurs from around us, but I don't give a shit what they think. All I know is Lan's lips on mine, his tongue stroking mine and telling me that I will never be without them again.

"Get off her!" the Ambassador snarls, and I pull slowly back, no longer afraid of him with my soulmates so close.

I turn to look at the man who has been my nightmare, who has ruled my life, and feel nothing but apathy for him.

"You don't get a say in my life anymore," I tell him, my own voice strong and sounding like the woman I always wanted to be. "And you will never lock me in the dark again."

His cheeks flush as the murmurs of the crowd grow louder, and a smile grows on my face at the fact that I have some power over him, even if it's small. Dismissing him as he always did me, I turn my back and go to Blaine.

"*Hola, mi tesoro,*" he says in that delicious voice of his, and I give him a quick kiss too, just to assure myself that he, too, is real. Then I turn to Forest, my brows pinched as I take in the pain he's clearly in.

"Forest?" I ask, but it's more of a whisper, and ignoring his injury, he pulls me into him, his scent of rose, gin, and leather tinged with copper.

"I'm here, sugar. As if we'd ever leave you," he whispers into my ear as I stifle a cry and cling to him. "Come now, let's take you home."

Nodding, I wrap my arm around his waist, wanting to help support his other side and grateful for the wide aisle that allows me to do that.

"Don't you dare walk away, Aspen," the Ambassador snarls, and I pause, looking over my shoulder at him. His face is mottled, his hands clenched into fists at his side, but it's not frightening, it's pathetic.

For a moment, I want to say something, to rage at how poorly he's treated me my whole life. Then I realise that he doesn't deserve anything more from me, that the worst thing I can do to him is act as if he's of no consequence. So, like he doesn't matter at all, which he doesn't anymore, I turn back to the front and we make our way down the aisle and into the sunshine.

CHAPTER 35

"ELEPHANT" BY FREYA RIDINGS

ASPEN

We take a car back to the Pound, the place that feels so much more like home than the huge Ambassador's residence ever did. I have to swallow the lump in my throat when we walk towards the door and Bolt comes bounding up to us, rubbing his head against my hand for scratches.

"You doing okay, Duchess?" Lan asks when I pause in the doorway, blinking rapidly to stop the tears that have gathered from falling.

"I thought I'd never see this place again," I confess in a whisper, looking around at the small space and feeling relaxed for the first time in over a week.

Blaine turns to face me after helping Forest get settled on the couch. "It's your home now, for however long you want it."

"Always," I tell him without missing a beat, earning one of his rare smiles.

"In that case," Lan says, his lips twitching as he hoists me into his arms, bridal style.

"What are you doing?" I giggle, wrapping my arms around his neck and letting him carry me into the room. He kicks the door shut behind him, never loosening his hold.

"Well, this is what you do with brides, Duchess," he tells me, his condescending tone earning him a slap on his ridiculously hard pec. The fucker just laughs, bending down and placing me in Forest's lap.

"Careful!" I admonish as Forest winces slightly, but he just wraps his good arm around me and pulls me closer, my dress flowing over us both and pooling on the floor.

"I'm okay, Little Lady," he assures me, kissing my cheek lightly and taking a huge inhale. "The worst part of almost dying was thinking I'd never hold you again, so let me enjoy it."

"What happened?" I ask softly, brushing my fingers around the bandage.

"Albert's pops shot me," he states, casual as fuck. I rear back, eyes wide.

"He did what? Why aren't you at the hospital? Jesus, Forest, has anyone—" He cuts me off with a finger to my lips, a broad smile on his face, though frankly, I don't see what he's grinning about. He was shot, for fuck's sake.

"We took Forest to a guy we know, who always patches us up when shit goes south," Blaine informs me, handing Forest a glass of whiskey and then passing me one before going back for his own.

"You've needed his help often?" I ask, nibbling my lower lip when I think about any of them hurt and needing to be patched up. I've only just got them back, it's too raw to think of the possibility of them being taken away so soon.

"Hey," Forest murmurs, setting his glass down and brushing his fingers over my cheek. They come away glistening. "We're okay, sugar."

"T–they told me you were dead, and I didn't—I couldn't—" My words end in a whimper, and I bury my face in his neck as I just let go. The pain and misery of thinking that they no longer walked the earth washes over me, mixing with the sheer relief and discovering they are alive and breathing.

"It's okay, Duchess," Lan breathes in my ear, his body pressed against mine from behind, Blaine's large palm stroking up and down my arm as Forest holds me tightly. "We will never leave you, Saint's promise."

I chuckle, although it's a watery-sounding laugh. "Saint's promise?"

"Yep." Forest grins when I look up at him. "It's more sacred than a pinky promise." His eyes sparkle, even if there is an edge of pain.

"You should be resting in bed," I say, letting him once again wipe the tears from my cheeks.

"I'll go to bed if you join me," he counters, and a spark of heat flares in my core, but I tamp that shit down.

"Only to sleep, you're injured," I tell him in a stern voice.

"Sure, sugar," he says, but the smile playing around his lips makes his words a barefaced lie.

Still, Lan helps me off Forest's lap, and Blaine helps him off the couch, then we all head in the direction of the bedrooms. Lan takes us to his, and I smile when I see the beds still pushed together. I like the idea that they've been sleeping together, even if I'm not here.

Blaine takes Forest around to the side, and I watch as he undoes Forest's belt, popping each button slowly in a tease that has my breath speeding up when Blaine pushes Forest's jeans down his hips, exposing the hard length of the other man's dick.

"Will you let us celebrate the fact that we're all alive and together?" Lan whispers in my ear, his fingers tracing the line of small pearl buttons that fasten the back of my dress.

"Yes," I breathe out, unable to deny his request even if I worry that it might be too much for Forest.

My breath catches when Blaine sinks to his knees, taking Forest's cock in his hand and guiding it to his lips. He licks the head, Forest groaning deep and low when Blaine swallows him down whole, Forest's hand grabbing a fistful of Blaine's thick hair.

"Fuck, Big Daddy," Forest moans, and my dress pools at my feet, my attention so taken up with the erotic scene before me that I'd missed Lan undoing all my buttons.

"I hope you weren't wearing that for him, Duchess," Lan growls, running a finger down my ivory lace corset. I wasn't even really aware of what was being put on me this morning, too lost to grief and my chest tightens with the reminder. "No matter, you're ours now and we get to reap the rewards."

My lips part as he runs his tongue up my neck, placing small, teasing kisses on my skin that have me lifting my chin and arching into him, closing my eyes just so I can feel him better.

"Fuck, Little Lady, you look exquisite," Forest breathes, and I open my lids to gaze at him with hooded eyes, an expression of pure desire on his beautiful face. My arms come up and I pull Lan closer, eliminating any space between us and he rumbles his approval, sucking my neck harder, marking me as his.

"Forest, lie down on the bed so our girl can ride you," Lan orders in a low voice, and I watch as Blaine pops off Forest's dick, helping him to do as Lan commanded. "You're going to show him exactly why he fought to stay with us, aren't you, angel?"

"Yes, sir," I whisper, slipping out of my heels, but pausing when Lan grabs my arm.

"One moment, Duchess." He lets go and then takes out a flip knife from his pocket, my heartbeat crashing in my ears as he flips it open. "Don't move."

I stand still as he slides it underneath the side of my lace knickers, quickly slicing the fabric and repeating the same on the other side. They fall to the floor, leaving me in just my lace corset, suspenders, and stockings, and the look he gives me is borderline animalistic, especially as he's still covered in his friend's blood. The sight only has my core clenching, heat lighting up my body.

"Good girl, now go and ride my boy," Lan orders, and I switch focus to the bed where Forest waits, naked with Blaine's hand around his dick, leisurely pumping it up and down.

"God, you're a fucking vision, sugar," Forest rasps as I crawl over him. Lowering my lips, I kiss him like it's the first time, like I could lose him at any moment and this is how I want to remember us. He grabs the back of my head and pulls me tighter to him, uncaring of the wound in his shoulder as he fuses our lips together and kisses me back just as fiercely.

I feel him nudge my entrance, and without taking my lips from his I sink down, gasping into his mouth as he fills me up.

"Fuck, Forest," I moan when he's fully seated inside me, my fingers clawing the bed either side of him. "Don't ever almost die again. You are not allowed to leave me." I move my hips and he groans this deep low sound that has wetness flooding between us.

"Saint's promise, beautiful," he murmurs, his good hand coming up and grasping my hip, helping to guide my movements.

We get lost in each other for a little while, my skin growing slick as he builds me up towards an orgasm that I know will destroy me in the best way possible.

"Think you can handle two of us in that pretty pink pussy, *mi amorsita*?" Blaine asks in my ear, and I moan a yes as my walls flutter around Forest at the idea of having them both inside me.

"Fuck, she wants you, Big Daddy," Forest gasps, helping to pull me closer to give Blaine the room he needs behind us. "You're such a good fucking girl for us, angel."

His lips crash onto mine, swallowing my gasp as Blaine pushes alongside Forest. The stretch is almost too much, my body trembling, the rough lace of my corset rubbing my nipples and adding to the overstimulation as I press against Forest.

"You good, *mi tesoro*?" Blaine rumbles, his voice strained as his fingers dig into my hips.

"More than good," I gasp as he thrusts all the way in, holding there while I shake and gasp around them both. "Please, please fuck me. Show me that you're mine."

"We were always yours," Blaine murmurs in a deep, gravelly voice, pulling out only to thrust back in and send me rocking on Forest.

They fuck me hard, punching into me with their dicks until I'm crying and begging for release. A hand wiggles between us, and I turn to see Lan lying naked next to us, his fingers finding my clit at the exact moment that our eyes meet.

"Come for your Saints, Duchess," he commands, and my body follows his decree without thought, my orgasm crashing over me and spraying all over the two men buried inside me. It's like the stars realign themselves, the world ceasing to exist outside of these four walls, outside of us and the magic that our bodies are creating.

"Fuck, baby," Forest hisses, holding me down on his dick as he groans out his own release, Blaine fucking us both through it, his hand a vice that holds me in place as he seeks his own climax.

I can't breathe, can't think, only able to focus on the movement of Blaine as he thrusts inside me, stretching me and prolonging my pleasure until I almost black out. With a guttural cry, he stalls, buried deep inside me, and I swear to god I feel him coating my insides with his release, Forest groaning underneath me as Blaine triggers another orgasm from my wrung-out body.

Panting, I collapse on top of Forest, trying to be mindful of his injury but unable to hold myself up any longer. My whole body feels alight, like I have lights under my skin and every inch of me tingles. Blaine pulls out, causing a shudder to run through my already overwrought body.

"Still one more Saint to fill you up, Duchess," Lan utters in my ear and I shiver, barely able to crack my lids and look up at him.

I gasp as he pulls me from Forest, lying me down next to him and smothering my body with his, entering me in a single, smooth motion. My body ignites, flickering with the promise of the pleasure that Lan is giving, even if I can barely move.

"Lan..." I moan, my voice husky and also desperate.

"Shhhh, Duchess. I got you," he whispers, moving his hips in a slow and sensual rhythm that has my hands grasping his shoulders, my fevered voice begging him not to stop. "Never, angel. Not until you come again for me like the good girl I know you are."

Lan makes love to me, building me up slowly until I burst into flames, crying out his name as tears squeeze from my eyes and I cling to him like a lifeline. He moans my name as he buries himself inside me moments later, holding me to him as if he's scared to let go.

"I love you, Aspen Buckingham," he purrs in my ear several moments later, kissing the side of my face.

"I love you, Landon," I breathe out, turning my face and catching Forest's gaze. "I love you, Forest."

He beams back at me, his smile the kind of thing angels weep over. "I love you back, sugar. So fucking much." Leaning over, he captures my lips, uncaring that Lan is still nestled inside my core like he never wants to leave.

Pulling back, I'm breathless but look to find chocolate-brown eyes staring at us, a warm smile on his face.

"I love you, Blaine Garcia. From that first night in jail." I huff a laugh, realising how much has changed since that night, but not Blaine. He's been my constant, my guiding star bringing me home.

Forest moves and Blaine leans in. "I knew you were mine from the moment you stepped into that cell, knew I needed you as much as you needed me, *mi princesa linda*. I love you with all my blackened heart. You make me, you make us, whole."

Tears stream down my cheeks and he brushes them away before kissing each one, and then his lips are on mine. He kisses me like we have the rest of our lives to do just this, to be in each other's arms, and I know that I'm finally home.

CHAPTER 36

"BECOME THE BEAST (PREDATOR REMIX)" BY KARLIENE

BLAINE

We clean ourselves up, Lan having showered, and he and Aspen making us all something to eat as I change Forest's dressing and check on his stitches. At least they held up, given the vigorous exercise he just took part in.

"I'm glad you're alive, Pup," I tell him, my voice thick as I smooth the edge of the bandage down. The memory of him passing out, blood seeping from the wound in his chest will be added to my nightmares for years to come.

"I'm glad too, Big Daddy," he replies, taking my trembling hand in his and placing a kiss on my knuckles. "All thanks to you, and now we have our girl back, all's right with the world."

I glance over my shoulder at her, Lan's arms wrapped around her from behind as she helps him chop something. He whispers in her ear and the blush that steals across her cheeks just makes her more beautiful. I love how easily we can make her colour up.

I watch them while they finish up whatever it is they are making, it smells delicious as Lan's cooking always does. She belongs with us, perfectly fits into our space and our lives as if she was always here.

"Grubs up," Lan declares a few minutes later, taking a pot to the table as Aspen carries large bowls and spoons over. "Grab the bread, would you, Blaine?"

I help Forest over to the table, then do as Lan asked and set the fresh loaf and butter down next to the steaming bowl.

"Italian skillet chicken," Aspen declares proudly as she lifts the lid and the smell increases tenfold.

"Smells almost as delicious as you, Little Lady," Forest comments, taking a bowl from her that she's just spooned some chicken and vegetables into.

"Lan did most of it." She blushes, and I smirk at the colour. So damn easy.

"You did great, Duchess," Lan says, kissing her cheek and helping her to spoon the rest out while I cut hunks of bread and pass them around.

After several moments of silence as we tuck in, I know that we need to address the elephant in the room sooner rather than later.

"The Ambassador needs to be dealt with," I state, wincing when Aspen's spoon clatters against her bowl.

"Y–you mean killed, don't you?" she asks quietly, and I nod, not wanting to sugar coat it.

"Even if we take all the evidence we have against him to the police, he has diplomatic immunity, never mind the fact he's probably paying them off in some way," Lan tells her, taking her hand in his and squeezing it. "This way, we don't have to run or hide for the rest of our lives either."

"Plus, he hurt you, so he has to die," Forest adds, and I grunt my approval. Forest's green eyes are hard, his usual smile missing from his face as he looks at our girl. "No one hurts you and doesn't pay for it."

Her eyes soften, and I love that she doesn't look at us with disgust or judgement, just love. "Will he suffer? Will he be terrified like he made me all those times he locked me away?"

Lan and Forest grin, a look that is pure devil, and I know that I have a matching one on my face.

"He will feel every second of terror and pain that he inflicted on you, Duchess," Lan vows, and I know that what he has planned is going to be good.

"Then I want in. I want to be there to see him suffer," she replies, and I have to adjust in my seat, my dick suddenly twitching in my sweats.

"It won't be pretty, angel," Lan warns, cupping her beautiful face in his large palm. "It may haunt you."

"Not more than what he did," she tells him, rubbing her face into his touch. "And I need to see with my own eyes that he's gone."

"Okay," I say, her eyes sliding to mine as her face lights up with a grateful smile. "You'll be there."

"Thank you." Her gaze goes back to Lan, and she leans in to press a kiss on his lips, then she twists, his hand falling away as she kisses Forest too.

"Let's make him rue the day he ever tried to mess with the Saints," she declares, holding up her water glass in a toast. *Coño*, she really is perfect for us.

"INTO IT" BY CHASE ATLANTIC

ASPEN

A few days go by and it's blissful. I relax the more I don't hear anything from the Ambassador and just live in bliss with my Saints. We don't go to school, though on Wednesday afternoon there's a light knock on the door, and Lan gives me a wink before going to open it.

"Aspen Buckingham, you bitch!" Aoife scolds as she storms in, handing Lan several bags and then rushing over to haul me into a hug. "Ghosting me for two fecking weeks, not telling me about a wedding until we get the fecking invitation, and then running into the sunset with gangsters! Let's begin there, shall we?"

She pulls back and I grimace, not really knowing what to say.

"I've been a terrible friend," I confess, and she scoffs.

"Yep, but luckily for you, I'm the forgiving type and as long as I get all the sordid details and some ice cream I'll forgive you," she assures me, pulling me down onto the couch, which I just stood up from, Blaine scooching over to make room. "Lan, be a doll and go get us some ice cream."

My eyes go wide, trying to contain my laugh as Forest doesn't even bother and howls from the chair. "Best do what she says, Daddy. I hear the Irish can get real mean when they're mad."

My gaze darts to Lan and I mouth sorry at him, but he just rolls his eyes, and somewhat to my surprise, drops the bags she brought on the table, grabs his keys and jacket, and heads out the door.

"Now, you two make yourselves scarce, it's girl time," she instructs, waving her hand.

"Yes, ma'am," Forest salutes her, trying to ease himself up. I wince as he grimaces, wanting to go to him, but Aoife has my hands in a vice-like grip.

"We'll just be down the hall, *mi tesoro*," he tells me as he gets up, brushing a kiss on my cheek, then going over to Forest to help him out of the chair.

Aoife sighs as we watch them disappear down the short hallway. "I guess that's the best we're going to get, they've not left your side since the wedding, have they?"

"Well, they are a little protective," I tell her softly, and she huffs a laugh.

"Girl, they stormed your wedding, covered in blood I might add, and practically threw you over their great big shoulders!" I chuckle, then stop.

"You were there?" I ask, guilt feeling like lead in my stomach when I realise I didn't even notice.

"Yep, though I just knew that you wouldn't ever marry that twat if you'd had a choice." Her gaze softens and she squeezes my hands. "What happened, Aspen? And what did you mean when you told the Ambassador that he'd never lock you in the dark again?"

I take a deep breath, then tell her my sorry tale, including stealing from the mall and getting arrested, then meeting Blaine and the others for the first time. Lan comes in halfway through, leaves the ice cream and two spoons on the coffee table, then goes into his bedroom with the others, giving us space so I can finish. She's quiet for several moments after I've recounted the last of it, and it's as if a weight has been lifted from me, like telling another soul has eased the shame I feel at the way my parents treated me.

"Jesus, Aspen, that's...feck, that's shite," she splutters, tears swimming in her eyes. "I'm so fecking sorry, if I'd known..."

"It's okay, you barely knew me, and I guess I was ashamed to tell anyone. Plus, I didn't want the Ambassador to target anyone else. Your dad's job could have been in jeopardy." She's shaking her head before I've even finished.

"He wouldn't have given a shite about all that. Family is the most important thing in the world to him, he would have taken you in," she tells me, and I heave a sigh, pulling her into a hug.

"Thank you, Aoife," I whisper as she hugs me back. "For being awesome."

"Well, leaving Albert at the altar and running off with three gangsters is the stuff of romance novels, that's main character energy right there!" She laughs, pulling away and then wagging her brows at me. "And I bet the sex is pretty incredible too?"

My cheeks burn, which just makes her laugh harder. We spend a bit longer catching up, and after making me promise to get back in touch when my love fest is over—and telling me that she wants all the gory details—she leaves, apparently, she had Bobby bring her over after threatening him bodily harm if he didn't.

That girl really is something special.

THAT EVENING, FOREST TURNS ON THE NEWS AND I FREEZE TO see the Ambassador's face all over it.

"It has been discovered that the British Ambassador has not only been running illegal dog fighting rings, but human hunts with many of his associates. It's believed that this is how Albert Pennington the Second lost his life, a hunt gone wrong..."

My wide eyes find Forest, who is smirking and looking all too pleased with himself.

"Keep watching, sugar," Forest tells me, using a finger to turn my head back to the screen. It's footage of the Ambassador's house.

"The Ambassador seems to have gone to ground, no one having set sights on him since the scandal of his daughter leaving Albert Pennington the Third jilted at the altar, though our sources tells us that she was being forced to marry the boy, though she, too, has disappeared since that day, supposedly on the arms of her three lovers."

I turn back to Forest, my heart racing as I stare at him.

"This was you?" I ask, my mind trying to work out what all this means.

"Well, technically, Alfonso and his guys had a hand in it, but yes.

We leaked the story to the press and it seems like they're having a field day with it." He chuckles.

"And the part about me running away with you guys?" If anything, his smile grows wider and although I want to be cross, I can't stop my lips from twitching.

"The gossip columns had that last week, it was a sensation, darlin'," he tells me, pulling me onto his lap while ignoring the injury in his shoulder. "But I would tell the entire world of our love if I could."

Any ire I have disappears, and I melt into him, our lips meeting just as the apartment door opens, letting in the chill evening air.

"You've seen the news?" Lan asks as he strides in, and I pull back from Forest's lips, the latter pouting at me and squeezing my arse with his hand, the other still in a sling to stop him from pulling the stitches.

"Yes," I tell him, noting the serious look on his face.

"Good, tonight we finish this," he tells me, not looking away as my heart thuds painfully in my chest.

"Tonight?" The word is a breath as I try to work out if I still want to cross that line. If I can watch them kill the man who tormented me my whole life.

His gaze softens and he comes towards me, crouching down until he can take my hand in his.

"You can leave at any moment, Duchess. One of us will take you if it becomes too much," he soothes, rubbing his thumb back and forth over my knuckles. "But the Ambassador will die tonight, by our hands."

I take a shaky inhale, squeezing his hand and nodding, making my choice. "I want to be there. I'll be okay."

"That's my girl." He smiles, pressing a kiss to my lips before getting up and heading over to the kitchen. "Now, let's have a nice meal together."

I take a deep breath, wondering when this became my new reality, when I became okay with the idea of killing a man. I guess we are all a product of our upbringing, and mine was designed to shut me away and make me detached from people. Only it backfired, because I've found the love I always craved, and the only one who I feel nothing for is the man who doled out my punishment.

We're sitting down to eat when I place my fork down and look up at each of them.

"So, I know we haven't really discussed my contribution to the household," I start, holding up a hand to quiet the protests that I can see on each of their lips. "But, my grandmother left me quite an inheritance that I'll come into when I'm nineteen in a couple of months. It's enough that I can help pay my way or if we want a bigger place one day..." My cheeks flush and I catch Blaine's smirk, my blush deepening when I remember our conversation in the gym back at the Ambassador's residence.

"We're fine where we are," Lan states, his tone brokering no arguments. "And we can take care of you, Duchess. It might not be what you're used to, but it's always been enough for us." I wince at the hurt in his voice, the way he won't look at me. Opening my mouth, I start to try and tell him that's not what I meant, but Blaine beats me to it.

"She means when she starts having our babies," he says, a possessive growl to his voice, and I swear I'm the colour of a tomato as my eyes widen and my mouth hangs open.

Lan freezes, turning to look at me, his eyes intense and so dark that they really do look like the night sky.

"You want to have a child with us?" he asks, his voice so deep that chills race across my skin and my core heats.

"I mean, maybe not right now, but, like, in the future, I—" I stumble over my words, my face growing hotter, and I see out of the corner of my eyes Blaine breaking out into a full-on grin, Forest's chuckle sounding around us.

Lan places his fork down next to his plate in careful movements, then he gets up, looming over me. His fingers grip my chin, tilting my face up until I'm drowning in his eyes.

"Do you want us to fill you so full of our cum that your belly grows big with a child, Duchess? Yes or no?" He's so still, his eyes never leaving mine, dragging the answer past my lips.

"Yes." Heat sears my insides at my confession, but it's nothing to the feral growl that rumbles from his chest as he bends down and scoops me out of the chair.

My legs wrap around his waist, my arms around his neck as he strides from the room.

"Lan! I've got a coil for fuck's sake! I can't get pregnant, and I'm not even nineteen yet," I rush out, squeaking when he throws me down on the bed, covering my body with his, his solid length pressing into my core. Blaine's T-shirt rides up my body—I've been wearing their clothes for the past week, even though Aoife bought me some clothes—and only the thin cotton of my knickers covers my rapidly dampening core.

"I can deal with that, Duchess," he growls, silencing me with a kiss that is full of possession. It's a claiming, pillaging my mouth and leaving me breathless and desperate. "Gonna fill you so full," he murmurs against my lips, tearing the fabric of my underwear and then shoving inside me in a matter of seconds.

"Fuck, Lan," I moan, my legs wrapping around his hips, pulling him deeper as he thrusts into me over and over again.

"Shit, Duchess, fuck, you always feel so fucking good," he rasps into my ear, fucking me harder, my nails digging into his shoulders as electricity races up and down my body.

My core tightens at his praise, the piercing at the end of his dick dragging along my inner walls in a way that leaves me trembling in his arms, my orgasm cresting and dragging me under. Sparks fly behind my closed lids, my body going rigid as Lan fucks me through it, seeking his own release which he finds moments later, buried deep inside my heat.

We lie there, still mostly dressed but panting, holding each other as bliss coats our skin. His lips press kisses over my face and neck.

"One day, when all this is over, I will fill you with a child,

Duchess," he tells me in a husky whisper, his dick twitching inside me.

"What if I'm no good as a mother?" I whisper, biting my lower lip as I voice the worry that I've always had. "I didn't exactly have a good role model."

He leans back, staring deep into my eyes. "You will be a wonderful mother for that very reason, beautiful. You love us, despite all of our flaws, and I know that your heart is big enough for many."

He kisses me so sweetly that tears spring underneath my closed lids, and I bask in the glow he gives me, trying to take his words to heart and letting them soothe away my concerns.

I need to sort out my issues first, my past trauma will not stay buried forever, and although I've not felt the urge to steal for a long while, I know that it's something I might have to deal with for the rest of my life. Mental health struggles are like that, they don't just disappear, but now that I have the support of these hard men. I know that I can face anything as long as they're by my side.

CHAPTER 37

"VIGILANTE SHIT" BY TAYLOR SWIFT

ASPEN

After a shower and eating the meal that Lan prepared before he went all caveman on me, we hang out for a few hours watching movies, but there's a tension in the air that has all of us on edge.

Finally, Lan looks at his phone as a message comes through.

"Our guest is ready for us," he states coldly, his eyes fathomless, and a chill runs down my spine. I know who the guest is, the Ambassador, and I can only imagine what he means by him being ready for us. "Remember, if at any point it becomes too much or you want to leave, Duchess, you just tell us. Okay?"

"Okay," I whisper back, getting to my feet. I'm in dark, high-waisted jeans and a black, polo-neck sweater, the guys all in black too. They were in the bundle that Aoife had dropped off, and I couldn't help the ironic chuckle at the appropriateness of this outfit when I put it on earlier. She'd see the funny side, her preemptively giving me an outfit to commit murder in, because she's badass like that.

"Good girl," Lan praises softly, a different kind of shiver travelling over me this time. "Forest, you're with Blaine. Duchess with me."

We all head down to the bikes and climb on after Lan pulls on my helmet and a leather jacket that he insists I wear when riding with them. The cool night air whips past us as we take off, making our way out of Fairview and towards the countryside that surrounds us.

We drive for what feels like ages, my fingers freezing as they grip Lan's jacket, and then we're pulling up in front of what looks like an abandoned cabin in the middle of some woods.

"Where are we?" I ask, getting off the bike. Blaine's hands are there to steady me and help take my helmet off. I like that they're always fussing over me, helping me when I don't need it but I love it nonetheless.

"Just a place we use when we have these kinds of...jobs, *mi tesoro*," Blaine murmurs in my ear as he pulls me into his side, his large arm wrapping around my shoulders. I snuggle into the warmth of his huge body, taking a deep, calming breath of his woodsy scent and letting it calm me. My blood still thrums in my veins, but at least I'm not feeling nauseous or shaking like a leaf which I worried I would do.

"Hey, boss," Reg greets, his brows set in a hard line. "Blaine, Forest, Miss Aspen. Good to see you all."

"How is our guest?" Lan asks, and an evil sort of smile crosses Reg's face.

"He's been pretty responsive to the noises, keeps muttering to himself, and flinches anytime we start up again," Reg tells us, a gleam in his eyes.

"Noises?" I ask in an uncertain tone.

"As he liked being around dogs so much, we've been playing the noises of dogs barking, snarling, and growling pretty much nonstop for the past week," Forest tells me, taking my cold hand in his. "Seemed fittin' that he should get a taste of his own medicine."

I blink, taking in what he's just told me. "You've had him this whole time?"

"My uncle helped bring him in. After we gave him all the evidence, he agreed that our debt to him was cancelled and that we could deal with the Ambassador as we saw fit. He was happy to lend a hand, but we have to decide what happens to him." Lan's voice is devoid of all emotion, and I swallow hard, wondering if I'll ever be so detached.

"You doing okay, *mi princesa linda?*" Blaine whispers in my ear as Reg and Lan chat some more.

"I think so," I tell him honestly, my thoughts a jumbled mess. I know that I should feel something, horror maybe at what has happened and will happen to the man that gave me life, but I just don't, and that's the thing that's bothering me.

"Everything that you're feeling, or not, is okay, sugar," Forest assures me, placing a light kiss on my cheek.

My shoulders loosen as his words give me the permission I needed to let go of my worries about being so damaged that I don't feel normal human emotions. This is the man who repeatedly tried to break me, tried to manipulate and abuse me. It's no wonder that I don't care about his pain, maybe even relish the idea of him being the powerless one for once.

"Let's bring him out, shall we?" Lan asks, Reg giving a nod and then going into the cabin. Moments later, Reg and another Saint are dragging out what looks like a homeless man.

It takes me a moment to recognise him, to see that he is the Ambassador, just stripped of all his imposing power and presence. He's not even fighting, just dragging his heels, his suit dishevelled and stained. As they bring him closer, I wrinkle my nose at the stale, acrid stink that wafts from him.

The two men dump him in a heap before us, stepping back with matching looks of disgust on their faces. No one says a word, all of us looking at the broken man before us, a shadow of his former self.

Slowly, he gets to his knees, lifting his head, his eyes dull and flat as his gaze swings between us, settling on me. His eyes widen, then the shadow of a sneer crosses his gaunt features.

"You disobedient bitch!" he rasps, his voice cracking like they barely gave him any water in the time he was locked up. Good. I hope he felt every second of his body craving what was being denied. My heartbeat picks up, but I don't feel the blind terror that I once did at his harsh words.

His head snaps to the side when Lan delivers a swift backhand that sends him reeling to the floor.

"You don't look at her," Lan seethes, his body trembling with pent-up rage. "You definitely don't speak to her, you pathetic fuck."

The Ambassador goes to argue, then Forest steps forward and barks, and the older man screams, scrabbling back as a wet stain appears at his crotch.

"Fucking disgusting," Forest spits out, coming back to my side and wrapping his arm around my waist so that I'm sandwiched between him and Blaine.

"Now, we have a deal for you," Lan states, strolling to where the Ambassador lies quivering in the dirt before he crouches down. "If you can evade capture until midnight, you get to walk free." My head snaps up to stare at him, my eyebrows knitting together. Before I can ask what the fuck is going on, Lan continues. "We'll even give you a head start. If you can't, well, then your life is ours to do with as we see fit." Lan glances at his watch. "Time starts now, *Ambassador*."

He gets up, turning his back on the older man, and sauntering back over to us, his ebony eyes on mine. I look past him to see the Ambassador stumble to his feet, unsteadily hurrying away, weaving around the path that disappears into the dark woodland.

"We're letting him go?" I ask, my chest tight with the idea that the man who has been my tormentor might walk away with just suffering for a week. My jaw tightens, a sudden rage making my hands ball into fists at my sides.

"Of course we're not letting him go, Duchess," Lan tells me with an arrogant smirk, stepping right into my personal space. He's so close that I have to tip my head back just to keep looking him in the eyes. He dips his head, bypassing my lips like I think he's heading to, and instead presses his to my ear. "But giving a man hope makes it all the more delicious when you rip it away."

A flash of heat tightens my core at his words, at the dark promise in them that shouldn't be so hot, but looks like my kitty kat is all for some protective alpha crazy. I flinch when a scream sounds in the night, the sound like that of a wounded animal.

"Looks like he didn't watch out for bear traps." Forest chuckles darkly, and after placing a soft kiss on my cheek, Lan steps away, the pulse in his neck throbbing as a wicked smile curves his lips upwards.

"Time to put this dog out of his misery," he declares, spinning on his heel and heading in the direction that the cries are coming from.

"Still want to come along, *mi amorsita*?" Blaine asks me as Forest swaggers after Lan.

I take a deep inhale, Blaine's arm a comfort that I appreciate more than I could say.

"I need to see this to the end, to see that he will no longer haunt my life," I tell him, sliding a glance up at his beautiful face. There's no judgement there, only concern in his lowered brows and set jaw.

"Let's go then, but you stay with me okay?" I nod, a glint of satisfaction making his chocolate eyes sparkle. "Good girl," he rumbles, darting down and kissing my lips. He keeps it quick but still manages to leave me breathless, chuckling as we head after the others, Reg and the other Saint following us behind.

We come across Lan and Forest not far from where the cabin is, the Ambassador writhing around on the floor and his leg at an awkward angle, the teeth of a bear trap digging into his ankle.

"Please," he begs, snot dripping out of his nose and tears falling from his eyes as he looks up at Lan. "Please, you can have whatever you want. Just let me go."

Lan sniggers, a dark kind of sound that has the hairs on the back of my neck standing up. "I already have exactly what I want. There is nothing else you can give me aside from your death, old man."

The Ambassador gives a small whine, his breathing sawing out of his chest as Lan pulls out a gun, aiming it at his head.

"Lan," I say, my voice clear as I step out of Blaine's hold. Lan's gaze swings to me, his aim never wavering.

"Yes, Duchess?"

"May I?" I ask, gesturing to the gun. His eyebrow twitches, then that devilish smile is back on his lips.

"Of course, angel," he says, taking a step back and opening his arms. "But I'm going to hold you as you take his life."

"No fair, Daddy," Forest grumbles, and a shocked giggle escapes my lips when he adjusts himself in his jeans. "Why do you get to be pressed up against her while she kills him?"

"Because, Pup, I'm the leader," Lan retorts, and I roll my eyes at their antics, advancing towards Lan, my heart racing. He moves behind me when I reach him, caging me in his hard body as he places the gun in my hands, his own pulling me in so that not a breath of air is between us. "Now, Duchess, you're going to shoot him right between the eyes like a good girl, aren't you?"

He flexes his hips, his hard length digging into the top of my arse, distracting me for a moment. I'm reminded of the time back at Maria's, when I shot that can off his head and then he fucked me raw with the barrel of the gun pressed to his temple.

"Yes, sir," I breathe out, focusing on the old man before me. My pulse pounds loud in my ears, a mixture of lust and excitement thrumming through my veins and leaving me a little lightheaded.

"You don't have the courage to shoot me," the Ambassador snarls, sweat beading his skin. "You were always weak, Aspen. A scared little mouse that needed correction and even then you were a failure."

I release a long, measured exhale, his vile words washing over me like water. They don't touch me, not anymore. Not since I found the Saints who made me believe I was worth more than I'd ever been shown.

The shot rings out, loud in the quiet of the night, and I watch his wide eyes, the light in them dying as the space between them drips red.

"Good fucking girl," Lan breathes in my ear, rubbing his face along the side of mine and placing teasing kisses on my cheek. "Fuck, you are so perfect, you know that, angel?"

"Bullseye, sugar!" Forest crows, taking the gun from me and cupping my face in his warm palms. "Do you know how hard that made Daddy?"

He takes my lips in a fevered kiss, and I return it, groaning into his mouth as his tongue massages mine. Shoots of pleasure flash over me, and although a small part of me wonders if this is okay, if I shouldn't be more upset about just killing a man, a larger part screams in victory.

Forest pulls back, both of our chests heaving, my cheeks tingling as I stare into his forest-green eyes.

"It's over," I whisper, the fact that I am finally free hitting me like a punch. My knees wobble and Lan catches me, holding me even tighter as I lean on him.

"It's just beginning, *mi tesoro*," Blaine rumbles from next to us, and I twist my head to see pride making his chocolate eyes gleam in the dark like jewels.

"Reg, get rid of the trash," Lan sneers, scooping me into his arms even though I know my legs can carry me now, but I don't complain, I like being here too much.

"Yes, boss," I hear Reg say, but I don't look back. I've had enough of the man that used to be my living nightmare, I don't want him to have anything else from me.

"Let's get you home," Lan suggests, heading back towards the bikes.

The cool breeze blows across my hot face, and there's a smell of spring in the air. It really is as Blaine said, a new beginning. There's a lightness in my chest, a breathlessness at all the possibilities that lie before us, and I intend to grab every single one of them with both hands, with my Saints by my side.

EPILOGUE

"YOUNG AND BEAUTIFUL" SCOTT BRADLEY'S POSTMODERN JUKEBOX

ASPEN

Two months later...

I take in a measured breath, exhaling slowly and then another, wiping my damp, trembling palms along my red sequin dress, much good that does me. The low murmur of the crowd beyond the curtains buzzes in my ears and makes my pulse jump, my muscles quivering.

"You ready, *mi tesoro*?" Blaine asks quietly in my ear, his large palm landing on my waist and squeezing gently. Some of the tension leaves me at his touch, and I lean back into his warmth, soaking in his steadfastness, using it to lend me strength.

"I think so," I breathe out, smiling when he places a kiss on my cheek.

"And now, we welcome to the stage here at Tailor's Ruin, Miss

Aspen Buckingham accompanied by Mr. Blaine Garcia," the MC announces, and the crowd erupts into wild applause, the sound making my heart thud loudly in my chest.

I take a final breath, then step out from behind the curtain, a smile on my red-painted lips. Stepping up to the old-fashioned microphone, I pause a moment until my eyes land on Forest, Lan, and Aoife sitting at the front, the boys dressed in nineteen-twenties suits looking too fine for words. Aoife is in a black-beaded flapper dress and looks stunning, the style really suits her, and I see more than one man glance her way.

"Good evening," I say softly, and Forest wolf-whistles, my cheeks heating at the attention of my two men. "This first song is dedicated to my Saints."

Giving the band and Blaine a nod, I start singing a cover version of Lana Del Ray's "Young and Beautiful," the crowd roaring their approval, couples getting up to dance, and all the while Lan and Forest keep their heated gazes trained on me.

As I sing the final note, they're the first to leap to their feet, along with Aoife, clapping and cheering, and my cheeks ache with how wide my smile is. We launch into the rest of my set, and by the end, I'm so high I swear I'm walking on clouds.

Coming out from the dressing rooms, I head to the main bar to find all three of my Saints talking to the owner of the speakeasy club, Lark Taylor, and her four husbands. They have the same air of danger as my Saints, but when I catch Lark's eye, she rushes over, pulling me into a hug. Her small, rounded stomach presses into me, and a pang of longing runs through me, reminding me of the time Blaine forced me to admit that I did want them to put a baby inside me one day.

"You were fucking incredible!" she gushes, letting me go but keeping my hands in hers. She's beautiful, with tumbling, auburn hair and an emerald-fringed dress, and I'm reminded of the Christmas ball they held where she wore the same colour. She has an interesting tattoo across her sternum, birds holding chains in their beaks, as well as several others I can see across her exposed skin. "Tell me you'll come back to sing again?"

"Of course," I answer quickly, my heart racing at the possibility of performing here again. "I'd love to."

"You were wonderful, Duchess," Lan says in my ear, I hadn't even noticed him sneak up behind me. A shiver cascades across my skin when he presses his lips against my neck. "And you look fucking stunning."

Lark gives me a wink, squeezing my hands then letting go and stepping back as the other Saints surround me, Aoife joining us.

"You were fan-fecking-tastic!" she tells me, pulling me into a quick hug and kissing my cheek.

"The crowd loved you, sugar, as I knew they would," Forest says as Aoife releases me and steps back. He has a wide smile on his face as he leans in and brushes his lips against mine. "You are a sensation."

"Thank you," I reply, leaning back into Lan. Blaine takes Forest's place, Forest moving aside as Blaine hands me a champagne flute.

"Happy birthday, *mi amorsita*," he says in that deliciously deep voice.

Lan steps out from behind me, holding his own glass up, Forest and Aoife doing the same. "To new beginnings," I announce.

"New beginnings," they repeat, the chime of our glasses like a promise.

I look into each of my guys' eyes, all sparkling like jewels as they gaze at me with so much love that my chest feels tight. They might be Tainted Saints, but they saved me in so many ways and became the guardian angels I needed to take me from the dark and show me how to live in the light.

NOT QUITE READY TO LET THE SAINTS GO?

Click HERE for an extra smutty scene between Blaine and Forest...

Do you like dark fairytale retellings? Then you may enjoy Tarnished Embers, a dark Cinderella stepbrother story.

Want to get to know Lark and her Tailors, owners of Tailor's Ruin? Look no further for their first book, Addicted to the Pain is here and waiting for you!

ACKNOWLEDGMENTS

I wouldn't be here, writing all the extra bits for my ANOTHER FUCKING without the help of many simply wonderful people.

My gorgeous alphas and betas who give me incredible feedback, help the story to grow and tell me there is never too much sex. You are all so appreciated and your comments are more precious than gold.

My wonderful editor Polly who literally gives me life with her comments! She makes these books shine and I honestly would be lost without her.

I'd also be totally lost without Julia, my wonderful PA who does so much more than she gets paid for!

And my lovely Rosebuds and Darlings, my Arc readers and Street Team. You guys don't know how much you do, giving me awesome reviews and recommending my books. I love you all!

To my wonderful Patreon supporters Nicola, Rebecca, Amy, Elizabeth, Krista, Nicole, Amanda, Amanda, Breanne, Brenda, Emmi, Kelle, Kymberlie, Lexi, Mandy and Stephanie. You are wonderful supporters and cheerleaders and I love our chat group where we share all the things. Reading your comments on my posts is awesome and I adore sharing my work with you guys. I can't wait for more shenanigans with you guys and thank you so much for being part of my tribe!

And of course, my amazing husband who supports me in all that I do, and enjoys the benefits of being married to a steamy romance author (you all know what I'm talking about!). I genuinely wouldn't be where I am today, as a person, craftsperson or author without him.

About the Author

About Rosa

Rosa Lee lives in a sleepy Wiltshire village, surrounded by the beautiful English countryside and the sound of British Army tanks firing in the background (it's worth the noise for the uniformed dads in the local supermarket and doing the school run!).

Rosa loves writing dark and delicious whychoose romance, and has so many ideas trying to burst out that she can often be found making a note of them as soon as one of her three womb monsters wakes her up. She believes in silver linings and fairytale endings...you know, where the villains claim the Princess for their own, tying her up and destroying the world for her.

If you'd like to know more, please check out Rosa's socials or visit
www.rosaleeauthor.com
Rosa's Captivating Roses
Linktree

Also by Rosa Lee

Also by Rosa

HIGHGATE PREPARATORY ACADEMY

A dark whychoose romance

Hunted: A Highgate Preparatory Academy Prequel

Captured: Highgate Preparatory Academy, Book 1

Bound: Highgate Preparatory Academy, Book 2

Released: Highgate Preparatory Academy, Book 3

DEAD SOLDIERS VS TAILORS DUET

A dark whychoose enemies to lovers romance

Addicted to the Pain

Addicted to the Ruin

THE SHADOWMEN

A dark gang & mafia whychoose romance

Kissed by Shadows

Claimed by Shadows

Owned by Shadows

STANDALONES

A dark whychoose Lady and the Tramp(s) retelling

Tainted Saints

A dark whychoose stepbrother Cinderella retelling

Tarnished Embers

A dark whychoose mafia romance Co-written with Mallory Fox

A Night of Revelry and Envy

Printed in Great Britain
by Amazon